PEARLJAM

The More You Need - The Less You Get

US EDITION

HENRIK TUXEN

captainkiddbooks.com

PEARL JAM
The More You Need – The Less You Get
by Henrik Tuxen

Translated by Michael Lee Burgess

Translator's note: Most of the interviews with Pearl Jam in this book are translated back to English from Danish, as the original transcripts were not available. I've tried to get as close to the way I hear Stone, Eddie, Mike, Matt and Jeff speaking in my imagination – I hope that these translations read smoothly and credibly. Thanks to Henrik and Marie for choosing me to give voice to this story in English. Thanks to Maria Elena Preciado for reading early drafts of my translations and helping to sharpen things up. This translation is dedicated to Sidsel, Gabriella, Elliot and Alvin.

Translation from Danish to English made possible by the support of Roskilde Festival Charity Society. Production is supported by 250 Kickstarter backers from November 1 to December 1, 2017.

Cover photo: Danny Clinch © 2013 Monkeywrench Records
Cover and sleeve design: Lisbet Krøll
Image editor: Morten Larsen Photography
Proofreader: Greg Bennetts
Editor: Marie Rose Siff Hansen

Copyright © 2018 Captain Kidd Books
ISBN: 978-87-999374-2-4
First US edition
Printed in the United States of America

For information about special discounts, press or booking Tuxen for a book event please visit www.captainkiddbooks.com. Danish edition was printed for the first time in Denmark in 2016.

This book is dedicated to the memory of Henrik Bondebjer, Carl-Johan Gustafsson, Lennart 'Leo' Nielsen, Allan Tonnesen, Jakob Folke Svensson, Fredrik Thuresson, Anthony Hurley, Frank Nouwens and Marco Peschel.

"Lost 9 friends we'll never know,... 2 years ago today
And if our lives became too long, would it add to our regret?
[...]
Love boat captain
Take the reins,... steer us towards the clear.
I know it's already been sung,... can't be said enough.
Love is all you need,.. all you need is love,...
Love,... love,...
Love."

Love Boat Captain
Lyrics: Vedder
Music: Vedder, Gaspar
©2002

Contents

This book is supported by

Erik Claeson, Anders Selander, David Svensson, Luke Ruane, Patrick E. Kitchell, Paula Barte, Jennifer Poinsot, Kelly Collier, Pernille Ravn, Vincenzo Salvatore Pannone, Cecilie Bolgen, Julie Peck, Jane Jaqué, Scott and Bobbi Roberts, Seija Korhonen, Allan Hommelgaard, Rebecca Driver, Francesco Chetta, Jill M. Franklin, Karsten Hahn, Janice Clarke, Stuart & Kristina, Levon Garfunkel, Emeline Sophie MACAUD, Ulla Klejs Tøttrup, Buru, Michael (Given2Flyimages) Young, Joyce van den Bogaard, Charlotte Mai Jacobsen, CG, Geoff Marshall, Mikko Kyyrö, Juliet Dewhirst, Christopher Boudreau, Thilo H. Ahl, Steve "Mookie2210" Rubin, Gretchen Rehnelt, Kathy, Christopher Weiss, Jérémie Plume, Nichole R Bechel, Heide Marx, Ingsefi Tuxen, Debbie Carmichael, Stein Andersen, Nicole Reysen, Yuri Beckers, Zak Zerby, Rita Guillot, Laura Baiguera Tambutti, Torben Jacobsen Matz, Christopher Anthony Troupos (P34RL J4MM3R), Marco van den Hout, Donna S., Matt Jacobson, James Neal, Dawn Mulligan, Darrin Puckett, Robert Bannister, Reeta Jalonen, Mark Tarnuzzer, Brynda Cotton Howell, Petri Pietikäinen, Clarisse Boutin-Duquesnoy, Shawn D Hood, Kristin Nielsen, John E Jones, Peter Veenhoven, Nis Westphall Breddam, Dirty Frank Slitti, Luciano Oscar Becerra, Brian Mulvany, Abraham Esparza, Marianne Sondergaard, Rogan Hennie, Reiko Liermann, Lis Søndergaard, Samantha J. Nieman, Jan Hogenberg, kusine Ingrid, Tom Pugh (Given To Live), Rebecca Pecsok, Henrik's dad, Rita, Valeria Segatore,

Tom Rinkus Jr, Martin Gammeltoft, Anne Mette Degn-Petersen, Jarl Mengers Andersen, Mark Daak, John, Paul Hiyake, Thomas Charlie Pedersen, Simona, Tyler Hanson, Morten Fivel, Jamie "Jambo" Davis, James Crisan, Stefan Campagnolo, felix rossbach, Thomas ODIN, Stefan Zander, Debbie Strozier, Tina Taylor, Jeff Albright, Brian Reilly (BR), Robbie Keenan, Fiona Wares, BJ Peace, Janet Kinnear, Mike Layman, Ana Garibay, Ryan Byrne, mackoMM - Touring Poles, Lisa & Cav, Paula Voiseux, Dave and Julie Greenberg, Keith Law, Antonino Morici, Brodie Verwoen, Jessica E. Nevil, Bill Kurnik, Josiah Lilly, Jason Lilly, Christel Van Grootel, Larry Meyer, Arjan de Jongste, Chantel Asbury Blankenship, Leanne Martin, Liz Peterson, Victoria Rowlands, Justin McLoughlan, Brian Plona, Nicholas DiNicola, Schnurstein, Mickey Biezen, Dawn Grealish, Lynsey McLean, Joseph Boudoumit, Emma Comerford, Martin Russell Davies, Abhishek Rao, Mike Baillie, Juliana Ferrari Müller, @CindyinCO, Damian Kenley, Bryan Emery, Meg Kenning, Matthew Zoch, Jorge Rojas Campos, Ben & Caroline Jones, Gilson N. Missawa, Ted Shumaker, Star Charise, Kenny Krebs, Erik Jacobs, John Bowman, Natascha Hermans, Matt Kessler AKA Too Many Records, Brandon Lewis, Garrett D., Louise Riddle, Erin R Kelly, Marco Labbate, Sam Giammona, Lars & Rikky, JESPER THUSGAARD, Given2fly from NY!!, Ben Schaefer, Luke Malloy, Jay Russell, Mikko Litmanen, Antti Ansas, Darren Ball, Copper Tom, Keri Jensen, Yanta Fernandes, Dimitri Sponselee, Jon Towslee, Rafael Carneiro, Kaushal Lapsiwala, Nic Dolas, Jason Van Auken, Ricky Mills, Marko Leinonen, Tolva., Anthony Angrisano, Mike Pastorello, Mark Augspurger, Andreas Haller, Mike Iavasile, Jussi Ertiö, Simon Niemiec, Dave Gavin, Sophie Wallas Rasmussen, Andrew McGhie, Ivana El Assadi, JD Zack, Wendell M., Christian Blücher, Tobias Ydestrand, Allison Buchtien, Matthijs Veld, Simon Johansen, Yuliya Nikiforova, María Gabriela Alvarez Aragón, Gitte Meier Nielsen, Shannon Hindahl, Ana López Boccassino, Richard Liet, Gleebs, Dadylle Sandins Yetti, Rossy Hernandez, Robin Petersen, Graham Klusener, Fredrik, Kimberly McGauley, Haukur Gunnarsson, Craig, Joshua R. Smith, Nathan Lind, Paul Martin, Warren Johnson, Fetter Peter, Peter Hermanrud, Chris Schultz, Nate Macy, J.B. Hoage, Koscik.photos, Renee C., Jamie Wester, Christinna Ciric, Lykke Kælepunker Svendsen, Renata Fonzar Ferreira Gama, Miska Kaukonen, Kössi Rehmonen, Nuno Pereira, Greg and Marcy Plourde, In Loving Memory - James Martin III, The Martin Family, Joshua Emory Opmeer, Sushant H. Amin, Thomas Stephen Holley.

5

"I would like to say a word about safety to all those who might read or hear about this book. Think about safety, think about each other, take care of each other, and get out of trouble in time. Help others when you can. I would like to say that to everyone. We don't want something like this to ever happen to anyone again. You don't want to rob anyone of their enthusiasm, but be careful. I would like you to write that. That's from a mother who lost her son."

Birgitta Gustafsson, mother of Carl-Johan,
who lost his life at Roskilde Festival 2000.

Prologue

COPENHAGEN

Sitting in my apartment on a Friday night in Copenhagen. My daughter Lulu's out for a jog after we've had dinner and re-watched David Lynch's mind-bending *Lost Highway.* Otherwise, we've spent the evening as we often do – playing guitar together. I had my old acoustic Levin restored and gave it to her a short time back for her eighteenth birthday – and tonight we've hammered out the perfect laid-back beat so *Daughter* flows just right from the acoustic guitar. We play a bunch of different stuff and a lot of Pearl Jam, mostly according to what she feels like playing. She's a child of her times and listens to everything around her, yet some passions have proven hereditary. The same can't quite be said for big brother Tobias, whose musical tastes are less rock-centric. He'd rather listen to Chet Baker, John Mayer or Kanye West. But he's born and bred with rock'n'roll, gets Led Zeppelin, dabbles occasionally in harder stuff, loves *Into the Wild* and can hit every note of the fingering in *Guaranteed.* But Pearl Jam has seeped deeply into Lulu's bones and she sings songs like *Light Years* and *Better Man* brightly and pitch perfect, not to mention a sea of obscure Pearl Jam numbers, including some I don't even know. Big sister Celine has always had a taste for all-out guitar, but the Red Hot Chili Peppers are ideal for triggering her karaoke reflex.

I could point to any random day and there'd be something that somehow relates back to that band from Seattle.

The 1990s

Pearl Jam is part of a wave that's shaking up and seriously reinvigorating music if you ask me. Riding in on the heels of a decade composed of pompous poodle-glam hair, disco in a can and melancholy, black-clad martyrs – a time when my personal playlists were more The Who and Motown – the metal-funk of Red Hot Chili Peppers, the melodic primal force of Metallica and the raw power of the Seattle wave came as a soul-soothing relief. (Later I came to appreciate more of the '80s vibe.) For the first time in eons, there was no need to look back retrospectively to the acid-heads of the 60s and punks of the 70s to get that liberating kick. The present was suddenly chock-full of vital rock'n'roll – and not just some peripheral subgenre for incarnate freaks, but chart toppers filling the airwaves. Unbelievable!

I indulge in this sudden bounty, finding myself particularly moved by the power of Nirvana, the Chili Peppers, Soundgarden and Metallica. Pearl Jam is just one band of many. Their blockbuster debut *Ten* is pretty good, but doesn't move the needle much for me. When *Vs.* is released in 1993, I'm taken aback by the sheer force in a song like *Rearviewmirror*; but I'm even more blown away by Soundgarden's *Superunknown* the following year. Later on in 1994, when a friend enthusiastically puts on Pearl Jam's third album, *Vitalogy*, I find it hard to relate to at first. But I feel a special connection with the whole Seattle wave, because at the time I'm playing in the band Sharing Patrol with two guys from Seattle – former housemates of Pearl Jam bassist Jeff Ament, whose room allegedly consists of 200 hardcore punk records and a bed. We're planning a move to Seattle, the rock mecca of its time, as a steady stream of inspiring anecdotes flows from the city to our ears.

In January 1996, Sharing Patrol records an album in Seattle and later that year I latch on as guest roadie in Spain for a couple of concerts by our producer's band, Fastbacks. They're the warm-up act on Pearl Jam's European tour. Eddie Vedder spends most of his time in Fastbacks' band room, and I soak in the inviting, non-hierarchical atmosphere between the supporting act and headliner. But it's not until Pearl Jam takes the stage that the real transformation begins. I feel it within the first few seconds of the opening number *Wash*. I'm sold. In the blink of an eye, I'm a fan in a way I've never been before – a lightning bolt, igniting an enthusiasm and devotion unrelenting to this day. This is at the same time that Pearl Jam's sales take a huge dive, and at the age of 33, I would appear to be far too old for such silliness. But ever since, I've followed them through thick and thin – first from the sidelines and later on closer terms, which leads to me standing on the side of the stage during their Roskilde Festival concert in 2000, where nine young men lost their lives.

Two years later, I interview Eddie Vedder. At his request, I arrange contact with the Danish families of the deceased, resulting in a heartfelt yet brief e-mail correspondence. But when Stone Gossard contacts me the next year (in 2003) and shares his desire to meet the victims' families and friends (if the feeling is mutual), I become personally involved in a altogether different and deeper way. The contact, the meeting, the friendship, the relationship, the love between Pearl Jam – especially Stone – and the surviving Scandinavian relatives, is a pivotal axis in this tale. And the trust and permission bestowed upon me by Pearl Jam and the families to tell their story as I have witnessed it first hand – including the unbearable sorrow and pain of the families – is the very reason that this book ever came to be.

2005

We never wanted anyone to write the official band biography, and we still feel that way. But if you choose to write your own interpretations, based upon all the things that we have experienced together and about what has happened, I would like to participate in any way that I can. I think that would be an interesting read and an important story to tell. I greatly appreciate your discretion throughout it all, which has also been important to the families, but I had actually expected that you would write something at some point.   *– Stone Gossard*

And so here we are. A personal journey more than 20 years in the making. On the release date of my first book about the accident, "In Pearl Jam's Footsteps – Before and After Roskilde" (published in Danish), I get an e-mail from Roskilde Festival's spokesperson, Esben Danielsen, who writes that on behalf of the festival he appreciates the book's portrayal of the festival's role. In the aftermath of that book, I've received hundreds of e-mails from people, some of whom were right there in the crowd and have the accident etched in their memories. Many of them express some form of recognition, others a sense of liberation from reading the book. One person writes that he's read the book six times – and a few years later, Veronica Bravo writes to tell me that she wants to translate the book into Spanish because South Americans love hard rock – not least Pearl Jam – but fans and audiences are generally younger and much more raucous than in Europe, and safety is rarely something they think about. As Veronica puts it: "Everyone here loves Pearl Jam, but nobody knows about the accident at Roskilde." Those who know the story of that day also know that things can go terribly and fatally awry. That's why Veronica wants to share the story with Chileans – and perhaps the Spanish-speaking world in general.

Her fears are rooted in tragedy: examples include four fatalities at a punk rock concert in Santiago in April 2015, and the Cromanön fire in Argentina in 2004, which claimed the lives of 193 concertgoers. And when I see the band in a tightly-packed stadium in Chile in November 2015, the people in the front rows couldn't get water, which could have ended fatally. All of which underpins the continued and unfortunate relevance of the somber parts of this book.

Veronica Bravo

When I first got her message, I just replied "OK and thanks" and didn't think much more about it – after all, I didn't know her before she wrote to me about the translation. But we stayed in contact and met up one afternoon while I was on summer vacation in Norway.

Veronica was born and raised in Santiago, Chile, but the threat of the military dictatorship spurred her to take flight to Norway in the mid-80s. Veronica raised her two children in Norway and now commutes between the two continents.

A couple of years later, Veronica writes to me again. The time has come. She has a contract with her publisher in Chile and suddenly the Danish Embassy also lends its support. The book will have to be translated to Spanish for release in Chile, and I just need to write a short chapter or two with the latest updates to the story. If only it were that simple.

The story is continuing all the time, but for practical reasons we only manage to add a concluding epilogue to the Spanish version. In this edition of the story you're reading now, our journey ends in early 2016, after the first incredible trip to South America for the release of the Spanish translation of the original book in Chile in the autumn of 2015.

There was plenty to write about back in 2005, and since then things have just snowballed. Meanwhile, dilemmas abound: just how up close and personal can I get, and what if Pearl Jam doesn't appreciate the results and feels like I'm violating their trust?

I write to Stone and offer to give him an oral translation of the whole book via Skype; if he or anyone in the band has the slightest objection or just a bad feeling about the project, I would then drop it immediately. When I wake up on October 1, 2014 in a hotel room in London, four hours before an interview with my lifelong hero Jimmy Page – and the same day that Pearl Jam is starting their US tour – I get an e-mail in a recognizable, brief and precise style: "Sorry, slow. It's all good. Do your thing. I trust you. Love to you. I'm on tour. All is well. Love S."

"Don't you ever get tired of seeing Pearl Jam?"

A friend of mine asked me that question a long time ago. And my answer came without a second's hesitation: "No." Because even though I can go for stretches without listening to Pearl Jam, I always come back. And every time I think I've seen and heard it all, something pops up: a new song, a new interpretation, a YouTube clip, a new connection, a cover or an original rarity. I couldn't imagine going through life without Dylan's catalog. I love The Beatles and Led Zeppelin, but I don't excitedly await new songs from their hand. And PJ concerts are always epic journeys with familiar and surprising elements that always relate back to the city and country where the concert is taking place. Every time I gain a little more wisdom, enrichment and joy.

My mentors

Just for the record: I'm still a fan. To me, Pearl Jam is still the world's greatest band. To me, it's the most complete band – a single band whose catalog embodies so many aspects of the very reason I listen to music. Anger, strength, power, passion, intensity, humor, insight, euphoria, unity, love and the four elements.

I've found my mentors in Pearl Jam – on a human, musical and personal level. A way of being, with an underlying base of humility and respect for others. They've given me an education in reading situations and staying calm, reserved and relaxed – even under pressure. It's become an essential element of my continued work as a journalist and, I would hope, my dealings with fellow humans. I do my best.

The more you need the less you get

I have the utmost respect for the people who take care of the band, especially Eddie, and sometimes I've had moral scruples about pushing for too much. On June 28, 2014, the day after the concert in Stockholm, I write to Stone to tell him that I've had the most incredible experience with them on tour (seeing 5 out of 11 concerts on the 2014 European tour), but that I wanted to express my respect for Smitty and Pete, two of the closest people behind Pearl Jam on tour for the past 20 years, and to apologize if I sometimes get too boisterous. I receive the following reply: "In general it's always good to try to be low key backstage, so I appreciate your thoughts about Smitty and Pete. They are just making sure Ed doesn't get swamped by people, 'cause he wants to visit with everyone but this isn't always possible. I think in general, with us, the more you 'need' the less you get. If that makes any sense. All right enough of that talk and more Rocking in Free world. Love to you big fella."

The more you need the less you get. A statement that's largely true in every aspect of life, and an edict that I'm often amazingly bad at living by, but I usually have the most mind-blowing experiences when I do.

The book

This book presents a relatively chronological look at a never-ending story spanning two decades of following Pearl Jam and meeting countless incredible people along the way. Parts of this story were previously published in the Danish music magazine *Gaffa*.

It's a personal eyewitness account based on the things I've seen and experienced through a combination of random events and personal initiative. This results in some pretty serious variation between the individual chapters. Sometimes I'm visiting the families, other times I'm at concerts around the world – often performing my "normal" work as a music journalist.

I make no attempt to cover – or to assess – the events surrounding the accident at Roskilde from a legal or liability perspective. Nor do I attempt to present the stories of every surviving relative or the significance of the judicial aftermath for those affected.

As of 2015, I have attended 22 Pearl Jam concerts; the band has given me the chance to fulfill the dreams of many of my friends with once-in-a-lifetime experiences. And every time I find that the music magically brings together and unites people. The music is the healing power.

Chapter 1

1996–1998: SEATTLE. BARCELONA. SAN SEBASTIAN. MAUI.

SEATTLE, JANUARY 1996

Sharing Patrol's Seattle stay in January 1996 was one of the more seismic events in the history of our band. We'd trudged through the preceding couple of years in Denmark: a dynamic rock band with an uncanny flair for being in the wrong place at the right time. Johnny Sangster and Jonathan Stibbard took flight from Seattle in 1984 at the ages of 19 and 20, respectively. In their words, it was wasteland barren of rock music, thanks to draconian age restrictions and other barriers. We turned our amps to full blast in Denmark in the mid 80s, doing all the legwork ourselves and carving out a niche at record companies more interested in the latest in Danish easy listening than the raucous The Jam- and The Who-inspired garage rock we're pumping out. It was pretty much unheard of at the time, but we toured throughout Europe as an underground band with a sound, style and music from a completely different dimension than the popular trends of the 80s. In 1990 we finally landed a record contract and managed to make two albums with good producers. But we're also handcuffed as a major label band and excluded from seizing all the smaller opportunities that arise along the way in neighboring countries. We have to sit by and patiently wait for the record company's gargantuan foreign departments, who vacillate like a pendulum from promising us the land of milk and honey to not lifting a finger. Two years later, we're squeezed out by a big merger and back on DIY planet. Keyboardist Jakob Palitsch had joined the band for a period of about five years, but now we're back to a trio.

A short time later, our drummer's wife dies tragically, casting a dark cloud over the band. Going back to our roots, we release the musically raw EP *Yikes* in 1994 and we feel revitalized and back at home. Meanwhile, guitar rock is once again "in" – even in Denmark – with a slew of bands about 8–10 years younger than us taking the spotlight. Further down the road, a lot of these musicians become close friends and partners, but at the time we're mostly on the sidelines.

Despite our continued underground status, there's plenty of reason for enthusiasm: the concerts are good and the new songs keep flowing. A new, young and talented management team adds some new wind in our sails and in 1995 we suddenly have a handful of contract offers to choose from. They're by no means gold-plated, but useful nonetheless. We make a decision, negotiate the budget and book studio time – but a few days before we're supposed to get started, the record company pulls the plug and tries discrediting our manager to cover its own back.

We don't waste a second. In no-time we mobilize plan B, landing a new contract, a pared-down budget and a killer producer in Seattle. Although lurking for years, the thought of returning has been complicated by my status as a university student and the fact that I already had my first child at the age of 24. But I get my master's degree from Roskilde University the same week that we sign the contract, and my son is about to go on a long vacation with his mother. In other words, the road is paved for me and my two bandmates to revisit the city of their birth.

The recording sessions, the concerts we play and the social rock'n'roll life in Seattle are all incredibly inspiring. For the first time in what feels like forever, it seems that we're in the right place at the right time. It's a fantastic time – and the beginning of the end for Sharing Patrol. Front man Johnny is so happy to be back home that he moves back permanently the next year.

Although some of the force of the historically prolonged Seattle wave had dissipated by this time, there's still a huge focus on this relatively small city and its exhilarating musical scene. Soundgarden, Alice in Chains and (especially) Pearl Jam continue to sell millions of records, and the biggest alternative act in the country at the time is the local band of jokers, The Presidents of The United States of America. Meanwhile, the rock scene in Seattle is like a cozy little village where everyone knows each other and plays together. We borrow drums from The Presidents, have guest performances by Scott McCaughey (The Young Fresh Fellows, R.E.M.) and Ken Stringfellow (The Posies, R.E.M.), meet members of Mudhoney when we go out, etc. During our four weeks in Seattle, we never meet anyone from Pearl Jam, but we're told that two members of the band attended one of our concerts – to this day, I still don't know who. Based on the stories people tell about them, they sound like some pretty cheerful and social guys who really give all the payback they can to their local music scene. Stone Gossard runs his own record company, Loose Groove, all of the band members are in local part-time bands, they play local benefits of all kinds and take lesser-known local bands with them as warm-up acts on their major tours. Rumor has it that if you see a short guy at a rock concert with his head covered by a big hat, there's a good chance that you'll find Eddie Vedder's curly locks under that hat.

One day I'm out enjoying a burger and a game of pool with a friend from Seattle and we run into a couple of guys who want to know what brings a Dane to the Pacific Northwest. I tell the story and one of them proudly says that he went to school with Stone Gossard, who he says is a totally ordinary, nice guy. We hear similar stories all the time. People are proud of their native-born sons, who are never shy to give back to their hometown in the form of benefit concerts and more.

Pearl Jam vs. Nirvana

But Seattle also has its share of rivalry. I'm familiar with the shade Kurt Cobain's cast on Pearl Jam in the international press, calling them commercial hypocrites in fake alternative packaging, characterizing their music as "corporate rock" and saying that the only thing that Jeff Ament and Stone Gossard have ever been about is making bank – in other words, light years away from the politically correct punk rock ethos. Pearl Jam's self-ironic response was both disarming and humorous. After Cobain's statements, I remember seeing a picture of Eddie Vedder in a T-shirts with the letters "Corporate Rock" plastered in huge letters on the front, as a response. But about seven years later, Mike McCready and Stone Gossard tell me that the Cobain rift really hurt.

Mike – Kurt really said those things, and the media blew it up big time. Facing that corporate rock thing, calling us corporate rock, that hurt. I liked Nirvana as a band, and it hurt me and taught me that that's not something I should do to other bands. We never really responded to it. I really wanted to sometimes, but we never did. It faded away over time.

Stone – It's the same type of gossip that you see in small cities with a lot of bands. But in this particular case, the press was on hand to snatch every little bit of what was said. You know, we all spew off a bunch of shit every single day that we would be embarrassed to see in print. You say something about someone or something that you're not particularly fond of, and if it suddenly gets blown up in newspapers and magazines, you might not be all that proud of it. But over time, you become more aware of how it all works, and I think that Kurt felt the same way. Just the whole transition of figuring out how to give interviews and getting used to people asking you about all kinds of stuff – and often about other bands. I can see how easy it must have been for him – or for anyone in that situation – to spout off stuff like that. And there was some truth in what he said. We were aggressive in our own way – now whether we were pure poison, which is pretty much what he said – that's another matter. Maybe it was a good experience for us to go through, maybe it was good for us to get that experience and understanding; it's made us very careful ever since.

Back among the rock people in Seattle in the winter of 95/96, I encounter great respect for both Nirvana and Pearl Jam – as well as those who take umbrage with all the fanfare. In the classic underground sense, everything embraced by popular culture is no longer cool and enthralling to spend your time on. And you pretty much couldn't point to a more popular band than Pearl Jam at the time. The old Nirvana vs. Pearl Jam polarization also plays a part, as does the fact that the members of Pearl Jam – unlike Nirvana – have been visible and popular figures in the local rock scene for years.

The city's take on Pearl Jam is encapsulated by an anecdote shared with us by Kurt Bloch's good friend and one-time girlfriend, Mary-Ellen, who's always got insider dirt to dish on the rock scene:

Mary-Ellen – When those two groups really broke through, I was in the Nirvana camp, and I didn't have much interest in Pearl Jam. But later on I got to know them and discovered that they're really cool guys. The last time I was out with them, we were smoking some weed and they were all totally cool and relaxed and extremely funny.

Kurt Bloch

Our producer and good friend Kurt Bloch – who previously shared a practice space with Cobain – holds a unique position in the city and is held in high esteem for his musical qualities, mild-mannered disposition and well-developed sense of humor. One of his many nicknames is "Sir Grunge-a-Lot" because of the numerous records he's produced in the genre. He's also a full-fledged composer and guitarist; during a concert with his other main band, The Young Fresh Fellows, he "Kurt-played-through" the show, which means that his hands remained glued to the neck of the guitar for the entire concert. Kurt's voice is almost falsetto, but he also manages to pull off the deepest bass, especially when delivering an ironic joke. Being with Kurt in Seattle is like having a free pass to everything and everyone in the rock scene stamped on your forehead. The jovial musician knows and is known by everyone in the community. Among his many friends are the members of Pearl Jam. I later discover that on the only day we didn't spend together during our stay in Seattle, Kurt played with Eddie Vedder at the Sundance Film Festival in Utah. At the time, I find this amazing, but Kurt hadn't mentioned it in the slightest. Kurt, who always makes a point of treating everyone equally, doesn't think it's all that important to talk about. After all, I didn't ask.

Copenhagen

Full of impressions and enthusiasm, Sharing Patrol returns to Denmark for the release of *Take You There,* and we embark on a big tour. A lot of the concerts are OK, but the vibe can't measure up to the ebullient atmosphere we got a taste of in Seattle. In Denmark, it's a time dominated by watered-down "Battle of the Bands," with event organizers and audiences fixated on local competitions featuring largely uninteresting bands – unfathomably provincial and pedestrian in our view, and a gradually accelerating turn for the worse. The rock scene is dead, and any shred of positive interaction between bands or with audiences is a distant memory as far as we can tell. Our countermove is a live concert featuring guests from an array of other bands, which is later released as the album entitled *Live at Vega* 22.10.96. We're surprised to discover that we're capable of drawing 1,200 people. The concert is by all means a great event, but it also proves to be the band's swan song.

Meanwhile, my girlfriend and later wife Anne is pregnant and I've been hired for the temporary full-time position of journalist for the rock magazine *Wild.* One of my first jobs is to write a review of the new Pearl Jam album *No Code.* I'm really surprised by the album's generally acoustic and subdued tone, but I'm also captivated and astounded by the music; it feels like I'm sitting with some sort of modern Neil Young record in my hands. At about the same time, Kurt Bloch gets in touch to tell me that he and his band Fastbacks will be the warm-up act on Pearl Jam's upcoming European tour. In addition to Kurt and drummer Mike Musburger, Fastbacks features the diminutive and enchanting firecracker Lulu Gargiulo on bass and vocals, and the ultimate rock'n'roll chick, Kim Warnick, on guitar and vocals. They're a dearly loved and remarkably charming band that more than any other embodies Seattle's rock history through the 80s and 90s – the underlying essence that never reaches a global audience. Kurt produces countless under-ground bands from the local area, Lulu shoots a bunch of films and videos with her husband, Kim works at SubPop when the grunge wave explodes, and if you take any random band from the area during that period – or even today – there's a pretty damn good chance that Mike is sitting or previously sat at the drums.

BARCELONA, NOVEMBER 1996

As a newbie music journalist, I'm toying with the thought of trying to pull some strings and hook up with the Pearl Jam/Fastbacks tour. I run the idea past my editor at *Wild.* His eyes light up. It would be a bona fide sensation if I could get on the tour and write an "on-the-road" report from the inside. A lively fax correspondence with Kurt Bloch ensues. He's generally amenable to the idea, but isn't sure if the details can be worked out. Meanwhile, there's commotion on the home front: *Wild* is going straight into the toilet, Sharing Patrol is about to record the aforementioned live album, and my girlfriend is very pregnant. But after a bunch of legwork, everything falls into place and on November 21, 1996

I find myself in the airspace above Barcelona with a live album of my own making hot off the presses in my bag and a picture of my 14-day-old daughter Lulu in my wallet. What's next to come is less clear. Kurt only communicates by fax, so it's been impossible to get a hold of him lately, which means that everything is completely up in the air. I don't even know if there's a ticket waiting for me to that night's concert. The only thing I have is an address to a hotel in town where Kurt is supposedly staying, and a return ticket home four days later.

Arriving in Barcelona, I head straight for the hotel. The first person I meet in the lobby is Kurt Bloch and he looks really, really tired. Nonetheless, we're both psyched to see each other and he says that I can sleep on the sofa in the hotel room he's sharing with Mike the drummer if I want.

A couple of hours later, I go to the Olympic Arena with Kurt – the site of that night's concert. It's a basketball arena surrounded by fans waiting to get in, and there's a sunny warmth in the air even though it's late autumn. Many of the fans recognize Kurt and give him approving pats on the shoulder. We enter the dome-shaped hall with a capacity of 8,000, which according to Kurt is one of the smallest venues on the tour. I get a "Pearl Jam Crew" sticker plastered on my shirt and start heading towards the sound. Pearl Jam doesn't normally do a soundcheck, Kurt says, but today is more of a practice session – a session now considered legendary among die-hard PJ fans. They play snippets of new songs and a version of Neil Young's musings on the death of Kurt Cobain, *Sleep With Angels*. But I'm not just here to be enjoying myself. The deal is that I'm gonna be assistant guitar roadie for Fastbacks. After Pearl Jam's mini session, I get a run-down of Fastbacks' stage setup during the band's quick sound check. Eddie Vedder has stated on the record that Fastbacks is his favorite band, and he's most at home in their company, as I will very clearly experience firsthand over the next few days. He shows up right after Fastbacks' first sound check. Afterwards there's a group dinner where all the members of Pearl Jam dine side by side with crew members, Fastbacks, friends, partners and children. The atmosphere is calm and relaxed.

An hour before Fastbacks hit the stage, there's a knock on the wall to the supporting act's band room and I hear Eddie Vedder ask if we can tone it down a bit while he talks with a journalist from the *LA Times*. He's giving what at the time was one of his very rare interviews. *Rolling Stone* had just printed a long article entitled "Reinventing Eddie Vedder," digging up people from Eddie's schooldays to provide a "true" portrait. Eddie himself was vehemently opposed to the article and refused to comment for it. The lengthy article strongly questions Vedder's authenticity as a spokesperson for a neglected generation of kids beleaguered by divorce. Despite Pearl Jam's status at the time as probably the world's biggest and best-selling rock band, they haven't given any interviews or produced any videos for their last three albums, while only playing a limited number of concerts. But Eddie decided to break the silence for once.

Fastbacks zoom through their set without letting off the gas and the concert goes fine, but the packed arena is naturally awaiting the headliners. Throughout the concert, Pearl Jam guitarist Mike McCready sits with a mini-cigar type of thing hanging from his lips and looks on approvingly from the side of the stage. When we return to the band room, Eddie Vedder drops by quickly and says laughing:

Eddie - I was laying there for half the concert behind Kurt's amp and waiting for you take a break so that I could run on stage, take the mic and say "Be quiet! We're trying to conduct an interview!" But you never take a break between songs!

Two minutes later, Pearl Jam's on stage. The sound is exquisite. I'm standing on the side of the stage with Kurt, his bandmates and other crew. The audience is all-in and the band goes from zero to full throttle in an instant. Pearl Jam deftly plays material from all four albums, improvises and experiments, and the audience reciprocates with a level of participation and engagement that I've never before experienced at a concert. The band plays six songs in its encore, continuing beyond the set list, which sends the roadies scrambling. The guitar that Eddie needs for *Around the Bend* is already packed away. When the poor guitar roadie finally comes running with the axe in hand, Eddie goes matador in front him with a white towel in his hand. We're in Barcelona, after all! The séance repeats itself five or six times to the unbridled approval of the crowd, who erupt in chants of "olé olé!" The atmosphere is ecstatic and in the course of one evening, I've undergone a transformation from a musical sympathizer to a full-fledged disciple. The concert lasts about two and a half hours, Vedder skillfully charming the masses every step of the way.

Back in Fastbacks' band room, spirits are high, even though both Kim and Lulu have gone back to the hotel; in their own words, they're suffering from a serious "rock'n'roll overdose." Kurt and Mike, on the other hand, are bouncing off the walls and five minutes after Pearl Jam has left the stage for good, Eddie's once again in their band room. He's in a great mood, but doesn't mention today's concert or Pearl Jam for the rest of the night. Instead, he walks around pouring wine for everyone in the room. We stay there for a few hours, with intermittent visits along the way by Pearl Jam's manager, Kelly Curtis, guitarist Stone Gossard, drummer Jack Irons, a couple of insistent groupies and others. The talk drifts from Barcelona and Gaudi's masterpieces to Eddie Vedder's collaboration with (now deceased) Nusrat Fateh Ali Kahn on the soundtrack to the Tim Robbins film Dead Man Walking. Eddie re-enacts how the legendary Qawwali singer at one point lays his hand on Eddie's shoulder and says, like master to apprentice, "You have a really good voice!", causing most of the people in the Barcelonan backstage room to burst out laughing.

Despite the enjoyable atmosphere and exclusive company, fatigue begins to set in for me. It's been a long day and a really hectic period leading up to my departure from Copenhagen. I doze off for just a moment, but awake with a jolt as some guy jumps into my lap and wraps his arm around my shoulder. Confused, I look up into Eddie Vedder's smiling face, while Kurt Bloch acts as photographer. A friend of Fastbacks is clearly a friend of Eddie Vedder, and a fill-in guitar roadie for the supporting act is just as welcome as the front figure for the main attraction.

Eddie asks where I'm from and Kurt tells him that I'm a good friend and that Sharing Patrol is a "kick ass trio." I take the opportunity to give Eddie our freshly minted live album, which he "can't wait to hear," said with emphasis and as far as I can tell without irony – after which he turns back the clock to Pearl Jam's chaotic performance at Roskilde Festival on June 26, 1992. On that crazy evening, Denmark won the European Championship in soccer[1] and Nirvana also played. Eddie stage dove into the audience, got into a physical scuffle with the security guards and later yelled at the guards from the stage. This dramatic and chaotic concert led to Pearl Jam cancelling the rest of their tour and pushed them to the brink of a split, amounting to the turbulent culmination of their upheaval from underground musicians to superstars in record time.

We're the last ones to leave the building through the backdoor at 2:30 a.m., but many fans are still lined up and waiting outside. A girl begs Eddie to take a picture with her – I think of the line "Take my hand, not my picture" from *Corduroy*, which Eddie sang on stage earlier that evening. And sure enough, Eddie discreetly lifts his left hand to hold her at bay and instead gives her the bottle of wine he's holding in his right. Then, he and photographer Charles Peterson – who closely covered the entire Seattle era – hop into a waiting bus. I go with Kurt and Mike to the nearby hotel and soon after I'm sleeping like a log.

The next day, I drive with Fastbacks in their small band van to San Sebastian. The mood in the van is pretty pissed off along the way because Lulu's extremely expensive camera had been stolen. She's furious and we drive around Barcelona to find a police station where she can report the theft. Along the way, Kim Warnick tells me about her close personal relationship with Pearl Jam's lead singer:

Kim – He comes to our band room before and after every single concert. So there's always a shitload of people in that room, because everyone knows that if they need to get in touch with Eddie, then their best chance of finding him is being around us. I've known him for a long time. It all began when Stone and Jeff told me that they had found an amazing new singer for their band Mookie Blaylock [PJ's original band name – and the name of a then-active NBA player]. I didn't hear anything from the band at first, but they began playing a bunch of small concerts and word spread that something big was up and coming. One day, we played a concert and this little guy came up to me and said that he was a big fan of Fastbacks. "Thanks," I said, "and just who are you?" "My name is Eddie Vedder," he

1. You probably can't fathom what a huge deal this was for Denmark, but it triggered one of the biggest spontaneous assemblies of people in Copenhagen's streets ever – an estimated 300,000 people. It's probably similar to what Chicago was like when the Cubs finally won the World Series in 2016, only bigger.

Henrik's first meeting with Eddie Vedder. Here, arm in arm with Kurt Bloch, from the supporting act Fastbacks – one of Eddie's favorite bands. Earlier that year, Kurt produced Sharing Patrol in Seattle, which opened the door to Pearl Jam for Henrik. Photographer Charles Peterson lurks in the background. Barcelona, Spain. November 22, 1996. Photo: Henrik Tuxen.

answered. Since then we've been friends, even though I wasn't all that crazy about Pearl Jam in the beginning. But Eddie is a person you can really trust. Recently, I was totally down after my divorce [from Ken Stringfellow]. Drunk and sobbing, I came knocking at the door of Eddie and Beth [Eddie's then wife] in the middle of the night. They welcomed me in, made a bed for me to sleep in, helped me settle down and saved me in a situation where I had totally lost my self-control. Eddie's a really good friend that you can always count on.

Our van makes it to Basque Country and we approach San Sebastian, where the bands will be playing that evening. Despite sold-out concerts everywhere, Kurt tells us that the tour is still losing money, largely due to Pearl Jam's new drummer, Jack Irons, formerly of bands including Eleven and Red Hot Chili Peppers. He's also an old friend of Eddie Vedder from San Diego, and the man who originally recommended him as a vocalist to Stone Gossard. Jack has back problems, which means that he can't play more than two days in a row and no more than four times a week. Pearl Jam has fully accepted this situation, which means that the concert caravan is running on a deficit. It has also given Fastbacks quite a few days off along the way, and in some cases they've played their own concerts at smaller clubs. One of these days off is in Groningen, Holland. After the sound check in Groningen, Fastbacks are surprised to find an old friend in the band room.

Kurt – A couple of weeks earlier, we'd talked with Eddie about playing some Who songs together. Eddie was psyched about the idea, but we never talked about it again. But then, there was Eddie, sitting in the band room. He had hopped on a train from Amsterdam to Groningen and asked if we still had a deal to play together. We formed the band on the spot and The What warmed up for Fastbacks: Mike on drums, me on bass and vocals and Eddie on vocals and guitar. We played three Who songs: *Naked Eye, The Kids Are Alright* and *Can't Explain*, and the Pearl Jam songs *Lukin, Not For You* and *Rearviewmirror*. A total blast.

SAN SEBASTIAN

Backstage in San Sebastian, I'm having a bite when I suddenly feel a hand on my shoulder. It's Eddie Vedder, who just wants to say thanks for yesterday, after which he rubs his temples and laments having had a bit too much to drink the day before. I remember sitting on the floor, leaned back against the wall, talking about and showing pictures of my newborn daughter. Eddie smiles attentively and looks at the picture of itsy bitsy Lulu for a long time. It's something that happens every time I meet Eddie, whose first question is almost always "How are the kids?"

Johnny Sangster's sister-in-law has arrived from Seattle with a friend to celebrate her thirtieth birthday in the company of friends from Fastbacks. It later turns out that she also went to elementary school with Mike McCready, but apparently they haven't seen each other for ages. It doesn't take long before anecdotes and old tales from the past fill the air.

Fastbacks take the stage in a packed arena and this show goes significantly better than the day before in Barcelona. I have some work to see to, getting Kim's extra bass ready. In keeping with tradition, Eddie shows up at Fastbacks' band room right after the concert and jubilantly flaunts a poster where Pearl Jam is presented together with *The Kim & Lulu Band.*

Pearl Jam later takes the stage with a musical hurricane. The set list is completely different from the day before and tumultuous scenes quickly sprout up. The security staff diligently pull the most raucous concertgoers over the barriers along the stage pit. The staff is prepared to use CPR, first aid, leg locks or whatever the situation may call for. A guy who originally seemed pretty groggy turns furious when the security staff won't let him back into the audience right away, so then his friend hops over the barrier and starts pounding the security guard. People are going nuts, but the guards eventually get the situation under control. I'm standing in the front row of the audience even though I have a backstage pass, but the frenetic situation makes me a little nervous and I decide to take in the rest of the show from the side of the stage.

The crowd's energy is astonishing and even surpasses the previous day in

Barcelona. The band plays tight, with Eddie dynamically leading the proceedings. At one point he starts hopping and suddenly 15,000 people are hopping in rhythm with him, causing the entire arena to begin undulating. The crowd is like a lump of clay he can shape with his hands. It's both fascinating and frightening. Later, Eddie talks to the audience about taking care of each other and takes a moment to pay tribute to his friends in Fastbacks, eliciting the audience's approval. The concert's intensity reaches unfathomable heights and culminates during the encores. As the ecstasy reaches its peak, Eddie throws his microphone as high as he can into the air. On the second try he manages to get the microphone and cord over the gigantic lighting rig suspended about 30 feet above the stage. Eddie jumps out and hangs from the microphone cable, which is wrapped around the lighting rig, and swings back and forth. Suddenly, everybody's jaw drops – audience and crew alike. The rig starts swinging uncontrollably, and everyone in the arena instinctively shares the same thought: "How much would it take for the whole damn thing to collapse?" Before the shock subsides, Eddie gets a running start and swings out once more in pure triumph.

After the concert, the party is again in Fastbacks' band room. Everyone from Pearl Jam is there except for Jeff Ament, and once again the atmosphere is pleasant, relaxed and by no means unruly, which almost seems counterintuitive given everything we've witnessed over the past three hours. Kurt tells jokes about Mike McCready's old band Shadow, which McCready wants to reunite on the spot with Kurt as guest guitarist, and he also wants to pin down an exact date for going second hand CD shopping with Kurt. Jack Irons is enjoying himself, but has his hands more than full trying to keep his 5-year-old son reined in. Meanwhile, I have my first conversation ever with the cheerful Stone Gossard. With his big smile, short hair and glasses, he looks more like a physics student than a composer, guitarist and founding member of the 90s' biggest rock band. Stone talks about the new album and the band's upcoming plans, but another subject comes up when he learns that I'm from Denmark. It turns out that he's a devoted fan of author Peter Høeg, and he delves into details of what makes Høeg's books, such as *Smilla's Sense of Snow* and *Borderliners,* so special. Stone then introduces me to a smiling and well-dressed older couple, who are also big fans of Peter Høeg. They turn out to be Stone's parents, who took the trip from Seattle to Spain. Stone's mother tells me how good it is to see Eddie in such good form and high spirits. There's no doubt that the vocalist's mental constitution has been dark for long stretches before and after the death of Kurt Cobain, and that many of those close to him have feared for his well-being.

Mike McCready joins the conversation; like the others, he has read most of Peter Høeg's works. He's stoked when he finds out that I live on the street Strandgade, where half of *Smilla's Sense of Snow* plays out. But apart from *Smilla*, Denmark and the 1992 Roskilde Festival don't trigger the best memories:

Mike – We were totally far out, and I remember feeling like I was going completely insane. Everything had happened way too fast for us. It was only the second band I'd ever played in, and everything just exploded around us. It was way too much to take in way too short a time. After the concert, we just couldn't do it anymore and had to cancel everything. That was the night Eddie jumped into the crowd and couldn't get back on stage again. Nobody had anything under control.

Eddie joins the conversation and recalls Roskilde, the European Championship final match and how everyone deserted the festival grounds to watch Denmark win, and how everybody went absolutely batshit afterwards. Despite it all, the band seems to agree that Denmark is a place worth checking out, and Stone Gossard concludes that Denmark should absolutely be among the destinations on Pearl Jam's next European tour. That will turn out to be quite another story.

My trip winds to its end, following a couple of monumental, breakneck days in the company of Pearl Jam and Fastbacks. I thank Eddie Vedder for the concerts, and he says that I've seen two very different concerts in Spain. He congratulates me on my newborn daughter, thanks me again for the Sharing Patrol album and asks if we might be interested in opening up for Pearl Jam if they come to Scandinavia. "Yeah, I think we could probably figure something out," I stammer, overwhelmed by the prospect. After a couple of approving pats on the shoulder and a "See you somewhere," I find Kurt and Mike's hotel room. I drop to the floor like pile of bricks. I was actually planning on booking my own hotel room, but I had overlooked the minor detail that "Pearl Jam in town" equals sold out hotels within a considerable radius of the venue.

The next morning, Pearl Jam is gone with the wind, and Fastbacks are on the way to the band van for the last concert in Lisbon. I say goodbye to Fastbacks and apologize to Kurt for the months of badgering him to join them on tour, to which he simply says, "We needed someone like you to come along."

After a short stroll through San Sebastian, I take the train to Barcelona. I find myself seated next to a teenage couple plastered with Pearl Jam merchandise and CDs. On the trip to Barcelona, they manage to sing every word of every verse to 25-30 PJ songs, helping me to comprehend some of the more complicated lyrics that I hadn't previously been able to decipher. Shortly before arrival, I get their attention to ask them for directions in Barcelona, but the boy and girl both shrug their shoulders dejectedly. They don't speak English. I experience the same situation repeatedly about 20 years later in South America. Pearl Jam's lyrics carve their way into the minds and hearts of even those who don't speak the language.

The mag goes out of business

Back in Denmark and inebriated in the wake of everything I've just experienced, I pen a tour diary for *Wild* magazine. Judging by the response from my colleagues, we've got a veritable scoop on our hands. In fact, there's a growing backlog of good stories at the magazine, but the management suddenly pulls the plug. *Wild* is shutting its doors for business, while the teeny-bopper magazines *Mix* and *Vi Unge* are merging under the same owner and will continue with a joint editorial staff.

I'm mostly preoccupied with getting the article published in its entirety, regardless of the magazine. As with every estate, there's a big rush of events before the burial, and I have to push hard to make sure that they don't just publish a few watered-down excerpts for 13-year-old readers of Mix. Wild dies and I get the article published in *Gaffa* in February 1997.

The excitement stemming from a memorable experience usually resides for a time in one's thoughts, only to slowly fade out and make room for other events. This time however, the opposite is true. It feels as if the intensity of the experience, the impressions and my enthusiasm continues to grow. My ensuing correspondence with Kurt just amplifies the feeling. The day after I return to Copenhagen, the tour concludes with a show in Lisbon, where The What plays four Who covers with Eddie Vedder (wearing a mask) on vocals and Jeff Ament on guest bass; and during Fastbacks' set, Stone Gossard takes the stage to sing Pearl Jam's *Mankind*.

Back home in Copenhagen's Christianshavn district, with two school-age children and a young infant, it's hard to forget the rush of Spain. My fascination evolves into a minor obsession. From infancy, my daughter is brought up with Pearl Jam blasting from the stereo and lulled to sleep by her daddy's guitar renditions of PJ ballads like *Around the Bend* and *Better Man*. Wall space traditionally reserved for family portraits and the kids' creations are instead bedecked with personal photos of me with Eddie Vedder and Kurt Bloch.

In Pearl Jam, I've found an unprecedented combination of the traits that attract me most. First off, there's the pure, overwhelming force. At the age of nine, I was addicted to Black Sabbath, Deep Purple and Led Zeppelin; and for 13 years I've played semi-professionally in a tinnitus-inducing, Who-inspired rock band. In my ears, Pearl Jam takes the intensity to new heights that I haven't heard before or since. Then there's the wild and hypnotic mass psychosis. The drama and tension in the mass phenomenon of everyone being moved and captivated by the same thing. The crowd in Spain didn't just come to see a concert. These are dedicated disciples who insatiably soak in every iota emitted from the stage, and who already know every word of every song. Despite the commercial success, Pearl Jam manages to maintain a clearly alternative bent in its sound and attitude that people find fascinating. A punk tone and vibe – with explicit social awareness I haven't heard since The Jam – a touch of noise rock, a Neil Young-like troubadour and the influence of heavy 70s rock. And in purely lyrical terms, we're dealing with an intense and expressive band that speaks from the core of its soul – from darkness and light – with a vocalist whose words and voice I still find hypnotically alluring to this day.

At the same time, I'm entranced by the sincerity and authenticity that permeates every aspect of the band. The mix of political activism, wild abandon, pain and beauty in the music, combined with the inspiring sense that there's always more to discover and things I haven't caught or understood on previous listens, intensifies my fascination.

And perhaps more than anything, the relaxed and unpretentious attitude that I've experienced firsthand backstage, firmly rooted in dignity and respect. Add to this the latent tension that it could all potentially collapse at any time. I've seen Eddie Vedder relaxed and chipper, but there's no doubt that external pressures and daunting inner demons can suddenly stop the party on a dime.

The Who

Then there's also our shared love of The Who, which is somewhat surprising to me, since it's not a band I would immediately associate with Pearl Jam in purely musical terms. I discover that Eddie Vedder's love of The Who dates back to his youth in a way that uncannily mirrors my own. I was born the year after Vedder, so we were both light years behind the popular music scene of our time. Sharing Patrol's greatest inspiration is The Who – equal parts melodic and explosive – mirroring our fundamental musical ideal. The Who writes the most beautiful pop songs, they're the most amazing instrumentalists and the most insane and destructive band, always smashing their gear, their hotel rooms and themselves, while the indefatigable Pete Townshend endeavors to decimate all imaginable artistic limits, often taking him to the edge of a breakdown. I read that Eddie's favorite album for years had been The Who's *Quadrophenia*: the same double LP I listened to ceaselessly in my late teenage years, and an album that's stuck with me ever since.

The 1973 concept album tells the story of Jimmy, a "Mod" (fashion-conscious youth culture in 1960s England) and fan of The Who in London in 1964. Jimmy's not schizophrenic, but rather has four dueling split personalities – quadraphonic – representing the four members of The Who. *Quadrophenia* is Pete Townshend's unrelenting lifestyle and subculture, delving deep into fundamental questions of identity and reckless youth culture. The album chronicles intense confrontations between Townshend and his fans, as reflected in the "who made who" dialog of *The Punk and The Godfather*. Townshend takes a philosophic approach to intro-spection, depicting himself as both a charismatic leading figure in a dynamic subculture and, on the other hand, a helpless cog in a machine, as a group of doomed youth (yet again) drowns in ennui. "The Punk" attacks "The Godfather": "You declared you would be three inches taller / You only became what we made you" and "We're the slaves of the phony leaders / Breathe the air we have blown you." The oeuvre culminates with The Godfather's parting shots to The Punk, sung by an utterly melancholic Townshend:

26

I have to be careful not to preach
I can't pretend that I can teach,
And yet I've lived your future out
By pounding stages like a clown.
And on the dance floor broken glass,
The bloody faces slowly pass,
The broken seats in empty rows,
It all belongs to me you know.

Lyrics: Pete Townshend
Music: Pete Townshend
© 1973

Quadrophenia hits the silver screen in 1979 as a film and soundtrack. Things go horribly wrong for the dedicated Mod, Jimmy, as conflicts escalate with his family, workplace, girlfriend and friends, until he suffers the ultimate loss: being let down for being a mod. Foreshadowing the road movie *Thelma & Louise* (released more than 10 years later), the film ends with Jimmy riding his Vespa scooter full speed over the cliffs of Brighton and being swallowed by the English Channel hundreds of feet below.

Vedder undoubtedly drew on the words and thoughts of Townshend more than once through the 90s as he – whether he likes it or not – became the spokesperson for the "lost" generation that seeks to express and discover itself through loud and melodic rock music.

The Who is as dynamic, pugnacious and dysfunctional as any band in history. Four hugely distinct personalities who combined equal parts mutual affection, internal jousting for status and merciless rivalry to create unforgettable art and insane rock'n'roll anecdotes. Sitting in the wake of my experiences in Spain and listening to one Pearl Jam CD after the next at home, I read to my great excitement that The Who will be performing *Quadrophenia* as a show, and the tour will be coming to Denmark. In connection with the tour, I land an interview with Roger Daltrey, who's 53 at the time but looks more like he's 35. I invite Johnny Sangster to join me on the interview. We give him Sharing Patrol's album, declare our trio's lifelong love of his band and have a fantastic chat with The Who's lead singer. The tone turns surprisingly personal as, without a hint of irony, Daltrey says a lot of stuff along the lines of "You know how Pete is, he never listens to what I say," only to declare his great love for Pete in the following breath. At the time of this writing, they're the only surviving original members of The Who – and they're the duo that reaches out three years later to help Eddie Vedder at a critical time in his life.

Yield

From afar in the Danish capital, I follow closely in the comings and goings of Pearl Jam. I accumulate extensive knowledge of the band's catalog, side projects, fan sites and anecdotes, discovering along the way just how strong the fan culture surrounding the band is, and how much PJ does to give fans special offers, exclusive fan club singles not available in stores, security at concerts, etc. I also get frequent updates from my sources in Seattle, but otherwise there's no closer contact.

I enjoy delving headlong into my rabid fandom, while at the same time I'm almost embarrassed by how preoccupied I am with this one band. From the sidelines, I know that Pearl Jam is in the process of recording a new album in 1997. When I'm the first person in Denmark to get my hands on a white label copy of *Yield*, I'm decidedly nervous as I put the CD in my Discman. After all, what if it's shit? It's not.

Being part of the music magazine *Gaffa*, I'm used to having a good shot at getting interviews with international stars, but the response to my Pearl Jam request is unsurprising yet devastating: *Forget about it.* I try to get into direct contact with Eddie Vedder through Kurt Bloch. Sure, we were in close contact in Spain, but everyone who meets him personally probably feels that way, I think. I know that Kurt forwarded a "letter" I wrote to Eddie, but I also know not to put any more pressure on Kurt to engage in distasteful rock star/press maneuvering. In fact, I've already gone a bit too far by pulling strings through my close friend and tapping into his great aura of respect. Kurt's goodwill – and pure rock'n'roll heart – comes from him never pressuring or taking advantage of others, while treating everyone fairly and equally.

MAUI, FEBRUARY 1998

The year 1998 is still a good era for the record industry. Digital downloading is more of a future threat than a reality, and a golden catalog from the days of vinyl can still be converted to CD format, triggering renewed sales. So if Sony's biggest rock'n'roll golden goose of recent times doesn't want to talk, other means become necessary: such as sending journalists to Hawaii to see the band's two low-key test concerts before the upcoming US and Asia tour. I manage to land a spot on the delegation at the last moment. So as winter ravages little Denmark, I am greeted with flowers and alohas at Hawaii's Maui Airport on February 20, 1998.

There's an outbreak of fever on the idyllic Pacific island. Pearl Jam fever. One of the world's biggest names in music playing two concerts on such a little island makes a noticeable impression everywhere. As far away as the airport in San Francisco, I run into swarms of fans headed for the same destination. A Pearl Jam concert (or concerts) is the main attraction for about half of the passengers on this flight to Hawaii. The steward boasts of hailing from Seattle, quickly whipping up a rowdy atmosphere, while a male voice from the cockpit begins singing *Alive* over the PA. Next to my party of travelers is a young Italian guy named Marco, who's spent every cent he had on the trip; he's planning to sleep on the beach.

Upon arrival in Maui, Pearl Jam is everywhere: people in T-shirts and various merchandise, and cars plastered with PJ stickers as far as the eye can see. There's a longstanding tradition of marquee bands dropping by the exotic islands, but these concerts are the biggest production in the history of Maui, even though it's not the first time PJ has played there. The original *Ten* tour concluded at the local high school about six years earlier. This time, Pearl Jam will be playing two sold-out outdoor concerts at a 4,000-capacity venue. Idyllic and scenic surroundings to be sure, but not exactly ideal conditions for good sound. The PA system is better suited for a garden party with Lawrence Welk than a full-blooded rock'n'roll concert with Pearl Jam. The sound is partly responsible for two concerts that are far from the power and intensity I experienced in Spain 15 months earlier. Nonetheless, it's both crazy and a blast to attend the concerts, where hardcore fans from around the world have convened to see Pearl Jam.

At the first concert, people scream things like "I've travelled 5,000 miles for this," waving banners with slogans such as "Save the Maalaea" – a world-renowned surfing area in Hawaii that was annexed for military purposes. Pearl Jam plays about 20 songs, both new and old, and despite plenty of highlights, the overall impression is disappointing, considering what the band is capable of. The band is all too aware of this, and after an exceedingly loose version of *Jeremy*, Eddie Vedder apologizes to the audience. Startup problems or not, the atmosphere is sublime. People yell and scream, crowd surf, pogo, drink and smoke. They've come from all over the world, they feel fabulous and they'll be coming back tomorrow. It's great to be in Hawaii.

I've joined a pleasant little travelling party of three others: two Danish colleagues, Jan Poulsen and Thomas Søie Hansen, and Sony representative Marianne Søndergaard, who came to Hawaii on the heels of a short tour of the US. After the concerts, we lay on the beach in the company of Pearl Jam freaks from near and far, taking advantage of all that Hawaii has to offer in our short time on the island: body surfing, flying in a helicopter over a desert, rain forest and volcanoes, venturing on a successful whale-spotting tour and fully enjoying exotic Maui. The only drag is my massive jet lag. We're 11 hours behind Denmark, and as the only one of us with a driver's license, I'm the designated driver – and a tight deadline means that I have to write my story right away.

The day after the first concert, we see at least nine humpback whales from a small sailboat. We leave behind the whales, Captain Willy "The Whale Magnet" and his beautiful deckhand Kitt, whose primary task consists of pouring drinks. She's so good at her job that we have serious trouble staying on our feet when the seas turn tumultuous. But the waves eventually subside and we turn to our preparations for another dose of Pearl Jam under the palm trees.

The concert is far better than the day before, and the sound is significantly improved. It's not a concert that will go down in the annals of Pearl Jam history, but it's certainly a nice exotic evening with many strong moments. The concert is followed by an outdoor after-party that we somehow get into. Neil Young and then-wife Peggy

The writer-to-be dozes off for a moment backstage after an incredibly long day, but wakes up suddenly with somebody hopping in his lap, wrapping an arm around his shoulder, looking him straight in the eyes with a laugh and saying something he doesn't comprehend a word of. Kurt Block reacts quickly and captures the moment on film. Henrik Tuxen & Eddie Vedder. Barcelona, Spain. November 22, 1996. Photo: Kurt Bloch.

Eddie Vedder promotes The Sharing Patrol. Barcelona, Spain. November 22, 1996. Photo: Henrik Tuxen.

Interview with Roger Daltrey in connection with the Quadrophenia tour. Denmark, 1997.

Maximum Rock'n'Roll Chicks, Lulu Gargiulo and Kim Warnick. San Sebastian, Spain. November 23, 1996. Photo: Henrik Tuxen.

The good life. Marianne Søndergaard, Jan Poulsen and Thomas Søie Hansen. Maui, Hawaii.
February 23, 1998. Photo: Henrik Tuxen.

The Sharing Patrol, Roskilde Festival.
July 4, 1986. Photo: Press.

are there with one of their sons who is in a wheelchair, and Chris Cornell is walking around in a dapper gringo outfit with his then-wife Susan Silver, who also served for some time as manager of both Soundgarden and Alice in Chains. Eddie Vedder stops by for an ultra-short appearance, but he's clearly uninterested in being accosted by the hordes. I manage to say hi and can see that he has to adjust his gaze a bit before he nods in recognition, shakes my hand and says thanks for the last time. Meanwhile, he's spotted a large mob headed towards him, so he quickly disappears into a band bus and doesn't make an appearance again that evening. On the other hand, I meet the tall, muscle-bound bassist Jeff Ament from Montana, who pays untethered homage to his friends from Fastbacks. Jeff freely admits that the first concert in particular was extremely substandard, he talks about the forthcoming *Yield*, and he tells us how great it is to snowboard in Utah. The conversation also touches on his old roommates and my former bandmates. Jeff asks why I'm in Hawaii. "To see Pearl Jam," I answer, which appears to come as a surprise. Jeff says that everyone in the band has been staying on the island for a while, and that apart from Eddie they're staying at a hotel downtown. Eddie's residing more incognito on another part of the island. I already know this to be the case from Kurt and others. Eddie never has the freedom to just walk around unbothered. Wherever he goes, there's always somebody who knows he's nearby and they hunt him down. "With the *Jeremy* video, he forever lost his anonymity," as Stone Gossard would say to me in a conversation later down the road. But the band and people around him are good at arranging things in a way that gives Vedder as much freedom as possible. The blue lagoons of Maui have always been one of the preferred destinations when the San Diegan surfer needs to recharge his batteries. The islands are also home to Boom Caspar, who has played Hammond-Leslie keyboard in Pearl Jam's live band since the early 00s.

Meanwhile, our Italian friend Marco from the plane ride to Maui manages to penetrate the iron curtain to the backstage area and approaches Jeff with his own CD in hand, which was probably the main purpose of his trip. Many of Jeff's friends (and others who would like to be) join the conversation. Before we head back to the beach, Jeff talks about how he doesn't care if people download and record Pearl Jam's music, as long as it doesn't lead to unauthorized middlemen making bank.

The next day, my travel companions depart a bit before my flight, so I squeeze in another whale-spotting trip and some ocean swimming. Departing from Maui, I find myself once again sitting next to a person who claims to be the world's biggest Pearl Jam fan. I join her in San Francisco for a round of sightseeing before continuing on to Copenhagen. Once again, I have Pearl Jam in my thoughts, words and headphones.

Chapter 2

2000–2001: DENMARK.
ROSKILDE FESTIVAL 2000.

From the time I get back from Hawaii until Roskilde Festival 2000, I'm never in direct contact with any of the members of Pearl Jam. They're no longer the world's best-selling band, but to me they're still the greatest thing going. Rumors had swirled for some time, but the celebration begins when Pearl Jam's upcoming appearance at Roskilde Festival 2000 is definitively confirmed. The concerts in Hawaii were more exotic than ecstatic, so I'm geared up for a night of PJ at the top of their game, on Danish soil for the first time in eight years. The last time they were here, at Roskilde Festival in 1992, the concert had been moved ahead two hours because of the European Championship final match between Denmark and Germany, but I didn't get the message. So when I reached the stage well ahead of the originally scheduled time, ready to experience one of the two headliners from Seattle playing that day, I only caught the last five minutes of the chaotic concert. This makes the news of Pearl Jam's appearance at the 2000 edition of the festival all the more sweet. A return to Denmark by the only superstar band of the Seattle era – the most important rock wave since the 70s – to have eluded pitfalls such as heroin, deaths, suicide, artistic stagnation and internal feuds.

ROSKILDE FESTIVAL, JUNE 30, 2000

The upcoming festival – and the PJ concert in particular – is the talk of the town in Danish rock circles, and the expectations are sky-high. I've landed a full-time position as co-editor at the music magazine *Gaffa*, but work-related duties at Roskilde are manageable and I make sure to keep my calendar free of encumbrances on the night of Friday, June 30. Two days before the concert, I get a call that just about knocks me off my feet. Lars Puggard, PR rep from Sony Denmark, calls to say that it's looking like they can get me a Pearl Jam interview at the festival, but that he can't make any solid promises. By any stretch of the imagination, we're talking about my number one professional dream. I would finally get a chance to follow up on the experiences in Hawaii and (especially) Spain on pre-arranged terms. I've already interviewed many big international stars by this time, but it's surreal to be sitting in the car and preparing questions for Eddie Vedder and company in the festival's parking lot. But some logistical cables get crossed and the interview is ultimately cancelled on the morning of the concert. It's a disappointment, to be sure, but not a big surprise. Nobody in the Danish media, *Gaffa* and myself included, had managed to get an interview with Pearl Jam when *Binaural* came out about six weeks before the Roskilde concert.

So instead, I meet up with my girlfriend Anne. She's at the festival and we've agreed to join some friends for a bite and then see some concerts together. She doesn't have the same bulldozer gene as me, so it goes without saying that our plan is to take a backseat rather than being on the front lines at the concerts. But I make it explicitly clear that things will be different when it comes to Pearl Jam: as sure as death and taxes, I'm going to be front and center, as close to the stage as I can get.

A few hours before the show, my cell phone buzzes. It's Marianne from the Sony team. My Hawaii travel-mate Marianne Søndergaard and promoter Lars Puggard have decided to give me one of their own stage passes for the Pearl Jam concert. They know what it means to me – but, obviously, not what it could have meant if they hadn't given me that pass. I meet up with Marianne and Lars and thank them profusely. One thing that I had completely forgotten until chatting with Marianne in 2015 is that I was really torn about whether to accept their generous offer. Obviously, it would be a rare opportunity to see the concert from the stage – but on the other hand, I had really been looking forward to standing with all the other fans in very front row singing along at full blast to every song. I can only say that I made the right decision that day.

Together with Anne and our friends, I start the day by watching the Swedish rock band Kent on the Orange Stage, followed by much of Travis' excellent concert at the festival's biggest tent stage, Arena, while keeping close track of the time every step the way. I leave the green tent, giving myself plenty of time to get back to the Orange Stage. Anne and I agree to meet up in the backstage area after the

34

Pearl Jam concert.

Wearing a Pearl Jam stage pass sticker, I stroll freely into the backstage area about ten minutes before the concert is slated to begin. In true stalker style, I manage to track down Eddie Vedder and catch his attention. He's wearing a slightly ripped sweater and looks a little tired, but he's apparently in good spirits and relaxed. I introduce myself from the days in Spain; he nods in recognition and smiles back to me. Afterwards, I give him the photo I took in Barcelona of him and Kurt Bloch, arm in arm and wearing silly hats, which he gets a kick out of; he thanks me profusely and says that he'll be hanging it on his wall at home as soon as he returns to Seattle. On my birthday 14 years later, my friend Susan, who's known and followed Pearl Jam – and Eddie in particular – since 1992, gives me a birthday card with all the photos she's taken of me and Pearl Jam members through the years. I don't meet Susan until 2004, but as Eddie's guest, she's there on June 30 and shoots a photo of this exchange. Prior to that birthday gift so many years later, I had no idea this moment had been captured on film. At the last minute before Eddie takes the stage, I finally manage to do something I hadn't in Spain or Hawaii – get an autograph. I slip Eddie my tattered copy of the *Vitalogy* CD for a personal dedication and autograph. Eddie confirms that they'll be playing *Rearviewmirror*, wraps up the conversation with a "take care" and gets ready to take the stage.

On the side of the stage, I meet Lene Westen, formerly of Sony and someone who shares my PJ passion. She's chatting with Mike McCready's guitar tech; we exchange an excited "here we go" look when she sees me. At first we stand on the side of the stage, about five or six feet from Mike McCready's amp, but we quickly inch out to the edge of the stage among the photographers and stage crew. I remember standing there, looking out over the seemingly endless sea of people. It's getting dark and the crowd is restlessly swaying back and forth in anticipation. I stand for a while, looking out over the crowd, not really noticing anything ominous or out-of-the-ordinary, apart from the buzzing crowd and an incoming storm that's growing in intensity.

When The Who's *Baba O'Riley* from *Who's Next* rings out from the PA system, we know that it's time for action! Pearl Jam takes the stage and busts straight into the rockin' *Corduroy*.

Shortly afterwards, a stage security guard orders us back to where we started, next to McCready's amps on the right side of the stage. McCready's cheerful guitar tech resumes his earlier conversation with Lene and shares short anecdotes between songs. We yell and sing at the top of our lungs. The festival grounds are jam-packed, but the response doesn't quite match our expectations. It's hard to tell whether the culprit is the wind, incoming rain and/or sound. Pearl Jam plays tight and on point, but not at the same level I've seen them reach both before and since. I'm having a blast and crooning my head off. Pearl Jam at Roskilde Festival –

it doesn't get any better than this! I'm at a concert with my favorite band, playing at the festival and stage that's home to my fondest and most enduring memories.

Pearl Jam manages to play:

Corduroy

Breakerfall

Hail Hail

Animal

Given To Fly

Even Flow

MFC

Habit

Better Man

Light Years

Insignificance

Daughter

During *Daughter*, the bad weather has turned miserable, with lousy visibility and rain blowing in on the stage. Jeff Ament's gentle tapping on the neck of his bass tells me that the next song is Pearl Jam's biggest hit through the ages, the "head-banger hymn" *Alive*. But right before the band gets started, there's some commotion on stage. A person comes in from the side of the stage and says something to Eddie Vedder; my guess is electrical safety problems due to the pouring rain and high voltage cables. But then I see it's something worse. Eddie tries to calm the crowd and get them to take three steps backwards. Then he announces a short break, after which Pearl Jam's tour manager goes to the mic and asks the crew to turn on the floodlights.

As we shout impatiently for the next number, we see Eddie break down on stage, apparently in tears. Lene complains loudly – "come on now!" – but stops abruptly as we begin to comprehend that something is terribly wrong. At first, Mike McCready is bouncing up and down a bit, impatiently ready to start playing again, but then he hears something that's clearly alarming and passes a message on to his tech. He then turns to us and says solemnly, "I think they killed a guy."

Every iota of ebullience and ecstasy evaporates instantaneously. Panic spreads through the crowd amidst the rising uncertainty about what's going on. Did somebody get stabbed, or what? As the number of people and bad news arriving at the stage grows, the concert gradually disperses. Those of us at the side of the stage don't get any specific information, but we can see by the activity and the faces of the band, crew and stage staff that something is terribly, terribly wrong. The areas on, in front of, and behind the stage are pure chaos. I cautiously walk out to the edge of the stage and see disfigured bodies being pulled up into the photographers' pit. Chaos and panic. When I look to the left, I see a young boy lying limp and know for certain that he is dead. I've never before seen a dead person, but I'm intuitively certain that the young man across from me has taken his last breath. There's no trace of blood, and his facial expression is more peaceful and passive than twisted with fear and pain. I later learn that the boy is 17-year-old Allan Tonnesen from Varde, Denmark.

The members of Pearl Jam mull around restlessly on and behind the stage. Drummer Matt Cameron passes me by with a stone-faced look of shock. In the midst of all the commotion, I've lost my stage pass, but none of the security staff check or ask about anything at all. Under normal circumstances, Orange Stage during a headliner's concert is akin to Fort Knox, and a lost stage pass would be a certain recipe for immediate expulsion.

There's a lot of hectic activity going on backstage. People are lying on stretchers and receiving emergency treatment from first aid staff in white uniforms. Ambulances begin arriving at the backstage area with sirens blaring. I discretely ask a first aid staffer how serious the accident is. "Right now, we're giving four or five people CPR – it's a serious as it could possibly be," he says.

Behind the Orange Stage, by the artists' backstage area, I see Eddie Vedder walking alone. He's in tears, with a look of desperation and torment on his face. He walks by me, not seeing or noticing anything. I see him run into the musicians' area, where he screams loudly and jump kicks a mineral water dispenser. An announcement is made from the stage that a serious accident resulting in fatalities has occurred, and that as of yet nobody has an overview the full extent. About 45 minutes after the concert has stopped, I leave the area behind Orange Stage to avoid getting in the way of the first responders.

Everyone I see and meet is clearly in shock. I exit the area behind Orange Stage and enter "Media City," the area reserved for media members, and I'm quickly swamped by feverish news journalists hunting for eyewitnesses. I tell a national news channel what I saw, but with the caveat that I want one hour to withdraw my statements – which, to the journalist's great chagrin, I do shortly after, in part on the advice of Marianne Søndergaard. Her point is that nobody has a full overview of the scope of the accident, and whatever you say now might be transmitted around the world and eventually result in backlash. At that point, we hear about four or five fatalities, but nothing is certain. The atmosphere in Media City is one of stunned bewilderment. My friend and colleague, *Gaffa* editor Peter Ramsdal, collapses sobbing into my arms. I don't shed a tear, but a dark feeling washes over me, ossifying body and mind alike. I find Anne, who is also visibly shaken by the unfathomable events that just unfolded before us. The evening evolves into a singular darkness and Anne drives us home in the early nighttime hours. After a

The moment Eddie Vedder learns that a tragedy has occurred. Roskilde Festival. June 30, 2000.
Photo: Johan Persson.

long, dark trip along a highway dotted with jubilant electronic signs declaring that the Oresund Bridge to Sweden is now open, we arrive at home in Gentofte. My answering machine is full of messages, all with the same worried queries.
My circle of friends and family knows that I had planned on standing in the very front row.

The day after

Having informed family and close friends of my continued existence, I return relatively quickly to the festival grounds following a restless and hazy night's sleep. The shocking reports of many fatalities and others still in critical condition completely dominate the Danish news. At the festival grounds, the mood is subdued and despairing more than panicked or chaotic. The most important task for editor Peter Ramsdal and myself is to write a lead article for *Gaffa's* website about the accident, including a take on the festival management's decision to allow the festival to go on. I'm extremely torn at the time – and I still am to this day. On one hand it seems grotesque, cynical and irresponsible to let the festival continue, while on the other hand it seems chaotic to stop it. Peter is more confident in his opinion and holds that it is important for the festival to continue, in part because of the logistical chaos that would be triggered by shutting everything down – people travel from far and wide to Roskilde – and in part to allow for collective recognition and mourning by the audience, artists and festival management. We write the lead article together that day and print an expanded version as the first story in the next issue of *Gaffa*:

The Culture Lives On

Year 0 – the end of a youth culture – Judgment Day.
The tragic accident at Roskilde Festival on Friday, June 30 has been given many names, while countless attempts to explain the inexplicable accident have emerged in the wake of the tragedy.
It is not *Gaffa's* errand to be the judge of whether the concert could have been stopped earlier, whether the festival's safety measures were optimal, whether the audience behaved too violently, or whether rain, sound or anything else was the decisive factor. Nonetheless, we present here a couple of comments on the events that transpired.
As *Gaffa* is Roskilde Festival's official media partner, we have worked closely with the festival management before, during and after this year's Roskilde Festival. *Gaffa* has been represented at the festival for years, and the majority of *Gaffa's* employees have attended Roskilde Festival since the early days of their adolescence. The same goes for thousands of others attending Roskilde Festival.
In other words, no other event has been as instrumental to the very existence of *Gaffa* as Roskilde Festival. To all of us at the magazine, Roskilde Festival is one of the social building blocks, right along side elementary school, the Danish Broadcasting Corporation, after-school youth clubs, summer vacations, the Danish national soccer team, Hans Christian Andersen, etc. It's the very fabric we are made of. And so the conclusion is also clear: An accident – no matter how tragic and meaningless – must not and cannot destroy 30 years of spirit and culture. The festival and life must continue.
The undersigned and all affiliated *Gaffa* employees have been deeply moved by the accident and have the deepest sympathy for the families and friends of the deceased.

The festive spirits came to a halt with the sounds of ambulance sirens, but in retrospect, the management made the right decision by allowing the festival to continue. Like everyone else, we talked about the accident at length in the following days. This collective contemplation, combined with the festival management's, festival-goers' and performing artists' respect for the deceased, made it easier to process the shock and relate to the tragedy. As Youssou N'Dour said from the Orange Stage the next day: "All over the world, people remember and respect the dead with song and music." That was also the case at Roskilde Festival on Saturday and Sunday, July 1–2.

In the wake of the accident, there has been a lot of talk that the audience behaved like soccer hooligans and that the rules of safety and audience behavior should be tightened up. We at *Gaffa* welcome every constructive and practical improvement in these areas. However, youth culture has no use for a moral or political overcoat. It is not the role of Roskilde's police chief or Minister of Justice Frank Jensen to dictate how a dedicated rock audience should dress and behave. The audience can figure these things out themselves. Ever since Elvis shook his hips, this form of mass culture has spread across the world in countless iterations – not with hands folded and rears nailed to a bench in holy silence, but with collective energy, physical expression and enthusiasm as the central driving forces.

Linking the accident at Roskilde Festival with organized violence, such as today's soccer hooliganism, is misleading. The audience attends a festival for the party, beer and music – not to beat each other to a pulp in organized factions.

That said, it is time for reflection among concertgoers. The existence of every (sub)culture is built on consensus about a set of unwritten rules – and the observance of these behavioral norms. At raucous rock concerts, this means that you catch those who stage dive, you help those who fall get up, you let people trying to get out through, etc. The community is what often makes concerts magic for audiences and artists alike – not the crushing force of one-man wrecking crews.

In a range of media and the first police report on the accident, Pearl Jam is cited as "morally co-responsible," as they purportedly have a habit of encouraging violent behavior. This is an insult to a band that throughout its entire career has gone to extreme lengths to ensure its fans optimal conditions, including the entertainment and safety conditions at concerts. Pearl Jam was without fault in the accident, and the band's subsequent indignation is fully understandable.

Cars and airplanes crash – these tragic events are covered in the media, but they do not trigger politicians to call for car-free cities or lead people to vacation by bike. We have long-since become accustomed to expecting a certain risk in connection with transportation. After the accident at Roskilde Festival, we must also accustom ourselves to expect a degree of risk when attending concerts at festivals.

One of the reasons the accident at Roskilde Festival garnered such widespread media coverage is the surprise that an accident of this nature could even occur. Nobody in their wildest imagination had envisioned an accident like the one that happened during the Pearl Jam concert, despite the fact that Roskilde Festival director Leif Skov said the following in an interview with *Gaffa* about safety at festivals just a short time before this year's festival: "I would say that the probability of an accident at our festival is not very big. But, of course, it can also happen at our festival."

Now the audience is warned. Now they know that from the moment they step onto the festival grounds, they are exposed to a certain risk, especially if they want to get up close to the stars near the front of the stage. One can also hope that the extra consideration shown at the concerts after the accident will be echoed in the coming years.

The efforts to do everything possible to minimize the risk in the future, to honor the dead, and to continue supporting Roskilde Festival are illustrated by the following initiatives and events:

–   The Roskilde 2000 Tragedy Memorial Fund has been founded to support research and development of health and safety measures, primarily in connection with music events. As of this writing, the festival management has already donated the concert fees originally allocated for Oasis and Pet Shop Boys to the fund.

–   The audience and relatives spontaneously created a memorial grove for the deceased, while the establishment of a permanent physical memorial is being planned.

–   Two of the deceased – and in one case all funeral attendees – wore fresh Roskilde 2000 admission bracelets during the funeral, at the request of the families.

Roskilde Festival will never be the same, but the spirit lives on. We'll see each other again in the summer of 2001.

Henrik Tuxen and Peter Ramsdal

Scapegoat

In the wake of the incomprehensible catastrophe, the court of public opinion and the mass media seek high and low for potential scapegoats. Strong accusations are hurled at Pearl Jam from various sources, including claims that they have a reputation for encouraging violence and exhibiting unrestrained behavior at their concerts. The police insinuate that these accusations come from a leading international agency for concert safety – a claim that multiple media outlets run with before doing their own investigations. The fact that Pearl Jam's concert eight years earlier at Roskilde Festival had been extremely chaotic only feeds the fires of what begins to resemble a witch hunt. The Danish newspaper *BT* publishes an article with a photo that seems to indicate that Pearl Jam intentionally encouraged the audience to cause a tumult at the concert. Upon further reading, the article refers to a conflict with a security crew that intentionally harassed the audience at a concert in the United States six years earlier. But how many people actually read that far? These were clearly grotesque and counterfactual rumors about Pearl Jam, a band that does everything it can to ensure its audiences proper, safe and entertaining conditions. With the support of Peter Ramsdal, I do my best to debunk these rumors through *Gaffa*.

The rest of the festival plays out in slow motion, permeated with grief yet imbued with a moving sense of togetherness. Returning home is almost unbearable, leaving the unanswered question of how to process the experience now.

I never personally shed a tear, but I feel heavy, tired and sluggish as scenes of the accident repeatedly play out in my mind's eye. I read everything I can find on the subject, taking everything in rather than keeping it at arm's length. Perhaps I do this to compensate for my emotional abyss and lack of catharsis. It's an emotional state that completely dominates the following months. While on vacation with my family in Norway, I lay down for long stretches, listening to the new Pearl Jam album *Binaural* in my headphones. The only thing I figure out for certain is that the song *Light Years*, which Pearl Jam played at Roskilde, is going to be played at my own funeral. It's a sudden realization about a subject I've never previously given a thought. And it's not because of the lyrics, but because of the mood and sound of Eddie Vedder's vocals, I think. In any case, I listen to it again and again, as it's proven to be the best way for me to get in touch with the incident and all the emotions it awakens. Pearl Jam themselves have often dedicated the song in honor deceased friends, including the band's close friend Diane Muus from Sony Music in the Netherlands, who died at the young age of 33 – a dedication that can be seen in the somber YouTube video "Pearl Jam - *Light Years* (Pinkpop 2000)", filmed in the Netherlands 18 days before the Roskilde concert.

Light Years
I've used hammers made out of wood
I have played games with pieces and rules...
I've deciphered tricks at the bar...
But now you're gone,... I haven't figured out why...
I've come up with riddles... and jokes about war...
I've figured out numbers and what they're for...
I've understood feelings... and I've understood words...
But how could you be taken away?...

Roskilde Festival. The day after. July 01, 2000. Photo: Per Houby.

And wherever you've gone...and wherever we might go...
It don't seem fair... today just disappeared...
Your light's reflected now,... reflected from afar...
We were but stones,... your light made us stars

With heavy breath,... awakened regrets...
Back pages and days alone that could have been spent,
Together... but we were... miles apart
Every inch between us becomes light years now...
No need to be void,... or save up on life...
You got to spend it all.....

And wherever you've gone... and wherever we might go...
It don't seem fair...you seemed to like it here...
Your light's reflected now,... reflected from afar
We were but stones,... your light made us stars

And wherever you've gone... and wherever we might go...
It don't seem fair...today just disappeared...
Your light's reflected now,... reflected from afar...
We were but stones,... your light made us stars

Lyrics: Eddie Vedder
Music: Pearl Jam
© 2000

43

In the days after the accident, I have no idea where Pearl Jam and their team are located. The only sign of life is their press release, which had the effect on me that I can never see or hear the word "devastated" again without thinking about the situation the band must have found themselves in following the tragedy:

Statement from Pearl Jam in response to Roskilde Festival Tragedy, June 30, 2000   *Copenhagen, Denmark*

This is so painful. . . . I think we are waiting for someone to wake us and say it was just a horrible nightmare. . . . And there are absolutely no words to express our anguish in regard to the parents and loved ones of these precious lives that were lost. We have not yet been told what actually occurred, but it seemed random and sickeningly quick . . . it doesn't make sense. When you agree to play a festival of this size and reputation, it is impossible to imagine such a heart-wrenching scenario. Our lives will never be the same, but we know that is nothing compared to the grief of the families and friends of those involved. It is so tragic . . . there are no words.
                                                                  Devastated, Pearl Jam.

Roskilde Police

Back home from vacation, I'm contacted by the Roskilde Police, who would like to speak with me. A jovial young officer comes by *Gaffa's* offices in Copenhagen a couple of times to get my version of what I had seen and believe happened. At the time, it's about a month since the accident, and my initial reaction is disbelief about how little the police apparently know. I also discover that determining the exact time of events is everything in police work. The officer is especially interested in knowing if I had been wearing a watch and if I happen to know what time the band played and how many minutes had passed before I saw the first injured and dead among the audience. The police are working with a 15-minute margin as to when the concert actually started. This seems a bit incredible to me, since there were about 50,000 people there. One of them must have checked the time. I can roughly estimate the start time of the concert, but the last time I looked at my watch was when I left the Travis concert in the green tent. I tell the officer that I saw the body of Allan Tonnesen right after the concert was stopped. The officer tells me that this is very important information and that my statement is now the earliest established time of any of the nine fatalities.

The officer is also very interested in hearing about my contact with Pearl Jam and the band's safety policy regarding audiences and fan contact in general. He says that two officers from the station will be travelling to the United States to see a couple of concerts with the band to see for themselves what a "normal" Pearl Jam concert is like – and he shares his deep disappointment that he won't be one of the policemen taking the trip.

I have a couple of nice conversations with the officer and try my best to recall as much as I can, but a lot of it has already dissolved from my memory or is repressed. I contact Lene Westen, who I stood next to at the concert, thinking that she probably saw something that I couldn't recall, but she isn't interested in talking with the police – or, for that matter, with anybody about the traumatic incident.

A couple of weeks later, I'm contacted again by the same officer, who asks if I would be willing to write an appendix to the police report. I find the question a bit confusing. It turns out that the supposed American safety expert Paul Wertheimer has written an appendix focusing on safety problems in connection with large rock concerts and the specific risks he believes apply to Pearl Jam's concerts. My task would be to write some sort of counterargument, accounting for Pearl Jam's safety and audience policy, and fan relations in general. I churn out a long spiel that is apparently included as an appendix to the case. I've never seen nor heard anything about the appendix since. Somewhere around October of that year is the last time I'm contacted by the police, apart from a Christmas card I receive from the Roskilde Police during the holidays a couple of months later.

Besides Pearl Jam's official statement "Devastated," I didn't find any official statements from the band, who used manager Kelly Curtis as their spokesperson. But the band is still active, as evidenced by the band's live CDs.

For years, Pearl Jam bootlegs on cassette, vinyl and CD have been a lucrative business for unauthorized middlemen. More than anything else, Pearl Jam has always been a "fan band" whose faithful followers want to get their hands on everything they can. To ensure audiences high-quality recordings of the group's live concerts at reasonable prices, the band decides before the *Binaural* tour to record and release all of their concerts on CD. Most of them are only available through the band's fan club, Ten Club, but some are also released for sale in retail stores. One of the more memorable recordings is the live concert on November 6, 2000 in Seattle. It's the second of two benefit concerts in Seattle, where old friends Pearl Jam and Red Hot Chili Peppers raise more than a half-million dollars for the homeless in Seattle. At the concert, Eddie Vedder talks a little about the tragic accident in Denmark, and about how Pearl Jam later came into contact with the Australian victim Anthony Hurley's family and friends, who visited the band in Seattle. He dedicates the following ballad, *Off He Goes* from *No Code,* to the memory of Anthony Hurley, as the song is said to have been one of his favorites.

"Time heals all wounds" is one of the biggest clichés in the book, but the accident slowly resides from my thoughts. And, of course, I didn't get hurt or know any of the victims. I see my role as giving voice to Pearl Jam's social commitment and unique fan relations. No charges are filed against the band, and the clamoring pundits who pointed to the band as the villain in the days and weeks after the accident never gain ground in the public discourse. I follow the band's autumn

2000 US tour from my computer online. In the summer of 2001, I travel to Seattle with my family for a month, but I don't meet with anybody from the band.

Autumn 2001, Telephone interview with Stone Gossard

On the fateful day of September 11, 2001, Pearl Jam guitarist Stone Gossard releases his first solo album, *Bayleaf*. I'd met the calm, cheerful and eloquent guitarist in Spain five years earlier, and through Sony I managed to arrange a telephone interview with him in October 2001.

After a good talk about his new album and Pearl Jam, the conversation shifts to a heavier note as the inevitable topic of Roskilde Festival 2000 comes up. Pearl Jam's manager Kelly Curtis previously spoke with the Danish newspaper Politiken and DR (Danish Broadcasting Corporation), but this is the first time that a band member discusses the accident with a Danish media outlet:

Stone – It's extremely difficult for me to talk about, since we all still feel genuinely sad and upset about what happened. Questions like "How could it happen?", "What brought everything together that made this possible?" and "How could us standing up there and playing some songs lead to a situation like this?" still hang in the air. On one hand, it feels like we were witnesses to a terrible car accident, but on the other hand we were participants – we were a part of that event. We participated in a context where something really terrible happened, and in some way we bear some form of responsibility. I know that we will play in Denmark again – I'm certain of that. It will be a very emotional experience. It's really painful to talk about, but it's important. We have to do something for Denmark, but I think that all of us in the band still need some time to really understand and live with what happened. I think we will do something concrete in relation to the accident at some point.

The interview then turns on its head as Stone asks a lot of questions about how the Danish public is dealing with the accident. I tell him that it has been, and still is, a huge case in the media and the subject of many conflicting views, accusations and disagreements. But I also tell him that the 2001 edition of the festival went well, with improved safety and in a respectful setting with understanding for the victims and their families.

Stone – The only thing I can think about is the families of the victims; how it has changed and impacted their lives. That's the only thing. It's only natural that people try to figure out what happened and why. But the only thing that really matters is the families, how their lives changed that day, and how everybody's lives changed.

Gossard specifically says that Pearl Jam will never again play at a festival of that size and will never play if their own crew does not have full control over safety, stage preparations on, in front of, and behind the stage, the medical tent, etc. Then he concludes:

Stone – Our highest priority is the safety of the audience at our concerts. Making the necessary decisions is up to us. Unfortunately, it's too late in terms of what happened at Roskilde.

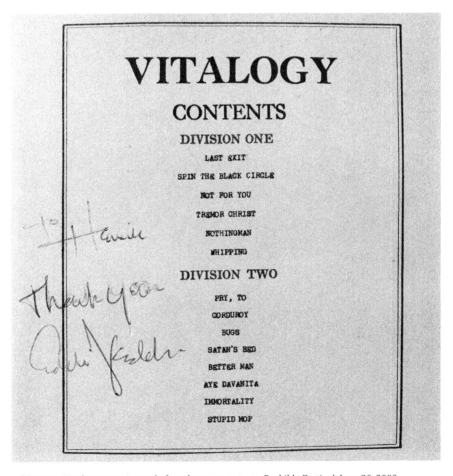

Eddie signs Vitalogy ten minutes before the concert starts. Roskilde Festival. June 30, 2000.

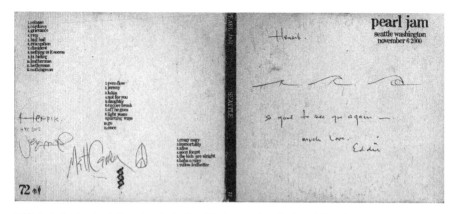

Eddie's dedication to Anthony Hurley before Off He Goes. Seattle. June 11, 2000.

Eddie and Henrik check out photos from Barcelona 1996. Roskilde Festival June 30, 2000.
Photo: Susan Nielsen

Chapter 3

2002: PEARL JAM. NEW YORK CITY.

"Can you fly to Seattle the day after tomorrow?" asks the voice in the telephone one day in early September 2002. It's Marie Hecht of Sony Denmark. "It's crazy! You can get a solo interview with Eddie Vedder." Well, OK then. No biggie – just the call I had been waiting the last six years for.

Against all expectations, the door's been pried open through official channels, probably due to Pearl Jam's more relaxed attitude towards the press.

I accept the invitation right away, but three hours before departure I get an emergency call: "The interview is cancelled." Great. Fortunately, it turns out to just be a postponement, not a cancellation. A couple of weeks later, I find myself in a steel bird high above the Atlantic, with a course set for New York City.

The interview doesn't have anything to do with Roskilde Festival. It's firmly a part of PR activities for Pearl Jam's recently released studio album, *Riot Act*. Yet we do end up discussing the events at Roskilde, and I step from the ranks of pure fandom into the role of sounding board and liaison between the band and a number of relatives of the deceased.

Things fall into place pretty rapidly after arrival in NYC. At the reception desk of my hotel, there's a Discman with the new CD in sealed packaging and a note with the time and address of the interview the following day.

When I step through the doors of the Soho Grand in Tribeca, I remember being in precisely the same place three years previous for a Beck interview. The surroundings are ideal: the rooftop balcony of a luxury hotel on a warm and sunny day, with a bird's-eye view of Manhattan. Eddie Vedder has cut his long locks –for a brief period prior to this interview, he had been sporting a Mohawk in protest against the US aggression against Iraq. He seems calm and in good spirits. I mention the concerts in Spain six years earlier. Eddie nods and says he remembers me: "Same haircut." "Yeah, I guess that's not where I channel my great originality – except for the part where it falls out over time," I shoot back.

I've brought the old *Gaffa* article I wrote about that trip in Spain, which includes photos of Eddie with Fastbacks and me. To my great surprise, he already has the article, which he recently found while cleaning up his archives and kept because of the photos. Eddie takes a brief look at the article, triggering a few joking barbs at the expense of Kurt Bloch and Fastbacks. I thank him for the good times in Spain and go on to praise the new album, *Riot Act*. Although I only had the chance to hear the record for about 24 hours before the interview, one thing stands out: the many songs about the complexities and pains of love:

Eddie – Yeah, first comes love, then the pain, and we're all a bunch of spinning tops. But who controls us – is it the big hand from above, or where does that drive come from? So about love, yeah, or about trying to compensate for the love you didn't get, or the search for love you've read about other people experiencing. It never ends. The top never stops spinning.

In a way, Eddie's words are a more positive extension of the desperate hit from *Vitalogy, Spin the Black Circle*. The interview then inevitably turns towards the darkest chapter of Pearl Jam's history. "That's right, you were on the stage. Now I remember," says Eddie after I briefly mention the tragic evening and tell him that my answering machine was full of messages when I got home. "To make sure you were OK," adds Eddie, before his voice gets weak and somewhat disjointed. He puts his hands to his head I see some tears in the corners of his eyes:

Eddie – It's weird. I've talked about it in every interview over the past two weeks, but the fact that you were so close to it all brings back some really heavy things. I've tried to tell others what happened, but since you were actually there, there's almost nothing I can say about it. Maybe we can come back to it later. It all just hit me suddenly.

We change the subject and Eddie talks about how difficult it was to enjoy success in the early grunge days, when people were constantly surrounding and chasing after him. It was impossible to go anywhere, but now that the audiences "have thinned out a little bit," it's much easier to keep his head high and look people in the eye, communicate and enjoy the music and the atmosphere.

To the question of why Eddie – unlike so many of the stars of his era – made it through the rock'n'roll centrifuge in one piece, and how Pearl Jam managed to survive and stick together as a band, he says:

Eddie – One of the things that I do personally is to disappear into nature for long stretches without being in contact with others. A 20-foot whale don't give a fuck who I am. Being in such direct contact with nature for longer periods is a big and humbling experience, and I'm usually bursting with new energy when I come back. Another reason is that nobody ever offered me heroin. And I think the fact that all five of us love playing in the band, but we also do other things: play in other bands, all kinds of humanitarian work, etc. As individuals, we aren't defined by the band, we have a life outside – although the guitar is an extension of Mike McCready's body.

It's a description that certainly fits Eddie. He's a surfer, painter, sportsman and political activist on a wide spectrum of issues. Despite superstar status, he's always fought doggedly to be able to look himself in the mirror.

Eddie – Without saying too much, I feel like I've tried to treat our planet right. But I have to say that there have also been some really difficult challenges in my life in recent years, even before Roskilde. [Eddie went through a tough divorce with his teenage sweetheart, Beth Liebling, after the two filed for separation the month after the accident at Roskilde.] I know that it sounds self-righteous, but I felt like I had a certain amount of good karma. When such big challenges come your way nonetheless, it's something you have to deal with – there's no way around it. Even before Roskilde I had gone through things that weakened my foundation and that night was so completely and insanely intense. Forty-five minutes before taking the stage, we got a call from the United States. Chris Cornell's wife [Susan Silver – the couple divorced in 2004] had just given birth to a daughter. I was so happy on his behalf that I had to leave the room for a moment to shed a few tears of joy. Chris is one of my closest friends, I love him dearly and they had been trying to have a child for a really long time. I had even thought about saying something from the stage – not name any names, but just welcome this new child to the world. Obviously, it also really meant a lot to Matt [Cameron, Pearl Jam's drummer, who also played in Soundgarden with Cornell]. I was really moved – and 90 minutes later we see the other side of life's cycle play out before our eyes. But no matter what I say about our thoughts and feelings, I don't want a single word to be written before making clear that it's nothing compared to what the families and friends of these young people, whose lives were so brutally cut short, have had to go through. After the accident we were in contact with the friends and family of the Australian boy, Anthony Hurley. We invited his sisters and some of his friends to Seattle. They showed us family photos, told stories about him and so on. It helped to deal with something that seemed unbearable. And if there are any other family members that want to get in touch with us, we are more than willing to do that.

I put the tape on pause and say that if I can help in any way to arrange contact with the Danish families, that I would more than willing to do so. Eddie responds positively to my offer and seems very open to the idea of establishing contact with friends and family of other victims, if that's something they're interested in. I'm surprised to discover that at this time, more than two years after the accident, such contact is essentially non-existent. Eddie tells me that he hasn't heard from any other families than that of the young Australian, Anthony Hurley. It's a subject he approaches with the greatest of caution and he asks me to do the same: "The last thing I want to do is to create any form of unwanted attention." We agree to discuss the practical details after the interview. As Eddie rewinds his memory, he is again overwhelmed by the events of that fatal evening and has to search for both the words and his voice:

Eddie – If I just could have ... It's hard not to regret things, even though we couldn't have changed them. It was also the way that the stage was set up. The audience on the stage side of the barricades were actually placed pretty high up, which made it hard to see past them. If you listen to the tapes from the earlier concerts on that same European tour, we probably stop the concerts 20 times out of 30, and it was no problem. There are a lot of questions that come up, and I'm sure that everything has been investigated. One thing is that it feels like the chain of command was unclear. Maybe some of the security staff weren't very familiar with the conditions. Our own security staff weren't working the show; they've never had a problem waving to me if something was wrong. My impression is that people saw something but felt they couldn't stop because there were 50,000 people there, which is almost understandable. But that's the type of situation we're used to handling, and I still think that if we just could have seen what was happening ... the rain was pouring straight onto the stage, and I had spotlights in my eyes.

Eddie was far from the only person who didn't know that something was terribly wrong. Even members of the audience who were in the close vicinity of the accident had no idea what was happening, and as for me, I thought the concert was stopped because of technical problems caused by rain on the stage.

Eddie – I just wish it had been for any reason but that. When we really realized what had happened, it felt like the worst nightmare imaginable was playing out before our eyes. When the attack on the World Trade Center happened, I felt like I knew how it must have felt to be here in New York or to have a family member in one of the buildings. The tragedy at Roskilde felt like it was on that level for us, and of course that's how you also experienced it in your city. You have to be very careful when you create a situation where people can see, hear, do and drink whatever they want, so you create a "communal vibe." You can't assume that people can take care of themselves. Whatever the price, you have to do everything imaginable to ensure the necessary safety conditions. Like in an amusement park.

You invite people in, they pay money to enjoy themselves and to be safe. But that's probably something that Roskilde has learned now. Maybe things had gone too well for too long, maybe some things were taken a little too lightly. I think that they should have stopped the festival. Because there wasn't enough time to establish a better and safer situation, and because the weather was still bad – but also out of respect for the victims.

I think back to that chaotic atmosphere behind the Orange Stage and how the band members looked so stunned and Eddie Vedder crying and taking out a water dispenser with a roundhouse kick. After the accident, Pearl Jam remained in Denmark for a few days before leaving. During that time, in the midst of their grief, the band received psychological assistance from some of the only people in the world to have experienced something similar first hand. On December 3, 1979, 11 people were crushed to death during a concert by The Who in Cincinnati. Since childhood, Eddie Vedder has had an extremely strong affinity for Pete Townshend – an affinity that only grew after two met personally. As Pearl Jam's popularity grew, the two bands frequently performed together, with Vedder and Townshend becoming close friends. Upon hearing about the incident at Roskilde, Pete Townshend and Roger Daltrey immediately took a direct flight to Copenhagen to give the kind of help that only people who have been in the same situation can offer. Vedder says that this mental assistance helped a great deal.

Eddie – One thing that was really important in my process of moving forward was the conversation I had with Pete Townshend in Copenhagen the day after the accident. I could barely speak, but I said to Pete that I couldn't understand it in terms of karma. We had always done everything in our power to create a safe setting at our concerts and to take care of our fans. I thought it was strange that it could happen to us. Pete said: "Maybe it happened to you because you can handle it. Karmically speaking, it happened to your band because of the respect you enjoy and because you are really and truly considerate and take care of other people." It was an interesting thought that turned everything around 180 degrees in my head. But at the time I didn't think we could handle it... and we can't, I will never be able to handle it. Afterwards, we returned home to Seattle and the band and crew created a kind of internal security system, and we called each other all the time, because it felt like we couldn't talk to anybody else about what happened. Friends and family showed us sympathy, but we couldn't relate to them for months. For us, it went from something you thought about once every five minutes to once every fifteen minutes. It was impossible to eat, we couldn't talk about anything else, and if anyone talked about a basketball game or an album, it was impossible to listen – it wasn't important. We couldn't get it out of our minds and it was there constantly during our subsequent concerts in the States. We were really unsure about whether or not we should cancel. We played, because it was important for us and our crew to be together and to work through the tragedy together. When we played the first concert in August, I went up on the side of the stage and watched Sonic Youth, which was the opening act. They played *Teenage Riot*, and that was the first time I had smiled since the accident. It gave me strength and a belief that there is a force and a joy in music that makes it worth it continuing in spite of everything. Now we've put the story into music with *Love Boat Captain*. I imagine that we'll be playing that song every night in our upcoming concerts. It gives us an opportunity to remember and honor the victims, which will feel good.

Love Boat Captain

Is this just another day,... this God forgotten place?
First comes love, then comes pain. Let the games begin,...
Questions rise and answers fall,... insurmountable.

Love boat captain
Take the reigns and steer us towards the clear,... here.
It's already been sung, but it can't be said enough.
All you need is love

Is this just another phase? Earthquakes making waves,...
Trying to shake the cancer off? Stupid human beings,...
Once you hold the hand of love,.. it's all surmountable.

Hold me, and make it the truth,..
That when all is lost there will be you.
Cause to the universe I don't mean a thing
And there's just one word I still believe
And it's

It's an art to live with pain,... mix the light into grey,..
Lost 9 friends we'll never know,.. 2 years ago today
And if our lives became too long, would it add to our regret?

And the young, they can lose hope cause they can't see beyond today,...
The wisdom that the old can't give away
Hey,...
Constant recoil...
Sometimes life
Don't leave you alone.

Hold me, and make it the truth,...
That when all is lost there will be you.
Cause to the universe I don't mean a thing
And there's just one word that I still believe and it's
Love,... love. love. love. love.

Love boat captain
Take the reins,.. steer us towards the clear.
I know it's already been sung,... can't be said enough.
Love is all you need,.. all you need is love,..
Love,.. love,...
Love.

Lyrics: Eddie Vedder
Music: Pearl Jam/Gaspar
© 2002

Later that day, while talking with Stone Gossard, he confirms the song's importance to the band:

Stone – The most intense moment for me after Roskilde was probably the first day we all sat together again, when we started our US tour. We toured for the next three months and it was really hard. When Ed wrote *Love Boat Captain* at the end of that period, it all suddenly came back to me. Discovering that he possessed such abilities as an artist was really significant. He got it out in such a beautiful way. That was the last song we recorded for *Riot Act*, and it was unfinished until the last day in the studio. But it did get done and the minute Eddie began singing the song for the first time, I knew that something good had happened.

Back to the rooftop terrace. I've now been in the company of Eddie Vedder for just over an hour and to put it mildly, the original plan is way off schedule. I was originally allotted a half-hour interview, which Vedder extended to more than twice that by telling the band's press manager Nicole Vandenberg, "I think we're gonna go for a bit longer." I need to run back to my room and get my bag with extra questions, but Vedder accompanies me and asks if I'm interested in taking a picture of the two of us together. For once in my life, I actually remembered to bring along a small point and shoot camera in my bag, so we pose in front of the Manhattan skyline as Nicole Vandenberg takes our picture.

When interviewing rock'n'roll icons, I usually try to get an autograph to bring back home for my son. After Vedder's story about his meeting with Townshend, I tell him that my weakness for The Who has been passed on to the next generation of my family. At this point, my son Tobias is 14 years old and has practically seized my Who albums. Without telling me, he wrote a big school assignment about The Who – and he later spends most of the summer of 2005 watching and re-watching the movie *Quadrophenia*. Eddie takes out a pen and paper:

Eddie Vedder's regards to Tobias Tuxen.

THE BACK CATALOG

Virtually all my encounters with Pearl Jam have been marked by a seriousness, insight and depth, as well as the flipside of their passion: Seattle humor at its best. I experience this humor that same day in an interview with Mike and Stone. And we have such a rollicking time that they ask if I'll drop by again the next day, which of course I will. Here's a rundown of my stellar séances with these two brothers in arms and soulmates, as they insightfully and jovially retrace their steps through Pearl Jam's back catalogue.

Ten (1991)

Stone – Ten is a record that everyone... When you meet a hard-core Pearl Jam fan – no not a hard-core but a general Pearl Jam fan – comes up and says "That record affected me." That record, still to this day, more people than not will say is their favorite of our records. For us it was a slightly difficult record to make. It was "over rocked." We were novices in the studio, and spent too long recording – we spent way too much time. Doing different takes on the songs, killing the vibe and overdubbing tons of guitars. It was just a difficult record to make, especially having made the Temple of the Dog album right before, which was the easiest and most beautiful record that we've ever been involved with [Temple of the Dog's lineup is close to that of Pearl Jam today].

Stone – Get Chris [Cornell] in the band with us and we would be unstoppable. Oh man. I would love to do a Temple of the Dog show at some point. That would be really cool.

Mike – I went through that the last time I talked with [Chris].

Stone – Goddamn it, let's do some Temple of the Dog! [Stone starts singing and imitating Cornell Cornell from *Your Savior*.] "Are you afraid... And you whisper my fate."

Mike – He is a very tall and handsome man.

I know. I interviewed him in Seattle in connection with his solo album Europhoria Morning. *Great album.*

Stone – Absolutely. There's that line, "I'm down all the time" – that's one of the greatest lyrics, and most beautiful songs.

Can you talk a little about the guitars on Ten?

Stone – We did it. There's a lot of reverb on the guitars, there's a lot of reverb on that record.

Vs. (1993)

Mike – On *Vs.* I think that we were a little bit more together. The band was blown up pretty big and everything was pretty crazy, and this record was kind of our reaction to that. It's probably my favorite record of ours; I always go back to this one – *Vs.* or *Yield. Vs.* is really fresh, there's more energy to it, and there's less reverb going on. There's different stuff like *Daughter* on it.

Stone – *Go* is still one of the heaviest songs we've ever written. Sounds killer. We got our "heavyosity" out on that record. Eddie's scream on *Blood* was the first one of his over the top screams.

I always loved Rearviewmirror.

Mike – Yeah, that one is always fun to play live.

Stone – Is that on that record? I thought it was on...

It is.

Mike – That was just a wild time in our lives. I remember when we finished it, me and Stone drove back to Seattle in Stone's car and we went, "Let's listen to our new record."

Stone – Let me tell you about this too – 'cause we had smoked pot. We thought it was kind of rock'n'roll to smoke pot, and for some reason we were driving up this mountain going up over Sacramento. I was driving, and at some point I couldn't figure out whether I was going uphill or downhill, and I had to pull over to the side of the road (laughing). I was having some kind of a massive anxiety attack.

Mike – I was really up. (laughing)

Stone – Wow yeah, we drove home together in my old Volvo Station Wagon with a DAT player.

Mike – And we stayed in Portland, Oregon for a night.

Stone – Made quiet love to each other.

Mike – Yeah, we only had one room, and I remember panicking a little about that.

Vitalogy (1994)

Stone – *Vitalogy* is the first one where Ed is playing guitar, and he wrote three or four songs on that record. I remember thinking, "This is so different from what we've done before, is anyone going to like this?" Ed started doing a lot more of the writing, and I was starting to figure out how I was going to fit in the band. All of a sudden I had to play more complimentary parts rather than writing parts. That was a big shift for me, and one that I wasn't comfortable with, necessarily.

You wrote most of the songs on Ten, *right?*

Stone – Yeah, and it was kind of a changing point in general, and at the end of the session, I was going, "I don't know if I like this record." I remember it coming out, receiving all these great reviews, and then you started listening to it three or four months later, and it was "this record is great," and thank God we went through that change. Ed started playing a lot more guitar, and it just had more of a punk feel to it, with real simple songs. A lot of the stuff recorded really quickly.

In many ways, it seems like Vitalogy *established an approach used on many of your following albums.*

Stone – Yeah, and I think it was mainly because Ed started to explore the guitar, and how his aesthetics kind of enter the thing, which now is an amazing aspect of our repertoire. Had he not started to play guitar, we could easily have become kind of one-dimensional, I think, doing the same kind of formula.

Mike – For me *Vitalogy* was just a fucked up time 'cause I was pretty drunk. That's a shameful time for me to think about, it was a bad time for me. I was having trouble getting into the studio. It was a big blur honestly. I like the record now, but I couldn't listen to it for years – it was a bad time for me.

I think it's my favorite album, but it took a while before it sunk in.

Stone – I kind of had less to do with that record doing it, but now to have it be such a great record – I didn't see it originally, but I understand it today.

No Code (1996)

Stone – That was a change. The first one with Jack Irons kind of being the main guy on drums. It was a whole new... It didn't really feel like we had put together a great record, it felt really... But it's another one of those records where people are coming up to me saying... "oh *No Code*." I think there are great words on that record.

You say that it was around the time of Yield *that you really got accustomed to playing with Jack Irons. That's interesting, 'cause some of the songs on* No Code *are really written for his way of drumming, like* In My Tree *and* Who You Are.

Stone – Well, Jack wrote *In My Tree*, or he actually recorded that whole drum take just by himself, like, "Here's some percussion kind of feel, do you want to add something on top of it?" We never even played that song, which is one of the reasons why it is hard to play [Pearl Jam started playing it on the *Riot Act* tour]. And *Who You Are* was something he and I came up with in the studio, which is a cool thing to do. When Jack is doing his thing, he really is an exceptional drummer. We have had three different drummers, but Jack is so distinctive, he's almost like a Stewart Copeland [drummer in The Police] kind of guy. He really has a unique style.

Sort of shuffling?

Stone – Yeah, he's got some great grooves for sure.

Yield (1998)

Mike – *Yield* was the first album since *Vs.* where I actually got to write some stuff. I wrote *Faithful* – well, Stone helped me out. I had two different intro parts, and Stone helped me out putting together the verse. I called him up on the phone and I think he just hummed.

Stone – Yeah, it was kind of a hard part to put together.

Mike – Yeah, Stone did that over the phone. It was just a great chance for me. I got more of my stuff on that record than I'd ever had in the past. [McCready also wrote the music for the opening song *Brain of J* and the hit single *Given To Fly*.]

I remember talking to you, Stone, after No Code, *and you said: "Next time I'd like to do a pop record."*

Stone – Did I say that after *No Code*? Yeah. Well I think in many ways we did. It was certainly "poppier." It had a little bit more structured and arranged songs. I don't know if it was really poppier, but it seemed more professional, if that's a good word or not.

Mike – So personally it was cool. It was also just a fun time. Jack was really getting involved with the band.

Stone – Yeah, we'd gotten into a groove with Jack. It was a much more comfortable record to make in terms of everybody sounding good together. It seemed to be much more focused after *No Code*.

Did Jack end up stopping in the band because of his back problems?

Stone – Well, he had gone through a really stressful time in his life, and had a real problem touring and being away from his family. I think it was more of a personal decision of his. As much as he wanted to be in a band and be a part of it, he found himself struggling with keeping up with the schedule, and kind of doing everything he wanted to do. And being away from his family was a real problem for him. And him bringing his family along with us turned into kind of a zoo for him. [*No Code*'s closing track, *Around the Bend*, is a kind of lullaby written by Eddie Vedder for Jack Irons' son, who was 5 years old at the time.] It just didn't work out, but it certainly was a musically enjoyable time.

Mike – Jack called us up some time before the '98 tour and said that he couldn't go on the road. We kind of had a tour booked and we wanted to do it. Soundgarden had broken up, so we called up Matt and he was interested in learning the songs, and he learns very, very quickly.

Stone – Yeah, he doesn't screw around.

Binaural (2000)

Mike – A hard one for me.

Stone – I think it was a little bit tough on everyone. I think that Matt, at that time, was still trying to figure out what his role was going to be in the band. For me personally, that was kind of difficult 'cause I was so used to having whatever it was – one for all, all for one – I was kind of struggling with that a little bit. I think Matt struggled too. I think we were just all a little tight making that record. There are some really nice songs on there, it was a success, but it didn't come out as quickly and with such genuinely good emotions as *Riot Act* did.

I'd say that Light Years *is one of your best songs ever.*

Stone – Yeah.

Mike – Hmm.

Stone – Yeah, that's a good one.

Mike – I think that *Nothing As It Seems* is a good one. That really shows you how dark lyrics Jeff Ament can write. For me, that was the first example of his dark side, which I hadn't really known. And I was going through some really bad personal problems at the time. Drugs and all kinds of shit. So my mind was more on trying to hide all that shit from the rest of the band. It was a terrible time for me, terrible.

I can see that you're looking a lot better now.

Mike – Thanks, I've been clean for 2 years and 8 months, except for cigarettes, and I feel good. Luckily, I'm still around, and I'm thankful that the band never kicked me out.

Stone (smiling) – We still have him.

Mike – I'm very grateful about that. Every day.

Was the entire time around Binaural *bad for you?*

Mike – Oh yeah – well the tour was great though, except for Roskilde. I was strung out when we recorded the record.

Unlike the previous four albums, you didn't work with Brendan O'Brien as the producer – why was that?

Stone – I think we were just ready for a change. We'd just heard a lot of records that Tchad Blake had worked on, you know, stuff he'd done with Los Lobos and Tom Waits, and a whole variety of albums. He's done a lot of beautiful sounding records. We were really super enthusiastic, and I think in the long run that we made a really cool record. But I think that due to the fact that Mike wasn't all the way there, and maybe there was still a little "getting-to-know-you" thing going on with Matt, it wasn't all of us showing up and being confident.

Riot Act (2002)

Mike – For me, going from *Binaural* to *Riot Act* was total opposites. To me, Matt was a 100% more involved. He brought in three songs and he was there, he was really excited and played amazing.

Stone – He played freely, and Mike did as well. I think those are the two main differences. The songs can be great, but they need to be opened up and brought to life. Matt can play straight and tight, and maybe he decided "I can come in and play like a studio drummer. I want to make Pearl Jam songs the best they can be," when he was making Binaural. He was really careful in not trying to step on anyone's parts, but on this record he just played like he was free, which he does when he gets excited. That's the difference between a great and a good rock performance. So he's full of life and free, and Mike had all this energy and freedom because of the arrangements, and because of how quickly things went down. And on top of that, Ed wasn't going through any kind of block in the middle of the record, but for song after song he just kept finding new things to write about, and was just genuinely excited about the whole process. We all fed on that. We all felt really comfortable and safe like, wow, "let's work on this song". You really felt like Ed was making everybody feel part of it, and that's the stuff that really feeds on itself. If everybody is in a good mood and comfortable, the playing gets better, and you start to have a little bit more swagger, and I think that's what this record has. Like, we're confident, we're not being safe. Binaural is a little safe, it just feels a little contained.

There aren't as many political statements as you'd expect from an album called Riot Act.

Stone – No, there's *Bu$hleaguer*, and on *Green Disease*, Eddie chants g-r-e-e-d over the music.

Mike – Well, the title *Riot Act* sounded cool.

Stone – It looks cool with the picture, which is kind of these king and queen metal chess pieces that Jeff helped design. It looks and sounds good. We'll have to do a song called *Riot Act* now. Isn't that cool when you have an album title and next album has a song called...

Mike – Pretty Zeppeliny. They did that with *Houses of the Holy* and didn't they do that one more time?

[A little Led Zeppelin history: *Physical Graffiti* contained the song *Houses of the Holy*. Their next album was *Houses of the Holy*, which contained the song *The Song Remains the Same*. Their next release was a live album called *The Song Remains the Same*.]

Speaking of Zeppelin – Riot Act*'s opening song,* Can't Keep, *sounds like the Zeppelin III-era.*

Stone – It's very Zeppeliny. The groove and drum sound is very John Bonham-like. In the guitar it also has a grey chord in Jimmy Page-style.

It sounds like Riot Act *was an easy nut to crack.*

Stone – This was a good one. This was one where we all felt that it was really good. When Brendan [O'Brien] came to Seattle and started mixing, and Ed was finishing up the vocals, and we could hear how it all sounded, we were like: "Oh wow, this is exciting, this is all fresh. We didn't labor over anything." It seems to me that the album showcases all of our things. There's the really simple kind of rock songs, which we could have been writing in the earlier era, but it just pretty successfully covers all the different times and dynamics, and has some really different songs on it, but still holds together.

Mike – I played lots of leads and enjoyed the process. I felt more like a part of the band than I had for a long time.

Stone – Mike got to show his stuff.

Mike – I love playing leads. (Stone and Mike start singing imitation guitar leads.)

Ground Zero - Year 0001

And of course, I couldn't make the trip all the way to New York without having a good chat with Jeff Ament and Matt Cameron. After all the interviews are in the can, I run into Jeff Ament outside the hotel. We walk down to Ground Zero as he shares stories, including about playing with the recently deceased bassist for The Who, John Entwhistle. Jeff's a sports and music fanatic, spry and straightforward and totally easy to talk with every time I meet him. It's a special moment standing there with Jeff and looking at the world's most talked about plot of land in many years, almost completely barren exactly one year after the twin towers collapsed and global politics took a historic turn. A few days later, on the flight back to Denmark from JFK, I'm not just filled to the brim with impressions and material for the articles I'll be writing in the time to come. I've also undertaken the responsibility to help establish contact with families of the Roskilde victims, without so much as an inkling about the nature, scope and achievability of this task.

Thoughts

My initial reaction is a mixture of shock and surprise. Why doesn't Pearl Jam have contact with these families, considering how much the accident weighed on their minds, shaping their adult and professional lives more than any other single event? Especially Eddie Vedder, the face most people associate with the accident. My surprise is all the greater because I know that the band has developed close relations with the Australian victim Anthony Hurley's family and friends.

The best explanation I can come up with is, on one hand, Eddie Vedder's statement about not wanting to draw unwanted attention, and on the other hand, the mental prison inhabited by celebrities of Eddie Vedder's ilk. In theory, he has access to everything and everyone, but in practice he can't lift a finger without it landing straight on the front pages of the tabloid media. And then there's the extreme sensitivity, understanding and discretion required for a task such as this. If the press gets the slightest whiff of contact between Eddie Vedder and the Danish families in the time after the accident, it would make a big commotion, producing a backlash that could have the exact opposite effect of the underlying good intentions.

In New York, Eddie Vedder says unequivocally that he has never received any letters or other contact from the Danish or Swedish families. It's unclear what happened in this very chaotic and vulnerable time after the accident, which involved many different parties. I later realize that letters were sent, but for reasons that remain unclear they didn't make it into the hands of the band members. Meanwhile, the band's management sought to spare the musicians from vulnerable confrontations for a time after the accident. Nicole Vandenberg of Curtis Management, Pearl Jam's publicist and personal friend, explained to me in early 2003 that Curtis staff attempted to shelter the band from the repercussions for a time after Roskilde:

Nicole – Every time the subject comes up in one way or another, they get so sad, depressed and introverted that it's almost unbearable.

Which is fully understandable. Pearl Jam is long on the brink of breaking up as each band member reacts in very different ways, but all of them are deeply impacted by the accident. Any attempts by the band in terms of new initiatives, creative endeavors, general joy and love of playing music can be punctured by the mere mention of the word "Roskilde." Whatever the reason, early contact between the band and the families of the victims didn't happen.

Manhattan Skyline. Henrik Tuxen & Eddie Vedder. September 19, 2002. Photo: Nicole Vandenberg.

Pearl Jam. 2002. Photo: Danny Clinch/Sony BMG.

Chapter 4

2002: THE MERLUNG REPORT.
THE DANISH VICTIMS.

Back in Denmark, the next step is to take a deep breath and embark on this mission with the greatest of care. During this same period, the public prosecutor's investigation of the accident concludes with an exoneration that frees Roskilde Festival of legal liability. The ruling sparks controversy, extensive coverage in the Danish and Scandinavian media and widespread public debate.

Immediately after the accident, the police chief of Roskilde heads an investigation of the events leading up to the tragic event. The Roskilde Police Department concludes that an unfortunate combination of circumstances led to the accident, with the primary cause being the panicked and violent behavior of the audience. The report concludes that no single organizational body or individual, including Roskilde Festival, can be held liable for the accident.

Some journalists, relatives and other organizations chastise the investigation. As the ultimate police authority at the festival, the Roskilde Police played an active role and could ultimately be held liable, which means that it has essentially investigated and acquitted itself.

THE MERLUNG REPORT
In response to this criticism, then-Minister of Justice Frank Jensen of the Social Democratic Party commissions an independent investigation by the public

prosecutor. With the assistance of the travelling investigative unit of the Danish National Police, public prosecutor for the Danish island of Zealand, Erik Merlung, interviews and questions more than 450 people. The investigation is tasked with exploring any potential criminal liability on the part of the festival management, police, audience, Pearl Jam and/or attending medical professionals. After 18 months of investigation, the Merlung Report is released in June 2002. Merlung is critical of the festival management's lack of an emergency response plan, but he does not find grounds for pursuing criminal prosecution of any organization or individual involved in the accident. The key findings of the Merlung Report are outlined below.

On the role of the festival's management

"The festival's management has not drawn up guidelines on when and how a concert is to be stopped. It must be assumed that the festival's personnel responsible for the performance of the concert and the leading security personnel did not know how they were supposed to respond in a situation such as the subject of this investigation, and they were unaware of who had the power to decide that the music must be stopped."

"In my assessment, it took far too long from the time that security staff recognized the severity of the situation until the music was stopped. The main reason for this, in my view, is the lack of clear guidelines as to who was supposed to do what. The preparation of such guidelines and the communication thereof to relevant personnel is, in my view, a managerial task. Thus, the festival management must bear some responsibility for the fact that 20 minutes pass from the time the large group of audience members collapses until the music stops."

"... it must be assumed that no overall emergency response plan was prepared for the festival; thus, there was no plan for collaboration between the individual medical functions in the event of an accident such as the subject of this investigation, and therefore the results of efforts by emergency staff were not optimal."

"However, nothing indicates that an overall plan for the emergency medical response would have changed the scope of the accident."

On the role of the police

"The processing of the permit application submitted to the chief of police in Roskilde was largely based on oral communications, personal relationships, experiences from previous years' festivals and trust that the festival management would meet the standard of previous years in terms of the number and qualifications of security and medical personnel. The police did not conduct any checks of compliance with safety requirements."

"The fact that it is not subsequently possible to document the details of the police's processing of the festival's permit application is unsatisfactory. The same applies to the police's failure to check for compliance with the stipulated safety conditions."

On the role of the audience

"There are no grounds for assuming that the number of audience members in the area in front of the stage was the cause of the accident. There was clearly sufficient space in the area between the mixer tower and the pallet platform."

"There were multiple groups among the audience that employed very aggressive and incendiary behavior on their way towards the stage."

On the role of Pearl Jam

"There are no grounds for assuming that the band Pearl Jam, in its conduct or by encouraging the audience, was a cause or a contributory cause of the violent pushing and wave movements among the audience."

On the role of medical staff

"The treatment administered to injured persons by doctors and nurses, aided by police officers, security staff and first aid volunteers, including the first aid administered, was the correct treatment based on a medical assessment. Thus, nothing indicates that there was any incorrect treatment or the like in connection with the accident."

"In my view, it can be assumed that there was a quite extensive medical response team at the festival in the form of doctors and nurses associated with the Stage Doctor function, doctors and nurses associated with the volunteer medical professional function and first aid volunteers from the Danish Red Cross."

Conclusion – no punishable offenses

"In the view of the public prosecutor, no reasonable suspicion has been established regarding punishable offenses in connection with the processing of the festival permit application, in connection with the accident itself, or in connection with the subsequent rescue efforts. The public prosecutor has therefore decided that no charges will be brought against any of those involved in this case."

THE DANISH VICTIMS

I am fully oriented on the report's conclusions, but apart from *Gaffa* reporting on the findings as part of its news coverage, I don't have anything to do with the report in a professional sense. My task at hand is of a different nature: finding the names and contact information of the victims' families. I begin by getting in touch with Roskilde Festival's new spokesperson, Esben Danielsen, to ask about the names and addresses of the families. Esben, who I already know very well at this point, is generally receptive to my request, but he is either not allowed or not willing to give me the names of the relatives – I can't remember which, but I don't get the information in any case. My luck isn't much better when I contact Roskilde Police, but there is plenty of help to find from Dorte Palle Jørgensen, a journalist at the Danish Broadcasting Corporation (DR).

Dorte had produced two excellent radio features about the festival accident by this time. The first is a reconstruction of the course of events using a pirate recording of the concert juxtaposed with interviews with festivalgoers and security staff who were in the crowd and escaped unharmed. The second program is a portrait of the 22-year-old victim, Lennart. Known among friends as "Leo," he was an inveterate Pearl Jam fan who pitched a camp at the festival with the same group of close friends every year. It's a dramatic tale of a son of Jehovah's Witnesses who turned his back on the congregation – and vice versa – in favor of rock music and his friends. In the course of her work, Dorte interviews more than 100 people, primarily young people who were present at the concert.

Through Dorte, I manage to get a hold of addresses and telephone numbers to family, and in some cases friends, of the Danish and Swedish victims of the accident. The next step is much more serious. Keeping in mind Eddie Vedder's words about "unwanted attention," I dial the telephone number of Leo's friend, Tore Rasch, as slight trembling courses through my body and voice.

My fears prove unwarranted. Tore Rasch is friendly and open to my inquiry, but also surprised and very emotionally moved by our conversation. In principle, he welcomes the opportunity, even if the idea of being in direct dialog with Eddie Vedder seems a bit abstract.

Tore says that he'll contact Leo's closest friends, including his childhood friend Matthias and Leo's former girlfriend Astrid. Leo and Astrid broke up well before Roskilde 2000, but had remained close. When I talk to Tore again a couple of days later, he says he felt so strange since our last conversation that he couldn't bring himself to go to work the following day because everything had so vividly washed back over him. The friends Tore contacted have reacted similarly, but their general attitude about corresponding with Vedder is very positive. On behalf of himself and his friends, Tore expresses gratitude and respect for the front man's desire to establish contact.

About Lennart "Leo" Nielsen

The story of Lennart, or Leo, is the story of a young, enthusiastic and vibrant personality castigated by Jehovah's Witnesses as a teenager and subsequently estranged from some members of his own family. He was a person you remember, or as all of his friend would agree: you'd either love him or hate him. About two years after Eddie Vedder's correspondence with the Danish friends and families of the Roskilde accident victims and Stone Gossard's visit to

70

Lennart "Leo" Nielsen. Private photo. *Shortly before the concert. Lennart "Leo" Nielsen (right) and friends. Roskilde Festival, June 30, 2000. Private photo.*

Scandinavia, I get a call from Leo's sister, Benita Rasmussen, who's interested in the articles about Pearl Jam that I wrote for *Gaffa*. Over the course of many long conversations on the phone, she gives a nuanced portrait of her little brother and their upbringing. Benita is now married and has two young children. She's still a member of Jehovah's Witnesses, but not the type that only knows about life within the confines of the church community. She is more than well aware of the wild lives of Danish youth and she's a lover of music, with a particular fondness for the bands Depeche Mode and U2. Like an open book, she talks about times good and bad in a dysfunctional childhood home shaped by violence, substance abuse, mental illness and love.

Benita – My little brother and I were very close, especially since we were born only 14 months apart. We've also been through a lot and had some really turbulent years in our childhood. When my mother was very young, she travelled all around Europe with a man. They returned to Denmark and had my older sister, Desirée, in 1975. But their relationship went bad and she found a new husband – Lennart's and my father. We all lived together with our dad for the first five years of my life. He was mentally ill and really violent, both towards us children and towards our mother. In the end, we fled from him in the darkness of night, after which things just went downhill for him. He later committed suicide by overdosing when Lennart and I were 13 and 14 years old. My mother got involved with Jehovah's Witnesses and started seeing another man when we were seven and eight years old. He also turned out to be mentally ill, along with everything that entails. Today I can see that he couldn't control it, but back then our daily lives were super erratic and filled with uncertainty. My

71

stepdad and Lennart didn't get along and were often in conflict. Lennart was really intelligent and eloquent, and a true master of provocation. He was the type of person who could take an oral exam with a hangover, without having read anything all semester, and come out with an A+. My stepdad wasn't nearly as eloquent. Lennart could really provoke him and cause him to lose face, which made him furious. Our stepdad, Jakob, tried to make things work with the limited resources he had at his disposal. But when we went on vacations, trips, etc., the conflicts were always bubbling under the surface and things almost always went bad. My mom and stepdad had two daughters: Liv, who was born in 1984 and Jennifer in 1990. Lennart was especially fond of Jennifer. It was really complicated, because he was in heated conflict with a man who was the father of his biological half-sister, who he loved with all his heart. Lennart and Desirée's relationship was also marred by longstanding conflicts, so it was a turbulent home where Lennart and I stuck together and leaned on each other for somebody to talk to.

Leo's mom, Sharon, had previously lived a relatively wild life in a family and network of friends where drugs were a part of everyday life. She turned to Christianity, in the form of Jehovah's Witnesses, and a more ascetic life before Lennart and Benita reached the age of ten. Obviously, it was a decision that influenced life in the family, but the siblings made their decisions about religion at a later age.

Benita – In Jehovah's Witnesses, we baptize adults, not children. Lennart chose to be baptized at the age of 15 and had actually wanted to do it earlier, but my mom and stepdad thought it was too early. When you choose to be baptized as an adult, you have to live by certain ethical and moral rules. As Lennart grew older, his way of life increasingly went against those rules. It was things like sex before marriage, drinking, drugs, etc. The Elder Council, which has a duty to expel members of the congregation who do not live by the church's ethical and moral rules, contacted Lennart numerous times and warned him, but he didn't change his lifestyle. At one point after he had moved out and was about 18 years old, the Elder Council decided to expel him from the church. But at the same time, they encouraged my mother to let Lennart move back in and asked her to take care of him and support his efforts to get back on track and in control of his life. But my stepdad refused, which really upset Lennart.

Benita (cont.) – After that, we saw him less, but both my mother and I still loved him. I always wrote a lot of letters to him and felt that he just needed time to find himself again and take control of his life. And after he passed, I found all the letters I had written to him, neatly arranged and kept in a small box in his apartment, which really warmed my heart. But Lennart was probably burdened by the effects of neglectful fathers, because he really went to extremes. He was an angry young man who wanted to do the right thing, but who needed to get something out of his system first. On the one hand, he was an outgoing and charismatic guy, and on the other hand a person who was looking for trouble. He started getting involved in petty crime, apparently owed some drug dealers money, and so on.

Benita goes on to say that when he was young, her brother had a strong charisma and ability to take charge with his intelligence and ability to speak eloquently. Combined with his explicit anger, Leo was able to take on and live out various roles in various contexts. Sometimes it was more than he could control.

Benita – Sometimes he seemed like two different people, depending on the company he was in. He was really wild when he was with his partying friends. I get the impression that his circle of friends really looked up to him. He was a born leader who always got people to join him because he was funny, intelligent and did the craziest things – for example, I've heard that he was on LSD at Roskilde. I think he tended to get stuck in a role that he actually wanted to get away from. He was a very complex person who went back and forth quite a bit. Lennart had a girlfriend that I think he loved very dearly. Her name is Astrid and she's a really sweet girl. I didn't get to know her until after the accident, but I think he was really counting on the two of them lasting for a long time. He had promised her that he would work things out by going to a psychologist. There were also a lot of other signs that he was in the process of getting things in his life smoothed out. It's sad that he had so much personal baggage to deal with. Of course, I've been through the same things, but people react differently. A boy also has a greater need for a father role than a girl, and I had my religion to support me. There's no saying whether Lennart would have returned to the church at some point, but I know that he was in the process of re-reading the Bible. After his death, I found it in his room with a bookmark in the middle and the corners of a lot of pages were folded in the first half of the book.

When I later talk to Astrid, she tells me that she's certain that her former boyfriend was never going to return to the church. In the time around the break with the church, Lennart moves from Randers to Aarhus, where he enrolls in a college preparatory program. He builds a large new circle of friends and spends his time writing, listening to music and partying. By all accounts, Leo has a sharp pen. He is a frequent write-in contributor to one of Denmark's most popular radio programs for young people featuring dedications. He also writes an application to Denmark's national college of journalism, but his printer is broken and he never gets around to actually sending it in. "Typical Leo," says Astrid Rørdam with a smile.

Astrid and Leo were together for about a year and a half. They broke up a while before the festival in 2000, but they remained in contact and on good terms. Astrid says that the intense break with the church and much of his family significantly impacted Leo's personality and that he went through a few very difficult years afterwards. She says without a doubt that, at the time of his death, he was 100% finished with the church, but not with some of his family members.

Astrid – Over the years I've developed a good relationship with Leo's mother, Sharon, and his sister Benita. I never met them when I was with Leo, but I know that there was a strong love on both sides in spite of the conflicts. There was also a great love in the anger, and I know that his mother was plagued by a strong feeling of guilt in the years after the accident. I still think about Leo a lot – he was a wild and extreme person that you either loved or you hated. His personality was probably best summed up in the eulogy written by his old friend, Matthias Forrest Clausen:

"Live now," you always used to say, Leo, and you were one of the few people who actually lived by those words. And as person who chose to turn away from a fundamentalist Christian background at a young age in your life, you knew all about the often unbridgeable gap between words and action – and this knowledge shaped your unique personality and commitment to doing what you believed in. I doubt that anybody who even peripherally knew you has forgotten you since, because you were so persistent in every aspect of life. When you were there, you were there ... And when you bolted, everybody could hear it. Like now. On the one hand, you were a master provocateur, and on the other a gentleman to the fullest. You were naughty, charming, uncouth, witty and almost frighteningly intelligent. But first and foremost, you were there. Now you're not anymore, and that's hard to fathom. But out of respect for the person you were, we – your friends – must reciprocate your loyalty and live now. That's how you would have wanted it. Being true to your memory is drinking a beer instead of shedding a tear; holding a party instead of sitting and mourning; being naked instead of clad in black. You knew all about pain and therefore you understood that it was all about "chilling out" and "feeling good," as you often preached. You practically lived for Roskilde Festival – the place where your hated civilization is temporarily disbanded and people live in the present. Your favorite band was Pearl Jam. The symbolism is clear and really quite beautiful – if you knew you had to die, this is the way you would have chosen.
- Lennart 'Leo' Tobias Nielsen died at the age of 22.

Whereas his love for his mother, sister and brother remained strong in spite of severe disagreements on lifestyle and religion, all of Leo's friends echo Benita's story that Leo's relationship with his stepdad was toxic. Leo was a die-hard Pearl Jam fan and especially captivated by *Vitalogy* and the song *Immortality*, and according to Benita, his favorite song was *Better Man* from the same album.

After having heard the stories from his sister and friends, it dawns on me how much Leo's story resembles the childhood and youth depicted in Eddie Vedder's autobiographical lyrics. Leo's anger and rebellion has striking similarities to that of Vedder. On *Alive*, Vedder relates the time when, at the age of 13, his mother tells him that the man he had always thought was his biological father was actually his stepfather. His biological father is a friend that sometimes visited the house, but who unfortunately died two years earlier: "*Sorry you didn't see him, but I'm glad we talked!*"

As connoisseurs of Pearl Jam know, young Eddie was not as relieved by the conversation as his mother, instead tumbling into an existential and emotional morass – an experience he movingly and intensely recounts in many of his lyrics. His mother's revelation is perhaps the single event, which, given the autobiographical content of *Alive* and the overall impact of Pearl Jam and the grunge wave as a whole, ultimately symbolizes the parental neglect that ultimately fueled much of the Seattle wave's fury.

Eddie's relationship with his stepdad – both before and after his mother's revelation of his biological origin – is thoroughly broken and drives him to take action. Eddie drops his stepdad's last name, Mueller, adopts his mother's maiden name, Vedder, and describes his hatred of his stepdad in the songs he writes. One of the best-known examples comes from the hook line of *Better Man*: "She lies and says she's in love with him. Can't find a better man." Eddie originally wrote the song while living in San Diego and playing in his first band, Bad Radio, many years prior to the advent of Pearl Jam. *Better Man*, released on the album *Vitalogy*, has since evolved into one of Pearl Jam's biggest hits. When Pearl Jam played the song for the third time during a globally transmitted live concert on April 3, 1994 at the Fox Theater in Atlanta, Georgia – three days before Kurt Cobain's suicide – Eddie leads into the song with the salvo: "This song is dedicated to the bastard who married my mama."

Whether Leo adopted Eddie's words as his own is something we'll never know, but the similarities in attitude and expression are striking. Based on more than 100 interviews and thorough research, Dorte Palle concludes that the evidence indicates that the crowd at the Pearl Jam concert collapsed as the band played *Better Man*.

Better Man

Waitin', watchin' the clock, it's four o'clock, it's got to stop
Tell him, take no more, she practices her speech
As he opens the door, she rolls over... Pretends
to sleep, as he looks her over
She lies and says she's in love with him, can't find a better man... She dreams in color,

she dreams in red, can't find a better man...
Can't find a better man
Can't find a better man
Ohh...
Talkin' to herself, there's no one else who needs to know...
She tells herself, oh...

Memories back when she was bold and strong
And waiting for the world to come along...
Swears she knew it, now she swears he's gone
She lies and says she's in love with him, can't find a better man...
She dreams in color, she dreams in red, can't find a better man...
She lies and says she still loves him, can't find a better man...
She dreams in color, she dreams in red, can't find a better man...
Can't find a better man
Can't find a better man

She loved him, yeah...she don't want to leave this way
She needs him, yeah...that's why she'll be back again
Can't find a better man (can't find a better man)
Can't find a better man (can't find a better man)   Lyrics: Eddie Vedder
Can't find a better man (can't find a better man)   Music: Pearl Jam
Can't find a better...man...   ©1994

It was an absolute given that Leo would be standing front and center in the crowd at Pearl Jam's concert at Roskilde 2000. The festival is one of the unequivocal highlights in Leo's life. Leading up to the festival, his euphoria is especially pronounced because Pearl Jam is scheduled to play Friday evening. Leo arrives at the festival campground on Monday, three days before the four-day main event is slated to begin, joined by three friends from Aarhus: his old friend Tore and two good "partying buddies" from Aarhus, Martin and Asbjørn. As planned in advance, the group joins a large Aarhus camp that has been at the festival every year since 1997, and is home to about 20–25 similarly aged festivalgoers from Aarhus. Just like Leo, his friend Asbjørn Auring Grimm is enamored with Pearl Jam; the upcoming concert on Friday is a frequent topic of conversation and the event they are most looking forward to at the festival. Although Asbjørn and Leo mostly know each other from meeting at clubs and bars in the city, they have good chemistry and end up hanging out together during Roskilde 2000 – and Asbjørn plays a central role in the turbulent course of events at the festival following the accident. I later meet Asbjørn, who talks about his close friend's death on that fateful night.

The 2000 edition of Roskilde starts strongly – and moistly – for the crew from Aarhus. On Friday the 30th, they take things up a notch, drinking liberally from the time they emerge from their tents in the morning. Leo and Asbjørn warm up for the evening's concert according to all the precepts of festival ritual. They go out to eat at one of the festival's restaurant tents, and buy whiskey and cigars for dignified enjoyment as they prepare for the festival's highly anticipated climax. The agree to take in the Swedish rockers Kent from a distance at the Orange Stage before moving all the way to the front to get the best possible view of Pearl Jam. But Asbjørn is already far too inebriated before they get that far. At four in the afternoon, he has to lay down in the camp and take a nap. He doesn't wake up again until 45 minutes before Pearl Jam is scheduled to take the stage, and Leo is gone with the wind. Asbjørn hurries from the campground towards Orange Stage and tries to find Leo. The only thing they've talked about is standing close up on the right side of the stage, but when Asbjørn arrives at Orange Stage, it's physically impossible to get all the way to the front. He settles for a spot pretty far towards the front of the massive crowd and enjoys the concert from there. The crowd is tightly packed and there's some pushing and shoving, but nothing out of the ordinary for a headliner concert when you're standing so close to the stage.

When the concert stops, Asbjørn thinks that it's because Eddie Vedder stage dived into the crowd or something of that nature. He doesn't realize that an accident has occurred until an announcement is made from the stage that The Cure is cancelled because of fatalities in the crowd during Pearl Jam's concert. Asbjørn goes back to the camp, where the mood is fucked, to put it lightly. It's been several hours and Leo isn't back yet, and everybody knows where he was headed when he left the camp earlier that evening.

Time passes without any news and there is an increasingly worried and chaotic atmosphere in the camp, and among the festival as a whole. Asbjørn falls asleep around four or five in the morning, but wakes up a few hours later. Since Leo hasn't yet returned to the camp, Asbjørn decides to find an answer to his unshakable misgivings. He stands in line for 20 minutes at one of the emergency camps established on the festival grounds. When he gets to the front of the line, he asks the police officer on duty whether a young man named Lennart Nielsen has been injured or hospitalized. The officer cannot say whether Lennart was injured during the concert, but he can say with certainty that Lennart was not among the dead. All of the deceased have been identified, says the police officer, and the name Lennart Nielsen is not one of those on the list. Asbjørn runs back to the camp and trumpets the good news: "Leo is alive!" A sense of relief spreads through the camp, people smile and curse about Leo not letting anybody know he was OK. They talk about whether it's time to break camp and return to Aarhus, or if they should stay at the festival. The group agrees to stay together and not leave the festival prematurely. The hours pass and Leo still doesn't show up. A group of campers go to a concert at noon, but despite the police officer's categorical reassurance earlier that day, they grow uneasy once more.

Asbjørn – My brother and I, together with Leo's friend Martin and his girlfriend decide to go to another emergency center. We find out that not all of the victims have been identified, contrary to what I had been told previously. We get descriptions of a person with tattoos that could be, but is not necessarily Leo. The police ask us to remain seated and it feels like a long time passes. After a while, a festival staffer comes and says that they would like to speak with one or two of us, as they need to fill out some official paperwork for the sake of documentation. The request sounds really strange, I remember thinking. But I go with my brother, Jon, and we are driven to a nearby school. They ask about the name of the missing person once more. I confirm that his name is Lennart Nielsen, and then the policeman says: "That's him." My brother just flips out, while I remain calm at first. I ask if the members of our camp can be driven back to Aarhus, but that's not possible. The police drive us back to the entrance to the campgrounds, and Jon and I walk back to our camp in shock, holding hands, while somebody nearby yells "faggots!" at us. We gather everyone together in our camp. I tell them what's happened, and then I totally break down. I start drinking, I'm totally out of my mind and can't comprehend what's happening. Some people around us pick up on what has happened and they come over and pack up our camp for us. I refuse any kind of crisis counseling and I just want to get away from there. Somehow we manage to gather together and travel back to Aarhus, where the entire camp moved into the collective where I was living. We cry, laugh and get drunk together. Our spirits ebb and flow, but it helps that we're all sticking together. We make it through the funeral, we see him lying in the coffin, and Bo – one of Leo's friends – and I play and sing *Immortality* [the song from *Vitalogy* whose closing lyrics are almost morbidly prophetic in mirroring Leo's fate: "Truants move on... cannot stay long/ Some die just to live..."]. Afterwards, we hold a wake at the home of Leo's old friend Tore.

    I didn't try to facilitate contact between Benita and Eddie Vedder in the autumn of 2002 because I wasn't yet aware of her existence, but a number of Leo's friends get into contact with Vedder at that time. Tore Rasch and others from Leo's circle of friends take the initiative to write to Eddie Vedder via Curtis Management. About two months after contacting him, I receive a very thankful e-mail from Tore. He and his friends – Matthias, Jakob and Astrid – have all received personal e-mails from Eddie Vedder. Tore expresses his joy to have received this personal letter, but also a sadness to discover the heavy sense of guilt that plagues Vedder,

78

Astrid also recalls the very somber, cautious and sincere tone of the letter from Vedder. Everybody writes back, but none of them hear anything more from the rock'n'roll icon. Astrid loses the e-mail address and changes her own, and later she can't precisely recall the exact course of events. A positive and heartwarming contact was established, but without any follow-up, which Astrid says came as a disappointment to some of the friends in Leo's circle.

About Jakob Folke Svensson

For years following the accident, Jakob Svensson's family declined any form of public contact or coverage of their son's death at Roskilde Festival in 2000. So in my initial efforts to facilitate contact with Eddie Vedder, I instead contact Jakob's best friend Michael Berlin via Dorte Palle. Michael stood next to Jakob for much of the Pearl Jam concert and escaped unharmed from the tumult at the last moment. At the time, Jakob was 17 years old and Michael 18, and they were both plumber's apprentices. Close friends since day care, they played soccer on the same team and later listened to music, went to parties and chased girls together. Michael's voice remains calm as he tells the tragic story.

Jakob and Michael are staying in a large tent in the festival campgrounds together with their childhood friend Thomas. Thomas goes with them to the Pearl Jam concert, but quickly moves further away from the stage when he feels the pressure of the tightly packed crowd. Jakob and Michael are both big Pearl Jam fans and have their sights set on getting as close to the stage as possible. They succeed in their mission, but Michael grows uneasy and exhausted, and decides to get out. But the crowd is packed like sardines and he can't budge. Michael says that he panicked at first, but that the feeling largely dissipated because Jakob was taking it all in stride. Nonetheless, Michael eventually runs out of mental and physical stamina and decides to get out. He only manages to get out when Jakob and a German guy they were standing with join forces to lift Michael up so that he can crowd surf up to the security guards in front of the stage.

About six months later when he is interviewed by police about the accident, Michael identifies the German who aided Jakob in getting Michael out of the claustrophobic sea of people. It turns out to be the German victim of the accident, 26-year-old Marco Peschel. The last time Michael sees Jakob, he's smiling, hands raised high above his head and signaling that it's cool his friend is crowd surfing. Arriving at the front of the Orange Stage, a doctor checks to ensure that Michael is OK, and he quickly feels ready to rejoin the crowd. But in the meantime, all hell has broken loose right where his friends are still located. Before returning to the crowd, Michael looks up to the stage one last time. He sees Eddie Vedder sitting on the stage crying, and he understands that something has gone terribly wrong.

79

The concert stops and Michael goes back to the tent, where he finds Thomas. They worriedly talk about what might have happened, and then they fall asleep. Or at least they try to. They don't get much sleep, because every time they hear a sound they think it's Jakob. But they are the only two in the tent that night. As the two friends are on their way up to buy breakfast the next morning, they see the headline of Politiken's daily festival newspaper and realize that people died at the previous evening's Pearl Jam concert. They have the same first thought: "Jakob." But they agree that he probably went over to his cousin's camp for the night. After a while, they get a hold of Jakob's cousin, who says that she hasn't seen her cousin. Jakob has yet to return to the camp, so Michael and Thomas report him missing at the festival's information center. When they return to the campground, they see large LED signs encouraging festivalgoers to contact their families. Michael and others around him call home to relay the news that they're unharmed. The parents of one of Jakob's other friends have been close with Jakob's parents for years, so everyone in the camp agrees that this friend should call home. He gets a hold of his parents and asks them to contact Jakob's parents and tell them that Jakob is still missing. The couple quickly calls Jakob's parents, who they then accompany to a hospital in Roskilde and later to Roskilde County Hospital. After providing a description of Jakob at both hospitals, the four adults are referred to Rigshospitalet, the National Hospital of Denmark, where all of the deceased have been transferred. At

Michael Berlin. Roskilde Festival, June 30 2000 Photo: Jakob Falke Svensson.

80

Rigshospitalet, Jakob is identified by his parents. At 5 pm, the friends of Jakob's parents call their son at the festival and tell him what has happened.

That call was like a bomb, says Michael, who recalls hectic aftermath:

Michael – I was on the cover of the national newspaper Ekstra Bladet three days after the accident. It was mostly my mother who had complained because we couldn't get any group crisis counseling or anything of that nature. Our parents had come to Roskilde to meet us, but they couldn't get crisis counseling because they didn't have festival bracelets [all attendees of Roskilde are given a festival bracelet that must be presented at all checkpoints]. They were suspected of trying to cheat their way into the festival. But what are the guards thinking when there are two young kids bawling because their childhood friend is dead? We couldn't get a referral to any place that could help us, so we went to the psychiatric department of Roskilde County Hospital on our own initiative. The article in Ekstra Bladet was primarily about my story, and the headline was something along the lines of "He saved my life, but died five minutes later."

In the years after the accident, Michael has had a varying degree of contact with Jakob's family. After our conversations in 2002, Michael contacts the Svensson family, but they are not interested in getting in touch with Eddie Vedder. Michael is also uncertain, but ultimately decides to contact Vedder via the rock star's agent. Michael sends two e-mails, but never gets a reply.

About Allan Tonnesen

17-year-old Allan Tonnesen from the small Danish town of Nordenskov was one of the nine young men who died at Roskilde Festival. In my efforts to contact the families on behalf of Eddie Vedder, Allan Tonnesen's parents, Eunice and Finn Tonnesen, were the most visible relatives in the media after the accident and therefore the easiest to establish contact with. The couple has harshly criticized Roskilde Festival and remains of the belief that the accident is largely attributable to a combination of poor emergency response planning, the management's unwillingness to admit their misjudgment and organizational negligence. They maintain that the festival should assume responsibility for the accident. Allan, the younger of two sons, was a cheerful and outgoing young man, Finn Tonnesen tells me.

Finn – He was a really happy kid with a drive and appetite for life. He was extremely social and had a big circle of friends who often visited him here at our house. A lot of his old friends still drop by to visit us. He was a Boy Scout in his youth and spent a lot of time fishing in the creek, mountain biking with friends and generally having fun. Allan wasn't that crazy about school to begin with, but in 10th grade he went to Flakkebjerg Bording School in Slagelse and he loved it. He was really popular at the school and played in two bands – he played both guitar and drums. The school's students had a long tradition of attending Roskilde Festival at the end of the school year. They went in 1999 after completing 10th grade, and Allan loved the sense of community, the music and the atmosphere in general.

Finn (cont.) – After the summer, he started in an agricultural studies program, which included attending school in Silkeborg and working on a farm in North Jutland. It really meshed with his interests and it was a choice he was really happy with. He was supposed to begin a pig farming internship at a new farm on July 1, 2000, but he arranged for a postponement until July 3 because he just couldn't stand missing Roskilde Festival. My wife Eunice is from Kenya, and the whole family has a tradition of visiting Kenya all summer – my wife and I still do, actually. Allan hadn't joined us the previous two years, but in 1998 I climbed Kilimanjaro with him and we went to Zanzibar together. In 2000, we left for Kenya and said goodbye to Allan on the Friday before Roskilde Festival. He left for the festival a couple of days later and spent the whole week in the camp leading up to the official opening. He pitched a camp with friends from the boarding school, but he was also joined by a couple of old friends from back in Nordenskov. The thing he was looking forward to more than anything else at Roskilde was seeing Pearl Jam in concert. A long time later, when I built up the courage to look in the program he had in his pocket at Roskilde, I could see that he had marked the concerts and other things he wanted to see at the festival. The catalogue was dotted with checkmarks and underlines, but there were a bunch of stars next to Pearl Jam. It was obviously going to be the highlight of his summer. When we later looked through his CD collection, we also saw that the Pearl Jam CDs took up a whole row.

Finn (cont.) – Allan went to the concert with his really close friend, Nikolaj, who is also from Nordenskov. They had gone to school together for all nine years of Danish primary school. The two of them started out on the edge of the crowd. Nikolaj thought it was too hectic and didn't want to try to get any closer, but Allan said that he wanted to go up to the front. He laughed and waved to Nikolaj and then started pushing his way forward, or however it was that he made it to the front. Later, he was identified by his older brother Alex, who lived in Roskilde and watched the same concert from further back in the crowd.

When I contact the Tonnesen family for the first time in the autumn of 2002, Eunice Tonnesen is receptive to my inquiry regarding Eddie Vedder, but also somewhat doubtful because the family had already made an attempt to contact Pearl Jam. After the accident, the Tonnesens sent a letter addressed to Eddie Vedder to a Danish media agency that was responsible for coordinating contact between relatives, public authorities and Pearl Jam's management. Enclosed with the letter were private photos of Allan Tonnesen, but the family never received a reply, despite repeated inquiries to the agency. The idea of a private letter with photos ending up in the wrong hands still bothers Eunice Tonnesen.

After talking with Eunice, I unsuccessfully try to track down the missing letter. But I can assure her that the letter never made it into the hands of Eddie Vedder, and that it's not a reflection of his or the band's arrogance that she never received a reply.

But since I was the one who contacted the family, I feel a responsibility to do my best to get to the bottom of what happened to the missing letter. At the time, I'm having difficulty getting in touch with Nicole Vandenberg at Curtis Management. So I ask my old bandmate Johnny Sangster in Seattle if he would contact Stone Gossard directly. Not long after that, I get an angry letter from Johnny; Gossard apparently prefers that all contact go through the management, whom he trusts in full. Johnny feels that I've used him as an errand boy in relation to Gossard, and somehow attempted to stab the band's management in the back.

Personally, I feel an obligation to explore every possibility since I've contacted the families on behalf of Eddie Vedder and not vice versa. I clarify my position to Johnny and at almost the same time I get a call from Nicole Vandenberg, who is now in contact with the Tonnesen family.

Eunice and Finn Tonnesen later tell me that they received a long and very warm and positive letter from Eddie Vedder, in which it is very clear that the accident still weighs heavily on his mind. It's a letter that Eunice and Finn greatly appreciate, but no subsequent efforts are made to arrange a face to face meeting.

Eddie Vedder's contact with the Danish families

During his visit to Denmark in 2003, I ask Stone Gossard what he knows about Vedder's contact with the families of the Danish victims. Stone isn't quite sure, but he believes that the correspondence has ceased.

Stone – By nature, he gets deeply and fully involved in other people, launches initiatives and does everything he can to help them. Then, sometimes he gets completely overwhelmed and backs out. Eddie's an extremely open, happy and outgoing person, but he's also a very vulnerable and private person who sometimes isolates himself from the outside world.

Without being entirely certain, Stone believes that something of this nature occurred in relation to Eddie's correspondence with the Danes. By this thinking, Vedder probably felt overwhelmed and overcome with grief, and felt compelled to push it away.

Stone's description of his good friend and bandmate causes some of the missing pieces to fall into place. I remember how intense my first encounter with Eddie Vedder was. As an active rock journalist, I've regularly met one-on-one with superstars, including nearly all of my personal idols. But none of them made nearly the impression that Eddie Vedder did. Of course, I was a bit newer in the field back then and probably more impressed by suddenly finding myself in the eye of the hurricane, but the instinctive impression of greatness and charisma was striking. Thinking back on it stirs up the same sense of allure and integrity. I've heard that Bill Clinton possesses a photographic memory and the ability to make everybody he meets feel like the center of his universe. When I meet Eddie Vedder after the concert in Barcelona in 1996, it dawns on me that he has a similar radiance, and that every person he comes into contact with must feel like they have a special connection and share a mutual understanding. Eddie is the type of person who addresses you directly and attentively, asks questions and listens sincerely, but it appears that he's not always able to manage his degree of involvement, so sometimes he gets overwhelmed and compensates by shutting down and withdrawing. Things are only further complicated when you're one of the biggest rock stars of your time, unofficially anointed as a spokesperson for your generation, and can't walk the streets in peace.

This conversation with Stone takes place at a much later date. At the end of 2002, I have a sense that my role is finished in this matter, and that the parties are communicating to the extent they mutually desire.

Over the next seven or eight months, the Roskilde accident gradually fades more and more from my thoughts. But in September 2003, things shift in a completely different direction. At first, I'm on the verge of deleting the e-mail because the strange sender address makes it look like spam. But on closer inspection, I realize that it's a message from Pearl Jam guitarist Stone Gossard.

Chapter 5

2003: STONE GOSSARD IN SCANDINAVIA.

In 2003, Stone Gossard reached a point in his life where he felt the need to do something in relation to the Roskilde accident. If nothing else, he wanted to see Denmark and Scandinavia once again with his own eyes – and, if any of the friends and families of the victims were at all interested in meeting with him privately and with no expectations, he would be more than willing to do so. In his e-mail to me, Stone asks if I think that any of the families would be interested in such a meeting, and if so, whether I can help him by facilitating contact. He also asks me if I can give him a more detailed explanation of how the matter of responsibility for the accident is viewed in Scandinavia, the degree of media coverage, and so forth. That's the essence of Stone's message.

As an incarnate rock fan, it's pretty amazing to suddenly be in direct e-mail contact with the guitarist of my favorite band, but this sense of awe quickly takes a back seat to considerations of a more practical nature. There's no doubt that Stone means business. He got my e-mail address from Johnny Sangster and he's determined to do "something," in one form or another, on his own – not as a representative of the band or management, but as a private individual.

Over the course of the following month, we engage in a bunch of transatlantic communication via e-mail and telephone. By agreement with Stone, I begin contacting the Scandinavian families. I also offer to accompany Stone as a translator and/or mediator on these visits, if desired – an offer that Stone appreciates and accepts. This display of trust from one of my absolute heroes comes as a great honor, but it also presents a very unique and potentially difficult situation.

Thoughts and emotions and ebb and flow in my mind as I think back to the interview with Eddie Vedder about ten months earlier. What will the families say? What should I say and how should I present myself? Will they be appreciative, furious, or hurt? What kinds of questions do I need to be able to answer, how should I answer, and how exactly should I phrase it? Will it be easy or difficult – and will I even be able to get in touch with anybody? And then there's the question of time. Stone and Liz will be landing in Copenhagen about two weeks after I make the very first phone calls.

Hello, this is Henrik...

I start with the easiest calls, which are to some of the people I've already met, and who share a musical culture with Stone and me: Leo's friends. I've gotten to know them well, especially Asbjørn, who I've met at concerts in town, and who was working at the club and concert venue Stengade 30 in Copenhagen. Leo's friends were generally really appreciative of the e-mail exchanges with Eddie, so the first person I call is Asbjørn. And he doesn't have the slightest doubt – he and his friends would really like to meet and talk with Stone about their feelings, views, the grieving process and their deceased friend. It's just a matter of arranging a time and place.

Next, I reach out to the Tonnesen family, with whom I've already spoken at length and who expressed appreciation of Eddie Vedder's heartfelt letter. They're also open to the idea, but mention that they're in the process of suing Roskilde Festival and that the members of Pearl Jam might be summoned to testify, which may present legal issues that could complicate any plans to meet. Stone doesn't think that it presents any problems, since he wants to meet with them as a private individual and not as a party to a legal suit. The Tonnesen family would like to meet with Stone on this basis, but only with him alone and at their home in the Danish town of Nordenskov.

I leave a detailed message on the answering machine of Jakob Svensson's parents, but never get a response. Unfortunately, I've lost all of the contact information for Jakob's friend, Michael Berlin.

At this point, I haven't been in touch with any of friends and family of the Swedish victims, and I pretty much only know the victims' names and ages. Things are further complicated by the fact that it's now 3½ years after the accident and I have no idea about who they are or their grieving process. But I promised Stone to give it a try, so the only thing to do is give them a call and hope for the best.

I start by calling the Thuresson family, who reside near Malmö, the large

Swedish city right across the Oresund Strait from Copenhagen. I get in touch with the older brother of the deceased Fredrik Thuresson, who doesn't mince his words. He is certain – also on behalf of his father – that the Thuressons aren't interested in any form of contact with Pearl Jam. Somewhat reluctantly, he jots down my telephone number anyway, in the unlikely event that they change their mind.

The next call doesn't go much better. I get a hold of Henrik Bondebjer's father, who promptly questions the reasons for Pearl Jam's sudden interest in talking with them now, three years after the accident. I do my best to relay Stone Gossard's reasons for seeking this contact. Sven-Anders Bondebjer says only that he will discuss the matter with his wife, Ann-Charlotte, and the rest of the family and call me back if they have any interest in such a visit.

The last call I make is to the parents of Carl-Johan Gustafsson, who live in the town of Tranås, Sweden. I get a hold of a very friendly woman's voice on the answering machine, who tells me that they are unfortunately not home.

Almost immediately after leaving a message and hanging up, my telephone rings. It's Sven-Anders Bondebjer. The family would like to invite Stone Gossard, Liz and me to lunch on the express condition that there is absolutely no press coverage of the meeting at all, which I can naturally guarantee in full. Sven-Anders tells me that the family has been treated horribly by the press, which has continuously invaded their privacy after the accident, and that they have only had terrible experiences with both journalists and authorities representing Roskilde Festival. He also says that the three Swedish families have helped each other and formed a little network, meeting a couple of times a year. To the question of whether I've contacted the other families, I tell him about the rejection from the Thuressons and the Gustafssons' answering machine.

Sven-Anders tells me that the tragedy has taken an especially hard toll on Gert Thuresson. In 1999, Gert lost his wife and then just one year later his 22-year-old son Fredrik. So it's no wonder that the oldest son, who I spoke with on the telephone, is very protective of his father. But Sven-Anders wouldn't be surprised – despite the son's assurances to the contrary – if I hear back from both Gert Thuresson and the Gustafssons.

And, in fact, not more than a few hours pass before I get a call from Carl-Johan's mother Birgitta Gustafsson, a warm, thoughtful and calm woman who would very much like to invite Stone and Liz to their home in Tranås – and they would also welcome my presence as a translator. Later that day, Gert Thuresson calls me after having spoken with the Bondebjergs. He would also like to meet with Stone and Liz.

Suddenly, almost everybody is in and I have a logistical puzzle to work out. It feels good – I'm both relieved and nervously excited about how everything is going to go.

At the suggestion of Eunice Tonnesen, I also contact Allan's big brother Alex, who lives in Copenhagen and attends Roskilde University. Eunice asks me to be cautious when speaking with him, because his brother's violent death and the aftermath have been very hard on him. I quickly get a hold of Alex, who would also like to meet with Stone – and like his parents, he's not interested in my participation as a mediator.

I e-mail Alex's contact info to Stone, but later I get an angry e-mail from Alex, who hasn't heard back from Stone. But not long after, direct contact and positive dialog is established between Seattle and Copenhagen.

During this time, Stone sends a number of movingly eloquent and thoughtful e-mails to me. He also asks for my thoughts about the fact that he's considering contacting Roskilde Festival's Leif Skov and the head of Roskilde Police's investigation of the accident. I write to him that I definitely think it's a good idea, because there are many sides to any matter and a direct dialog with Leif Skov would probably add to his understanding of everything that happened.

But since their schedule is already pretty jam packed into the course of just one week, we agree that I should focus on contacting the families and friends to begin with, and then possibly contact Leif Skov and/or the police and authorities when Stone and Liz are in Denmark.

STONE GOSSARD

Stone and Liz catch an earlier flight to Copenhagen than expected and check into a hotel in central Copenhagen on October 31. After getting a night's sleep, the couple asks the hotel concierge if Christiania is a good and safe place to visit. Christiania, a historic military base in Copenhagen, was occupied by squatters in 1971 and later became a "Freetown" recognized by the Danish government – and one of Denmark's most popular tourist attractions, known for its laissez-faire approach to marijuana, DIY architecture and direct democratic decision-making. The concierge says he thinks it is a very bad idea, after which Stone asks him to call a taxi to take them to Christiania. The Americans explore the Freetown on their own and spend the remainder of the day resting and adjusting to jet lag. In the meantime, I've filled their calendar with appointments and carefully planned transport logistics. I meet with Stone and Liz that evening.

Stone is feeling fine and shows no signs of fatigue despite the long journey and the fact that Pearl Jam played four concerts earlier that week. Liz is a friendly, relatively reserved and very calm American. The two began seeing each other a couple of years earlier, and met one another outside of the usual rock'n'roll circles. Liz says that she never really had any kind of connection with Pearl Jam, but she met Stone at the wedding of a mutual acquaintance. They are clearly fond of one another and seem thoroughly harmonic. Liz works in the field of environmentally-friendly design of workplaces, buildings, etc. Not exactly classic rock'n'roll, but perfectly in line with Stone's great commitment to various types of philanthropic and political work.

We start out by having a bite to eat and then take a walk in wintry Copenhagen as we chat about assorted things, including the latest Pearl Jam news. Just three days earlier, Pearl Jam completed their *Riot Act* world tour with four benefit concerts, the last of which was quite unique because of the show's line-up and set list.

On October 28 in Santa Barbara, California, Pearl Jam played a benefit for a prostate cancer center, featuring the following guests: ex-drummer Jack Irons, Red Hot Chili Peppers guitarist John Frusciante, the folk singer Jack Johnson, David Crosby and Chris Cornell. Cornell also plays solo and some Audioslave songs, and for the first time in 11 years, the band plays two Temple of the Dog songs – the band that started at the same time as Pearl Jam and was convened as a one-time tribute to the deceased vocalist Andrew Wood, who fronted the true forerunner of Pearl Jam, Mother Love Bone.

In addition to the core members of Pearl Jam, Temple of the Dog included the Soundgarden members Chris Cornell and Matt Cameron, who became Pearl Jam's drummer in 1998. This one-off project went on to stratospheric acclaim, but at the time of this conversation it only existed in the form of a debut album and the aforementioned recent concert in Santa Barbara.

A lot of Temple of the Dog has been played on various occasions since then. In March, April and May 2016, I see Chris Cornell play three or four Temple of the Dog songs during three solo concerts in Copenhagen, right around the time that the band announced their first tour ever in the fall of 2016. Returning back to 2003:

Stone – Now we have Matt in the band, and since Chris was making a guest appearance, I said to the others, "Let's play some Temple of the Dog." We ended up playing two songs [*Reach Down* and *Hunger Strike*], but if it had been up to me, we would have played five or six.

That same week, Pearl Jam played an acoustic set for the sixth time at Neil Young's annual Bridge School benefit concerts, which included an appearance by Young himself. After chatting for some time, we return to the matter at hand.

As Stone requested, I tell him a bit about how the accident had been covered in the Scandinavian media and how hard it has been for a great number of people. Stone's expression turns somber as it suddenly becomes very tangible that he's once again in the country where, three and a half years before, he played an involuntary part in a national tragedy that reverberated around the world. He takes a deep breath and gathers himself before we begin to review the program for the next six days. According to the plan for the following day, Stone and Liz will meet with Alex Tonnesen and visit with a number of Leo's friends at Asbjørn's apartment in Copenhagen.

I talk to Stone later the next day, after he and Liz met with Alex Tonnesen. The three of them were quickly on the same wavelength and it marks the first time that Stone and Liz had the opportunity to meet face to face with one of the family members of the Roskilde accident victims. The conversation was so good that they decided to squeeze another meeting into their tightly packed schedule.

Later that day, they visit Asbjørn's apartment, where a lot of Leo's friends have convened and spirits are high. Asbjørn and the others clearly appreciate the visit by the American rock star. According to Stone, the friends share a bevy of stories about Leo's personality, his relationship with Pearl Jam and Roskilde Festival, which they all still attend annually. Stone and Liz stay for a couple more hours than originally planned, and they do more than just talk. Leo's friends suddenly put a guitar in Stone's hands and ask him to play the chords to *Immortality* from the death-centric album paradoxically entitled *Vitaology* – and the song played at Leo's funeral.

Leo's friends think the time has come, right now at the dining room table, to hear the real McCoy from one of the musicians who wrote the song. Stone takes the guitar and several of Leo's friends sitting around the table strum along. Stone later tells me that he had to concentrate a bit, since he'd forgotten some of the chords, but he makes no bones about the fact that it was a deeply personal experience with a strong connection between all those present in the apartment.

Asbjørn remembers that Stone played the song way too slow, and he later says with a smile that it was actually pretty embarrassing. Later that evening, Leo's oldest friend Mattias builds up the courage to ask whether Stone would mind writing a few words to Leo.

Stone writes a dedication to Leo on page 26 of the *Vitalogy* liner notes, alongside a photo of a Native American and the lyrics to *Immortality* from Eddie Vedder's old typewriter, as featured in the liner notes for almost all Pearl Jam albums. Stone's dedication is framed and laid at Leo's grave in Aarhus, where it remains for some time.

Immortality

Vacate is the word...vengeance has no place on me or her
Cannot find the comfort in this world
Artificial tear...vessel stabbed...next up, volunteers
Vulnerable, wisdom can't adhere...
A truant finds home...and a wish to hold on...
But there's a trapdoor in the sun...

Immortality...

As privileged as a whore...victims in demand for public show
Swept out through the cracks beneath the door
Holier than thou, how?

Surrendered...executed anyhow
Scrawl dissolved, cigar box on the floor...
A truant finds home...and a wish to hold on too...
He saw the trapdoor in the sun...
I cannot stop the thought...I'm running in the dark...
Coming up a which way sign...all good truants must decide...
Oh, stripped and sold, mom...auctioned forearm...
And whiskers in the sink...
Truants move on...cannot stay long   Lyrics: Eddie Vedder
Some die just to live...   Music: Pearl Jam
Ohh...   ©1994

That same evening, I've invited Stone and Liz to my home for dinner. My wife Anne has made sure that I've completely straightened up the house and cleaned, because no matter how nice and relaxed I've told her that Stone Gossard is, we're going to be hosting an American millionaire after all, as she says.

The kids are all here too. The girls, ages 7 and 12 at the time, are mostly there because they've understood that one of our guests is a celebrity – which is all that really matters – as well as my 15-year-old son, who's infected by the rock bug passed on from his father and wants to be Jimmy Page when he grows up. Since we're about to be welcoming such prominent guests, it's only natural to break out the very finest the house has to offer. But everything's been super hectic in the past few days, so the menu humbly features soup – made with organic beef, but still. Nonetheless, our guests are just as easygoing as expected and you would think there were no bounds to how wonderful that soup tasted. Yet the combination of the nine hour time difference and the emotionally intense meetings are making their mark. This isn't going to be an all-nighter.

The kids are thrilled with the visit. Both Stone and Liz are visibly attentive to my youngest daughter Lulu, and they show great interest as they converse with each of the kids individually. Stone also has an invincible trump card up his sleeve for Lulu. He knows the drummer for her biggest idol, Avril Lavigne! At the Vote For Change concert the next year, Liz asks about Lulu, smiling and calling her "some kid." Liz says that Stone often talked about my then 7-year-old daughter.

I take the opportunity to play albums by various Danish bands that I hope will be to the pleasing of our guests. Stone is receptive and after *Honeyburst* has been playing for a while, he mentions that you can hear Tim Christensen's affinity for Pink Floyd. When we later listen to and talk about the Danish band Kashmir's *Zitilites*, I recall the last scene of the documentary *Rocket Brothers*, a portrait of Kashmir, where the camera steadily zooms out from a close-up to a panorama shot of the band playing *The Aftermath* at Roskilde Festival 2003 – a scene that nicely illustrates the new and improved safety measures at the Orange Stage.

I eagerly suggest showing the clip to our guests, but I quickly sense that it's far from the best idea that's ever dawned on me. Seeing a film clip from that stage at that festival is not exactly what Stone needs this evening.

We call it a night a short time later. A long day awaits us tomorrow. All three of us will be driving to Sweden to meet with the Bondebjer family and later with the Gustafssons.

On a biting cold November day, I have the honor of being the driver of our rental car, given that I'm the local in our party. I've brought along a stack of Danish CDs to introduce Stone to the strong development of Danish rock, but of course there's no functioning CD player in the car. But that hardly dampens our spirits as our little Ford Focus rambles up through Sweden. A good night's sleep has clearly reinvigorated the Americans. Stone and Liz have gotten off to a good start and speak of mutually healing experiences with the people they've met so far, despite the tragic circumstances that brought them together.

First stop: Henrik Bondebjer's family

The plan is to meet Sven-Anders Bondebjer at a gas station near the town of Falkenberg, which is about a one hour drive south of Gothenburg. From there, he will escort us to his home, where we'll have lunch with Sven-Anders and his wife. Apparently I forgot to mention this to my fellow passengers, because when we meet our hosts at the gas station, Liz comes out of the store devouring a newly purchased hamburger. We're greeted at the gas station by Mr. Bondebjer and his two sons, 29-year-old Lars and 20-year-old Johan.

Sven-Anders Bondebjer is a gray-haired, stocky and physically strong man in his fifties, who cordially welcomes us to Falkenberg. It's about a ten minute drive to the family's home, a large and rather exclusive single-family house on a farm. They're obviously comfortable, financially speaking. Yet it becomes readily apparent that ever since the fateful day of the Roskilde accident, the family has suffered emotional anguish and lived as a shell of their former selves.

Before we go from the car to the house, I remember to tuck away my bag with a "Roskilde Daily" logo in the car – *Gaffa* had produced the daily festival newspaper for the past three years at that point. "Probably a good idea," Stone says as I do so. I'm also bewildered by the fact that I could have been so thoughtless as to even have that bag with me on this trip.

The family kindly welcomes us. Once we've all sat down on the sofas in the living room, Stone gently begins by thanking them for the invitation and conveying his great sympathy with the family and the unthinkable tragedy they've suffered. He shares with them how difficult it has been for himself and his band – and, of course, that their pain is nothing in comparison to the loss of the families. He stresses that he has come as a private individual without an agenda of any kind, and that I am there as a good friend of the band and not as a reporting journalist.

In the home of the Bondebjer family, the opulent arrangement of delicacies on the lunch table in the room next to us cannot mask the somber mood permeating the air. Simply put, the Bondebjer family's lives have stood still since June 30, 2000. Sven-Anders Bondebjer does the speaking as his two sons listen quietly. He tells us that his family has been raising pigs at this farm for six generations. As he begins speaking of his deceased son, Henrik, the strong and robust man breaks into tears on multiple occasions.

No efforts are made to hide the fact that Henrik was the central hub of the family. He was accepted and understood by everyone to be the favorite son of the family. Henrik suffered from an eye disease that left him with just 10% of his vision in one eye and completely blind in the other, and his hearing was impaired. In spite of his significant visual and hearing impairment, Henrik was intelligent, social, outgoing, highly loved and a passionate music fan. He was also a talented swimmer, did well in school and was studying engineering at a technical college in Lund, Sweden – none of which was a small feat, given his disabilities.

Henrik was the shining light of the family and he was dearly loved by his friends. Among his many interests, Henrik was an avid traveler. The year before the accident, he visited London with a friend to see the Rolling Stones at Wembley Stadium. Despite the family's worries, the trip exceeded all expectations – Henrik had a fantastic trip and was really happy. According to his father, Henrik loved going to concerts and was a passionate rock fan, with the Rolling Stones and Pearl Jam among his favorites.

So the announcement that Pearl Jam would be playing the 2000 edition of . Roskilde Festival presented Henrik with the opportunity to fulfill two of his biggest dreams: seeing Pearl Jam in concert and attending Roskilde. With the positive experiences of the London trip fresh in their memory, Henrik and his schoolmate Anton decided to make the trip to Denmark – and because of Henrik's exuberance following the successful trip to see the Rolling Stones, the Bondebjer family had no objections to their son's plans.

Henrik regularly called his parents back home in Sweden during the first days of the festival, telling them about what a good time he was having. On the evening of Friday June 30th, he arrived well ahead of the scheduled start of the concert and found a good spot close to the stage, before making what would be his last call to his parents. He was in great spirits.

The following morning, the family is visiting Gothenburg when they hear about the accident for the first time on the radio. Like all other friends and family of the more than 100,000 festivalgoers and staff at Roskilde Festival, the Bondebjers are worried about their son. They call his cell phone, but the voicemail picks up. A short time later, Henrik's brother Lars calls his parents and tells them that Henrik has been reported missing, and that the family needs to drive to Roskilde immediately. Henrik's travel companion, Anton, tried to contact the Bondebjergs to no avail before getting a hold of Lars. Sven-Anders Bondebjer says that Anton had already identified Henrik's body by that time, but he had been strictly ordered by the Swedish police not to tell the family that their son had died.

Henrik's parents turn the car around immediately and head directly to Roskilde. They say that the trip to Denmark felt like an eternity, mired in the uncertainty about their son. A couple of hours into the approximately four-hour drive to Roskilde, they get a call redirecting them to a new destination. One of the two or three Swedish police officers who are traditionally stationed at Roskilde Festival calls the family and tells them not to drive to Roskilde, but instead to the Forensics Department of Rigshospitalet, the national hospital in Copenhagen.

The atmosphere at Rigshospitalet is extremely chaotic, and they're suddenly inundated with information. Without any warning, the coroner asks the couple to identify the body of the young man on the stretcher in the room next door. They're asked to confirm that it is their son, Henrik Bondebjer, and they are asked not to stay in the room too long, because the staff is very busy and other people need to do the same after them. Petrified with despair, they stand looking at their lifeless son Henrik. His mother tells of a face contorted in unimaginable pain, bearing witness to a violent and torturous death.

In the midst of this paralyzing shock, the Bondebjers are quickly asked to leave the room, and Swedish police authorities are waiting to question them. The Swedish policeman heading the questioning of the Bondebjers begins by giving his condolences for their loss, only to add in the same sentence that the family is partly to blame. Personally, he would never send his own children or youngsters to Roskilde Festival, says the policeman, calling the festival a cesspool of narcotics and crime. After the questioning, the stunned couple returns to their car and drives home to Falkenberg.

An hour later, the doorbell rings. Mr. Bondebjer opens the door and standing before him are two unannounced reporters from the Swedish newspapers *Expressen* and *Kvällsposten*, who request an interview with the grieving family.

As Sven-Anders, with occasional input from his wife, tells us of the family's nightmarish days and the brutal insensitivity of the authorities and press in the wake of the accident, the family's youngest son, Johan, sits and nods silently. The story now comes to the point where the parents face the impossible task of telling their other two sons of the tragedy that has befallen the family. At the time, Johan was in Colorado as an exchange student on a Rotary stipend.

Johan speaks for the first time: "For some reason, I couldn't sleep that night. I turned on CNN and heard about the deaths at Roskilde Festival and immediately had a sense that Henrik was involved. I knew that he was at the festival with a friend. So when the phone rang and it was my parents, I knew right away why they were calling," Johan says, breaking into tears.

He quickly boards the first plane for Sweden and his stay as an exchange student comes to a sudden end.

Around the time of the funeral, everything is chaotic for the family, who in the midst of their unfathomable grief feel violated by the relentless press. Sven-Anders points through a window to the road in front of the house. For days, that road was jam-packed with cars from an array of uninvited media, their cameras monitoring the family's every step.

Meanwhile, their relationship with Roskilde Festival isn't much better. Apart from flowers at the funeral, the Bondebjers don't hear anything at all from the festival. At a later date, the family receives a letter from then festival director, Leif Skov, who offers to meet with them. After some correspondence between the festival and Bondebjers, Skov visits the family five and a half months later to talk about the accident. It's a very difficult situation for both parties and far from a reconciliatory experience for the family in Falkenberg.

Sven-Anders – We never really liked Leif Skov and he came across as really arrogant when he visited us. He refused to take responsibility for the accident at any point in our conversation and he didn't seem regretful in the least. For us, it was terrible – not because we were demanding huge financial compensation, but for the sake of our inner peace it meant a great deal to us that the festival was willing to take the blame for the lack of safety measures that led to the accident. But Leif Skov maintained the festival's innocence. It doesn't make sense to us that nothing was wrong in 2000, if you just think about all of the new safety measures that have been introduced since and all the changes that have been made. Our oldest son, Lars, attended the festival before Henrik and he's told us about the lack of safety.

Later, the Bondebjer family would go on to start a foundation in their son's name to support other young people with the same disease as Henrik. The family writes to Roskilde Festival regarding a potential donation, given the festival's philanthropic activities. The family's request is met with a rejection, which according to Sven-Anders is formulated in legalese and cites formal tax obstacles to such a donation. To the Bondebjergs, it's yet another slap in the face from Roskilde Festival. Like all of the other families – except for the Tonnesens, who send the money back – the Bondebjers later receive compensation from Roskilde Festival for their funeral and psychological counseling expenses.

Also at a later date, the festival offers to pay the family DKK 40,000 for pain and suffering, and to close the matter with finality. On the advice of their legal counsel, the Bondebjergs reject the offer, in part because it would amount to a legal gag, and in part because the family wants somebody to be held responsible, not financial compensation. Sven-Anders concludes by saying that they've only had negative experiences with the festival and he shows me documents, including a letter from the festival's attorney asking the family not to contact the festival again.

I'm sitting there all the while with a lump the size of a softball in my throat – and when I look over to Stone and Liz, Stone has a very pained look on his face and tears are flowing down Liz's cheeks. We sit in the form of a horseshoe in the Bondebjers' large living room, and for long stretches of time the conversation descends into complete silence. I feel extremely uneasy and know that I have to measure every word with minute precision.

I can hardly imagine how Stone is feeling and experiencing these long, silent minutes. Rarely, if ever, have I been witness to a person being in such an emotionally vulnerable situation. It's as if Stone represents the culture and lifestyle that stole the life of their beloved, talented, joyous and resilient son.

After he's finished sharing their harrowing story, Sven-Anders stands up and asks us to join him for lunch in the dining room. The atmosphere seems to lighten up a bit, and the pickled herring arrives at the table. The sons begin asking Stone a bunch of "rock star questions" that he cheerfully answers: "Yeah, I guess we've sold 40 million albums" [an official press release from the record company in May 2005 estimated Pearl Jam's total album sales at 55–60 million]; "I don't really know if we feel old, but there are a lot of kids today who have no idea who we are"; "No, we don't really trash hotel rooms and go wild"; "I prefer a good dinner and a bottle of wine with good friends," and so on.

At one point, I'm in the kitchen to get a plate and have a moment alone with Ann-Charlotte Bondebjer, who pulls me aside and asks: "What do they want to get out of being here? These American rock stars can't understand what we're going through." I answer that she's certainly correct, but that they sincerely want to help start a dialog that might be able to slightly relieve some of the pain. Ann-Charlotte nods silently.

Sven-Anders tells us about life in Falkenberg and on the farm. As a sixth-generation pig farmer, there's an unspoken pressure on the two sons to fill the space left vacant by the death of the family's favorite son. Sven-Anders and Ann-Charlotte convey how the family's life came to a halt on 30 June 2000, and that nothing has been the same since.

Ann-Charlotte – When we sit here and eat, his spot at the table is empty. When we're on vacation, we miss his company. His spirit is there always, but we miss him so dearly.

Ann-Charlotte proudly tells us of Henrik's academic feats in school, overcoming the obstacles caused by his disability, and she fetches a large framed photo of her son in his graduation robes. She's the only one in the family who's remained composed thus far, but as Ann-Charlotte stands with the photo of her dead son in her hands, she yells, on the verge of crying: "I was his eyes, I was his ears!" Liz, who's standing closest by, gently lays a hand on Ann-Charlotte's shoulder. What can you say or do in a situation like that?

96

Things lighten up once more as we flip through photo albums featuring Henrik, including a picture of him smiling ear to ear at the Rolling Stones concert in London.

The time then comes to say goodbye. We have an appointment to meet with the Gustafsson family near Jönköping, which is about a two and a half hour drive away. Right before we leave, Sven-Anders tells us that they've been contacted by the Danish attorney Tyge Trier, who has offered to file suit against Roskilde Festival on behalf of the families at no charge. He also adds that he informed the attorney of Stone's visit, and that Trier might want to contact Stone. That's fine with Stone, so I give Sven-Anders my cell phone number. The Bondebjers ask us to give the Gustafssons their regards, as the two families meet up at least twice a year.

Sven-Anders and Lars drive in the car ahead of us to show us the way back to the main road, and after about five miles, Sven-Anders pulls off to the side of the road. He gets out of his car, walks back to ours and gives me directions to our destination. He thanks Stone and Liz once more, and says directly to me: "You've done well, Henrik," once again breaking into tears for a brief moment.

Overcome with the emotions and events of this visit, we drive on silently towards Jönköping.

Second stop: Carl-Johan Gustafsson's family

I think we drive for about 15 minutes without any of us saying a word. But after some time on the road, the conversation slowly resumes. We talk about the emotional visit and whether we've just made things worse. Personally, I choose to take Sven-Anders' closing remarks at face value: "Thanks, this has reopened all our wounds once again, but it's been a positive experience. It has helped."

Stone expresses his appreciation of the planning of the visits, and says how good it was that they met with Leo's friends and Alex Tonnesen on the first day – young people who in many ways live a life and pursue interests closer to those of Stone himself, and people for whom the loss is not a lingering abyss of sorrow that has practically brought their lives to a standstill. Although certainly marked by a serious and grave tone, the encounters with the young Danes the previous day were also filled with music, a sense of unity, political discussions, etc. Stone and Liz stress the importance of those uplifting experiences as a precursor to the meeting earlier that day.

During my two-day interview the previous year in New York, I discovered that Stone's arsenal of sharp and witty comments is as much a core element of his personality as his guitar playing. From the fifteen years I've been close with people from the Seattle music community, I know that a very particular form of absurd humor is at least as much of a trademark as the grim outlook on which the grunge movement built its fame.

Stone takes on the role of joker, constantly making fun of my driving and sense of direction. And, honestly speaking, much of it is well deserved. I completely botch a roundabout near Jönköping, which significantly prolongs our travel time. Liz says, "I can hear that you two have a lot more in common than just music."

We stop and get a hot dog at a gas station. We're all pretty darn tired and frazzled, but we carry on in hopes that we don't arrive too late at our destination in Tranås. I call the Gustafssons from my cell phone and ask if we should wait until the next day because we are so late, but they say "Just come. You can get here when you get here, no problem."

We head back to the car and drive off towards our destination. Stone sends his warmest regards to the most famous band to come out of Jönköping, The Cardigans, who are among his (and my) personal favorites. There's still a ways to Tranås, and the conversation glides over to Pearl Jam's ongoing activities. Stone humbly concludes, "We are very, very lucky." The band doesn't sell on the same scale as when Seattle ruled the global world of rock, but we're still talking in the millions. And in a time when all of the era's other bands have either broken up, ODed or committed suicide, the same core four of Pearl Jam have persevered through the years. Or, actually, core five, since the band's drummer since 1998, Matt Cameron, is an old friend who originally played drums on the demo tapes that Stone Gossard sent down to Eddie Vedder in San Diego at the suggestion of Jack Irons in the summer of 1990.

Despite Roskilde and personal ups and downs, all of the band's members are healthy, happy and still going strong, and the band enjoys virtually unparalleled loyalty among its fan base, drawing huge audiences anywhere in the world they choose to play. Liz mentions in passing that the recently concluded Pearl Jam tour in the US, with its 70 concerts, was the sixth-highest grossing tour in the nation in 2003. And on another occasion, when discussing the concert in Mexico City on the same tour, it's mentioned that they played to an audience of 25,000 people. "So you played there one night?" I ask. Nope, they played to a sold-out stadium three days in a row. Stone says that some cities and areas are better than others. For example, Boston is one of the better cities; on the aforementioned *Riot Act* tour, they played for a crowd of 80,000.

No more than two hours after departing from Falkenberg, attorney Tyge Trier calls me after having spoken with the Bondebjers. I quickly hand over the telephone to Stone, who confirms that he would like to try to meet with Trier later that week, if his tightly-packed schedule allows. After hanging up, we converse on matters big and small until suddenly, we've arrived at the home of Ebbe and Birgitta Gustafsson in Tranås on the drearily-named street Regnvädersgatan – which literally translates from Swedish to "Rainy Weather Street."

Birgitta has asked me to participate in the meeting as translator. But it turns out that my assistance in that regard is completely unnecessary. The couple's

English is absolutely at a level that allows for a precise and meaningful conversation.

Birgitta and Ebbe greet us warmly and offer us beer and sandwiches. We spend a couple of good and heartwarming hours in the company of the harmonic couple. Birgitta does most of the talking, but we sense a mutually agreed distribution of roles, with her as the outgoing and talkative one, while Ebbe is the quiet and stable support – complementary yet different, both in personality and physique. Birgitta is small and dark, Ebbe is tall and has a very light complexion.

One of the first things Birgitta says is that she wants to emphasize that the family has never at any time blamed Pearl Jam for the accident. Not long after we sit down at the table, Birgitta asks Stone if he would like to see Carl-Johan's (known among friends as Kalle) room? While Stone visits the son's room, which is still relatively intact, Liz and I speak softly with 53-year-old Ebbe, who has worked for most of his professional life as a fireman and since the accident has also done volunteer work with socially disadvantaged youth.

As opposed to the Bondebjer family, the Gustafssons have chosen to forgive. And it has been – and still is – a challenging and merciless struggle. Every life is unique, and the story of Carl-Johan Gustafsson's far too short life is a tragic and fateful tale. For generations, the Gustafssons have been active members the Pentecostal church (a branch of evangelical Protestantism), living devoted Christian lives with strong involvement in the church. Like his older sister by four years Sandra, 20-year-old Carl-Johan was raised within the traditions of the church, but despite a strong Christian faith, other and sometimes conflicting forces captured the fancy of the tall and handsome young man. To his parents' dismay, one of these forces was a strong passion for melancholic and hard rock – with a special affinity for Pearl Jam. The songs from *Ten* frequently blasted from his teenage bedroom, and he rejected his mother's well-intentioned advice to listen to less violent and calmer music. Carl-Johan's parents tell us that Pearl Jam's CDs got plenty of airtime on his stereo.

Birgitta and Ebbe bring out their photo albums, showing us pictures and talking about Carl-Johan. They loved their son, but didn't share his fondness of rock music and a lifestyle that sometimes lacked direction. For the same reason, they didn't even know that he was at the festival – he didn't tell them he was going.

Eight months before the festival, Carl-Johan moved from Tranås to the larger and more exciting city of Jönköping, enjoying the life of a young bachelor with his good friends. He lived with a couple of roommates and, in many ways, was just beginning to figure out what he was going to do with his life. They went out on the town and were regulars at Bongo Bar, played and listened to music, read books and went to school. They lived life. The tall, dark and friendly young man from Tranås was naturally popular among the girls and his friends, blessed with a face and an aura that also proved lucrative. In the last part of his life, Carl-Johan worked as a model and was believed to be on the brink of very promising career.

Although he had previously lived with pronounced lack of money, he didn't let his newfound modeling income control his life. In the early summer of 2000, he was offered a lucrative and prestigious modeling job in Stockholm that he turned down because he had other plans.

Together with his friends Patrick and Tomas – who would later identify Carl-Johan's body – he doesn't head north to Stockholm in June of 2000, but rather south to Roskilde. Meanwhile, his parents are on the way to a short vacation in Germany. Patrick later tells me that Carl-Johan was overjoyed while at Roskilde Festival, frequently shouting "This is the life!"

Friday is the big day for the two friends. They begin by dancing in the rain to the reggae sounds of Ziggy Marley, and then await the absolute highlights of the festival. First off is Patrick's favorite band, the Swedish rockers Kent – who Carl-Johan also likes – followed by Carl-Johan's greatest musical love, Pearl Jam, on the very same stage. The two friends have stuck side-by-side for days since their departure from Sweden. First they see Kent play together, but then they lose each other in the crowd. Patrick has since wondered why they hadn't agreed on a meeting place before the Pearl Jam concert, but they didn't. Patrick watches the concert from pretty far back in the crowd, and he has no idea that something is amiss until the concert is suddenly stopped and the announcements start trickling out. Carl-Johan Gustafsson is the first victim to be transported to Roskilde Hospital, where he is declared dead at precisely 12 midnight due to asphyxiation caused by a compressed chest.

That same day, Ebbe and Birgitta are in the vicinity of Roskilde completely by chance. Their road trip to Germany has been somewhat delayed by the inclement weather. And since there is no prospect of improvement, the couple decides to return home to Sweden a couple of days earlier than originally planned. In the late morning of June 30, the couple drives up through Denmark, passing by road signs pointing the way to Roskilde Festival and the many LED signs declaring that the Øresund Bridge to Sweden is now open. Upon arrival in Helsingborg, Sweden, Birgitta calls Carl-Johan's cell phone, which is turned off. Later, she calls his apartment in Jönköping and one of his friends says, as instructed in advance by Carl-Johan himself, that he has gone out into town. Back home in Tranås on Saturday morning, Ebbe and Birgitta see the live TV broadcast of the official opening of the bridge, and the speaker says that they will now hold a minute of silence for the victims who died at Roskilde Festival the previous day. This marks the first time the couple hears of the accident, and they talk a little about the sad event, but with a distance typical of tragedies far removed from one's life that are reported in the mass media. During the day, Birgitta repeatedly laments that her son hasn't called back. But Ebbe and Carl-Johan's older sister Sandra, who is at the house, are more relaxed about it. As the day progresses, Birgitta tries to call some of Carl-Johan's friends' parents, but doesn't get a hold of any of them. It's apparently impossible to find out where Carl-Johan is.

At 11 p.m. that night, the doorbell rings. Birgitta opens the door to find the priest from their church, Daniel Alm, together with two of Carl-Johan's friends' mothers, who are both crying. The family's priest is a good friend and knows that it's pointless to prolong the suspense, so he says compassionately and directly that Carl-Johan has died and that he is one of the – at that time – eight fatalities from the Roskilde Festival accident.

Three and half years later, Birgitta and Ebbe are both calm and collected as they once again recall the worst moment of their lives. Daniel Alm's words leave Birgitta paralyzed by shock. She stands stiff as a statue without emotionally comprehending what's happened, while Ebbe and Sandra collapse to the floor screaming.

Everything in the following time feels surreal for the family, as they are embroiled in a whirlwind of deep sorrow, personal blame and the constant intrusive presence of the press. The family goes through the painful processes of finding a burial site for their son and holding his funeral. Grief weighs heavily on the family, who receive tremendous support from friends, family and the congregation – particularly their priest, who continuously does everything he can to help and support them.

Birgitta develops insomnia, is unable to work and often breaks into sudden, uncontrollable crying. She says that it felt like she was sinking into a abyss. Ebbe is calmer and more collected, despite the enormous difficulty of accepting the death of his son. Birgitta grows physically ill from grief and has to call an ambulance that autumn when she finds herself unable to move. Birgitta gears down to about 10 hours a week at the office supply store where she works and only performs administrative tasks. She doesn't want any direct contact with customers and she generally feels increasingly shy. She reads everything she can find that is related to the accident, which only contributes to her deteriorating mental well-being and physical health. Ebbe continues to work as a firefighter, but switches from emergency response to daytime tasks at the fire station so that Birgitta is never alone at night. He is the one who keeps the family going, but he loses his sense of joy for life.

The summer creeps ahead slowly. On August 21, which would have been Carl-Johan's 21st birthday, his friends gather and hold a moving memorial concert in Jönköping, where a number of bands play. As a form of occupational therapy, Birgitta works that autumn on the interior plans for the family's soon-to-be-built holiday home, which leads to the unexpected discovery of Carl-Johan's detailed diary. She can't resist looking in the diary, and what she reads is like a stroke of lightning: "Yesterday I read a book about heaven. It will probably be fine in a couple of years, or whenever it is that Jesus comes," wrote Carl-Johan in May 1998. Birgitta says that all her life she felt that she wouldn't have him forever, and that despite his great love of life, it appears that Carl-Johan also felt that his life on Earth would be of a limited duration.

A half year after the accident, the only contact the family has had with Roskilde Festival is the flowers sent to Carl-Johan's funeral. The otherwise mild-mannered Ebbe Gustafsson is infuriated when he reads an interview in which Leif Skov stresses the importance of being in personal contact with the families of the accident's victims and that he has personally been in contact with all of the families.

Ebbe gets a hold of Leif Skov's e-mail address and writes a indignant letter to the festival director. Leif Skov responds quickly and is understanding of Ebbe's anger. It turns out that the festival has written to the family to no avail. The only legal way for the festival to contact them was to write via the police. The police sent the festival's letters to Carl-Johan's address in Jönköping and they never reach the Gustafssons in Tranås. Leif Skov offers to meet personally with the family, if they so desire.

To the Gustafssons, Roskilde Festival represents all the evil that took away their son far too soon – and the face of the festival is Leif Skov. But in spite of their doubts, pain and odious sentiments, the family maintains a conviction that forgiveness and reconciliation is the only solution – even when it is easier said than done. After extensively considering his offer, Ebbe and Birgitta invite Leif Skov to Tranås in January 2001. Leif Skov arrives and rings the doorbell at the exact time they agreed to meet. The Gustafssons say that Leif Skov comes across as humble, solemn and open. The festival director brings photos of the Memorial Grove and discusses a range of topics, including the accident, safety procedures and how his daughter was bullied after the accident because of her father's position. Daniel Alm is present at the meeting and conducts much of the dialog with Leif Skov, and he explains on behalf of the Gustafssons that, as Christians, they are committed to reconciliation. Ebbe apologizes for the angry tone in his original e-mail, and Leif Skov conveys his understanding. The Gustafssons later send an e-mail to Leif Skov, expressing great gratitude for his visit and understanding of his own grief. They also write that they now keep him and his family in their prayers.

During our visit, the family stresses that this meeting and contact with Leif Skov has been an essential part of their grieving process. Later, the festival donates DKK 50,000 for youth activities in the church in response to an application submitted by the Gustafssons. Ebbe asks me to give the family's warmest regards to Leif Skov, a greeting that I have the opportunity to pass on a year and a half later.

In the first six months after the accident, the focus is on Birgitta and Sandra's grief. Ebbe has done his utmost to remain strong and hold the family together, but in the spring of 2001, things start to crumble for him. He's lost about 20 pounds and the once hyper-fit sportsman now finds that even brief runs leave him short of breath. As a firefighter, he's seen his share of human catastrophes and he's a mentally and physically strong person, but it feels different when the tragedy hits so close to home. Although Ebbe once again discovers an inner peace and joy during his annual ski vacation with friends, he awakes in the hotel bed one night, screaming after a nightmare. Shortly after, he collapses physically with heart problems, leading him to take sick leave and ultimately requiring hospitalization. At the hospital, Ebbe meets the priest Ronny, who becomes a close confidant and plays an important part in Ebbe's grieving process.

Time has crept by very slowly, but things are gradually getting better say the Gustafssons, even though there are still days when they are crippled by grief. The help of family, friends, the congregation and local community, their Christian faith – including the firm conviction that they will meet Carl-Johan in heaven – and a willingness to embrace reconciliation and forgiveness all help to make life more bearable. They also point to the importance of their contact with the other Swedish parents who lost children at Roskilde, as well as with a Swedish couple that now gives talks about loss and moving forward after losing their daughter in the 1994 sinking of the MS Estonia ferry, one of the worst maritime disasters of the twentieth century.

We say goodbye to the Gustafssons and, as a parting gift, they give us the personally dedicated copy of the Swedish-language book, After Roskilde – From Crisis to Reconciliation, in which Ebbe and Birgitta tell their story to journalist Jonatan Sverker. As our travelling party of three boards the rental car once more, it's with a positive feeling in our bodies and minds, despite the tragic and moving stories we've just heard. Having met two families on the same day that tackled the situation so differently almost comes as a shock.

Meanwhile, the question of the role of Roskilde Festival and Leif Skov remains ambiguous. Both meetings make a huge impression, and there's so much to digest that there's not much energy left in our tanks when we arrive at a small hotel in Jönköping about an hour later.

Third stop: Alan Tonnesen's family
The next day, Stone flies from Jönköping to Copenhagen and then takes a connecting flight to Billund, Denmark to visit the Tonnesen family in the small town of Nordenskov, while Liz and I drive the rental car back to Copenhagen. But first, the three of us start the day with breakfast at a cafe and read the morning papers, which feature yet another scandal in the long line of Courtney Love's escapades. Stone smiles altruistically and says that he doesn't know her personally, but that it must be a hard job to be in her shoes. The conversation moves on to Pearl Jam and the lack of single hits in the past several years. Stone asks whether Love Boat Captain made any kind of a splash in Scandinavia. I tell him that it hasn't really. Stone concludes with a smile and apparent satisfaction that Pearl Jam's

Ludde Ahlström and Henrik Bondebjer. Rolling Stones concert, Wembley Stadium, London. June 12, 1999. Private photo.

Carl Johan Gustafsson. Tranås, Sweden. Private photo.

time as a band with hit singles appears to be a thing of the past.

I meet with Stone and Liz once again the next afternoon. Stone tells us that his meeting with the Tonnesens went really well. In fact, he stayed there so long that he had to spend the night at a nearby motel. Stone also says that he will definitely be seeing the family again, not least if an upcoming suit against Roskilde ends up in court.

Fourth stop: Asbjørn and Dorte Palle

Earlier that day, Stone and Liz met with Leo's friend Asbjørn and Dorte Palle from the Danish Broadcasting Corporation. At Dorte's request, I had asked Stone in advance of his visit to Scandinavia whether he would allow the filming of any of his meetings with the families and friends – and particularly the meeting with Leo's friends. It was a pretty awkward request to pass on to Stone, but I felt that Dorte had helped me so much that I really couldn't refuse to give it a try. Dorte's journalistic philosophy and experience is that you can always ask – otherwise nothing will ever succeed and, after all, people can just say no.

I forward Dorte's letter and give Stone my warmest recommendation of her. Not surprisingly, Stone rejects the request to film his meetings, but he says that he would like to meet with Dorte and he expresses great respect for her work. The meeting is presumably an opportunity for Dorte to interview Stone, but to her surprise the roles are quickly reversed. Stone has a lot of questions.

Dorte – Asbjørn and I arrived for breakfast at Hotel Skt. Petri. Asbjørn was really nervous about meeting one of his idols again, but things quickly became a lot more relaxed. I could immediately sense that Stone and Liz are positive and friendly people, but I was really surprised by how little Stone actually knew about the accident. I think he started asking me questions because I'd interviewed more than 100 people, most of whom had been at the concert. He was really interested in learning about my conclusions, whether the people who were there felt that Pearl Jam shared some of the blame, whether the consumption of drugs and alcohol had impacted the outcome, and so on. I told him that nobody I spoke with in the course of all my interviews had blamed Pearl Jam for anything, but that a lot of the young people were dealing with a heavy burden of personal guilt. Of all those I spoke with, only one responded like a "hero" in the classical sense. That's just one person who understood what was happening in time and then began helping people get out of the crowd. Many people had pushed their way to the front of the crowd to crowd surf, and at some point they had a sense of standing on a sleeping bag or a purse – or some kind of foreign surface – and that others had seen people be crushed to death but were helpless to do anything about it. In retrospect, the "sleeping bags" turned out to be human bodies, and many people blamed themselves with questions like: "Was I just thinking about myself?", "Could I have done more

Liz Weber & Stone Gossard. Tranås, Sweden. November 3, 2003. Photo: Birgitta Gustafsson.

to save others?", "Why didn't I realize how bad things were in time?", etc.

Dorte adds that it's very difficult to tell all of these painful stories to Stone, and she wonders whether she's getting close to the limit of how much he can withstand hearing, but that's not the case.

Dorte – I stopped multiple times to get a feel for whether I should hold back, but he sat and nodded and kept asking questions. I told him that I spoke with a young girl who was deeply traumatized by her own reaction to the situation. She was

at the concert with a friend, but when everything suddenly got so chaotic, her only thought was to get herself to safety. With a lot of struggling and effort, she managed to fight her way out of the crowd. Not until she had made it out safely did she think about her friend. A lot of people who were there that day have suffered from similar traumas. I also told Stone that the autopsies of the deceased showed that the amount of drugs and alcohol in their systems was limited, which I was surprised to discover that he didn't know. Regarding the sequence of events, I told him that my research indicated that the first people were toppled during

Better Man. I expressed great sympathy with his actions, and told him how much it means to the families and friends that a rock star like him came to meet with them in a down-to-earth and humble way – which was readily apparent in Asbjørn, who was sitting next to me. It was a very positive meeting with a little bit of disappointment. Stone said that if he had known that things would go as well as they did, he wouldn't have minded if I had been there with a film crew. "I knew it," I thought to myself, but obviously that's just the way things had to be.

Fifth stop: Fredrik Thuresson's family

Despite Stone's jam-packed schedule, he manages to meet with the attorney Tyge Trier and he offers to testify about what he saw and experienced if the suit goes to court.

On the final evening before their return to the States, Liz and Stone cross the Oresund Strait to Sweden once more to meet with the Thuressons in the city of Malmö. Stone tells me that they met for dinner at the father's home, together with Fredrik's two brothers and the wife of one of the brothers. Stone describes it as an incredibly nice and positive evening, where the father, Gert Thuresson, is in good spirits despite the mournful circumstances. As with the Bondebjers, Gert Thuresson talks about how their home was surrounded by the press, and that the photo of his son was displayed pretty much every time Roskilde Festival was mentioned on Swedish television for about two years after the accident.

The journey home

Stone doesn't manage to meet with Leif Skov or representatives from the Danish police. However, he's so encouraged by his trip to Scandinavia that he mentions his thoughts about returning to Scandinavia with the entire band within the next six months. I say that if he and/or other members of Pearl Jam decide to come back, I would be more than willing to try to locate and contact the relatives of the two victims – Marco Peschel of Germany and Frank Nouwens of The Netherlands – that Stone and Pearl Jam have not yet been in contact with. Stone is very receptive to the idea, but we agree that I shouldn't do anything before Stone is certain about when or if he and/or the band will be returning to Scandinavia.

Throughout the week, I try to tend to my regular job to the best of my abilities, so I'm at *Gaffa*'s offices in Copenhagen when it's time for the Americans to return home. Before Stone and Liz go to Copenhagen International Airport, they manage to do some alternative sightseeing, which includes visiting me at *Gaffa*'s offices in the Copenhagen district of Vesterbro. Another huge Pearl Jam fan is at the office, so there's a bit of time to sign some CDs and share some concert stories.

On a side note, Stone doesn't really have a clear idea of where Pearl Jam has played and when, and his guesses about some of the concerts we mention are sometimes off by many years. Stone and Liz thank me again for my efforts, and I can only repeat that Pearl Jam, Roskilde and the accident are so much a part of my personal story that the efforts are at least as much for my own sake as that of others. On the way out the door, they give me an envelope as Stone smiles and says it "might come in handy." In the envelope, there's a gift certificate to a local electronics store in the amount of 13,300 Danish kroner – the exact price of a brand new iBook. My old one crashed and died a few days earlier.

To sue or not to sue

Following the whirlwind of events in the past few days with Stone and Liz, a number of positive responses start to trickle in. Sven-Anders Bondebjer thanks me for the meeting and asks whether we got in touch with Tyge Trier. He adds that he'll stop by the next time he's in Copenhagen. Eunice Tonnesen also calls to tell me that the family was really appreciative of Stone's visit and, around Christmas about a month later, I get just about the world's largest bouquet of flowers with warm greetings from the Gustafssons in Tranås.

At Roskilde Festival 2004, Leo's friend Asbjørn contacts me. He says that before Stone's visit, he and his friends thought they were done processing the tragedy, but it turns out that was not the case. Stone's visit gave all of them a heightened sense of peace and closure in a different and more complete way.

Stone also sends a number of e-mails expressing his appreciation and satisfaction with the results of the trip, and shares some information about his ongoing correspondence with a number of the families and relatives.

During the winter, the matter of a civil suit against Roskilde Festival returns to the front pages in the Danish press. The public prosecutor previously found that the legal liability for the accident itself cannot be attributed to any person or organization, but that it was instead the result of an unfortunate combination of circumstances. However, the Regional State Administration in Roskilde grants the Tonnesen family free legal counsel in their civil lawsuit against the festival, and grants the same to the parents of four victims in a parallel case, where they are represented by Tyge Trier. In response, via attorney Bruno Månsson, Roskilde Festival objects to the necessity of a lawsuit in the spring of 2004 on the grounds that the parents can obtain financial compensation without a trial.

The Tonnesens are of the view that it's not just a private matter, but rather in the public interest to determine whether anybody can be held liable for the accident. Tyge Trier's attorney argues much the same as the Tonnesen family.

A few months before their meeting with Stone, the Tonnesen family receives a check in the mail from the festival. It's in the amount of 40,000 Danish kroner and offered as support without assuming legal liability for the accident. The family is not interested in the check and returns it to the festival via their attorney.

In connection with the Regional State Administration's decision to grant the parents of the four victims free legal counsel, I write a news article for *Gaffa*. In the article, Tyge Trier is quoted as saying: "It's encouraging that we can finally move forward with the case. It hasn't been possible to do so in any other way, since Roskilde Festival has rejected all of my attempts to establish dialog between the parties. The court has the power to find that the festival is liable to pay damages for the grave tragedy suffered by these parents. This may include financial compensation to the families, but nothing significant in terms of the awards seen in other countries. The main purpose of this principled case is to force the festival to acknowledge its legal responsibility for the lack of safety at the festival, which led to the accident."

I also contact Roskilde Festival's spokesman, Esben Danielsen, who says:

Esben – We will contribute to anything that can shed new light and improve understanding of the accident in 2000. Therefore, we are awaiting the respective authorities' reaction to these lawsuits, and we believe that these cases should be litigated in court and not in the press.

In the same article, Stone Gossard, speaking on behalf of Pearl Jam, expresses his satisfaction with the decision that the legal responsibility will be determined by a court of law.

Chapter 6

2004: VOTE FOR CHANGE. USA.

In the year 2004, all eyes in the United States were on the November presidential election. Rarely, if ever before, had leading American musicians so actively entered the fray to support a presidential candidate – or to specifically oppose another. Pearl Jam joined with other prominent figures in the music industry to start the Vote For Change initiative, a travelling music caravan with the clearly delineated mission of getting John Kerry into the White House instead of a another four-year term for George W. Bush. The initiative raised money for voter registration efforts and for the grassroots organization America Coming Together, an interest group that engaged in public debate, hosted town hall meetings, wrote letters to the editor and more. Though history now shows that the effort proved unsuccessful, the initiative and events that took place were impressive nonetheless.

I follow Pearl Jam for about four days during the final stretch of Vote For Change – an experience about as far from Roskilde and the Swedish forests as you could get. Vote For Change consists of six simultaneous touring caravans that play on the same day in the same state in each of the election's swing states, concluding with a grand finale in Washington D.C. just three weeks before the election. The lineup features upper echelon American artists in genres ranging from rock and rap, to pop and country – names such as R.E.M., John Fogerty, John Mellencamp, Dixie Chicks, Bonnie Raitt, Dave Matthews Band, Jurassic 5, Pearl Jam and the ultimate scoop, Bruce Springsteen. The Boss thereby breaks 30 years of silence and letting his lyrics and music speak for itself by taking a direct political stand.

Pearl Jam is centrally involved in the planning and execution, particularly manager Kelly Curtis, Eddie Vedder and Stone Gossard. Stone serves as the musicians' unofficial spokesman to the media for the largest collective political initiative by American musicians in the nation's history. In other words, a project that's impossible for a music journalist like me to ignore.

I express my interest to Stone and quickly receive an invite to join in. Once again, Marianne Søndergaard from Sony Music plays an important role. There's no new album, so it's far from a project that the record company would typically fund. But Marianne does her magic, and suddenly I'm sitting in an airplane on my way to an all-expenses-paid trip in the States. I see Pearl Jam's final concert as part of the travelling caravan in Orlando, Florida on October 8, 2004, followed by the grand finale in Washington D.C. three days later.

Florida

As for me, it's my first Pearl Jam concert since the night of the accident, making it impossible for me to think about the concert in purely musical terms. All the concerts I've seen since Maui have been more enjoyable than fantastic, so I have to go all the way back to 1996 in my memories to find a mind-blowing PJ concert. I have my doubts about whether Pearl Jam still has the potential to reach its former heights – doubts that are absolutely obliterated after this evening in Florida.

My travel plans are botched by a long delay in Chicago and an inattentive taxi driver who drops me off at the wrong hotel in Orlando. I don't arrive at my hotel room until five in the morning, eight hours later than planned. The next day, my biological clock is off the rails and my capacity for logical or clear thought is heavily impaired. Despite it all, I think I've got everything under control, since the hotel's address is on the same street as the concert venue. But I forgot one little detail: American boulevards can stretch on ad infinitum.

Stone said me that he'd make sure there were tickets for me, minus the details of exactly where or when said tickets would be available. And being on a tour with concerts, daily political activities and press conferences, he's not the easiest guy to get in touch with. No concert tickets await me at the hotel and when I finally find the arena where they're playing, I'm told that no guest list tickets will be arriving until shortly before the concert starts. So I wait.

A picturesque scene unfolds outside the arena: 82 degrees in the shade on an October day ain't too shabby, and the crowd pouring in is fully primed for a party long before the scheduled concert starts. Three radio stations are broadcasting live from the event and various political figures and organizations have set up shop.

Any concerns about Pearl Jam's declining popularity are clearly unfounded.

I'm in the presence of hardcore fans. I don't recall ever seeing such a long and lasting line at a merchandise booth as the one selling Pearl Jam / Vote For Change wares – it's longer than the line to get into the concert. Probably around half the audience is already clad in various Pearl Jam T-shirts, maybe around 300 different versions in all, the vast majority feature designs from the hand of bassist Jeff Ament. The audience, which is somewhat younger than I had expected, streams into the arena when the doors open. But there are still no guest list tickets and no Pearl Jam. The near 10,000-capacity arena is completely sold out, so if all else fails, I have two options: either try my luck with a scalper, or return to the hotel. Right before I start to get really nervous, I check with the woman at the will call window once again. This time, she smiles and waves me over, handing me a nice envelope bearing my name that holds a ticket and an "after party" sticker.

While the early birds are just beginning to find their seats and long before the two support bands are scheduled to take the stage in the fully lit arena, a familiar voice comes from the stage. As so often before, Eddie Vedder has taken the stage solo with his acoustic guitar. He plays a Cat Stevens song followed by the Beatles hymn *You've Got to Hide Your Love Away*. The crowd is ecstatic. People rush into the arena. Before leaving the stage, Eddie introduces an old Republican senator in honor of freedom of speech. The senator rolls onstage in a wheelchair, looking like Peter Seller's Nazi caricature in *Dr. Strangelove*. He begins chastising Eddie Vedder before suddenly jumping up in an electric inferno. It's Pearl Jam friend and filmmaker, Tim Robbins, now joined by his furious punk band, Gus Roberts. Gus is followed by Death Cab For Cutie, the melancholic and atmospheric indie rock band from Washington state. In the dark and subdued arena, I doggedly resist my escalating jet lag. Soon after Death Cab For Cutie, I go looking for backup in the form of coffee. Suddenly, the stage lights dim and the supercharged tones of *Last Exit* blanket the venue in a wall of sound. Instantly invigorated, I run back to my seat with burning hot coffee spilling down my arms and legs – the previously half-empty arena is now filled to the brim. The sound is massive and crisp. Pearl Jam is definitely a band at the top of its game tonight.

As with the other Vote For Change concerts, the band's performance is split into three parts: a set of about 12 songs, a break, five or six acoustic songs, another break, a few songs at full tilt and then a final farewell. Pearl Jam rounds off this evening joined by Death Cab For Cutie and Tim Robbins for a rendition of Neil Young's *Rockin' in the Free World* (Young and his wife appeared as surprise guests with Pearl Jam four days earlier) before their familiar go-to closing number, *Yellow Ledbetter*.

The event is a diverse cornucopia of rock'n'roll, well-formulated encourage-ment to vote, atmospheric ballads, and unexpected twists and turns such as Tim Robbins and Eddie Vedder wrestling around the stage or Eddie slow dancing with Robbins' wife, the actress Susan Sarandon. The audience sings along on every song, just as familiar with the lyrics to *Do the Evolution* as to *Alive*. Pearl Jam has integrated a number of simple pop/punk covers, including Ramones' *I Believe in Miracles*, The Avengers' *The American in Me,* and Vedder's irresistible duet with Tim Robbins on *The New World*, a song originally recorded by the punk band X. It's vital, varied, political and liberating rock'n'roll. In spite of my general wariness to make sweeping statements, I don't remember having seen anything like it in more than 28 years as a concertgoer.

The concert is a textbook model of how Pearl Jam's concert performances have evolved. Their shows typically feature extensive and varied setlists, and are always speckled with surprises. Eddie may take the stage alone almost as soon as people start entering the concert venue, while support groups or guests may play on their own and/or with Pearl Jam. The headliner may rock all night from curtain

Tim Robbins, Eddie Vedder, Death Cab for Cutie. Kissimmee, Florida. October 8, 2004.
Photo: Kerensa Wight.

to curtain, or shift gears for long acoustic interludes. The audience never knows what surprises await them, or which songs they will hear that night. In fact, ever since their first show in 1990, Pearl Jam has never once played the same set at two concerts in a row. Jeff Ament tells me two days after the concert in Florida that Pearl Jam played about 100 different songs on the *Riot Act* tour and at least 60 different songs on the Vote For Change tour.

After the concert, it's time for a reunion with Stone and Liz – and their dog, who is tagging along on tour. They look happy and satisfied, and I've got nothing but praise for the fantastic concert. Pearl Jam's schedule is really tight, but Stone suggests that we might be able to meet up two days later in Washington D.C., the day before the big final concert, when he hopes to have a little time.

Washington D.C.

After making the rounds to the White House, Capitol Hill and other D.C. attractions on my own, I head for the band's luxurious digs, The Mandarin Oriental, which is also the abode of R.E.M. and many of the other featured acts at Vote For Change. I got a call from Pearl Jam's tour manager – and Stone's tennis partner – Mark "Smitty" Smith, who tells me where to meet the band. Smitty's been with the band forever and I clearly remember him from Spain in 1996.

When I get there, the whole band and some friends are present. Eddie Vedder sits on a chair, occasionally dozing off, but later greets me with a smile and can remember both my face and my name. He points to his throat and says he would have given me a big hug if it wasn't for "this" – I don't know what "this" is, but I'm guessing it's a cold or an injury from the rowdy wrestling match with Tim Robbins on stage in Florida two days earlier.

Stone and Liz are there too, together with a middle-aged Native American couple from an NGO whose name I have forgotten. They've never been to D.C. before, Stone tells me, so he decided to invite them out for the weekend.

A short time later, everybody piles into two vehicles and drives over to the gigantic MCI Center, where Pearl Jam is going to run through the following day's set. I drive with Stone, Liz and Eddie Vedder's partner (and later wife), Jill McCormick, who four months earlier gave birth to the couple's first child, Olivia. Stone tells me that Pearl Jam is going to hold a little meeting about the band's set the next day. There's some disagreement among them about whether to play *Bu$hleaguer*, a lambasting of the sitting president with lines like "He's not a Leader – he's a Texas Leaguer." The controversial number caused quite a furor when Eddie took off his George W. Bush mask and hung it on a mic stand (or as critics said, "impaled it") during the opening concert of their *Riot Act* tour in Denver the year before. Eddie Vedder is primed to play *Bu$hleaguer* in Washington D.C., says Stone, who doesn't seem quite as convinced.

It's just a short drive to the arena, and on the way to Pearl Jam's band room, we pass rooms with signs such as R.E.M. 1, R.E.M. 2, Dixie Chicks, Dave Matthews Band, John Fogerty and more. We can hear Michael Stipe's voice from the stage as R.E.M. runs through their sound check.

In Pearl Jam's backstage room, there's plenty of time for a little small talk with the band. Again I get the sense that once you're welcome among Pearl Jam, all doors are open. Mike McCready – the band member who has been through the most serious personal crises through the years – has never looked healthier. He greets me smiling with an ironic "Hey guys, have you seen? Henrik is here!", like a circus director presenting the evening's biggest sensation.

Smitty says to just let him know if I need anything or if he can help with anything. Nicole Vandenberg is there too, and I get some details from her for the Vote For Change article I'm going to be writing. She gives me some telephone numbers to key figures behind the event and says to mention her and say that "I'm with them." Jeff Ament is also really outgoing, talking about his latest artistic creations for the Vote For Change tour; he also tells me that he has a bad feeling about the upcoming election. But he gives a thumbs up for Neil Young, saying that the latter and his wife Peggy stole the show with their guest appearance earlier that week.

Eddie Vedder is friendly and attentive, and asks if I'll be coming to the concert the next day – which of course I will be. Stone introduces Eddie to the Native American couple, who Vedder greets with a humble smile. A man I haven't seen before comes and gives Eddie a large photograph that he's clearly grateful for. A number of others who are standing close by shower superlatives on the photo in the lead singer's hands. I peep over Vedder's shoulder to get a look at the black and white photo, which captures Eddie Vedder and Bruce Springsteen, arm in arm in front of the White House. If I had to guess, it looks like a classic black and white Anton Corbijn portrait, and maybe that's who is standing next to Eddie. I don't know what the Dutch photographer looks like, but given the conversations and reactions, it seems that the photographer is present. I later make an unsuccessful attempt to dig up the photo, which *Gaffa* hoped to use on the cover of its next issue.

There's still some time before Pearl Jam's sound check, and Stone asks if I'm interested in conducting an official interview. Talking about Vote For Change, Stone says that a number of bands, independently of each other, wanted to take action in connection with the election campaign. The project really took off when Pearl Jam's manager, Kelly Curtis, got the green light from Springsteen's manager that The Boss was on board. Considering the lack of a Republican counter among American musicians, Stone feels that Vote For Change is a valid and representative expression of American musicians' general opposition to George W. Bush. To the question of whether Pearl Jam's seemingly limitless political and philanthropic activities are starting to overshadow the band's music.

Stone – There's really an art to incorporating artistic ideas with political things. I think that Ed has an amazing ability to write songs that are highly political but still from the heart. They come from a place that is really genuine and direct without being pedantic or self-righteous. I think he's able to reach other people and help them understand and relate to situations and scenarios that they might have never imagined existed. He's also able to surprise and the band can still play its ass off. You saw a good concert yesterday. Nobody can accuse you of being too political if you still rock, which is mostly about having a good time, letting go and embracing life in a hopefully unpredictable way.

After a few words about Pearl Jam's greatest hits album, their work on the next album and upcoming tours, Stone says that the band still has a strong interest in playing in Denmark. It's important for everyone in the band to return and re-establish contact.

I take advantage of this change of subject to bring up another matter. As opposed to almost every other band of comparable or much lower acclaim, there is no official biography of Pearl Jam. Only a few books have been published, the vast majority of which are based on third-hand sources, while one includes quotes from the band's former drummer, Dave Abbruzzese, who often clashed with Eddie Vedder. But there is no official biography. I float the idea of writing a comprehensive piece on the band's recent history, with an emphasis on the band's fan relations, humanitarian work and the events surrounding and after Roskilde Festival.

Stone – We never wanted anyone to write the official band biography, and we still feel that way. But if you choose to write your own interpretations, based upon all the things that we have experienced together and about what has happened, I would like to participate in any way that I can. I think that would be an interesting read and an important story to tell. I greatly appreciate your discretion throughout it all, which has also been important to the families, but I had actually expected that you would write something at some point.

It's a somewhat different response than what I was envisioning, but interesting nonetheless. So there's plenty to think about as I later sit in the cavernous empty area and listen to Pearl Jam's sound check, which includes breakneck political punk and covers of the Dead Kennedys, among others.

Afterwards, I return to the Mandarin Oriental Hotel and go up to Stone and Liz's luxury suite with Jeff Ament, who's staying in the room next door. Jeff is tired, but says that he may come down to the restaurant later. Liz asks how it's going with my biography, after which Stone clarifies, "Kashmir". When the couple were in Denmark in 2003, I was working on writing a biography of the Danish band. Stone invites me to join them and Tim Robbins for dinner. Robbins proves to be riveting, humorous and the consummate anarchist. In the super posh restaurant, he's wearing a totally trashed outfit and loudly comments on the restaurant's no-smoking policy, on his son's band, where the father of one of the other band members is very pro-Bush and unappreciative of Robbins' adamant opposition, and on Sarandon's sister, who is coming to D.C. tomorrow – he's sharp as a tack, laid-back and hilarious.

Tim and Stone conclude with satisfaction that President Bush apparently feels threatened by the Vote For Change initiative, since he's synchronized his election campaign with the concert tour to capture the biggest local headlines. "Just think that a bunch of guys like us can scare the president. That's wild," philosophizes Stone with a smile. But as history would have it, Vote For Change ultimately came up short of its goal.

Masters of War

The next day is the big finale. For me, it's an incredible "all-American" experience. I've never been particularly intrigued by names such as John Mellencamp or Jackson Browne, but seeing them on their home turf in this context is remarkable.

Imaginative and colorful demonstrations and counterdemonstrations rage outside the MCI Center. Television, radio and newspaper reporters with microphones swarm the premises and it's like somebody dumped me into the middle of a classic Hollywood film.

All the featured acts exhibit passion for the cause, delivering one fantastic concert performance after the next. Almost all the bands have guest appearances from other bands. For example, Eddie Vedder drops in on R.E.M. and before each act leaves the stage they introduce the next in line.

I've got a seat among Pearl Jam's guests and am sitting next to Liz, who's exuberant. She tells me that she and Stone are now engaged, and that Pearl Jam is considering a European tour as soon as the spring of 2005 – they later change their plans when the work on their upcoming album drags out longer than expected. Stone and Mike McCready sit with us most of the night, except for right before and after their turn on stage.

Most of the bands deliver a parade of greatest hits, peppered with occasional zingers aimed Bush. But not Pearl Jam. They stick to explicitly political line throughout, from the opening number *Grievance* (*I pledge my grievance to the flag / Cause you don't give blood… then take it back again*) until the closing lines of Dylan's *Masters of War* (*And I'll stand over your grave / 'til I'm sure that you're dead*).

The event continues with strong appearances by Dixie Chicks and Dave Matthews Band, all of which is overshadowed by Springsteen's divine concert and a final all-star performance. The evening is quite simply American cultural history at its best.

Stone "Pinocchio" Gossard. The nose refers to Bush and Cheney's role in the Enron scandal. Vote For Change. Asheville, North Carolina. October 6, 2004. Photo: Kerensa Wight.

VOTE FOR CHANGE!
OCTOBER 11, 2004
BONNIE RAITT
BRUCE SPRINGSTEEN
&THE E STREET BAND
DIXIE CHICKS
DAVE MATTHEWS BAND
JOHN FOGERTY
JOHN MELLANCAMP
JACKSON BROWNE
JURASSIC 5
KEB MO
KENNY "BABY FACE" EDMONDS
PEARL JAM
REM
'10710
AMERICA COMING TOGETHER & MOVEON.PAC.ORG

All-American superstar lineup.

Vote For Change demonstrations for and against Bush. Washington D.C. October 11, 2004.
Photo: Henrik Tuxen.

CHAPTER 7

2005: FIVE YEARS LATER.
ROSKILDE FESTIVAL. THE TRIAL.

June 30, 2005 is the five year anniversary of the day nine young people lost their lives during Pearl Jam's concert at Roskilde Festival. It's a moment for reflection and remembrance for all those whose lives were touched by the tragedy. For many of the families, the summer of 2005 is largely dominated by the emotionally taxing legal aftermath of the accident. The findings of public prosecutor Erik Merlung's June 2002 report aroused criticism from many sides. After the release of the report, Eunice and Finn Tonnesen, represented by attorney Morten Vindsløv, file a civil suit against Roskilde Festival to hold the festival management fully or partially liable for the accident, seeking compensation for the family's funeral expenses and other costs, as well as DKK 70,000 for pain and suffering. Meanwhile, attorney Tyge Trier files a parallel civil suit against the festival on behalf of the parents of four of the victims. Both the Tonnesens and the parents of the four victims were granted free legal aid, after which the case was transferred to the Eastern High Court.

The first hearing in Tonnesen v. Roskilde Festival takes place at Denmark's Eastern High Court on August 8, 2005. The first order of business for the court is to determine whether there is a legal basis for filing the civil suit. The judge informs the parties to the case that a ruling on this question will be issued on November 8 at the Eastern High Court.

At this point, the public prosecutor has already found that no person or organization could be charged with criminal liability, making the cases civil rather than criminal disputes. However, the Danish courts have the power to award plaintiffs compensation in civil suits where there is no criminal liability.

At the August 8, 2005 hearing, the court has to determine whether there is a legal basis for such a suit. Roskilde Festival's attorney, Bruno Månsson, argues that no such legal basis exists. He holds that a civil suit would not contribute anything new, that the Tonnesens are seeking to determine a "moral" liability, which is not a matter for the courts to decide, and that the festival has already offered the Tonnesen family financial compensation, which the family has refused to accept. Månsson also cites the need for consideration of Roskilde Festival and the volunteers who were on duty as security on the night of the accident.

To this, the Tonnesens' attorney, Morten Winsløv, says "you probably don't need to be a great psychologist to understand that the loss of the family's son and the festival's responsibility is the primary matter in question, and that the compensation is secondary," and that "the dilemma for the court is whether greater consideration must be given to the festival's employees or to the plaintiffs, who lost a son in the accident."

The fact that the Tonnesen family does not want to accept financial compensation unless it is accompanied by an acknowledgment of responsibility complicates the case and, according to Winsløv, is unprecedented in Danish case law.

In regards to the matter of pain and suffering, attorney Tyge Trier cites 26 rulings based on the European Convention on Human Rights in which families have been awarded financial compensation for an accident that did not affect their person, but that of a relative. Månsson argues that the European Convention on Human Rights cannot be used to file suit against private individuals or organizations.

The ruling in the Tonnesen case, as heard by the court on August 8, 2005, will establish a precedent for the parallel suit litigated by Tyge Trier. Despite relatively small amounts of money at stake, the case may prove to be of great importance for interpretation of the law.

During the time around the five-year anniversary of the accident, the trial weighs heavily on the thoughts and emotions of all those involved. Over the past five years, I've been in contact with so many different people whose lives were impacted in one way or another by the tragic event. And now that it's clear that my story is taking shape as a book, it makes sense to contact the most centrally involved figures to ask about their thoughts and feelings on the matter.

Dorte Palle

No journalist covered the accident more in depth than Dorte Palle Jørgensen, who especially wrote at length about Leo's circle of friends. We meet on a blazing hot day in late June at her office at the Danish Broadcasting Corporation, and not long after at the 2005 edition of Roskilde Festival. Dorte feels that the story of the accident is just as relevant and important as ever.

Dorte – It would be fatal to forget the accident. In the time after the accident – maybe even for some years after – there was a heightened awareness of safety at concerts, and people in the crowd were careful to be considerate of one another. But the more time passes, the more it seems to be disappearing from the collective memory. This became really clear to me last year when I took my 14-year-old little sister to a Britney Spears concert. I told her that she had to wear sneakers, not let her hair hang loose, remember to drink water, and so on. She clearly thought that I was acting like a old, nit-picking aunt, so we talked about it a little bit. I told her that she shouldn't forget the accident that happened at Roskilde, to which she replied, "What accident?" That really came as a shock to me. In my mind, it was something that everybody knew about, but then I realized that many of the new concertgoers three or four years after the accident had no idea what had happened. No matter how good the general safety is at concerts, it's all-important that people in the crowd are attentive to each other and the situation, and that people are able to read any signs of danger so they can avoid similar disasters in the future. And in this sense, it doesn't help that people my age, who probably attend fewer and fewer concerts as they grow older, are attentive – we have to get the attention of the current and future concertgoers. It's important that they're aware of what can go wrong and that they remember to behave considerately towards others. But some things have changed. For example, you don't see stage diving or crowd surfing any more.

I have to correct Dorte a bit on this matter. Earlier that week I saw Queens of the Stone Age play at Vega in Copenhagen, and people were crowd surfing the whole time.

Dorte – OK, well, that just makes it all the more relevant. I think it's important as a journalist to work with this case. I also think it's good that the question of liability will now be considered in the courts. It's good to get everything out in the open, so the trial is a good thing. It will give the parents a real chance to see and understand what happened and what Roskilde Festival is all about. Openness is positive for everyone involved. That said, I also think it's incredibly important to avoid a conclusion along the lines of "Roskilde Festival is a bad thing" – instead, there should be a show of support for youth culture. For the same reason, I also think it's extremely positive that Asbjørn, Tore and his friends continue attending the festival. And personally, I'll be going again this year.

Leif Skov

I can't say whether former director Leif Skov, who worked for the festival through three decades, attended Roskilde Festival 2005. The accident dealt a severe blow to the former schoolteacher, who dedicated almost his entire career to making

Roskilde Festival what it is today, alongside a wide range of social work activities for youth. Given Leif Skov's central position during the accident and its aftermath, I contact him in connection with the five-year anniversary and the prospect of a pending trial. He does not wish to comment, but does request to be quoted in full as follows:

"In connection with the preparation of this book, Henrik Tuxen contacted Leif Skov to ask about his dialog with the families and his thoughts/conclusions five years after the accident. Leif Skov does not wish to contribute to any use or exploitation of the accident in a commercial or external context, and stresses that all meetings with the families have been of a confidential and trusting nature. As before, Leif Skov wants to contribute to relieving the pain and grief of the surviving relatives – and to amicable and clarifying dialog between the parties involved."

Following my correspondence with Leif Skov, I decide to contact Esben Danielsen, who succeeded Leif Skov as the festival's official spokesman in late 2001. In an unsolicited gesture of transparency, Esben offers me full access to all of the festival's documents regarding the accident, following the court session in the Eastern High Court on August 8, 2005. I choose to decline the offer because my mission is not to conduct an in-depth legal investigation of the accident. Based on the same reasoning, Esben does not have anything to do with this story, nor is he a person that the families or people in Pearl Jam's camp have mentioned during my interactions with them.

But considering that Esben is now responsible for carrying on Skov's legacy and representing the festival in the public sphere, I send him the book's introduction, outline, etc. and offer him the opportunity to comment. After some correspondence, Esben comes to the conclusion that neither he nor Roskilde Festival wishes to comment.

Lennart "Leo" Nielsen's friend, Asbjørn

Following a number of telephone conversations with Asbjørn in connection with Stone's visit to Denmark, I meet him in person for the first time at Roskilde Festival in 2004. Later, I run into him at one of Copenhagen's cult concert venues and night clubs, Stengade 30, where he had begun working as a booker. Since then, we've had steady contact. Asbjørn also has an ongoing e-mail exchange with Stone, who mentioned that he might be coming to Denmark in July 2005.

Asbjørn asks if I know anything more about the visit. I tell him that Stone said that he was planning to spend a week or two in Europe during the summer, but that I didn't have the impression that he would be coming through Scandinavia this time.

I also tell Asbjørn about my book project and ask if he would like to contribute. A short time later, we meet on Stengade 30's large outdoor deck. Asbjørn downs coffee after coffee as thoughts swirl around the topic of his deceased friend Lennart "Leo" Nielsen and the muddled aftermath.

Asbjørn – I'm really torn about the fact that many of the parents are now suing Roskilde. I fear that many of them have no idea what the festival is about, how strong and important a part of youth culture it is, and how much it has done and meant – and still means – for so many people. I think that's really important to understand and get a feel for. But I also think that Roskilde Festival should have done more to bring together all of the families and friends and communicate with them in a positive way. Not more than week after the accident, we wrote to Leif Skov, telling him that we supported the festival and didn't think the tragedy was their fault. We never heard a word back from them, and I don't think that was very cool. That's why Stone Gossard's visit was so incredibly important. It really meant something to us to see that it meant something to them. In a way, I've gotten over it completely, and on the other hand, it all comes back as we sit here talking about it. I like thinking about the fact that most of Roskilde Festival 2000 was the shit and that Leo, before he died, was also having a blast. I still visit his grave once in awhile and I still think about him. I also keep going back to Roskilde Festival, and every year I visit the Memorial Grove. It wasn't fun in 2001 – back then, it felt so overwhelming. But now it's a tradition and something I find important. My girlfriend and my parents don't really get it, but it's important to me.

Lennart "Leo" Nielsen's ex-girlfriend, Astrid

Astrid Rørdam Ibsen is among those who come to Asbjørn's apartment during Stone and Liz's visit, but otherwise she's not a part of the tightly-knit group of friends who were with Leo at Roskilde Festival 2000. I exchange some e-mails and talk on the phone with Astrid a number of times during the summer of 2005. Even though she had broken up with the unruly Leo some time before Roskilde 2000, she is still greatly moved when the subject of his death comes up. And while Asbjørn and friends continue to pack their tents and sleeping bags each summer and head for Roskilde Festival, she hasn't returned since the accident.

Astrid – I can't say that I feel like going to Roskilde Festival. Maybe someday, but not now. I think that I've really processed what happened a lot, and I don't need to dive any deeper into it. I can understand the parents who feel a need to have somebody held responsible for the accident, but it's not important to me personally. I think there are things where Roskilde Festival has promised the victims' families more than they could deliver, but I don't think you could say that the festival is responsible for the accident. It can provide relief to have somebody to be angry at, but I don't have a need to be angry at the festival.

But there's no doubt that Astrid's feelings for Leo remain strong. This is evident in the fact that she consistently speaks of him in the present tense as we talk, five years after his death. Astrid might also be the person among Leo's friends who was the most emotionally moved by Stone Gossard's visit.

Astrid – When I heard from Tore that he was coming, I had a hard time deciding whether to participate. I had previously received two e-mails from Eddie Vedder, which were very touching, but I stupidly lost his e-mail address. Actually meeting a member of the band in person seemed like it might be overwhelming. I ended up going, and it was a really good experience. But I was so overcome with emotion that I had to leave after a half hour. I hope he didn't take it negatively, because I certainly didn't mean it that way. He was very humble and clearly affected by what happened, and he came to us as a friend and was down to earth, which felt really nice and positive. And he had so many questions for us.

Lennart "Leo" Nielsen's older sister, Benita

During a visit to Aarhus in late summer 2005, I meet with Benita, who shows me her little brother's gravesite as she talks about the shock of Lennart's death, the difficult and prolonged healing process, and her thoughts about the complicated legal aftermath.

Benita – As a Jehovah's Witness, Biblical teachings have charted my course. You can't make it through losing someone without some scars, even with a religious background, but I received so much incredible support from other Jehovah's Witnesses. If you ask people in crisis if you can do anything to help, they often say no thanks, even though they actually have a huge need for help. That's not how things were in my case. People came and cooked for me, cleaned, did my laundry and talked with me as best they could. I also think that I received about a hundred letters of support from a wide range of people, many of whom I didn't know in advance. But in spite of all this support, I became physically ill for inexplicable reasons after the accident and was hospitalized two months later. I woke up in the middle of the night and felt an excruciating pain in all of my joints, and I've now been diagnosed with chronic arthritis in my back. I don't know what caused it, but it came in the wake of my grief.

Benita then thinks back to the day she was notified of her little brother's fate.

Benita – Lennart's death was the toughest blow of my life. Two police officers came to my mother's house and told her what happened on Saturday. I was at a party, but my mom called and told me everything. I can't remember it myself, but I was later told that I started screaming. Now that so much time has passed, it's strange to describe those days and the time after the accident, because now I can better grasp it all. At the time, it felt like you were in a deep hole that you just couldn't get out of. It was so surreal that everyone else just kept living their lives like they always had, while your own life came to a screeching halt. People around me seemed like ghosts that I didn't dare to approach. And all the headlines were about the Roskilde accident, which to most people was just a sad news story, but for me it had changed my life completely. I hadn't ever imagined – fortunately – that I would ever find myself in the situation of having to identify my beloved little brother, lying there cold and peaceful in a mortuary. There's something that breaks inside, and something that will always be there. Time is the best healer, but Lennart isn't here anymore.

But it's not only the church that helps Leo's older sister. Benita knows that she needs professional help.

Benita – I also decided to start seeing a psychologist about a month after the accident. My husband had been a faithful listener, but I was lacking what I needed to slowly put my life back together and get things under control. And I was really fortunate to find a psychologist who calmly and slowly gave me the tools I needed to process all of the impressions and emotions that were so difficult. It was as though I just needed to get through the first year and then things began to get better. It also helped to get some of my feelings of guilt under control: whether you could have done something better, whether he should have moved home with me, and whether you could have managed to say some of things that it's too late to say now. The person it was hardest for was my mom – she's always had a lot of guilt. But she's managed to channel the shock over the accident towards straightening things out in her life. She's thrown out my stepdad and has managed to treat Liv and Jennifer right and in their best interests. I wish Lennart could have seen how good we're doing now, despite it all – and that he could have been a part of it.

Although Leo's mother, Sharon, is represented by Tyge Trier in the lawsuit against Roskilde Festival and has made statements to the press, including an interview with the Danish Broadcasting Corporation's equivalent of *60 Minutes* in June 2005, Benita says she does not feel the need to make Roskilde Festival accept responsibility for accident when I talk to her in 2005.

Benita – In terms of the lawsuit, I don't have much of a need for somebody to be deemed at fault and liable. I have two young children and don't feel like I would have enough room for them if I had chosen to spend all the energy it must take to pursue the legal case to its end. For me, the most important thing is to spend time with my children. When I think about the beautiful flowers from Roskilde Festival at Lennart's grave, I don't view them as people with horns coming out of their heads. And when Leif Skov later visited my mother, he was really nice and very humble. But there are a lot of things about the way things happened that leave a bad taste in your mouth. I remember that we had a meeting with a doctor named Allan Horn, who was responsible for safety at Roskilde Festival. He had attended Roskilde Festival since the '80s and said that there had been problems for the last ten years with lifting people over the security fence, and that it was virtually a miracle that nothing serious had happened earlier.

Benita – And I didn't much appreciate the way the police tried to acquit themselves. At first, it was clear to me that the police put the blame for the accident on Pearl Jam – that's what we were told. It's also mentioned in the first police report, which was essentially Roskilde Police acquitting themselves. My family and I have never blamed Pearl Jam for the accident. I've always had great sympathy with the band. Back in 1994, Lennart told me that Pearl Jam had considered stopping after Kurt Cobain's death – which was followed by at least one copy-cat suicide – because those types of things could result from playing rock music. It's completely different than a band like AC/DC just playing on after six people have died in the audience. Back then I thought, "They're good people in Pearl Jam," and I haven't doubted that since.

Lennart "Leo" Nielsen's mother, Sharon

On a summer day in 2005, my telephone rings. On the other end of the line it's Lennart's mother, Sharon Nielsen. We arrange for her to send me a number of photos of her son and family. We go on to talk a few times after this phone call. One of the things Sharon tells me about is the time she experienced every mother's nightmare on the afternoon of Saturday June 1, 2000, when the police knocked on her front door.

Sharon – They told me that they were almost certain that Lennart had died at Roskilde Festival. Since he didn't have any identification on him, they had taken his fingerprints. I said that it couldn't be true and that it simply couldn't be him. The next day, the whole family went to the forensics department at the hospital and then on to Roskilde Festival to see where it happened. In my interactions with the police, they have been very measured and limited in what they say, perhaps to protect the management of Roskilde Festival. I was interested in knowing exactly what happened to Lennart, what he had done minute by minute. But I wasn't informed of very much at all. I think the police were insensitive.

Sharon Nielsen's relationship with the authorities doesn't get much better when she is later contacted by the national legal authorities.

Sharon – The court sent a letter asking if they could perform an autopsy on Lennart. I said no to the request, but they had already done it. They told me that they had the right to do it and I couldn't prevent them from doing it, but the law required them to ask.

Benita also says that it was visible on Lennart's corpse that the surgeons had cut open the back of his head. In the wake of her son's death, Sharon's view of Roskilde Festival has also been less than stellar.

Sharon – Roskilde Festival sent a letter and so forth, but I didn't want to have anything to do with them. When I heard about the nine birch trees, it seemed so ridiculous and I thought, "That won't bring them back to life!" Now that we're in the middle of a lawsuit, I don't want to get into details, but I've always felt that the festival and the police should accept their responsibility.

As with many of the other families and friends, the accident drastically changed Sharon's life.

Sharon – I would say that Lennart's death has changed my views on a lot of things. First and foremost, I'm probably much less rigid and am better able to accept other people's choices and differences. Looking back, we've probably been pretty rigid and expected that our children would choose the same faith as the one we felt was right for us. I've always believed that there is a God – it's not something that I was raised with at home, but when I read the Bible it gave me answers to a lot of the questions I had. Lennart chose a life diametrically opposed to what he was raised with, and I had a hard time understanding that. My youngest daughter, Jennifer, is now 15 years old. She's also been taught what the Bible says about different things, but it's her own choice, just as it was Lennart's. You have to learn to accept that as a parent, even though it can be difficult.

Jakob Svensson's friend, Michael

I'm a little disappointed that I don't get a hold of Michael Berlin when Stone is in Denmark, not least because he was the only person – as far as I know – who didn't hear back from Eddie Vedder. But I manage to track him down later on. Dorte Palle, who originally gave me his name, no longer has his contact information, and his name doesn't ring a bell for her. Since I can't think of any other way of getting a hold of him, I contact Jakob Svensson's mother in the summer of 2005. I know that she doesn't want to comment, so keep it brief and ask if she has the name and number of Jakob's best friend, with whom I had previously been in touch. She gives me his name and I find the rest using the phone book. Michael tells me that Jakob's mother came down to his workplace and told him that I had called. Michael then asked her if she has any objections to him commenting on this matter, to which she said that she does not.

I quickly re-establish contact with Michael. In retrospect, he's certain that he was on verge of ending up on the list of Roskilde fatalities. Michael tells me how the tragic event has significantly changed his life and attitude, about the images that won't disappear from his mind's eye, and about his annoyance with the prolonged legal aftermath.

Michael – I've been extremely annoyed by the lawsuit and the fact that people keep stirring it all up. It was an accident for Christ's sake! I was there. The fact that it's constantly being brought up and splashed on newspapers' front pages has made it harder to let go of. The first year, I was really mad about it, but I've had to accept it. Another thing that has disappointed me is the idea that everyone was on drugs. If I talk to somebody about the accident, the first thing they usually ask is, "Were you on drugs?" Irritating question. Of course, I can only speak for Jakob and myself. But we weren't, and we had hardly had anything to drink either. In a way, I've gotten it out of my system, but in another way I haven't. Every time I talk about it, I feel like I'm on the brink of sitting down and crying, and I still feel that way. But I'm open about it and I don't want to go around with it all locked up inside. In fact, I've become a much more open person in general after the accident. The first thing I did was to go visit all of our friends and tell them what happened – I just changed my clothes and didn't even take a shower. In the past, I'd been more of the type who's quiet and in the background while others are talkative, but now I don't have any problem being the first one to speak up. It changed at that point and it's actually stuck since then. But it's an experience that I'll never forget. And the more I've been told, the more I've also realized how incredibly close I was to dying. There are two pictures in particular that have stuck with me. The first is my last eye contact with Jakob, as I'm crowd surfing towards the photographers' pit, and the other is the picture of Eddie Vedder sitting and crying on stage. Those pictures have stuck with me and return in flashbacks, causing everything to come crashing back to me.

Allan Tonnesen's parents, Eunice and Finn

I've spoken many times with both Finn and Eunice Tonnesen, and I meet the couple in person for the first time at Denmark's Eastern High Court on August 8, 2005. They've both been very sharp and consistent about distinguishing between private grief and general responsibility and justice. In addition to the family's principled belief that it's in the public interest to determine whether any person or organization can be held responsible for an accident like this, they feel that Roskilde Festival has an ethical and credibility problem by paying for something they don't believe they are responsible for, simply to prevent a lawsuit that would determine whether they can be held responsible for the accident.

Finn – We were also offered more money from the festival, but we didn't want to accept it. Not like a gift that's given between friends. This matter shouldn't be settled by the power of money. We don't think that would be honorable for the deceased or for us, the families. If we are to receive anything, it has to be as compensation based on the festival accepting that it failed to meet its responsibility to maintain peace and order among the audience during the Pearl Jam concert. Whether that compensation is two cents or two million doesn't matter.

Represented by attorney Morten Winsløv, the couple lodges a civil action against the festival. At first, the couple chooses to sue on their own, because they do not accept the ruling of public prosecutor Erik Merlung, which absolves Roskilde Festival of criminal liability.

Finn – We strongly disagreed with Erik Merlung's conclusion. To us, it doesn't make sense that Roskilde Festival won't accept any responsibility for the accident. Nine people died, and afterwards a number of changes were made at the festival. Why did they do that if nothing had been wrong, and how could nine people die if everything was as it should be? How many have to die before you'll accept that you did something wrong and before you can be held legally responsible with a consequence for the extensive neglect and misjudgments such as those identified in Merlung's report?

When I speak with Finn and Eunice shortly after the session in the Eastern High Court, they're in a hurry to get back home, and they feel it's too early to comment on the court session. We agree to speak later that week, at which time Finn Tonnesen shares the following assessment.

Finn – We viewed the court session on August 8th as very confused and full of a lot of beating around the bush. But we feel that our attorneys [Winsløv and Trier] presented the case clearly in its simple nature. We have a handshake agreement to pursue this case to the end. But we try to keep things carefully separated. We don't want to be portrayed to the public as grieving parents seeking the pity of others. We keep the private things to ourselves – that's also why we're not interested in allowing any photos of Allan to be printed in this book. But we feel like we've been dragged into a case that no longer makes sense, and in this case we will fight to make it clear to the authorities and the public that something is wrong when nine people are killed and nobody is held legally responsible for the accident and nobody takes responsibility.

Even though the couple wants to keep the public and private aspects of the case separate, Eunice does talk about the positive meeting with their American friend.

Eunice – The meeting and contact with Stone Gossard has been nothing but a positive experience for us. He has felt deeply affected by the incident and has – in a way – felt like a perpetrator in a matter where we are the victims. We were very happy to meet him and hear about his experience and his telling of how he viewed the conditions on the night of the accident. It has also evolved into a close and personal contact that still exists, and which we hold very dear.

Henrik Bondebjer's parents, Ann-Charlotte and Sven-Anders

After the visit to Falkenberg, Sweden with Stone and Liz in the autumn of 2003, contact with the family has been incredibly positive. Sven-Anders is once again welcoming, honest and talkative when I get in touch with him a few days before the five-year anniversary and later when I speak with the whole family after the court session in the Tonnesen case six weeks later. The Bondebjers are one of the couples represented by Tyge Trier, and Sven-Anders is crystal clear about the family's intentions.

Sven-Anders – We don't want money, but we'd like to see that the guilty parties are ruled guilty. That those who are responsible assume and accept their part of the blame. That won't put an end to our grief, but I believe that we would have a little more peace of mind. Maybe we would feel a little better. We were never fond of Leif Skov, nor of the subsequent contact with Roskilde Festival. We had actually given up on the case, but then Tyge Trier contacted us and now we'll have to see what happens.

During the visit with the family a year and half earlier, Sven-Anders told us that the accident had fundamentally changed the family's life. Speaking on the matter once again, Sven-Anders elaborates.

Sven-Anders – Everything has changed. When Henrik was alive, we had a big social network, not least here in the local community, but today almost everybody is gone. When we see old friends or acquaintances in the city, it's as if they cross to the other side of the street to avoid meeting with us. Over the past few years, we've come into contact with an association called "We who have lost children." Everyone there says the same – our story is completely typical. At first you get a lot of sympathy and compassion from your friends and surroundings, but afterwards they reject you. You become isolated and your old friends and acquaintances avoid you. Our circle of friends is completely different now. We've been very actively engaged in "We who have lost children" in the past year and a half. We feel at home there and on the same wavelength as the people who have suffered fates similar to ours. We meet two or three times a month, and these meetings include everything from field trips to lectures and just general socializing. We've also become very close with the other two Swedish families that lost children at Roskilde Festival [Gert Thuresson, Ebbe and Birgitta Gustafsson]. At first we met two or three times a year, but now that's down to one annual gathering. This year we're the ones hosting the meeting. They're going to come and stay from Friday to Sunday in connection with the five-year anniversary of the accident. We've all dealt with the grief differently, but we've really gotten a lot out of spending time together, since we share a common grief. But when we meet now, we talk about everything but the accident. It's actually a topic that we discuss as little as possible, and that's probably a good thing. Earlier this year, my wife and I also attended Birgitta Gustafsson's 50th birthday party in Tranås.

Everything's been turned on its head since Henrik's death. I used to think that we lived a completely normal life, and that our friends were "real" friends, but that was not the case. I've realized that now. I couldn't say whether that's good or bad. We have suffered dearly and we continue to do so. It has also been really hard on our son still living at home, Johan, who has seen us suffer and has suffered with us.

After the first meeting with the Bondebjers in Falkenberg, I speak with Stone and Liz about how hard it must be for Johan, who returned home from the United States to live alone with his parents in the countryside. At that point, his older brother Lars had already moved far away to Stockholm and a job at an advertising agency. I don't know whether this put pressure on Johan to carry on the family farm, but there's no doubt that the tragedy has taken a heavy toll on him.

After the court session on August 8, 2005, Johan Bondebjer – who by this time is now a handsome and well-dressed young man – talks about his many skiing trips to the Alps, but he also seems affected by the atmosphere in the courtroom. Later that day, his mother Ann-Charlotte says that both she and Sven-Anders are worried about Johan.

Ann-Charlotte – It's also been hard for our oldest son, Lars, but probably a little bit easier, since he has lived in Stockholm the whole time. Johan has been at home with us and seen how we have suffered. We have changed. We have become two different people and Johan has had to get used to having a new mother and a new father. And he is so terribly worried about us. I got seriously ill after the accident and was hospitalized, and Johan took it really hard. He withdrew from school and he spends a lot of time helping his dad on the farm. He's almost reluctant to leave because he's always nervous that something will also happen to Sven-Anders. Fortunately, he works for much of the winter as a ski instructor in the Alps. I hope and believe that he enjoys getting a break from all the grief that continues to fill so much of our lives here at home.

Sven-Anders – Time passes quickly, and now it's five years since – but you're constantly reminded of your loss. At birthdays, Christmas and other holidays, we're always reminded of how much we still miss him. Life goes on, but it will never be the same, and our relationships with the outside world are completely changed. Stone Gossard's visit was a highlight for us. We had no idea what he looked like and we thought that he was going to be some kind of long-haired rock star in a leather jacket. But, of course, he looked completely normal and was nice, sincere and sympathetic. That probably changed our view of rock music and rock musicians in general. And also the thought that Henrik's idol travelled all the way from the United States to meet with us in our own home. We've talked a lot about that in the family, and it's also meant a great deal to our two other sons – it was really incredible.

Carl-Johan Gustafsson's parents, Birgitta and Ebbe

On June 29, 2005 – one day before the five-year anniversary of the accident – I meet with Ebbe and Birgitta for lunch in Helsingborg, Sweden. The Gustafssons are on summer vacation and will subsequently be spending the weekend with Gert Thuresson and the Bondebjers at the Bondebjer residence in Falkenberg. We had actually planned to meet on the Danish side of the strait in Elsinore the next day, but Birgitta tells me that it suddenly felt too overwhelming to be in Denmark on the five-year anniversary, and that the couple decided to spend that day together by themselves in Sweden.

Since we met for the first time a year and a half earlier, much has changed in their lives. That spring, Birgitta turned 50 and began studying to become a deacon – a person who provides counseling to people in the congregation and works in the church's social and health institutions, such as children's homes, nursing homes and hospices.

Birgitta – I told Ebbe that I needed something new in my life. I needed to engage more with people than I did in my office work. During my schooling, I've had Bible studies, psychology, etc., and I really hope to get work as a deacon when I'm done. I'm sure that this desire comes as a result of everything we've experienced in relation to losing Carl-Johan and the subsequent social work we've been involved in. I've discovered that a part of our grieving process is going out and helping others who have been in similar situations, by talking about our experiences. Unlike the Bondebjers, we haven't gotten involved with the "We who have lost children" association, but we give about two talks a year, based in part on our book. So far, it's all been within the church, but it could just as well be in other venues. We greatly value these experiences, but they're also emotionally demanding. We couldn't do it more often, but we've seen how it tangibly helps others who have suffered a similar loss. For example, we've been in contact with a couple who lost their daughter in the sinking of the Estonia ferry, and I've been involved in a group for mothers who have lost children in Tranås. Many of those who experience deep sorrow don't believe that they'll ever smile again. But although the wounds never heal, and we have both suffered physical illnesses as a result of the accident, we are doing better now, despite it all – we've moved on with our lives.

The family's strong Christian faith has helped the couple in the mourning process, but religion does not necessarily provide a shield against merciless trials and tribulations in life, and there's no guarantee of making it through these challenges intact.

Ebbe – We have our faith, but we are also like other people and we have the same emotions and reactions as everyone else. I also went to parties and drank beer when I was young, and I'm very familiar with the life that Carl-Johan lived. Just because we're Christians, it doesn't mean that we live cut off from the life that everyone else lives, nor from the joys and pains that life brings. But one thing that's probably important is that we're certain that we will meet with Carl-Johan again. But we haven't simply forgiven. We've faced great challenges. We have learned so much about ourselves and about others as people, even though we never would have chosen to go through what we have gone through if we had the chance to do things over. I feel much more at peace today, but in the past we were furious with Roskilde Festival.

Birgitta – The first time we heard from Leif Skov, our first thought was that we would never let that man set foot in our house.

Ebbe – But one day we made a decision that the end had come. We could feel how that bitterness was draining the life out of us. If we were going to move on with our lives, we had to forgive – being driven by bitterness is like walking backwards into the future. But we couldn't just change course with a single decision. It's been a long and hard process. There's a lawsuit underway that means a lot to a lot of people. It's fine if somebody is deemed responsible, but it's not particularly important to us.

Unlike the Bondebjers, the Gustafssons have not experienced a change in their social circles, but they are very familiar with the sense of being isolated from the outside world.

Birgitta – When you experience something like we have, you become very lonely in a way. It's almost impossible to communicate with others, since they don't understand what you're going through. A mother in my mothers' group said: "It's like you're sitting in a different train car than the rest of the passengers." On the other hand, our faith and the support we've received from our congregation and friends has meant so incredibly much. Despite our mourning, our circle of friends hasn't changed. Just yesterday, some of our close friends called to hear how we were doing and to say that they were thinking of us. When Sven-Anders and Ann-Charlotte Bondebjer attended my 50th birthday party, they both said that now they understood what we meant by the unity of the congregation. It's been harder for them to forgive – we know that and we understand. All three of us Swedish families have mourned and grieved in different ways, which is something you should respect. But we have greatly enjoyed each other's company, which has developed into friendship over the years. At first we met two or three times a year, but we found that too hard, so now we have our regular annual meeting. Despite the pain, I feel more calm and assured now. I've learned a great deal, and in some ways I now feel closer to Carl-Johan and the youth culture he was part of. To us, rock music and Roskilde Festival represented something negative for young people – a place where beer and drugs flowed freely. But Leif Skov told us how he dedicated his life to working to promote and strengthen youth culture through Roskilde Festival, which also conducts extensive social activities in the community. And the meeting with Stone Gossard was incredible. It was a great day in every respect when the three of you came and visited us in Tranås. I was so nervous before you arrived. We had no idea what he looked like, and we envisioned a man with long hair and so on. At the time, we didn't think about the fact that they had a website where you could see who they were, what they looked like, and so on. We know now – they're going on tour in Canada soon. But Stone's visit has meant so much to us. He just looked completely normal, and was calm and humble. We've had contact by e-mail about once every four months, and it's a contact we both value greatly. He's invited us to a Pearl Jam concert the next time the band plays in Sweden, and we're looking forward to it. That probably goes to show how much we've changed. It's no secret that I had ongoing discussions with Carl-Johan over the years about what is good and bad music, and what it is good to spend your time on and engage in. I always used to tell him to turn down that noise when he was listening to a Pearl Jam record in his room. I thought that he should pay attention to other values and other music. Once in a while, I look up to him now and say: "Just look – here's your old mom, writing letters and talking with Pearl Jam, and looking forward to being invited to a concert. You probably hadn't expected that." I feel like I can much better understand and see the values that attracted him to rock music and the youth culture he was a part of. In this sense, I feel like I understand him better now, and I would have reacted differently back then if had known what I know today. I wouldn't have complained about his Pearl Jam records.

Ebbe – Sometimes I even put on one of Carl-Johan's Pearl Jam records at home now.

Birgitta – I think it was an incredibly strong thing of Stone to do to reach out to us. The life we live and have lived is the life of normal people, far from fame and the limelight. He comes from a completely different world, a world that has been completely foreign and surreal to us. But when he came to our home as a perfectly normal person – and we met as people on equal footing – it felt like two worlds met and became united. It's been very moving for us and it really meant something.

Stone Gossard

I exchange quite a few e-mails with Stone Gossard in May and June, and all indications are that we will see each other that summer. Through official channels at the record company, I'm offered the opportunity to come to Seattle in late July to interview Pearl Jam. But these plans are cancelled a short time later because the band's work on their new album is taking longer than expected.

Stone writes to me in late spring that Frank Nouwens' family from The

Netherlands has contacted Pearl Jam, and he asks if I've been in contact with that family. I refer back to our previous agreement and say that I haven't tried to locate the family because Stone hadn't given notice of any new plans for him and/or Pearl Jam to come to Europe. Stone then responds directly to the family. In early June he writes to tell me that he and Liz will be travelling to The Netherlands to meet with the Nouwenses in July. In connection with that trip, Stone suggests that we meet in Amsterdam to go over things in detail. Unfortunately, the timing clashes with my family's summer vacation plans, so we agree to have that conversation by phone. Stone and Liz have a very successful meeting with the Nouwenses, who Stone also writes to Birgitta Gustafsson about in glowing detail.

Right before I'm on my way to Roskilde Festival for the 23rd time, I call Stone in the United States. It's June 30, 2005. Stone has just poured his morning cup of Joe and is sitting at Liz's parents' ranch in upper Washington state. Given the time difference, it's just a few hours before the exact time of the accident five years earlier. Stone's thoughts wander as he talks about what he's gone through personally and the things he's processed in relation to the accident.

Stone – In terms of time, on one hand it's five years ago, and on the other hand it's still like it happened yesterday – it sticks with me. For all those who were there – security guards, festival staff, the audience and everyone who participated – it has forever become part of their personal psyches. First and foremost, having met personally with the families that lost their sons at the festival has given me an important kind of relief and resolution. I can't say why I took the initiative to do all this. There are just some things that you feel an urge and a need to do. It was something that I felt driven to do. That's how I felt personally. Looking two years back, I didn't have any contact with any of these people at all, and I simply had an inner need to try to have some kind of connection to the feelings of sadness and loss suffered by these families, because I was part of the events that took place that day. I had a need to reach out a hand and see if anybody was interested in accepting it. By meeting with the families, I began to slowly comprehend and understand what they went through, and my hope was to contribute to creating a new space to remember and live with what happened. Here I'm not thinking of just the moment of the accident, but placing your experiences in a different place than the feeling of just sinking down without any form of hope or healing. To create a new platform, together, based on forgiveness and honesty. Without having formulated this in any way before or since, there was a vague sense in this direction that I hoped to help bring about. Basically, I just tried to flow with the process. When we got into contact with each other, I felt little by little that I could get in touch with the families through you. I thought, you are my contact and because of your understanding and connection with the situation, I had the opportunity to express my feelings and a new kind of situation and contact emerged. It gave a different sense of peace of mind to the situation, and I really appreciate the way you guided the whole process. It allowed me to send word "out there," and if anybody wanted to get in touch with me, it was possible.

There's no doubt that the five band members in Pearl Jam and many regular crew members have all been impacted by the accident. For example, Mike McCready got tattoos that symbolize the accident for him. Nonetheless, it's imperative for Stone Gossard to maintain that he acts as an individual and not as the band's representative.

Stone – Everyone in Pearl Jam has handled the tragedy differently. It's no longer something we talk about all that much, and we've each moved in different directions in relation to what happened. I've probably felt more personally driven to confront the tragedy that we all experienced. Everyone in the band tries to find a personal understanding of what happened, but it's not the easiest common memory to share. For me, there was suddenly a personal link to you, because we both know Johnny [Sangster], and I contacted you through him. In that way, it became more of my own personal journey than anything I did as a representative of the band. Originally, I didn't know what I was doing or who I wanted to get in contact with. I wanted to meet the affected families, but of course there were also a number of other factors that were part of the same process. For example, people from the festival and police, who investigated the accident, were important figures and I was curious to hear about their assessments. I think it's incredibly important that there's some kind of public acknowledgment of what happened, based on complete honesty, where every aspect is touched upon out of respect for the affected families. A lawsuit is currently underway, and I hope that such a statement will be the result. I think that an acknowledgment like that would give the families some feeling of closure, and help them to move on. Unfortunately, many aspects of this case have ended up in legal jockeying, which is sad. That also goes for Pearl Jam. At first, many people pointed to the band as responsible for the accident, which really scared us. So rather than engaging in a personal and open dialogue, it was our attorneys dealing with Roskilde's attorneys and so on. Given the confusing and tense situation at the time, that may be understandable, but I hope that now – five years after the accident – there's a willingness to look at all aspects of what happened before, during and after the tragedy. I haven't been in contact with any authorities or with Leif Skov afterwards. Personally, I hope for peace in the case, and that the legal responsibility is determined based on a new form of honesty about what happened. Although I don't even know whether I have the right to feel that way, I hope that Roskilde Festival will acknowledge a different form of responsibility than they have done thus far. And if some kind of meeting could be arranged between representatives and attorneys from Roskilde and Leif Skov on one side, and the families on the other, I would like to participate, if the starting point was positive. If, through some kind of joint solidarity, it could help to determine all of the factors and establish a clearer picture of the situation. Having said that, I personally feel that the more I learn, the more impossible it becomes to form a precise understanding of what happened, and who was responsible for the situation. But my primary solidarity is with the families. Many have suffered more than necessary and carried a burden of guilt that is not their responsibility. Speaking out publicly and turning to the court system has been the only way forward for some of the families, since nobody has been willing to take responsibility. My biggest fear leading up to the meeting with the families was about what role they felt Pearl Jam had played in the accident. Because although there were a lot of factors, like security, consumption and serving of alcohol, and legal questions in general, it's a fact that our band was up on stage. No matter what, we were a part of the events that day. Given that I'm the person I am, that's been the hardest aspect. Things like group dynamics and the fact that a lot of people loved the band played a role. That's been hard to handle, but I hope that all of these aspects are considered in the safety measures from now on.

One thing that struck me when I met Eddie Vedder in New York in 2002 and Stone Gossard the year after is how many of the basic facts they were unaware of. For example, the band had no idea that the autopsies of the nine victims showed either little or no alcohol and drugs. Stone readily admits that Pearl Jam was sheltered from hearing about the aftermath.

Stone – We've been totally isolated in terms of information. Personally, it took me more than two years to get started with this process, and it has progressed extremely slowly. Having said that, I think that the role of alcohol is a hot potato that nobody wants to touch. Crowds of people act differently when they have consumed large amounts of alcohol – that's a fact. It's as if people don't want to acknowledge the problem, out of fear that they won't be able to drink their beer in peace. I absolutely believe that alcohol is an element that must be considered in terms of understanding what led to the accident.

Although the passage of time and additional information have not necessarily given Stone Gossard a clearer and less ambiguous picture of the accident, the personal relationships are key to his own peace of mind.

Stone – It can't be overstated. It feels 100% better to have established contact – it has brought about a completely different sense of inner peace. I feel the accident every single day, and there are many others who also do. It's always in you, but now it's located in a different and better place than before. Facts and the realities of what happened cannot be changed, but I try to live my life in relation to the event and to pull through this existence with some form of spirituality about it all, and permitting myself to actively engage with these emotions rather than repress them. I just wanted to participate as one of those who was at the center of it all, to try to find a new place to deal with all of these emotions – to the small extent that I had the energy to do so. I felt that I had the power to do something, and based on the person I am and the role my band played in the events, I felt that it was the right thing to do. Personally, I followed my intuition, and in retrospect it's something I'm glad I did. I haven't wanted, and don't want, to look at all of this through analytical glasses.

Stone (cont.) – The biggest thing for me has been experiencing all of the families' kindness and courtesy towards me. I'm extremely grateful and humbled by this. Everyone has been hospitable and open, and has welcomed me with warmth and acceptance. After what they've been through, it must have taken great strength and compassion to welcome me into their own homes. That's given me an opportunity – as a band member – to establish a connection with these people. Each family, in their unique way, has found ways of looking at, understanding and dealing with these events. Getting so close to them and their stories has given me a new and better form of understanding.

Then we hang up so that Stone Gossard can start making breakfast for Liz and his mother-in-law.

ROSKILDE FESTIVAL 2005

Roskilde Festival 2005 commences on the fifth anniversary of the accident on June 30, 2000, but it's not something that's mentioned officially. Just like five years earlier, the Swedish rock band Kent is playing on Orange Stage. In this case, it's a couple of hours later than they played on the day of the accident – in other words, at the exact place and time. Whether the lead singer of Kent, Joakim Berg, doesn't think about the coincidence or consciously refrains from mentioning it is unclear, but not a word about the accident comes from the stage. When my colleague, Søren McGuire, asks what I thought of the concert, I mention my surprise about Kent's utter silence on the matter. Søren then tells me that he consciously tries not to think about it, because the accident affected him so deeply that he needed psychological counseling for a long time afterwards.

Søren McGuire

Five years earlier, Søren is standing and screaming to the guards to stop the concert from the very scene of the accident. Søren realizes how tightly packed people are when he lifts his own legs and just hangs in the air. People start to topple and at one point he sees a terrified girl who is about to lose consciousness as she's on her way down to the bottom of the pile of bodies. Søren is partially pushed down at the same place, but at the last minute he manages to pull up the girl. Drawing on all his strength, he manages to get himself and the terrified girl out of the crowd. For reasons that remain unclear to Søren himself, he then chooses to fight his way back into the crowd without realizing just how critical the situation actually is. A few hours later, he discovers what has happened and basically blacks out. He's totally shaken for the rest of the festival and unable to tend to his job at the festival's radio station. On the way back to his home in northern Denmark, things don't get much better.

Søren – At the time, there were two bands in my world: R.E.M. and Pearl Jam. When I got back to my dorm room in Aalborg, I couldn't resist putting on the darkest Pearl Jam songs, but I just couldn't handle it and sat there crying. The picture of Eddie Vedder stooping and crying on stage was chiseled in my consciousness and I couldn't escape it. I'd otherwise had a fine childhood and so on, but the accident triggered something in me, and afterwards I spent a long time in therapy with a psychologist. I had a phobia of large crowds, stayed away from the busy pedestrian street when it was crowded and I just felt horrible for a long time. Before Roskilde 2001, my psychologist strongly advised me to go back to the festival in the company of good friends, revisit the scene of the accident and see the Memorial Grove. The psychologist offered to accompany me, and we were in standby contact by cell phone the whole time. Some really wild things went through my mind as I stood down there in front of Orange Stage at the exact place that I had pulled that girl out of the crowd during the Pearl Jam concert one year earlier. I never met her again, but at one point I saw a letter to the editor where a mother thanked the man that pulled her daughter out of the crowd. But there could have been many others, of course. I've gotten over it today, but I have a completely different feeling about being in tight crowds and I always have to know how I can get out. In the past, the biggest problem about being in a big crowd was having to pee. Even though I'm fine now, it's something that has made a lasting mark and it comes up at various times. For example, I still can't really stand hearing Pearl Jam. Even now, five years later, it just feels too heavy.

It's a personal story I had no idea about until now, and yet another example of the enormous scope of the accident and how differently it affected and traumatized countless people.

The nine birch trees

In 2005, I'm at the festival as a concert critic and assigned the job of reviewing Brian Wilson's evocative concert late Sunday evening. But before pulling up the tent stakes after four great days with equal parts sun, music, beer and good spirits, just one thing is left. With sleeping bag and toothbrush under my arm, I stop by the nine birch trees in an open circle about 150 yards to the right of Orange Stage: the Memorial Grove for the victims. Festivalgoers have tied greetings, letters to the deceased and some photos on the trees' branches. There are flowers, newspaper articles about the accident, posters and flyers from Roskilde 2000, etc. Close to the sculpture in the middle, I find a densely written postcard with a sender name I can't make out. Rain and other moisture has smudged many of the words, but I can decipher the overall content. It's a word for word reproduction of the lyrics to *Light Years*. Suddenly, the symbolism overwhelms me as I stand for a long time with the postcard in my hands. I consider taking it home with me and possibly printing it in this book. Otherwise, I reason, it would probably just end up being thrown out and disappearing in the huge piles of festival trash. But what right do I have to take and use a greeting that another person – perhaps as part of their personal grieving process – has placed in memory of a deceased friend or relative?

Certain things are off limits and although, physically speaking, the postcard would disappear, it represents an event that will always remain in the minds of those affected, each of whom deals with the repercussions in their own, often unpredictable and not necessarily rational way. As Birgitta Gustafsson said a few days earlier, this is something that should be respected. I put the postcard back where I found it and head for the train station.

THE TRIAL

Judge Wegener announces his ruling in the Eastern High Court on November 8, 2005. The conclusion is that Roskilde Festival has already demonstrated a willingness to pay money to a couple who lost their son during the accident in 2000, and thus there is no ground for a lawsuit. On this reasoning, the Eastern High Court rejects the parents' request that the court consider the claim for compensation.

Regarding the Tonnesens' claim for DKK 70,000 in compensation under the Danish Liability for Damages Act, the three judges rule, based on the wording of the act at the time of the accident, that there is no basis for awarding compensation to the families of the deceased. Roskilde Festival is acquitted in this regard.

Chapter 8

2006: PEARL JAM HQ. SEATTLE. EDDIE. MIKE & STONE.

In early 2006, Pearl Jam starts ramping up its activity once again. The album *Pearl Jam* (perhaps better known as "The Avocado") is ready for release, and if I can find the time, Sony Music Denmark informs me that there's an opportunity to interview Eddie Vedder at PJ headquarters in Seattle on March 1 – which of course I can, so I pack my bags for Seattle – but that's not all.

At around the same time, Music Export Denmark (MXD) has invited me (as the only press representative) to join a nine-day North American tour with three Danish bands – Kira & The Kindred Spirits, The Blue Van and Figurines – who will be playing in Toronto, Ottawa, and Montreal, followed by concerts in Seattle and Portland. Personally, I've been going through a turbulent time plagued by poor sleep and general stress from a variety of sources. But I can't turn down a trip like this, so I soon find myself crossing the Atlantic with my safety belt fastened.

The first destination is Seattle, for the Pearl Jam interview. My spirits are high, but the combination of jet lag and my generally non-existent sleeping rhythm means that I essentially haven't slept a wink at my posh hotel in downtown Seattle. Fortunately, there's this invention called coffee. Combined with my elation about being at the heart of all things Pearl Jam, it takes quite a few hours before my body and mind register my extreme sleep deficit.

EDDIE

Pearl Jam's HQ in Seattle is a big factory building that's home to a wide range of operations: the entire Ten Club, including its warehouse and shipping facilities, a large studio and rehearsal room with an insane number of guitar cases, smaller studios where all of the official live concerts are mixed, and various offices and common spaces for the many people who work for and around Pearl Jam. I meet a lot of people I know and am warmly welcomed by Nicole, who shows me around the palace. There's a bit of time before the first interview is slated to begin, so I walk around and soak in the atmosphere and history, both with others in the building and on my own. I end up in a fascinating room decked out with framed posters from legendary concerts and other goodies, and then it's suddenly Eddie time.

Laid-back and in no hurry, we stroll around a bit, laughing and chatting. Eddie's good at making people around him feel comfortable, giving them something and creating relationships between people. Although our paths trace back to Fastbacks and 1996, where we had a blast, Roskilde is what connects us more than anything else, and our conversation centers around life and death – from the first sentence, there's a sense of gravity and importance to our talk.

Eddie understands why many of those who contacted me after Roskilde can't listen to Pearl Jam any more, associating the band's music so closely with the tragedy. It's a feeling he knows well from his own experience.

Eddie – Yeah, that's also how I felt about Kurt [Cobain]. Still to this day, I have problems listening to his music. But just the fact that we are talking about friends and families and their feelings. It's incredible here now, years later, to be able to talk about it and to have some kind of positive aspect to it also, that's incredible. The fact that something so brutal can still have some positive sides to it. Somehow there's always light at the end of the tunnel. Like Tom Waits said, "Did you know that if you are standing at the bottom of a well, you can still see stars at night?" It's so hard and you just can't count on it when you're going through it, because you've literally lost everything and your heart is broken. Your body and your mind and chemical reactions are taking place inside of you and you just don't know how to survive it. It's kind of testament that just through living, and getting through day by day, the ashes of something that once burned down flourish into fertile soil. Incredible, life is incredible.

Lust for Life

Should the lyrics to Life Wasted *be seen as a reflection of this realization? You know the dark, but refuse to be dragged down again and have made it through to the other side with renewed insight and strength?*

Eddie – It's almost like there's an energy which is emerging when someone else has passed away, for instance when you're attending a ceremony. In surfing we do a thing where we're 50 guys paddling out, passing the waves, holding each other's hands and dropping the ashes. I was involved in such a ceremony last week. We formed our surfboards in a huge circle, and said our words to him. This one in particular was intense 'cause the guy who passed away was a great environmentalist, especially for the oceans and a passionate surfer. He was a young guy who was taken by disease and we all paddled out early in the morning. It was this great gathering and this guy had him in a backpack. I saw this wave coming right in the back of him, and he caught it, so he gave him one last wave, and then paddled out to the rest of us, with no hands on the board and sat in the center and we all said our things, poured the ashes in the ocean, and then we all surfed in. Beautiful day. But you leave a ceremony like this and you're reminded of how fragile life is, and that's when you start thinking about these things. Life wasted. You're given this kind of lust for life when you've been this close to death, that you just don't want to waste a second, and yet that energy can be caught up with responsibility, your daily life and all sorts of things that easily pull you back into the grind. As powerful as that energy is, it seems to have a shelf life of less than a month sometimes. So this song is a reminder.

On the same note, there's a story going around that you and Jack Johnson's father were caught by a huge wave in a canoe off the Hawaiian coast a couple of years ago, and that you were extremely fortunate to be rescued by a fishing boat several hours later. Is that a true story?

Eddie – Jack's father and I were paddling between two Hawaiian Islands and the weather got hard. The tail winds were out and in the midst of trying to get this canoe upwind, a wave a couple of miles from the shore caught the boat and turned it around. We were six people altogether, and three hung onto the boat whereas three of us were left in the ocean, me and two women. We were out there for what seemed like quite a while, because there were fairly big ocean swells out there. This was in 2001 – I just never told anyone about it.

So, referring back to what we were just talking about, did this near-death experience give you a renewed appetite for life?

Eddie – I'd been living a jungle lifestyle for about a year when that happened. 'Cause when we got back after the [*Binaural*] tour and Denmark and all the personal things [Eddie went through a divorce from childhood sweetheart Beth Liebling shortly before Roskilde Festival], I just disappeared for about a year. While I was in a place where no one could find me, I was really becoming... well, part of my process surviving that whole period, the choices I made put me in a position where I stripped myself down to the basic animal type human being, living off the land. So when that happened, I just felt a connection with nature, I didn't really panic. If I'd been in Seattle working and took a little vacation, and an accident like that would have happened, it would have been completely different, as opposed to being out in the wild for a long stretch of time. I was feeling really at peace and trying to figure out how to get out of the situation. Actually, it was a fishing boat that saved us – the only fishing boat that was out that day because of the weather. It just happened to see us and only because we had paddles. The two girls had their paddles, they waved them and the fisherman's daughter saw us, because otherwise we were just heads on water, like coconuts you couldn't see. It was like, when something happens, don't react, respond! It wasn't until about two weeks later that I took a little boat out to visit the scene of the crime, to see how far we were out and the situation we had been in. When I did that, that was when I felt the urge to vomit, because it was probably way worse than I had imagined. When some of the Hawaiian fishermen heard of where it was and what had happened, they were saying "It's time for you to go back and do more benefits 'cause your karma has been spent."

You've played a lot of benefit concerts, and now you've got a brand new album that critics are calling the band's best in a decade. Where do you find the drive, given that you've already achieved so much more as a band than you ever could have imagined?

Eddie – That's an interesting question. I guess since what we are doing here is trying to dissect all these thoughts about music, in order to have a conversation about it. If I were to investigate the process of what I think is the end result when I hear this music, I think that we're trying to make the best music on the planet in regards to our own personal taste. Last night I saw a guy called Robert Pollard – from Guided by Voices. I also saw a show by him at the beginning of this record-making process which was about 14 months ago, and it was one of the best shows I've ever seen in my life. And now I saw him solo last night – Guided by Voices stopped, it was their final tour. And I listened to it and thought of how great this music is. And that's what we're trying to do. We're not trying to be the best band, we're just trying to make the best music. And how do we do that? It has to entertain us. We can see our favorite music and know that our band has reached its potential. What makes us confident and excited about the album is that I think we've reached our potential. We've worked hard, have argued and have had endless discussions, and without overthinking it, we kind of hammered it out. 'Cause in the past, we kind of recorded pretty quick. Someone brings in a song, everyone learns it and we record it the same day. And we were sort of proud of that work ethic. We didn't set out to do anything different this time, it just happened differently. I think what it is now, is that we know that we've reached the maximum potential at this time and we feel that we have more potential now than we did in the past, so we feel that this is our best record.

My first-hand impression of Pearl Jam *is that it harks back to the fast, punchy songs with a strong chorus, as well as a sprinkling of unexpected and strange chord progressions and vocal arrangements reminiscent of* The Beatles *or* The Beach Boys.

Eddie – Yeah, I had a little machine with me this time and an 8-track digital machine, which is the same size as a 4-track cassette, which I always used to work on. I had a few extra tracks and I've been carrying this machine around. I had my kid in one arm and the machine in the other, no matter where I went, you know. I could set it up in about four minutes and as soon as I got to a hotel or wherever at four o'clock in the morning, I'd find the best window, push the furniture around and set it up and it just became a friend. Usually it's a guitar or a ukulele that becomes a friend, and this time it was a piece of technology that really allowed me to work. I actually enjoyed the process, once we decided to take a little more time with it. This record was originally going to be out last October or something.

I remember Stone writing to me that you were counting on July 2005.

Eddie – I just said, if we took so much time on the music, you got to give me more time with the lyrics and vocals. I'm not going to just splash paint with this. I'm really going to stand back and look at this. I'm going to take a little brush, some big brushes, and that's where the background vocals came in.

Her world

The conversation drifts from the purely musical towards Eddie Vedder's political and humanitarian activism. At this point, 13 months into George W. Bush's second presidential term and with the allied invasion forces engaging in combat in Bagdad and various other regions, Eddie has plenty of objections to the current state of world affairs – not least because he now has others besides himself to think about.

You said that you had the machine in one hand and your daughter in the other. She's your first-born – for many people, becoming a parent is a life changer, both on a personal and artistic plane. Pearl Jam *is your first album as a father. Have you felt a change in that respect?*

Eddie – I think that what people say to you and what you hear before becoming a parent are very cliché things, like you relive your childhood and all this innocence will come into your life. All that is true, but what I didn't expect was, that as far as our country and its involvement on a world stage and the global health of our planet, I wasn't expecting to get so angry. Things that I was trying to be diplomatic about, as far as what goes on with world leaders and giving them the benefit of the doubt or whatever has changed. Now I'm angry, 'cause it's just not me anymore, it's her [Ed's daughter Olivia was born summer of 2004], and where the world is going to be in her adolescence and her middle age, now I'm furious. So it wasn't this peaceful, easy feeling of having a kid – it was different for me. Because you know when you have a child it's their world, it really is. Everything is new to them and it's their world. So me at my age, I realize that I have my own little world, this big world is all hers and I don't want these assholes fucking it up. It's her world they're fucking with, so now I'm pissed.

You've also said that the dire state of the world is one of the main reasons that the album is so relatively aggressive.

Eddie – Well, it's easy to complain and it's easy to rant and rave, especially after a few cocktails with some close friends, where nobody is questioning you. That's what happens with the Republicans and Republican radio and the media, which is biased towards the conservative where it is unquestioned, and it happens on the left as well, so it's easy to do that. What I think is a bigger challenge is, and what maybe our job is, is to make sure that these questions are being kept at the forefront. I would think that it's not complaining as much as it's a reminder, saying "Are we thinking about this stuff?" We certainly are, as a band, and I think that a lot of other people around the globe are thinking about this. But the volume of those conversations out in the world, especially in America, that's at a volume 3 or 4, but what's at volume 8 or 9 is just loads of trash and crap coming through the media, whether it's about celebrity gossip, whether it's politicians talking about non-issues – even in politics, they're spewing out crap that is diversionary tactics to what's really going on. To think that we're a country at war, that has maybe been responsible for creating an atmosphere where more than 100,000 Iraqis are dead, their lives, their resources and their way of life is worse than before we went in there, mind you, that when we went over there, they were suffering from sanctions and a horrible leader. Now it's even worse with the US occupation.

Which could easily lead to civil war?

Eddie – Yes, and we are choosing sides in fighting a civil war for them, 'cause we just want to be in control over that part of the world, in order to also keep control – or to have resources under our control in regards to other countries like China and India. That we will keep ultimate power over them. But if you add all these things up, our country is saturated with bullshit. Everyone is just thinking and talking about bullshit, TV shows and celebrities, reality TV, which is showing all the worst sides of human nature in little competitions, and they go out of their way to find people who are willing to exploit the worst of humanity. In a way, they're feeding people in need of something to keep their minds off what's really going on. We just can't get used to being a country at war. It's a horrible legacy and one that I certainly don't want to leave to my child.

Vote for Change

At this point, it's 16 months since I boarded a flight in Washington D.C. and headed home to Europe after a fantastic experience with Pearl Jam during the *Vote For Change* tour. In terms of the ultimate goal of the tour, it turned out to be a lost battle, but in a broader sense, it nonetheless offered many important victories along the way, bearing witness to the power of musicians to join forces and bring people together to influence major political decisions and create positive change.

Eddie – I think that, if nothing else this initiative maintained and kept alive that atmosphere of social commentary, and has been making sure that artists and writers can remain relevant in that process, in the sense of putting a mirror up to society. It was a fight to do that. There were very powerful people in media corporations and such who wanted to stop it. Part of the Republican playbook is to dismiss not the issue that the person is commenting on, but the person themselves. They'll say, "Why should we listen to Hollywood actors?" – like we were all the Hollywood elite or something. We don't live in Hollywood, we aren't part of that. So I think that it was a battle – that if it hadn't been undertaken, the future landscape would have been even less fertile for social commentary to be delivered through art.

So although you lost the battle, there were a lot of victories along the way. Has it provided a new kind of self-confidence?

Eddie – Yes, and you were questioning things people were saying in the pre-election, like questioning "We still feel safer with George Bush." But since the election, you've seen that things we were saying were right. Things like Hurricane Katrina, how safe did those people feel? How well were those people taken care of as Americans? All of these things have kind of revealed themselves, and I'm happy that there were voices out there who were trying to inform people and trying to give them information to make their decisions on. Looking back, you can't say "Why didn't we know about it?" 'cause actually, you did. Lots people now feel like, "OK, I see now." When you put out indispensable information, you can say something or hear something and maybe it won't resonate for years. You know, songs do that. A Pete Townshend song – not only did I know the words and chords, I could play it and everything. I'd play it by myself at 15 or 18 or whatever and age 32 it suddenly hit me what he was talking about. For instance, a song called "How Many Friends" I really got. I related to it as an 18 year old, but then at 32 I saw it completely differently – probably when I hit the age that he was when he wrote it.

It's the same with your own songs. New interpretations and aspects of your lyrics continue to unveil themselves as time goes by.

Eddie – Well, things can become evident because certain things are happening in your life.

149

You've mentioned Hollywood bullshit a few times today. But no matter how you look at it, you're a very famous person. I know that it has bothered you in the past, but have you gotten better at dealing with it over the years?

Eddie – It comes up in different ways, but in very small instances now. But back when we were in people's living rooms because of videos or however we were represented, we were more visible. I remember it causing problems in relation to your own personal space. Something that we all kind of felt demanding in our own little ways – in relation to other people, neighbors and so on. It just took some time to get used to. It was also just the level of it. But since the level got taken down to more of a simmer than a boil, it's something that I don't even think about. I'm pretty in touch with it and things like disappearing for long periods of time into nature helps. I do those things knowing that I am very fortunate to have this opportunity, although you could also do those things having no money whatsoever if you happened to be born on an island. If you are born in the Bronx, it's different. But I feel I'm pretty connected to what it's like being a human without regard to anything.

As my wide-ranging interview with Eddie draws to a close, he offers me his e-mail address and cell phone number without my asking. Then, in what feels like something of a ritual demarcation of this invitation into his inner circle, he pulls out his old Polaroid camera and asks if he can take a few pictures of me. He takes extreme close-ups of my eyes, one at time. Then I have to hold the two Polaroids up in front of my face as Eddie takes the last picture. It's the exact way that each of the band members is pictured on *Lost Dogs*. I feel a bit like I've just been admitted into a kind of club that I have absolutely no objections to being a member of.

Side note

About a week later, when I'm back in Seattle with the Danish bands and MXD, we come close to adding some additional stardust to the Danish musicians' first evening in the United States. On the day of the concert at the small Seattle club, The Crocodile, Nicole Vandenberg calls and asks when the concert is going to start.

Eddie would like to drop by. At first he thought that I was going to be playing, but he'd like to come anyway. Later that evening, I get a disappointing call. His daughter had fallen ill, and he can't arrange for a babysitter. The Danes are clearly bummed out, but not for long.

The next day in Portland, I'm in touch with my friend Scott McCaughey from Young Fresh Fellows, who has been a part of R.E.M.'s concerts and recording sessions for the past 15 years. He asks if we can put him on the guest list +1. We can. There are just eight people in the audience that evening, and on the way to the toilet in a dimly lit hallway, I think to myself: "Did I just walk by Peter Buck from R.E.M.?" Afterwards, I bump into Scott. He's in his typical upbeat mood and apparently didn't think it was worth mention that his +1 was Peter Buck.

The members of the Danish delegation are not only big fans of R.E.M., but might even be more into Minus Five and Buck's various other idiosyncratic projects. They exchange CDs and anecdotes, and Buck and McCaughey shower some praise on the Danish musicians.

MIKE & STONE

After the interview with Eddie, there's time for a another reunion with a couple of familiar faces. I know from past experience that there's never a dull moment in the company of these two guitarists – they're something of a dynamic duo, while also representing two contrasting poles in the history of Pearl Jam. A variety of internal sources, including Nicole, have told me that Stone is a very calm, stable and unifying force in the band, who also largely formulates and represents the band's values in dealings with collaborative partners and others. Meanwhile, Mike is indisputably the band member who's been through the most personal turmoil, apart from the external pressures on Eddie that he's had to deal with.

In Scandinavia in 2003, I ask Liz who she thinks Stone is closest to in the band, and she quickly answers, "Mike" – which was also really obvious to me during the interview with the two guitarists in New York about three years previous. Mike is deeply grateful for never getting the boot from the band during the times that alcohol and drugs ruled his life. It's also clear that Stone has provided enormous support through the years to Mike McCready, the lead guitarist blessed with a disarming and delightful sense of humor.

When I meet the guitarists this time around, they're both awaiting their first child and their girlfriends have due dates less than a month apart – and as luck would have it, one goes 14 days over, while the other is born 14 days early.

Mike and Stone themselves were born less than three months apart and have known each other since their early schooling, long before their high school days, when they traded photos of rock bands. Mike hits a personal roadblock in terms of the desire to play music, eventually losing interest in his role as guitarist in the band Shadow. But eventually, Mike gets back on track, largely thanks to the support of his old friend Gossard. Following the inevitable breakup of Mother Love Bone due to the death of Andrew Wood, Stone asks Mike if he'd like to start playing together again, and after a couple of months in the rehearsal room, Mike suggests that they ask Stone's old bassist from Mother Love Bone, Jeff Ament, if he wants to join in. The rest is well-known history. After more than 30 years of friendship and 16 years together in Pearl Jam, Mike and Stone both became fathers for the first time, in the same city, on April 12, 2006 – about a month and a half after the interview below.

One of Pearl Jam's many trademarks is the band's unique blend of guitars, with the flashy lead guitar of McCready out front, while the rhythm guitarist and

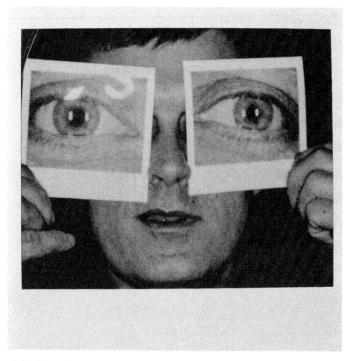

Club Eddie. Photo: Eddie Vedder.

composer Stone Gossard continuously charts new paths. Eddie Vedder, who also plays guitar on about half of the songs on the record, even admits in a *Rolling Stone* interview in connection with *Pearl Jam* that Gossard's innovative spirit sometimes drives him crazy.

In the same issue of *Rolling Stone*, senior editor David Fricke gives *Pearl Jam* high praise, including a previous oversight he fesses up to: "It reminds me that Gossard and McCready deserved to be on our 2003 'Greatest Guitarists' list. Permit me to admit it here: I screwed up."

At heart, McCready and Gossard are a pair of happy-go-lucky guys that love rock'n'roll. That's where we begin.

Mike – I spray painted a "Let there be rock" AC/DC logo on the back of a puffy jacket. It looked terrible.

Stone – That was back in '78, you were in the 7th grade. You were just rocking so hard so early, and doing the art as well, so that's great. I made a Zeppelin pillow in 7th grade 'cause we could make pillows in home ec class. The pillow was this big [stretches out his hands to indicate how big], and I spelled Led Zeppelin wrong [Mike and Stone break into laughter]. "Zepplin" – I missed the "e" – and it wasn't until a year later that I noticed. It was easy to spell wrong.

Mike – AC/DC is not too hard to spell wrong.

Stone – No too easy to spell wrong. Not too hard to spell wrong or not easy?

Mike – Exactly, it is too hard to spell wrong… ohh I can't even think.

Speaking of Zeppelin or Zepplin, you just played the House of Blues in Chicago with Robert Plant at a benefit concert for the victims of Hurricane Katrina. How was that?

Mike – Plant and Ed were harmonizing together on stage, improvising, it was great. We played *Little Sister* and the Zeppelin songs *Thank You* and *Fool in the Rain* [Mike starts singing].

What Pearl Jam songs did you play?

Mike – Well, we did a little side wave. We played *Given to Fly* going into *Going to California* [there are close similarities between the old classic from *Led Zeppelin IV* and Pearl Jam's song]. That sort of dressed up that entire situation. We did it live.

What did Plant have to say about that, or how did he feel about it?

Mike – Great, it was his suggestion. [Mike and Stone both start laughing and flinging ironic claims that *Given to Fly* and *Going to California* are completely different from each other.] We had a fun time. I went over to him on stage and he gave me one of those "fingernail Planties" [Mike stands up and mimics Plant's gesticulations].

Is he a nice guy?

Mike – Completely. He's the consummate gentleman.

I once interviewed him and Jimmy Page when I was still pretty new in the game. I said something along the lines of, "I've been waiting for this moment for 25 years," to which Plant said, "Let's see if we can get it over with in 20 minutes." Shortly before, he had just shouted, "Bring in the Dane!"

Stone – Just like in Monty Python ["Bring out the dead" from *The Holy Grail*].

Yeah, actually. I'd never thought of that before. Silly bunt.

Stone – That's hilarious.

Mike – Plant is really funny, and he just knows so much about music. We discussed blues for about 15 minutes after our sound check. He's like an encyclopedia.

Stone – And he tours in the strangest places.

Mike – He'll drive ten hours by bus out to some place in the African desert.
Stone – He still really loves music, and we were so honored that he would play a show with us.

Accessible album

Whereas Eddie almost always writes the lyrics, the musical compositions are more evenly distributed throughout the band. Stone wrote most of the early blockbusters, like *Alive* and *Even Flow*, Jeff wrote songs such as *Jeremy* and *Nothingman*, and Eddie started composing from *Vs.* onwards.

Looking at the new album, Mike, you've been working hard. It says McCready all over the liner notes.

Mike – Yeah, I was happy that I was allowed to bring some stuff to Ed and he was into it and everyone was. It wasn't a planned thing for sure. I was just going, "Well hope I can get a couple of songs on the album." This time it just kind of happened. It was a natural thing and everybody kind of helped me arrange some ideas, and that was rad. I was like "Wow." It kind of gave me a boost in my confidence, as far as writing. [For the first time in the band's history, Mike is credited as the lyricist for the final song on *Pearl Jam, Inside Job*.] For years, I felt very intimidated at times, like, well Stone writes songs all day and Jeff has written a lot of great songs, so it helped to feel I've done that too.

I really like the new album.

Stone – Good to hear. I'm glad it works for you.

My first-hand impression is that it's generally more accessible than Riot Act.

Mike – I agree with that. There's a lot of energy on the record, which in my mind brings me back to some of the stuff we were doing on *Vs.* The energy feels like that to me. There's an immediacy to it and there's all this up tempo stuff where Ed is singing like I've never heard him sing before in my life, doing crazy harmony stuff on top of it. Very passionate as he always is, but even more so on this one. It does seem more cohesive in a certain sense, something is happening. Maybe it's because we got a new record label, which creates a new excitement. We're still around.

Stone – We're still here. You've come over here, so we know that the writing's still on the wall. That's how we determine whether we still exist – the international press actually still keeps coming. It's not like the international press says no thanks. We don't have to travel to meet with them and then have an interview with a guy from their B-team instead of the usual guy.

Mike – Yeah, having to talk with the new, young Dane. The new Henrik!

Stone – The 17-year-old version of him [heavy laughter].

Maybe it's about time?

Stone – Nah, it's just us old geezers.

Mike – We've been together for a very, very long time [said in an imitation drunken voice].

The Thin Lizzy trick

Well there's definitely been a lot of excitement building up for this record – a "now it's really going to happen again" type of vibe. And there are definitely songs with commercial potential like World Wide Suicide.

Stone – For sure, the vocals are really strong there. I'm glad you like that. I think that's our first single – or actually, it is our first single [the song went on to spend three weeks atop Billboard's Alternative Songs Chart]. Would that also be your first pick for a single?

I think it's an excellent choice. It also seems that you've been working more with the harmonies than in a long time – both in the vocals and the guitar parts.

Mike – I'd been listening to a bunch of Thin Lizzy a year and a half ago and really got back into how they'd harmonize their guitars.

Time for some double leads?

Mike – Yeah, exactly. I always wanted to do that with Stone. I did some myself, but we actually did one [Mike is probably thinking of *Comatose* here].

Stone – We have two already working.

Mike – We've been joking about that for years, and now we're actually doing it.

Stone – And you'll see us when we do, we'll go "We fucking did this" [yelled in a falsetto voice]. We're as proud of ourselves as first-year guitar students.

Like the Thin Lizzy classic, Cowboy Song.

Mike – Exactly. There's guitar harmonies and the vocals following. On *Unemployable*, Ed's going [imitating his vocal]. The first time I heard it, I was like "That's a hook right there." Very memorable.

Vedder at work

It's accessible and doesn't sound like an album that was hard to make. But it must have been, since you've spent more than 14 months cutting it?

Stone – It wasn't difficult, it was just more of how we went about recording it. It was over a process of one and a half years, but we'd record for 15–20 days and then we'd take some time off. Sometimes we'd be really productive in that period of time and other times we wouldn't. Then we'd come back and hear it after some time. We might take a month off in between, where everything went away and you'd listen to it with fresh ears again. Then we'd get back, Ed could've been working on some lyrics, maybe we'd work on a new song. So in that sense, it didn't feel like a hard one to do. Maybe it did for Ed at the end, where he was really trying to get the lyrics down. It kind of ended up being in his lab for a while at the end, since a lot of the songs were pretty quickly recorded and had the rocking spontaneity. But in terms of the lyrics, he really spent a lot of time making sure they were right. It was probably some work for him, but it wasn't like pulling teeth for us – it was more being patient and just be easy on it and say, "Let's do another session, see where it goes, we'll add it on another song." Like the song *Gone* got added on at the very last minute. Ed wrote it when we were on tour in Atlantic City.

It's got an epic feeling to it. The liner notes send a thanks to "pt." I guess that must be Pete Townshend?

Mike – It's gotta be Ed's man, I'm sure.

Stone – It wasn't Peter Tosh?

Mike – Peter Tampton?

Stone – Who else could it be?

Mike – Paul Taft [the laughter and creative interpretations just keep going].

So there was a lot of pressure on the vocals. Ed also said that since you'd spent so much time getting the music right he didn't want to rush the lyrics.

Stone – Yeah, he likes the music raw, but he likes to spend time making the lyrics really right.

Mike – Yeah, there was also times when you'd be thinking, "Wow, I wonder if this record's ever going to come out?"

Stone – So it could be like, we've spent 20 minutes on a song and it works, with Eddie ad-libbing. But then when you get the final lyrics, it's like, "Fuck, this song is going to be awesome to play live for years to come." It feels so vital and meaningful because of Ed's incredible talents as a vocalist and lyricist.

Computer illiterates

There's a young guy running a Danish Pearl Jam site [now on Facebook], where there have been a few sneak peeks of the limited few new songs you've played live.

Mike – Yeah, there's been a little bit. *Comatose* with other lyrics and Ed's played an acoustic version of *Gone*.

Stone – It's great with young guys who are good at computers. Mike and I barely know how to check our e-mail.

Mike – I'm getting there. I don't hit my computer as much as before, but I'm still computer illiterate.

Live success

You've received rave reviews of your Canadian and South American tour [in the autumn of 2005], with Rolling Stone calling you "mightier than ever" and so on. Why do you think you've been able to grow so much as a live band?

Stone – I think we have a lot of songs we can play now from a bunch of different records, with people connecting to all these different songs for different reasons. But I think as far as Canada and South America goes, the fans are what made the shows happen. We hadn't really done a proper tour in either of those places before, in terms of going there and really spending time. And we'd be going out there every night and people would be going insane, to the point where we couldn't even believe it and it was just so easy to get going. It's a good time for us in general now – I think that we're playing well. I think that how Matt fits into the band and how we're all playing together is really starting to jell into something that really feels comfortable. We're finding a balance between the best of the old world and the new world. We're in a great space and I think that that energy comes across live. I think that the people can tell that we're really happy to be in a band together. The fact that our friendship and our musical collaboration are still intact is great and all, but the biggest backbone is the fans. When you go out there they're just not going to let you stop. They're singing the songs for you.

Mike – And they're singing the guitar parts, which I'd never heard before. Some nights, there'd literally be 40,000 people jumping up and down. We'd be like, "Wait a second – it goes all the way to the back!" I've never seen it like that before.

Why do you think that is? Considering, for example, that you're not selling as many records as you used to?

Stone – I asked someone in South America why that was, and he said the reason we were so popular is because we never went there. Like we were playing hard to get, so when we finally did show up, people were really coming out – meaning that if we go back again, no one is going to show up. [laughing]

Mike – What happened to the 40,000 people!? [Mike starts clapping as if he were the only person in an empty auditorium.]

Stone – The great sound of one hand clapping.

Flexibility

Do you think that it somehow helped to break from the traditional sequence of recording, releasing a record and then touring?

Stone – I think we just want to be more flexible altogether. We want to be able to play small clubs, we want to be able to tour. We don't always have to have this gigantic build up of touring for two years and then break up for four years. You can do things differently if you can figure out how to. Like us going to Canada and doing a tour for a month, it doesn't take that much. If that happens to be in the middle of recording, we can just go back and do some more recording. Even on this record, there's songs we haven't finished, we'd finish them later. I think we just really wanted to be as flexible as possible and luckily, we are able to be that flexible, because we can go out and tour for a month in Canada and South America, not having a record out and people still come out, which is totally a trip.

Well, you have to be in shape all the time, since you never play the same set. How can you remember all those songs?

Stone – If you listen to the [live] CDs, you'd notice that we don't necessarily know how to play all the songs. [everyone laughs] Usually we'll play them right before we go out, so we'll kind of have them in our minds. We can sit backstage and go, "We're playing this song tonight, and how are the chords in the B part again? Oh, yeah that's how it goes." And then you go out in the spotlight and you can't fucking remember a thing anyway! That happens so much that our fans have grown to accept the fact that it happens, and it turns into one of their favorite parts of the show, like "the part where Stone didn't know the second or third chord of the chorus, yet he kept playing the same wrong note, thinking that the rest of the band would eventually come around."

So now you're about to finally play in Europe again?

Mike – Yeah. I hope we get a good response. It's been a long time. I'm ready to play in Europe again, especially the new songs. I never have any idea whether a tour is gonna go well or not. I hope that this will be one of the good ones. We'll see.

After wrapping the interview, I leave Pearl Jam HQ to hook up with Johnny and the whole Sangster family. The following week, when I'm back in Seattle with all the Danes, Stone comes and picks me up in his anything-but-fashionable car, and invites me to join him for a bite to eat and a glass of wine at a nearby restaurant. I hardly remember what we talked about, but I think we basically just caught up on everything and enjoyed ourselves. Later that evening, I join the Danes and a bunch of Seattle friends at The Crocodile, and in the wee hours of the night we end up in the Figurines' jam-packed hotel room, smoking joints as we lean out the window – risking, yet ultimately evading, an encounter with the long arm of the law.

Chapter 9

2006: EUROPE.

I see Pearl Jam again less than two months later. This time it's on British soil, or more specifically, at the Astoria in London on April 20, 2006. As they often do, Pearl Jam is playing a warm-up concert before the real tour kicks off.

LONDON, ASTORIA

I'm in London as part of a Danish record company delegation for unrelated reasons, together with my good friend and colleague Signe Glahn as my guest. Back in the day, we worked in the same office, writing and editing *Gaffa* (including my first book in Danish about Pearl Jam), and developing a close and trusting friendship that's held up ever since. We share a strong passion for music, but not the same musical taste buds. Whereas I like old school prog-rock and the hard stuff, Signe has a distinct aversion to guitar solos. She loves The Cure, Depeche Mode, shoegaze and everything indie, introverted and nerdy, but her inner pop gene also perks up for the likes of Duran Duran. Tonight's Pearl Jam concert is Signe's first and the band's first in Europe since the accident.

It's very moving for me to see Pearl Jam in Europe for the first time in six years. The Astoria houses 1,600 people, and the last time Pearl Jam played on the continent it was in arenas and as a festival headliner. So, not surprisingly, fans line up like sardines along Charing Cross Road from early in the morning, even though the concert isn't scheduled to start until 8:00pm that evening. And it's not like there are any tickets for sale – they vanished in a split second on the Ten Club website. People are just standing in line to get in as early as possible to get a spot near the front, to perhaps get a glimpse of the band on their way in, and to eavesdrop on the sound check through the venue's walls. Suddenly, a commotion spreads like wildfire: "They're playing *Why Go!*" at the sound check. Total euphoria. Apart from two concerts in 2003, it's the first time the band has played the heavyweight from *Ten* in nearly 11 years.

Rockin' business suits

Signe and I get to the Astoria early on this beautiful spring day to take in the atmosphere. Once inside the Astoria, we buy a beer and scan the crowd; among the many classic PJ T-shirts are quite a few British businessmen in nice suits. When the music starts, the place is literally wobbling on its foundation and Signe just about drops her beer in shock at the sight of the wildly gesticulating suits losing their shit when the big hits start playing.

I smile and am not as surprised. People go nuts. I'd seen it before, in Florida and Washington D.C. two years earlier, where the crowd discovered that Pearl Jam hadn't forgotten the art of delivering a tight and compact live show – and once again here, after six years of European absence, the people in this crowd had far from forgotten their American heroes. The band starts with a series of new songs from *Pearl Jam*, still a week away from release, but the audience sings along to every word of *World Wide Suicide* like it was a classic from the early 90s. Pearl Jam indulges the insatiable crowd with a third encore, where the Brits get an all-in version of *Alive*, with Mike playing the entire solo on his back as Stone busts up laughing on the other side of the stage.

Afterwards, there's an after-party in the Astoria's Keith Moon Bar. Stone, sporting a brand new Avocado T-shirt (the first and only time I've ever seen him in PJ merch), is the first person to show up, but not long after the whole band is there.

Stone's in great spirits and fires jokes in rapid succession. He says how much he's looking forward to the upcoming European tour, but they have some disappointing news for me: the tour won't be making it to Scandinavia, it's logistically impossible. Mike, who's dyed his hair pink for the occasion, joins the party and the conversation. We're about 40–50 people in total, including all the members of Pearl Jam, who are mingling and enjoying themselves. Signe and I run into Jeff and end up talking with him for about a half hour, with Eddie joining the conversation after some time. The European tour is an obvious topic of conversation and Jeff says, unsolicited, that it would be unthinkable to play Roskilde Festival, even though the band will be playing at both Reading and Leeds, Pearl Jam's first festivals since that fateful evening in 2000. Jeff says that they discussed the idea of playing a small acoustic

Mike 'guitar hero' McCready. Photo: Susan Nielsen.

concert in Denmark and they ask if I think that's a good idea. Not really, I say. I think the Danish audience needs to see a full-scale Pearl Jam show with two encores and no fewer than 30 songs, surprising guest appearances and everything that makes the band's concerts unique – not Pearl Jam light. Jeff invites me to be a guest at the European concerts: "An offer you can't refuse."

Somebody grabs Jeff's attention, but Eddie's in a talkative mood and having a good time. It's so cool that everything is so loose and full of positive vibes – he and the others are clearly among people who allow them to relax. Signe, by no means a classic fan, later says that she was decidedly blown away by the concert and by how sincerely interested and friendly Eddie was at the party. I have a greeting to pass on to Eddie from our common friend Susan. She was going to be there, but couldn't come because of personal reasons. Eddie is sad to hear this news and asks me to give her his warmest thoughts. It's a greeting that will be very gratefully received when I pass it on back in Denmark. Like the others in the band, he's very positive about my book, even though they don't understand a word of Danish. But the book has apparently been praised along the way by those they've been in contact with. Eddie reasons that now that I've written the book, I clearly know more about him than he does himself, and he introduces me to people around us as "the writer."

And now I'm going to try something completely new: going home before the stars for the first time ever. Signe's always hard at work, and this exile in London hasn't changed that at all. She has to get up early to go to work, and she can't stay out a minute longer. I'm crashing on the sofa at her and boyfriend Peter's apartment. Although she says that I can just come later, I decide to join her instead: "Thanks for a great evening. Have a good one, boys, we're out."

PRAGUE, SEPTEMBER 22, 2006

Stone writes to me that I'm on the list +2 and that he'll make sure I get a couple of after-show tickets so we can meet for a drink after the concert.

As soon as I arrive at Copenhagen Airport, Pearl Jam is clearly in the air. There's a surprisingly large number of PJ T-shirts on the plane's passengers, and once in Prague and on the way to buy a bus ticket, I run into a familiar face from the Astoria. "Have you seen any of the other concerts," I ask the passionate Norwegian man. "Yeah, I'm on the tour," he says. He means that he's on one of the three or four shuttle busses following the entire tour from Dublin on August 23 to Athens on September 30. Then he starts giving me reviews of each of the concerts – a true fan.

The plan is that I'm going to meet up with Susan and her boyfriend Martin. Susan has already seen two Pearl Jam concerts in Italy and will also be seeing the final show in Athens. Susan's a die-hard fan and photographer who toured with Pearl Jam on their first European tour in 1992, before – or rather, while – the band had its international breakthrough with *Ten*. The members of Pearl Jam hardly fathomed their success at the time – an era in which the fastest form of communication was the fax machine. The band had two vans. Susan rode in one with Henrik the driver and drum tech, and the band rode in the other. The busses stopped at the same rest stops, where she frequently socialized with the band, including sharing chocolate cake with Eddie. One plate, two forks. Ed shows her photos of Beth Liebling, calls back home every day to "my girl," and every night after the concert, a beer's in the freezer with Eddie's name on it. Susan forms a close and lasting friendship with Eddie in particular.

I find Susan and Martin, and together we rediscover Prague's impressive historic district. Quite by chance, my parents are on vacation at the same time in the same place, and so all five of us meet at the Charles Bridge and drink an Urquell before they go to the Opera and we continue on to Pearl Jam.

The concert's in an ultramodern arena that's akin to an NBA arena in the States. Pearl Jam takes the stage after the supporting act, Tarantula Aid, and somewhat surprisingly opens the show with *MFC*. Unfortunately, the arena and it's less than stellar acoustics are better suited for the ice hockey matches it typically hosts. The sound gradually improves during the show, and the crowd's delight reaches new heights when Eddie speaks Czech from the stage. People love it, but we don't understand a word of it.

After the last encore song, we try to find the backstage area, which is often easier said than done. There's no cool bar, only more of a cold, white basement room. We find the people from the crew, who tell us that the band has already left the arena. But a short time later, the PJ staffer in charge asks into his head-set: "What was the name of that gentleman Stone left a message for?" "Henrik," somebody on the other end answers. He hands over a handwritten note with the address of the bar that Stone, tour manager Smitty and Nicole have gone to, followed by a "Hope you drop by."

As Susan, Martin and I are on our way out of the arena, headed for the bar in town, Susan recognizes somebody from the back: it's Eddie Vedder. He's holding a small suitcase in his hand and looks like he's headed out of the building. He sees Susan, who gets a big hug; then I get the same. He looks completely beat.

Ed says that it's been a great tour, but that the program has been a little too tightly packed for his tastes. He adds: "I'd rather play smaller tours and come back and play more often, and I'd really like to play in Northern Europe next time." The vocalist, who originally looked like he couldn't get out of the place fast enough, suddenly has plenty of time, and after a while he invites us to his personal back-stage room, which is full of stage clothes and everything else he's brought along on tour. He shows us pictures of his two-year-old daughter and takes his time, as always, asking how our kids are doing. We end up spending at least a half hour with Eddie in the backstage room.

It's Martin's first Pearl Jam concert, and Eddie gives him a memento of the

Martin, Susan, Ed, Henrik. Prague, Czech Republic. September 22, 2006. Private photo.

Ed with the setlist, including the songs that were never played that night. Prague, Czech Republic. September 22, 2006. Photo: Susan Nielsen

Eddie signs Ten and the setlist for Marcus. Prague, Czech Republic. September 22, 2006. Photo: Susan Nielsen.

DEADMAN
MAN OF THE HOUR
NOTHINGMAN
BETTER MAN
LEATHERMAN
ALIVE

(BU$HLEAGUER)
COMATOSE
GIVEN TO FLY
HAIL HAIL
BLACK
LEASH

Late night at Charles Bridge. Stone Gossard & Henrik Tuxen. Prague, Czech Republic. September 22, 2006. Photo: Susan Nielsen.

evening. Eddie shows pictures of his daughter Olivia in front of the Eiffel Tower, and fishes up the original setlist from the trash can, writes on it and gives it to Martin. Eddie also does me a favor. My dear colleague at *Gaffa*, Anne Sophie, is a huge Pearl Jam fan. But that's nothing compared to her boyfriend, Marcus. If I can get Eddie to sign the cover of *Ten* with a dedication to him, she's going to frame it and give it to him as a birthday gift. Eddie signs it, but not only that – he finds one of that evening's setlists, writes a greeting to Marcus and lets me take a picture of him holding the setlist. I had actually totally forgotten this story until I ran into Anne Sophie at a music festival in Denmark in June 2016. She tells the story as vividly as if it had happened yesterday – she framed the cover and, as she puts it, "I was Girlfriend of the Year."

We continue our conversation with Eddie. Not everything is rosy. Eddie tells me that he's been sick ever since the last time we met, which was five months ago in April. I'm not sure how sick he means, but it's certainly proof that you have to grit your teeth and bear it when you're a rock star. It has to be something major to bring the huge machinery of a concert production to a halt, not to mention an entire tour, when you're on this level and this type of budget, with so many people and organizations depending on you. He adds that Jeff has a 104-degree fever tonight. All things considered, it's baffling that we just witnessed an all-out, 29-song concert where the only problem was the less than optimal sound. "Yeah, I even noticed it from on stage," says Ed when I mention the sound.

Ed asks if there's anything we'd like to hear the next day in Berlin. I suggest *Go* and *Rearviewmirror*. Ed says that they've already played both songs a lot on this tour, which I take as a friendly no. Susan suggests *Last Kiss* and, especially, *Footsteps*.

We part ways with Mr. Vedder – "See ya soon, buddy" – and the three of us hail a taxi to find Stone's bar. The scene is picture perfect on this warm September evening right alongside the architectural masterpiece, the Charles Bridge, but there's no Pearl Jam guitarist in sight. On closer inspection, we find him, Smitty and Nicole sitting outside at a different bar on the other side of the street. He looks tired and a bit frazzled, but is in good spirits. He says that he was the first one to get sick, and now he's now healthy but has apparently passed it on to the rest of the band. I ask him about Liz and get the big news: she's doing great and the couple is awaiting their first child in April. All the while, a rather inebriated Australian girl persistently and desperately tries to gets Stone's attention, repeatedly interrupting our conversation until Stone kindly but clearly asks her to "give us a break."

There's absolutely nothing wrong with this September evening, but everyone is going to Berlin the next day, so it's about time to call it a night. Around this time, I take out the setlist Ed gave me and check it out. To my surprise, the encore list has three songs they didn't play: *Hail Hail, Leash* and *Black*. I complain jokingly to Stone and demand an explanation. "Well, partly because we're sick and partly because of curfew. The subway only runs 'til a certain time, so we had to stop the show earlier than planned. But if you want to hear them tomorrow, we'll play 'em," he says. Stone takes an extra look at the setlist and laments that *Bu$hleaguer* "sucked" and that they "fucked up" in *Comatose*.

BERLIN, SEPTEMBER 23

After a wonderful train ride from Prague, filled with signing PJ fans, it's time for some quality family time in Berlin. Tobias recently turned 18, which we celebrate with a father & son Pearl Jam/Berlin trip. I love Berlin and have had a long and storied relationship with the infamous metropolis since before the fall of the Berlin Wall. We're staying with my crazy photographer friend, the Dane Casper Helmer, who at the time is having an affair with the German capital. Tobias arrives by train from Denmark and we set up our crash pad in Casper's gigantic combination studio/apartment in Kreutzberg. It's the same day as the Berlin Marathon, and many of the participants are spectacularly dressed. Everything's great, apart from the fact that it's completely impossible to get to the other side of the street.

Nonetheless, we eventually make it to Wuhlheide, Berlin's legendary outdoor amphitheater located deep in a forest in historic East Berlin, surrounded by an array of small lakes where city slickers have waded in the summer for generations. I see a lot of familiar faces, including the merry Norwegian who's "on the tour" and many Danish friends and colleagues.

Wuhlheide is an amazing venue and one-of-a-kind experience. The concert begins in bright daylight and darkness slowly falls until the skies are pitch black, lit up only by moonlight, beer stands and people's lighters and cell phones. Not surprisingly, this spectacular place is one of Pearl Jam's personal favorites and by now a staple on the program whenever they come to Europe. The band sounds much better than the day before in Prague, and the audience is ignited from start to finish.

Not many European venues can compete with Wuhlheide on a warm day. The band plays 29 songs, and among the first five are both *Go* and *Rearviewmirror*. When a one-two punch of *Last Kiss* and *Footsteps* comes at the start of the encore, Susan and I both feel like we've had a hand in writing the setlist. There's no *Hail Hail* or *Leash*, but there is an unforgettable version of *Black*, with the audience continuing to sing the "du-du-du-du-du-du-du" for more than two minutes after the song comes to an end, as the band eventually just stands there laughing on stage. At first I was disappointed when I discovered that the Berlin concert would be outdoors, but after this experience, it will be hard for me to ever miss a Pearl Jam concert on a summer evening at Wuhlheide.

There's not much backstage activity after the concert. Sarah from the press staff invites us inside and passes on a greeting from Stone, but the birds have already flown the coop. Instead, I end up back in Kreutzberg with my son and colleagues, where we have a night on the town in true Berlin style. Tobias and I crash at Casper's place and the next day we make the trip home to Copenhagen.

The Gustafssons

2006 was also the year that the Gustafsson family got to know the other members of Pearl Jam. Based on extensive correspondence with Birgitta, I know that Stone had invited her and the family as special guests to the PJ show in Paris on September 11 – about a week and a half before I crossed paths with the band in Prague and Berlin. Birgitta expressed how much the family was looking forward to seeing Stone and Liz again, and how exciting it was that they were going to see Pearl Jam live and perhaps even meet the other band members.

Shortly before their departure for France, Birgitta received an e-mail from Stone, who wrote that he had just told the other band members (I recall that he originally told the others in the band very little about his trip to Scandinavia in 2003, if anything at all) and that they all said they were looking forward to having the family as their guests. Birgitta wrote that she was both excited and nervous about the prospect of meeting Eddie and the rest of Pearl Jam.

After the Paris concert, I read some of the fan mail from that night and got the impression that it been a tumultuous concert with a lot of pushing in the audience, so I feared that it might have stirred some dark memories for Birgitta, Ebbe and their daughter Sandra.

Fortunately, my worries proved unfounded. The day after the concert I got an e-mail from Birgitta: "We're back home after a fantastic trip that was absolutely perfect. The meeting with the band was an unforgettable experience. On Sunday we had dinner with Stone and Liz, and it was soooo wonderful to see them again. Stone asked if I had any requests for the setlist and I mentioned *Thumbing My Way*. He said that they had just practiced it a couple of days earlier, but that he couldn't promise me anything. On Monday, Liz picked us up at the hotel in one of their own cars with a personal chauffeur, who drove us directly to the backstage area. The first person we met was Eddie, who welcomed us with big hugs and warm words about how good it was to finally meet us. Afterwards, we met with the rest of the band, and they were all just as nice. The time flew by so fast, but we had time to talk some more with Eddie, Matt and Mike alone, which really meant a lot to me. Stone just sat there with a big smile and looked like he was having the time of his life. I'll never forget it. They told me that they'd be playing my request, and after that we were escorted to our VIP seats in the arena. Before they played *Thumbing*, Eddie said my name from stage in front of the entire audience. I felt so honored. After that, we went up front and saw the rest of the concert just a few steps from the stage. The concert was fantastic. Eddie really made us feel special the whole evening – he even ran off stage during the last song [*Yellow Ledbetter*] to give us one last hug, since we had to get back to the hotel. He also gave me his guitar pick and said 'That's the one I used when we played *your song*.' I don't think that any of us will ever forget that night."

A month later, Birgitta discovers that Eddie had actually dedicated the entire concert to the Gustafsson family from the stage, which only made the experience and encounter all the stronger. And when I met with him Prague, Eddie assured me that the warm feelings were mutual. He expressed how much he was moved by meeting the family and laughed about how he ran down to them all sweaty during the concert to say goodbye. He also said that meeting the Gustafssons, who all had such a positive attitude towards the band, would very likely make it easier to meet with the other families in the future.

When I brought it up while talking with Stone at the bar in Prague, he simply and succinctly said: "She's my savior."

Chapter 10

2007–2009: DENMARK. LONDON.

June 26, 2007. Pearl Jam at Forum, Copenhagen. The first concert on Danish soil since Roskilde seven years earlier. I've been going through a tough time personally and basically feel like the best thing would be to sit on a deserted island and pass the time staring at an albatross, but suddenly I'm in high demand because PJ's coming to town. A lot of people in Denmark see me as being the expert and a primary source who not only knows the band and was there in the eye of the hurricane at Roskilde, but who also has an understanding of everything that happened in the aftermath and is in close relations to the families and friends of the victims. I do interviews for a slew of long-read newspaper articles and radio and TV reports, where the recurring questions are: What is it like for Pearl Jam to return to Denmark? How has the accident affected the band? What are they going to play at Forum? And will they ever play Roskilde again?

As the day of the concert draws near, and given the many questions from journalists near and far – combined with ongoing contact with Stone, Birgitta and others – I also have a chance to reflect over everything that happened and to relive the strong emotions it all stirred up for me and so many others.

I'm frequently in touch with Asbjørn Grimm, Jacob Chapelle and others from Leo's old gang of friends. Asbjørn has maintained an ongoing friendship with Stone and, for a time at least, the two have exchange frequent correspondence. In the weeks leading up to the concert, I speak and correspond with many, many people directly involved or impacted by the accident.

News of the concert is also making waves far beyond little Denmark and the international press is here – rarely has a concert been laden with such strong and split feelings.

The concert venue, Forum, is located in central Copenhagen and has a capacity of about 10,000 – and a well-earned reputation for lousy acoustics, but it has actually improved a lot over the years. I'm on live TV in front of the venue, and as so often before in similar situations, once we're off the air and the cameras and lights are off, the journalist and TV crew bring up their personal experiences with Pearl Jam and their ties to the accident. This time, one of the country's most famous news reporters tells about his close relationship with Pearl Jam and the era when Seattle dominated the international music scene.

It's a whirlwind of a day, where everything is hectic, yet a bit trance-like. Birgitta, Ebbe and Sandra have come to Copenhagen, and on the day of the concert we meet for a quick lunch downtown – and in the midst of all the general commotion, combined with traffic chaos, I end up getting a parking ticket. All of these reunions and encounters are also wonderful. Stone is calm and, like the rest of the band, affected by the weight of the situation and determined to make it a special evening.

And special it is.

The Long Road

Shortly before the concert, Nicole Vandenberg tries to get a hold of me. They'd like me to translate something to Danish that will be said from the stage. At first I take it that they want me to go on stage and read something, but actually it's Eddie who's going to try his hand – and tongue – at Danish. Bathed in dark blue light, the band takes the stage, and after a few moody guitar chords, Eddie lays into a couple of familiar and well-chosen lines.

And I wished for so long, cannot stay...
All the precious moments, cannot stay...
It's not like wings have fallen, cannot stay...
But I feel something's missing, cannot say...
Holding hands are daughters and sons
And their faiths just falling down, down, down, down...

The concert begins, very fittingly, with *Long Road* – the beautiful melancholic hymn from the outstanding movie *Dead Man Walking*, which stars two of the band's close friends, Susan Sarandon (who won the Best Actress Oscar for her performance) and Sean Penn. It seems that everybody understands exactly why Pearl Jam chose to open the evening with this particular number. From there, the music speaks for itself.

171

As I remember it, they play about seven or eight songs before Eddie speaks between songs for the first time. *Love Boat Captain* captures the moving symbolic significance of the moment. It's a fully focused concert, but certainly on the darker side. Most of the more than 20 PJ concerts I've seen have some recurring ingredients. There's usually some kind of humorous bit from Eddie, social issues are addressed and there's a kind of wild physical abandon. But on this night at Forum, it's a far more subdued vocalist at the helm. There are plenty of classics: *Alive, Rockin' in the Free World*, and *Yellow Ledbetter* are all delivered according to every tenet in the rock rulebook, but the focus is somewhere else.

There is no closure

The choice of songs and Eddie's comments during the concert both suggest that something more is going to be said. But it's not until Pearl Jam returns to the stage for its second encore that the message takes shape. It's not a scripted or tight speech, but Eddie articulates the feelings that he, the band and probably most of people at Forum that night shared.

I just wanna say, to have you all here... you've been just great. Take care of one another, I know it's been really hot and they've pulled a few people out of here, passed out even – unnerving.

We were here as a band, but also our family – we all went through that together – all of our crew that we've been with for 15 years. And I know a lot of you were there, and your friends were there. Showing such strength to be here. I can't tell you, it is the highest honor, to have your presence here tonight – some of the family and relatives and friends of those who we've missed so much over the last seven years. Thank you so much.[Long round of applause from the band and audience.]

Somebody said to me that this would be good, that there would be some closure. I said no, there's no closure. There's no end of the street. We each have our own road, and we all have these roads and these paths, and they're still going. I see it, and we see it, as all of our roads meeting together here again after seven years, and meeting together and seeing each other down the road and gathering. And seeing that we're doing OK, and that we've learned things, and we've come closer, and we've become smarter and we've become better people, and more caring, and more understanding of the world, and more understanding of loss.

We're so glad we had this opportunity to connect like this. I imagine there's some healing happening. I feel it, and I hope you do to. Thank you so much.

- Eddie Vedder

The ensuing applause and cries of approval from the audience are emphatic and prolonged. Eddie's speech tails off into the familiar opening chords of *Better*

Man, as the audience transitions from applause to signing along: *"Waiting, watching the clock, it's four o'clock..."*

It's the moment everyone's been waiting for. Eddie speaks to what everybody can't help but think about. Emotions that never cease, never fade. As Eddie says, "There is no closure," but this has been an important step towards moving forward, together.

Backstage

The atmosphere backstage afterwards is warm, but it's also largely imbued with the gravity of what brought most of the people to this gathering. Accompanying me backstage are my wife and three children, my old photographer friend Morten, and his then 14-year-old son Mikkel, who is already quite the accomplished guitarist.

The whole Gustafsson family is there, as well as a big group of Leo's old friends, of whom I know Asbjørn and Jacob best. Others in the room include Danish supermodel Helena Christensen and a number of local luminaries.

Eddie goes straight to Morten, who introduces his son. Mikkel, who doesn't speak a whole lot of English, stands silent and star struck: "Hey, my name is Ed, who are you?" and so on. There's a peaceful calm about the setting, with people mingling and engaging in sincere conversation; the whole band is there and they're clearly taking their time. The accident is once again on everyone's lips and ever-present.

Tobias, Celine and Lulu meet the Gustafssons and Eddie for the first time, but then they mostly just lounge on a mattress on the floor, chatting among themselves and relaxing.

Clearly, this night as a whole is a highly emotional and momentous event for the families and friends of the victims, the band and the audience. For me, the concert isn't one of my greatest musical experiences with the band, but more an evening of strong symbolic importance.

LONDON 2009

I never really lose touch with Pearl Jam, but in 2008 I only have sporadic contact with Stone by e-mail and through our common friend Birgitta. I'm going through some very tough times in my personal life, and I have a lot of contact with Birgitta, who generously gives me great and dearly needed help.

After 14 years of marriage, Anne and I have divorced. And for reasons unknown, a tall, beautiful and funny woman, 22 years younger than me, comes knocking insistently on my door. I'm certain that she's got the wrong door – that she's looking for the neighbor or something like that – but she's on a mission. What on paper would seem to be a hopeless endeavor suddenly turns into an 18-month relationship and a lasting close friendship. Signe just gets Pearl Jam right off the bat – a trend that's actually true for most of the women I've known. Of course, I must let the women speak for themselves, but it's my clear impression that the band, despite its generally hard sound, has a really good grasp on their female listeners and are in very close contact with their feminine side. Case in point: the lyrics to songs like *Better Man, Daughter, Leaving Here* and *Why Go* speak for themselves. And quite exceptionally for the world of rock, Pearl Jam has had eight or nine women on their crew for years. It's a conscious choice by the band, in an otherwise male-dominated industry.

I know from my contact with Stone that the album *Backspacer* is coming soon. I've also heard a couple of pre-release songs, as well as talk of a possible European tour in the works. The rumors prove well-founded, and Signe's a decisive young lady, so we decide in record time to go see the band in London.

The day before the big day, on August 10, 2009, we meet up with Stone and the Gustafssons – this time including their daughter and son-in-law, Sandra and Johan – for dinner at an excellent restaurant somewhere in London.

"Hello again my friend, it's so good to see you," says Stone with a smile and open arms, welcoming us all to dinner. Signe, who's not exactly used to such famous and exclusive company, is an end-to-end smile the whole night.

It turns out that I've booked a hotel further from the city center than I'd gathered on the internet, which is a terrible combination with the fact that I recently killed my leg playing tennis and am limping around. London is suddenly much bigger than I remember. We eventually find our hotel, with its steam bath and all the frills.

The following day it's showtime and privileged exclusivity. The concert is at the legendary but relatively small Shepherd's Bush Empire, one of the coolest venues I know. I've been there three times before on assignment, twice to see Radiohead and once to see Scissor Sisters. But tonight it's no business, just pure unimpeded pleasure.

When we arrive with Birgitta, Ebbe and the family, fans line the building in hopes of getting lucky with a scalper. Many of them also missed out on getting a ticket to the band's already sold-out concert at the ten-times-bigger O2 Arena a couple of weeks later. We're greeted by a friendly and smiling woman who guides us into the building and our reserved seats.

Shepherd's Bush Empire is a historic theater with three balconies. We have great seats, each of which has a sheet of paper taped to it reading "Reserved Gustafsson." The seats next to us have similar notes with something to the effect of "Yusuf," but I don't really give it much thought. We get comfortable in our places about 40 to 50 minutes before the starting bell and, whaddayaknow, a familiar face from the day before shows up – Mr. Stone Gossard. He just wants to hear how our day's been, what we've experienced in London, and to make sure that everything is as it should be – that everybody has tickets for the afterparty, etc. After about ten minutes, he takes off again with a short "Wish me luck!" "Yeah, right," I say laughing, "It'll probably be really hard tonight!"

"Bra tjej" with a big heart

Of course, it's not at all hard for the world's best band, at one of the world's best venues, in unusually good company: making for pretty good odds that it'll be a decent evening. Son-in-law Johan, a very nice, calm career man in the IT world, whispers to me: "Have you noticed that it's Cat Stevens sitting next to us and smoking joints!?" Oh yeah, Yusuf – well, I finally made that connection.

The concert rocks out with a host of notable guest appearances. Simon Townshend plays guitar on big brother Pete's signature song *The Real Me*, and Ronnie Wood himself takes the stage with a cigarette dangling from his lips and that characteristic, rough and tumble boyish smile.

There's always something special about seeing a band in a place with a much smaller capacity than what they're capable of drawing. I've experienced it a number of times with Pearl Jam, but also with artists like Foo Fighters, Radiohead, Mumford & Sons and David Bowie. Small venues can be hampered by sound issues, but that's far from the case at Shepherd's Bush Empire, a legendary favorite for countless bands. Because there are several levels in the theater, it feels like you're close to the stage no matter where you're sitting and you can see everything. So there's this wild clash between being at a super intense rock concert in a historic music venue that has seen more than its fair share of original British 60s rock and punk through the years – epochs that stand as milestones in pop history – and at the same time a theater that exudes the grandeur, decadence and decline of the British Empire. In other words, it's mind-blowing to see Pearl Jam at Shepherd's Bush Empire. There's no two ways about it.

I feel like I usually do at Pearl Jam concerts: Amazing. The only confusing thing is, where's Signe? There's probably a line for the loo, I think, or maybe she thinks it's too loud – who knows? But she had really been looking forward to the concert, so it's really a bit of a shame. I think she misses about half the concert, but she comes back near the end of the set, eyes clearly a bit teary. Now Signe can be a bit of a "crazy party chick" who doesn't shy away from partying hearty – she has a track record of drinking healthily for eight days straight at Roskilde Festival. On the other hand, she's also a very empathetic and humanitarian nurse with a strong drive to go to the front lines and make a difference for vulnerable people and populations (later, in connection with the many Syrians seeking refuge in Europe in 2015, she made great contributions as a nurse for boat refugees in Greece). The reason for her absence during the concert has nothing to do with a bladder in need of relief or fear of lasting tinnitus. In the middle of all the joy and enthusiasm, it suddenly hits her why we're actually here. The reason that our little party has gathered here today, at this place, for this event. In other words,

Air guitar at the dinner table. Stone Gossard. London. August 10, 2009. Photo: Birgitta Gustafsson.

Good friends in good company. Stone Gossard, Birgitta & Ebbe Gustafsson. London. August 10, 2009.
Photo: Henrik Tuxen.

the accident at Roskilde Festival in 2000, where nine young men lost their lives and where one of the victims was 20-year-old Carl-Johan Gustafsson, son of Ebbe and Birgitta, brother to Sandra and the brother-in-law that Johan never met. Overwhelmed by the situation, she can't hold back the tears, so she finds a corner to cry her eyes out during the first half of the concert, while the rest of us sit and croon along with *Corduroy* and *Better Man*.

As Birgitta later says: "Signe is a *bra tjej* [Swedish for *a nice girl*]. She has a big heart."

The tears are wiped away and afterwards we partake in a really fun afterparty, where Mike, Jeff and Stone are in particularly festive spirits. Everyone talks and mingles, and Cat Stevens – sorry, Yusuf – enjoys another pleasant spliff.

Chapter 11

2010: ROSKILDE, 10 YEARS LATER.

My close friend and editor at *Gaffa*, Peter Ramsdal, had long been asking me to write an article in connection with the ten-year anniversary of the accident. Most of all, he'd like an interview with Birgitta Gustafsson and Stone Gossard to illustrate their unusually strong relationship and connection. Despite strong friendships with both of them – or perhaps for that very reason – I'm always cautious about asking for favors, especially those relating in one way or another to the Roskilde accident. I know that, regardless of the underlying intentions, this always has the potential to reopen the never-healing wounds.

I contact Birgitta and Ebbe first, and then Stone. All three say that they would like to participate. The result is an article that is disseminated widely, including all over the place at Roskilde Festival 2010. And later on, Nicole Vandenberg requests permission to translate the article and post it on pearljam.com. Here's the article in a slightly edited version:

A light in the dark

10 years ago, more precisely the 30th of June 2000, the unthinkable happened. Nine young men died in front of the main stage at Roskilde Festival in Denmark as Pearl Jam was playing – an incomprehensible tragedy followed by deep and dark shadows. But in the midst of the darkness, a warm and close friendship has flourished between Stone Gossard and one of the mothers of the Swedish victims. By coincidence, Ebbe and Birgitta Gustafsson drove through the city of Roskilde on the night of June 30, 2000, on their way home from a vacation in

Germany that was cut short by heavy rainfall and generally miserable weather. Unbeknownst to them, their son was at the festival, tragically at the epicenter of a disastrous accident. When their local priest came knocking on their door with the news of their son's passing the next day, the Swedish couple from the small town of Tranås felt their world come crashing down. Together with the eight other families, their lives changed forever that day. Drawing in part on their strong Christian faith, the Gustafssons have worked their way through the tragedy and rebuilt their lives, a story recounted in their moving book from 2003 (in Swedish), *After Roskilde – From Crisis To Reconciliation*.

The doorbell rings

Around the same time, Stone Gossard feels that the time has come and he has to do something. He feels a need to relate to the tragedy and to the families – that is, if they are interested in meeting with him. Up to this point, dialogue between Pearl Jam and the families has been limited to lead singer Eddie Vedder's contact with family and friends of the Australian victim, Anthony Hurley, and a couple of e-mails exchanged between Eddie and a few of the Danish friends and families. Seeking to break the relative silence, Stone travelled to Copenhagen in November 2003 with his then wife, Liz, visiting friends and families of five of the six Scandinavian victims during his week-long stay. Late one Thursday night in November 2003, the doorbell rang at Regnvädersgatan 3 in Tranås, Sweden – an encounter that would prove to be the beginning of a warm and lasting friendship.

Birgitta Gustafsson – It made a huge impression on us that he had traveled all the way from the US to visit us. I remember that I was terribly nervous. I didn't know what he looked like, and expected that a long-haired rock star would be walking through the door [after years of having a soldier-like cut, Stone has once again let his locks grow in recent times], but he was absolutely normal. It was as if he were just like one of us. It was an unforgettable night. He made a such a strong impression. He was clearly a warm, loving and open human being – we understood that right away. Even though we met on the background of a deep sorrow, it was an incredibly positive meeting. I immediately felt that this meeting would mean a great deal in the time to come, for him as well as for us. I asked for his e-mail address on that very first night, which he gave me. I still have the scrap of paper he scribbled it on.

Birgitta's positive impression was absolutely mutual, says Gossard on the eve of to 10-year-anniversary of the tragedy.

Stone Gossard – I can't thank Birgitta and Ebbe enough for the kindness and love they showed me. There are very few times in life when one meets a person with such a loving and spiritual presence. Birgitta's openness and love has had a profound impact on me. I think we have both touched each other in an unexpectedly beautiful way, out of this tragedy that is every parent's worst fear. I am very grateful for her.

A void

The unique friendship between Gossard and the Gustafssons is of course closely linked to the memory of the family's deceased son.

Birgitta – We value his friendship dearly. Just to think that a man with such a wide circle of friends would continue to maintain contact with us. Carl-Johan can never be replaced. He was our son. But Stone is filling a part of the void. That's the feeling I have, which is only made stronger by the warmth and love he always expresses when we exchange e-mails, talk on Skype or meet in person.

Given that you've been brought together by a tragedy, doesn't it keep reopening the emotional wounds by maintaining this contact?

Birgitta – No, not at all, on the contrary. We get his support and care, which helps to sooth our grief. It is always positive to be in contact, whether by e-mail, meeting up or seeing Pearl Jam in concert.

This sentiment is echoed by the Pearl Jam guitarist.

Stone – Birgitta and I have seen one another on multiple occasions now. She's come to shows, and she's met the band. We've shared meals and exchanged e-mails. At the end of each encounter, we share how thankful we are for each other, as we continue to feel and heal from the greatest kind of loss. After my visit with them, we started a friendship that continues to this day. Our shared spirituality and openness to each other has been a huge source of my own healing, and I have enormous gratitude to her for her love and forgiveness. It has helped me to feel and accept the tragedy of loss without losing faith in the goodness of the world.

Have you found a different kind of peace today in terms of what happened ten years ago?

Stone – Everyone in the band, and all those who work around us, experienced the Roskilde tragedy profoundly. It is always with us. It can be very intense to face, feel, acknowledge and witness the past, but each of us has taken that opportunity in different ways whenever possible and always will. We want the lines of communication between us and the families to be open always. Time, and meeting with and getting to know some of the families, has helped some in the healing process... but I can't say I'm at peace with it.

Pearl Jam – live

There's been a clear shift in the way Birgitta sees Pearl Jam and their music. At first it was inescapable noise from her teenage son's bedroom, but now she finds herself clapping along at their concerts.

Birgitta – Pearl Jam was Carl-Johan's favorite band – that's the reason he went to Roskilde. He always listened to their music loudly in his room, and meanwhile I often thought that he must be capable of listening to some more quiet and relaxed music. But today I understand his values and enthusiasm a lot better. We're more into more quiet and peaceful music in general, so in that respect Pearl Jam will never be "our" music, but they have a lot of great songs and it's fantastic to see them live. It has also been a great experience to meet the other band members. I've found them to be very sympathetic and humble human beings. We also know that they are making great efforts for a variety of philanthropic and humanistic causes, such as the environment, and that they're all for helping to create a better and more just world. They're not the type of people who put themselves first, but instead do their best to help others. When we arrived at the concert, Eddie welcomed us in the warmest way. He showed us pictures of his little daughter, and said that he couldn't imagine how he would react if something were to happen to her. The band generally took really good care of us and let us stand on the side of the stage during the concert. Eddie dedicated the entire concert to our family and they played the song that I requested – *Thumbing My Way*. Just as we were getting into the car that was going to take us to the hotel and we could still hear Pearl Jam playing their last song, *Yellow Ledbetter*, Eddie came running over from the stage, heavily sweating, to say goodbye while the band was still playing. It was a gesture and expression of compassion that just meant so much to us.

Are there any of their songs that you find it particularly hard to listen to? A lot of the evidence indicates that things went wrong at Roskilde during Better Man.

Birgitta – Well, yes, I think about when I hear that song. That was probably the last one Carl-Johan heard.

The audience has a tendency to react very intensely when Pearl Jam plays live. Doesn't it bring up bad memories when you're in the audience and the crowd is going wild?

Birgitta – Well, the band has such a positive charisma when they play, which inspires the audience. More than anything, it's a positive enthusiasm. But, yes, I don't like it when things are getting out of hand. In Paris and in London we had VIP seats, which shielded us from a lot of the pushing and shoving. We experienced it a bit more in Copenhagen, and that was kind of uncomfortable. I don't like it when people are stage-diving. If that happens, I try to look the other way. I also wouldn't want to stand in the crowd and watch a concert at a festival. But I know that Pearl Jam has really enhanced their safety precautions to ensure greater safety.

Improved safety procedures

In many ways it was paradoxical that Pearl Jam, of all bands, became part of such a tragedy, given that the band has always maintained extensive safety standards both before and during their shows. Following Roskilde, Pearl Jam announced that they would never play festivals again. This position has now shifted somewhat, but only when the band's own security standards are met to a T.

It's obviously impossible to turn back the clock, but was there anything you could have done in terms of preventing what happened?

Stone – Before Roskilde, the status quo when it came to playing festivals was to accept a festival's operational and security structures. Bands were considered "just performers" and didn't traditionally have much of a say in operations or security in the way they do with their own shows. Since Roskilde, that has completely changed for us. We have increased the standards of accountability for festivals to the same level we have in place for our own shows. Our contracts with festivals dictate our security and operational requirements. If they are not agreed to, we don't enter into the contract; if they are not adhered to, we don't take the stage. We mandate the right to review all operational, security and safety policies in advance, including barricade design and configuration and security response procedures, in order to ensure the safety of our fans. That includes proactive, advance review and oversight of the following [as confirmed by Pearl Jam Head of Security then and now, Pete Beattle]:

- The chain-of-command for festival security
- Adequacy and placement of EMTs (Emergency Medical Technicians)
- Barricade type, configuration and implementation
- Responsible alcohol sales
- Capacity
- Ingress/egress procedures
- Show-stop procedure

Had no idea

Pearl Jam did not have control over any of these factors on that evening at Roskilde Festival in 2000, at a concert that was seemingly like all others – nothing about the situation caused any alarm bells to ring in advance for the band.

Stone – We had no idea until our tour manager came on stage and told us something was wrong. I felt like I had been physically struck and an overwhelming sense of shock and pain as it became clear that people in the crowd had been trampled. That the people being lifted over the barricade were dead. Everyone who was there looked stricken. That this really happened. We sat and stared at each other at the hotel afterward, stricken and afraid.

Why did more than three years pass before you decided to contact the affected families?

Stone – We tried to convey our availability to the families immediately after the tragedy, but no real connections were made. At the time, I attributed that to the general chaos and everyone's devastation, but I later heard that some of the families had tried to reach out, unsuccessfully. I have always regretted that. Some of the first impressions in the press spoke of how the band had inspired this behavior and was to blame. It was at that point I think we all retreated. Eddie was the first to connect and share with one of the families. I heard that he had spent a couple of days with the Hurley family from Australia, where he wept with them and where he recognized and felt the intensity of their loss. I felt inspired by the courage and love he demonstrated. So three years after Roskilde, I reached out to you Henrik, as you were there on the stage that day. You graciously agreed to help me make contact with the families and let them know that, if they wanted to, I would like to meet with them. I am so thankful to all of the families who shared with me their memories, pictures, sadness and anger. Nothing could be more profound than their dignity and openness during these visits. All of the families were still devastated three years later. But they opened their doors graciously and hosted me. I will never forget how powerful that experience was. We did not share a lot of words, and you, Henrik, did your best to translate. I tried to convey our band's sadness and acknowledge and feel some of their loss. Maybe my visit was helpful in some small way.

Roskilde and the families

A number of the families were in contact with the festival management both before and after Stone's visit, and not all of them had positive experiences in the process.

Stone – I can only say that most of the families with whom I have met weren't happy with the way the festival representatives handled the tragedy, for various reasons. Some felt they should take more responsibility, some thought they should take legal responsibility. This is an important question that should be answered by each of the families, as I believe they each have had their own personal experience with Roskilde Festival and its representatives.

Do you think that the festival should have acknowledged legal responsibility for the incident?

Stone – I think that when people die or are harmed on your watch, you have to acknowledge your role in that honestly and fully, identify and learn from your mistakes, and implement measures to prevent it from happening again.

With the grace of God

A number of the families have filed lawsuits, unsuccessfully, to make the festival accept legal responsibility for the accident. These legal proceedings have found that the accident was caused by a culmination of unpredictable events, the responsibility for which cannot be attributed to the festival alone. These rulings have caused great bitterness and grief for many of the families. The Gustafssons have mostly stood on the sidelines of these legal actions. Although they feel for the families that have gone through long and emotionally arduous lawsuits, they chose a different course from the outset, mostly based on their deep-seeded Christian faith.

Birgitta - Faith in God has always been an important part of our lives and it was a huge comfort when Carl-Johan died. He held us during the hardest days of our lives. The Bible has taught us to forgive people who have done us harm and to seek reconciliation with them. We don't believe that the safety was adequate, and we still believe that the festival had a responsibility, and that it was their fault, but we have nevertheless chosen to forgive them. We believe that there's a difference between forgiveness and to say that what happened was okay. We decided to forgive in order to move forward in our lives. The opposite would be to go backwards in life. Our choice and our faith has helped us to move forward.

Before you met with Stone, you were in contact with Leif Skov [Festival Director at the time of the accident]. How did that go?

Birgitta - It was tough, but it was an important meeting for us. We told him that we wanted to forgive and reconcile with him and the festival – that they should know that. We believe that, as a festival, they have a responsibility for ensuring that people are not in danger. There were a lot of tough circumstances – bad weather, rain, problems with the sound – but still, the festival leadership had a responsibility to live up to. When Leif Skov visited us, he showed us the new safety procedures that were to be implemented. "Well, that's fine," I thought, "It's just a year too late." But still, it was good to meet and to reconcile with Leif Skov.

Book and lectures

In 2003, the book *Efter Roskilde – från kris til forsoning [After Roskilde – From Crisis to Reconciliation]* was released, in which Birgitta and Ebbe Gustafsson tell their story to author Jonatan Starker. Over the last decade, the couple has given a number of lectures, often in churches, where they share their story and how they live with their fate on a day to day basis.

Birgitta - The reason for writing the book was that it might help others in similar difficult situations, when life is tough. The main point is that there's light at the end of the tunnel, it's possible to go on with your life. We have been invited to give talks based on the book. It often feels quite heavy, but it has also been rewarding and has generated some optimism. We've made a lot of personal contacts through these talks and meetings that we treasure dearly. It's been a tough experience to go through the process of writing the book and giving talks, but it has helped a lot of other people in their life situations, and that's the most

Family. Stone Gossard and Birgitta Gustafsson. London. August 10, 2009. Photo: Henrik Tuxen.

important thing. But there's also a limit to what you can do. We don't do anything active to arrange these events ourselves, and we carefully consider it each time we're asked to come give a talk.

On an island in Venice

Birgitta, Ebbe and their daughter Sandra (accompanied the last few times by her fiancé Johan) have seen Pearl Jam in concert in Paris, 2006, Copenhagen 2007, London 2009 and they're soon heading for Italy.

Birgitta – Yeah, it's amazing. Stone has invited us all to Venice for Pearl Jam's concert in the city. We're going to stay three nights at a five star luxury hotel on an island. It's going to be an experience of a lifetime.

Stone had originally invited the family to Berlin, but Pearl Jam's show there is on June 30 – on the 10-year anniversary of the accident, which would be too much for Birgitta.

Birgitta – I don't want to see Pearl Jam on the exact anniversary. That day is always really heavy for me, and I don't want to go and see the band on a day that is so deeply connected with grief. It's different for Ebbe, he feels that all days are alike as far as that goes. But we have

186

a tradition of taking a little trip around the anniversary. We also visit Carl-Johan's grave and lay a heart-shaped wreath of red roses for him every year.

A blessing and a privilege

And, so it is that Pearl Jam takes the stage on June 30, 2010 at Wuhlheide, Berlin, the ten-year anniversary of the accident, which the guitarist sums up as follows:

Stone – It seems to me there is no escape from the past. Those families still ache deeply from the loss of their children. I hope to acknowledge the past and honor those who died and those who lost them. And to say again, as a band, that we still feel that loss profoundly, and we hope and pray that in time it will lessen or transform.

And Stone's reaching out to the families has made a tangible difference, not least for the Gustafssons, in their deep sorrow.

There's been quite a sea change in your view of Pearl Jam. What do you think Carl-Johan would say if he is sitting and watching from heaven?

Birgitta – He'd probably say "Well, done, mommy!" He would laugh and smile and he would see that I've changed. He would be glad that we were in contact with the band, and maybe a bit jealous!! One day, when Stone and I were talking, I said, "Just think if he's watching us right now." It was a very intense moment.

It's just one of the many examples of a bond and a friendship woven on the back of a tragedy, drawing people with vastly different lives so close together: the rock star through two decades, Stone Gossard, and the devout Christian office clerk Birgitta Gustafsson from Tranås in central Sweden – a connection that also encompasses Pearl Jam and Birgitta's family.

Birgitta – We've only encountered positive responses in our community when it comes to our relationship with Pearl Jam, even though many people may not exactly understand what we are feeling and experience. But even though Stone is a big rock star, he's totally normal on a personal level. We cherish our deep friendship and we want to keep and maintain it. We know a lot of people who have lost a child, but we have been given this contact with Stone, and for that we feel blessed and privilege.

Chapter 12

2009–2011: SEATTLE. PEARL JAM'S STORY. STONE GOSSARD.

In the period 2009–2011, Pearl Jam releases the album *Backspacer* and celebrates its twentieth anniversary, an occasion marked by Cameron Crowe's documentary *Pearl Jam 20*, a soundtrack and two anniversary concerts in Wisconsin, which are accompanied by an exhibition and supporting acts such as The Strokes and Queens Of The Stone Age. Meanwhile, *Backspacer* takes the band to the top of the Billboard charts for the first time since the release of *No Code* 13 years earlier.

I've spoken with Stone about *Backspacer* and PJ20 on a number of occasions, and each time his thoughts and tangents have meandered in new directions. The following is a compilation of my interviews and our regular conversations, with Stone exploring the many sides of Pearl Jam. Nicole Vandenberg once requested permission to use a lot of the following content for official Pearl Jam press interviews. I gladly granted this request, of course, but I'm not exactly sure how or to what extent Nicole and the band ultimately used these interviews.

Backspacer
So, generally speaking, where is Pearl Jam today?

Stone – That's hard to say, because we all can be in different places on different days. We don't know where we are before we get started on a new project, and then it just unfolds from there, you could say. Everyone has ideas about what they think could become a new song, and what might happen, but until we get together nothing is certain. We've learned not to think too much about what's going to happen the next time, but instead to stay more open – open to everyone's ideas and try to give it our best. I know that if I bring something to the table, the others will help me with my stuff. I think the possibilities are wide open as things stand now. We could make a very quiet folk album, we could make an up-tempo punk rock album, we could do mid-tempo rock, heavy metal, there's a lot we can do now. We'll probably use a combination of all these elements.

Backspacer *has been really well-received. What would you attribute its success to?*

Stone – I think it's a record that will come to represent a certain period for us. This time around, we succeeded in getting the band together and writing more material than we usually do before Ed got involved with the arrangements. We were a little more focused and had the opportunity to really give Ed something to work with. I think that gave us all self-confidence, which contributed to the creation of an album that's probably as simple and compact as we've ever made. We ended up having five or six songs under three minutes, which is pretty cool. I like that length. You can get a lot done in that time. The Beatles proved that again and again in terms of dynamic new sounds. Now I feel like a song that is four or five minutes is too long for me.

Backspacer *starts with a fury, but halfway into the album it becomes warmer, quiet and melodious.*

Stone – Yeah, that's true. I think the last number, *The End*, is one of the best songs Ed's ever written. Lyrically and musically, it's really fascinating. It's a bit of a Dylan-like folk song, but the guitar part is more interesting. Ed uses some unusual chords and melodies. Lyrically, I think *The End* is unbelievably strong.

Amongst the Waves... *is that you and Ed working together like you did on many of your hits in the beginning?*

Stone – To me, it feels like the perfect combination of our strengths: my ability to arrange and put together a piece of music, and his ability to write lyrics to match the music and take the song to the next level. It was really easy to play. I love the bridge, where Mike McCready sounds like Mick Taylor. It was a highly satisfying arrangement for me, and it felt like it had been a long time in the making. When you really come together on a song, people notice it. I really like that song.

The lyrics are generally pretty clear on Backspacer.

Stone – Yeah, I agree, and probably more than usual. Ed wrote in a pretty direct style. His approach varies – he likes to wander sometimes. Sometimes he likes the words to unfold slowly. He likes the puzzle part of it, making things a little hard to decipher. This time there was more "Let everybody in," and Brendan [O'Brien] also played a role in that respect.

Matt Cameron. Photo: © Danny Clinch/Universal Music Group.

What was it like having Brendan back as a producer?

Stone – Working with Brendan again was great. We spent a lot of time with him, and it was really good after not having worked with him for such a long time [Brendan produced *Vs.*, *Vitalogy*, *No Code* and *Yield*, in addition to working on other releases]. Everyone was very receptive to each other's ideas. We feel very fortunate and blessed in terms of where we are as a band. Because of that, we were all in good spirits when making the record. If you're in good spirits, I think you end up making music that is better than if you're stressed. I don't necessarily think that we're at our best when we're stressed.

Matt Cameron's drums are pretty wild, like on the opening number Gonna See My Friend. *It's like hearing Keith Moon with a steady beat.*

Stone – Yeah, that's exactly right. We talked about that song, and when we began playing it, I kept hearing Mudhoney. When Mudhoney broke through, they had this amazing ability to create a kind of chaos, where the drums churned out and there were guitars and fuzz everywhere. It's like Matt takes a Mudhoney beat, but beefs it up. The precision is incredible and at the same time it has kept this feeling of total chaos. It's very rare that a drummer who is so precise allows himself that freedom of chaos. Really good studio drummers tend to become pretty conservative in their playing style. They're used to working with producers who say, *keep it simple, it's a pop song,* and so on. Matt has held on to some of that childish instinct, where he just goes completely amok on the drums.

Backspacer went to #1 on the Billboard chart – your first #1 album in 13 years. What was that like for all of you?

Stone – It was exciting and very short-lived. [laughing] We were only there for a week. But it helped the album quite a bit. We could have debuted at #2 and it wouldn't have been a headliner, but since we came in at #1, it was a story and helped boost excitement surrounding the record. We're good now. We've learned so much, just by staying together and dedicated to each other. Now it's like we're more creative as a group in the sense that everybody's instincts have been incorporated into the whole. Everything is really wide open for us now. I get a big rush when I think about our future albums. Ed continues to write, his lyrics and his musical instinct are so unique. A unique combination of incredible poetry and singer-songwriter instinct, but also a love of rock and chaos, which is a very rare combination.

From sales comet to stadium rock
Your songs are getting shorter and shorter, and your concerts are getting longer and longer – in Philadelphia, you played a 41-song concert lasting more than 3½ hours!

Stone – Yeah, it's true. [laughing] The next time we do something, we'll have a chance to challenge *Backspacer*. I don't know what we're going to do, but I hope we end up experimenting a lot. Not necessarily in terms of song length, but in different moods and keep exploring the more unique aspects of *Backspacer* in terms of grooves and such. I hope we follow that path and continue moving in that direction.

Since No Code, *you haven't sold as many records as the first phase of your career. But on the other hand, it seems like you're playing bigger and bigger concerts, most recently with stadium concerts in Australia and New Zealand.*

Stone – In the course of three weeks, we probably played for the same number of people in Australia and New Zealand as if we had played a six-week tour at smaller venues. It's really nice that it's possible, because otherwise that's a long time to be away from your family. We've developed the self-confidence to play those concerts and to believe that we can do it. And we've been supported by our audiences every step of the way. There's so much signing along, and so much energy from the audience on every song. They're the reason we're able to play such big concerts. As soon as the audience starts singing along, it stops being about the band and becomes a communal experience. Then you're just there and playing a part of the bigger whole.

How many different songs would you guess that you've played this fall?

Stone – Probably about 115. We played four shows in a row in Philadelphia and probably played about 100 different songs at those concerts. Amazing! That's another interesting thing about this band that was probably never a product of my own instinct. I'm a little more conservative. I'm a little more like, "Let's play the big hits and make sure that people hear what they've come for." But Ed and especially Jeff, they're really committed to the mantra of, "We have to play different stuff every night, we have to keep the songs alive by continuously adding new material." It's been really cool to see how that's taken shape over a long period of time. There have probably been people who were hoping for songs that we didn't play, but now the audience expects us to play varied sets, and it's a big challenge for the band to learn so many songs and remember them. We fuck up half the time, but that's just the way it goes. It makes everyone feel loose and we kind of say, "It's OK to make mistakes once in a while, it creates an atmosphere of spontaneity." People are open to that, instead of expecting the same thing every night. It's a real luxury for us. It's a fantastic position to find yourself in.

There aren't really other bands that do the same, are there?

Stone – There are a lot of bands that change their setlists a little bit, but we usually change 15 songs every night. And there's a lot of rotation, so there may be songs that we only play once every fifth night, which is cool. So when you finally get around to playing it, it's like "Oh no, I can't remember it."

You've played songs like Black, Alive, Even Flow *and* Better Man *more than 500 times. How do you keep them fresh?*

Stone – You know what, that's actually kind of funny. We change songs so much that when we get to a song like *Better Man* or *Even Flow*, they're easy to play, because the sound and lyrics mesh musically. They're not a problem at all. What we're talking about is four songs out of the typical 27 that we play in a show. It's like a little island of familiarity in a big ocean. Sometimes there are very strange things on the setlist. We really enjoy that and can see that it triggers a response from the audience. Hearing the audience sing along is the greatest thing, because then the songs become a lot more about the audience.

I would hate to be in a band that played so many songs – I'm convinced that I wouldn't be able to remember them.

Stone – It's actually not that hard. You get used to it get, become acclimatized to having so many arrangements in your head. The human brain is actually pretty good at it. It seems impossible when you think about it the first time, but after you've learned the songs, it triggers your memory, which knows how they go. And it's easier to be a guitarist than a bassist, for example. That's the breaks. [laughing] If the bassist doesn't keep the foundation together, it gets derailed. But we've all gotten better at remembering a lot of different material. It's like riding a bike. Once you've learned a song, you can forget it, but if somebody shows you it for a couple of minutes backstage, it all comes back when you play it again. We can basically play everything, but if we don't get it right anyway, it's OK. It's one of those things about playing a different set every night. Your audience gets used to you not making it through without some bumps along the way – and it doesn't appear to bother people – maybe a few. But that's life being a live band like ours. In a way, we're still amateur musicians. Matt isn't and Ed isn't, but myself, Mike and Jeff – we're still amateurs. We're guitarists, we're good, we're OK, but there are probably a thousand guitarists in Copenhagen that are good musicians. We're just some guys that follow the beat.

Does Ed write the setlist before you take the stage, or how do you do it?

Stone – It's been different people over the years, but in the long run Ed's led the way a bit more, with the rest of us more contributing ideas and suggestions here and there. He has a talent for really getting the first three or four songs to work. He understands how to push himself, he knows every detail and knows the mental state he's in from song to song. He creates a kind of blueprint for each night by switching things up a bit. But he's got a good sense for the big picture, in terms of what songs we haven't played in a while, what would be fun, what covers would be cool, what songs would be a good fit for that night, and what would mesh well with the band's state of mind at the given time. So generally it's him writing a lot of the setlists, but he's always open to suggestions. Sometimes I've also written the setlist, which is a good process.

Looking at your core audience, does it seem like a lot of people have hung around through the years, or are there also a lot of new faces?

Stone – Well, there are definitely people at the shows who weren't born when the first record came out. They've probably heard about us from hardcore fans that have followed the band for years. I think it's a generational thing. If the music is being passed along and if people are discovering the band, that's great. But I really can't speculate as to who our primary audience is. I really don't know. I know that the feeling we get when we're out playing is one of humility, and it feels like being at home. And seeing people who are smiling and giving you warmth and support like a family member is a really amazing thing. We are very blessed to have a large and wonderful fan base that supports us. It has been a huge factor in our success. The belief in and love for the band has carried us through periods where we didn't necessarily feel on top of our game. A huge part of our success can be attributed to the fact that people have really loved and supported us. It never would have worked if it was just us making records and not having that kind of support.

Do you have some favorite Pearl Jam songs or albums, or is that like choosing between your kids?

Stone – Well, when I listen back, I think that *Vs.* is a really fantastic record. I love its sound and its heaviness vs. its mellowness. I think it's awesome. I love *Backspacer*, I think we did a great job on that one in terms of finding a lot of energy and bringing it out and then mixing it with the super folky vibes of some of Ed's ballads. There are things on each record that I appreciate for sure. When *Vitalogy* came out I was thinking, "I'm not sure if this is the best record," but today it's probably one of my favorites in terms of its rawness and how little we thought about that record while making it. It's very simple – simple chords, it just worked together, and Ed's fantastic lyrics. A key for us is not overthinking it, but finding the mood that inspires Ed to go to that place where he's willing and able to share a poem over some very simple chords that match his vocals.

If you were to choose, could you name five Pearl Jam songs that are special to you, and why?

Stone – *Nothingman* is probably the one I go back to the most. It's a song I didn't have much to do with making. I think it represents the blossoming of Jeff Ament's musical style. I think it was a journey for him. His songwriting really took off. I was a really strong personality in the beginning, dominating that side of things, so it took some time for him to get started. That song is an incredibly strong combination of music and lyrics. It's very simple and has a drone-like feeling that comes from Jeff tuning his strings down to create a slightly eastern, mystical feel, but the roots are very much pop with simple chords. It's a really cool combination to put some drone over some chords that would otherwise seem very standard. And I think that Ed is really good at understanding different types of people and writing from their perspective. That's something I admire him for and something that has a special magic. It's something that inspires all of us in the band. We try to put ourselves in the same place. Try to get into the mindset of someone else. It's pretty cool.

Stone (cont.) – And *Black* is a song that still means something special. It's a song that I wrote the music for before I met Ed – I had the chords. It's a classic Gossard song, going back and forth from major to minor. It's the dynamics. Major on the downbeat and when it goes to minor the song starts pushing. I think it sums up my writing style as it evolved at home in my bedroom. I didn't write lyrics back then, but I still had an idea about what it should say and where it should go. And then having Ed write those lyrics. At first I didn't really get it, but now, past the age of 40, I think that every line represents a movement in the story that keeps changing for me. It's very expressive and powerful. It's so easy to play, it never goes wrong, the arrangement feels perfect, there's never a time where you're thinking, "Oh my god, what's next?" Everything is simple A-B, A-B. I love that kind of simplicity.

Stone (cont.) – And then there's *The End*. It's so lyrically simple and ends on rhymes, without seeming forced or trying to be clever. It rolls off his tongue, and even though it rhymes, the words feel completely natural. That combination is rare in folk and rock music, where the perfect words almost write themselves all the way to the last moment, where the vocals hang alone in the air. That's probably the best song Ed's ever written.

Stone (cont.) – *Life Wasted* was one that I wrote for the "avocado" album, and I was convinced that it was the greatest piece of rock music I'd ever written, in terms of the individual parts. I brought it to the band and we played it, but it was a little tricky – there was too much math in it. I remember being incredibly disappointed and thinking, "Oh God, how could I have been so wrong about this song?" It wasn't nearly as direct as I had thought. Near the end of working on songs for the album, Ed said, "Let's bring that back again and work on it and see what happens." I was really surprised, because I thought that it had already been canned. But we started to play, Jeff suggested a few simple things, and suddenly it all just worked. And off we went. It had that cool arrangement, a super heavy vibe that I felt was good for the record. It proved to me once again how important the band is. Someone says to you, "Hey, you have something really cool here, chill a bit about it, let it live, feel your way out, don't make it too complicated." I think I can have a tendency to overplay an arrangement because I'm not the one singing it. So sometimes the things I bring to the band may be more stiff and complex than necessary. But I love that song and feel like it sums up my songwriting instinct. I love the melody and, lyrically speaking, it could have been on *Backspacer*. It's positive and reflects a more optimistic time for Ed. It's one of my favorites.

Stone (cont.) – The fifth. I would probably say *Yellow Ledbetter*. That was a song Mike McCready wrote when we were recording *Ten*. At first, I didn't hear much in it. I thought it was a bit too classic. I didn't think it was album material. We recorded a version and you can hear Ed mumbling a bit – his lyrics don't seem particularly worked out. He usually spends a lot of time getting his lyrics to be exactly like he wants them, but this was a case of him not being quite as focused. We started playing the song again a couple of years later, after people had heard it on the radio and had started talking about it. I was surprised and thought, "What's this all about?" It was Mike's start as a songwriter in the band. But we started playing it live, and slowly but surely the lyrics evolved day by day. I realized that Ed would never write finalized lyrics, which I found extremely interesting for a guy that spends so much time getting things, the lyrics, exactly right. OK, sometimes Ed writes lyrics in 20 minutes, but he's always very precise about getting the words exactly as he wants them, and here's a song where he was just playing with it and wasn't really worried about the final product, but instead let the words keep coming. I've never asked him, but I would imagine that even today he doesn't know exactly what the song is about, but that's part of its charm. It's a work in progress. I know that there's a specific meaning in the lyrics about a person who comes home from war, a soldier. The song is an example of how you can miss out on something important because of your own perspective. Ed has allowed the lyrics to be pretty open and, to some extent, intentionally without meaning, which for him is a much different approach than normal. I'm proud of Mike. He developed that song based on some relatively simple ideas, and it's become one of our greatest. The audience goes wild every time we play it. That song is a bit of a mystery to me – I never saw it coming. It didn't make it on an album until *Lost Dogs* [the rarities album from 2003] and then it got a lot of airplay in the States at the time.

Meeting Eddie for the first time

You got in contact with Eddie by hearing a tape with some of his vocals recorded on top of your instrumental tracks. What was your reaction the first time you heard his vocals with your songs?

Stone – The first tape had *Alive*, *Once* and *Footsteps*. I could hear that some of it was good, but in terms of vocal hooks, I was looking for something that was faster and more direct. He was so much of a poet that it wasn't about hooks for him. And I wasn't expecting his deep vocals at all. I hadn't heard anybody sing in that low register before. He had such incredible pitch, but to be completely honest, it took me a while to really understand him. He just had to get the message out in a way that felt right to him, whereas I was in a different world. I was used to singers who were more slaves to melodies. Right at the time, we were making *Temple of the Dog*, and I grew up with bands that played alongside Soundgarden and Chris Cornell. I knew Chris's style, and the *Temple of the Dog* album was incredibly easy to make. Chris had written most of the songs and allowed Jeff and me to write three songs, which he latched onto immediately. From start to finish, everything was done in two weeks. I love it, but can hardly remember that I played on it. So I was probably a bit spoiled at the time. Singing on Chris's, the bar is so high, but Ed proved to have his own style. He wasn't trying to sound like Chris at all. Ed was inspired by him, but definitely had his own thing. I think it was my blindness to his creative instincts. I was so young that it took me a while to understand it. But

Jeff was all-in and understood Ed right off the bat. It took me longer than any of the others to really appreciate him. The thing I value more than anything is his diverse lyrics, his incredibly varied approach to storytelling, his perspective and sympathy for the characters he depicts and the perspectives he presents. It's a reflection of how important lyrics can be in rock music. And his range is unbelievable. He can go from crooning to exploding into these wild rock screams. He just has such a cool ability to mix things up.

What were your original expectations when starting out? Did you realize that it was something out of the ordinary when Eddie joined the band?

Stone – We had already had a little bit of success with Mother Love Bone and Andrew Wood, and we knew a lot of bands that were starting to succeed on a bigger level, so I think we believed it was possible. I knew that Eddie was a great singer, you could hear that. He was very thoughtful and very kind, he had a genuine kindness about him, which was so refreshing, and he worked so hard in the studio. But it took me a long time before I understood how extremely talented he was and still is. He and I tend to hear things differently and can be at opposite poles from each other, which I think is good for the band.

Amazed by success
When did you realize that you guys had what it takes?

Stone – I had played for ten years without making a dime, so it took me a while to get used to the new situation. It was a thrill that we sold so many albums and were making money, but we were also a little bit uneasy about it all. It's kind of like, "Now we have to live up to what people say. A lot of people want to see us, but are we really that good?" I had my doubts. It's a lot more fun now than it ever was back then. There were good shows back then, but there was so much pressure. I never felt deserving of it all. Now I understand it all much better and feel worthy of the success. I understand the simplicity of it and know that anybody could do it. That makes us trust it all much more, and it's also a matter of all the time we've spent together. You have to be together as a band for 20 years to really get to that stage and that understanding. It's the hardest thing in the world and something that a lot of bands never achieve. They get short-sighted with regard to their nature and what people really love about music. Now we can look back on 20 years and say, "We did it!" and now we really can do it. We can completely relax and feel self-confident because of all that we've been through. We're in an enviable position. We can keep making albums and touring, and we can also take all the breaks that we need. We're the luckiest people in the world, and I feel like we're more thankful than ever for what has happened. We really try to be genuine in relation to the success we continue to enjoy, and we try to stay grounded in our creativity and not just continuing because there's money in it and it's popular. We try to be genuine so that people can relate to it. It's a challenge, but we're in the perfect position. I definitely think that's the case.

If somebody had said to you back in the beginning that you'd still be a band in 20 years, what do you think you'd have said?

Stone – I would've been delighted. If you look back at the old interviews and see what I said back then, it was along those lines. If we could stay grounded and keep going and avoid becoming short-sighted in terms of pleasing everyone, or doing something because we thought it would bring us success, instead of doing something because it was fun. I think that one of the major things we did in the beginning was to adopt some ideals as a band. Treating each other as equals, sharing things collectively is important, and doing it yourself is the best solution in the long term, instead of getting others to do it for you. Also in terms of playing on our albums, even if we weren't the most professional. I think those principles have made this band special. There are a lot of special bands out there and tons of incredibly talented musicians all over the place. I'm sure that you can go out tonight and see five guitarists in Copenhagen who are fantastic, vocalists with great voices, but can they come together and find a path and understanding of each other and their band? I think that's the hardest path for all bands to navigate – and getting through hard times together and making it through to the other side in one piece. I think that philosophy has been a key to the band's long-term success.

Did your massive success in the beginning put pressure on you, or did you always know that the band would survive?

Stone – I had strong doubts on many occasions. But every time, I would sleep on it, and when I woke up there'd be somebody who asked, "We're going to make an album in two months – are you in?" and I'd say "OK." You go through the process and suddenly you've made a new album and been on a new tour – and although there are problems along the way, we try to understand each other's personalities and views, and that way you can find a new way of reacting the next time a situation arises.

Do you think there will still be a Pearl Jam 10 years down the line?

Stone – I hope so.

Two epochs
It seems like there have been two epochs in Pearl Jam's lifetime. There was the first four or five years with extreme commercial success, and since No Code *in 1996, you've have stable sales that are good, but lower than in the beginning. Who changed: Pearl Jam or the mainstream?*

Eddie climbs up the stage scaffolding. He's survived every time. Photo: Susan Nielsen.

Stone – Yeah, you're right, there have been two epochs, with the change coming after *No Code*. People had a feel for our sound, but we didn't exaggerate our sound more and more each time to keep all the same people in our boat. I think that a band like U2 has been incredible in terms of finding that sweet spot where time and again they find a brand new single that is so focused and defined by the combination of rock and pop that they're so good at. They go for the biggest thing every time in their process. They're not interested in trying to scale it back or doing things in a fast and raw style. They made a choice at an early stage and have stood by it since then. They want to develop every single idea so that it reaches as many people as possible and gets as big as it can be. That's just never really been our aim. It's been more about letting our fingerprints change from one color and tone to another. And sometimes the colors are mixed together, they're unfinished and maybe somewhat unprofessional. But in the long run, that type of thing can sound pretty good. It's kind of like hearing *Black & Blue* or *Exile on Main Street* by the Rolling Stones. You know that they haven't played the songs 30 times – maybe they've only played them a couple of times, and maybe it was a jam. There's a special freshness in some of those Stones albums. Sometimes it's like they had practically just pushed record. I think that both methods make sense in their own right – and I think that we're in the process of changing a little bit again. Perhaps we're in a phase where we're a little more interested in developing our ideas more, which might appeal to more people in a way. Brendan O'Brien has been really instrumental in terms of this direction. But nothing stays the same forever. If you want to stay big, you have to work really, really hard to maintain that position, and we've never really worked particularly hard to maintain our position. We've worked hard to be a band, to be true to ourselves and to each other. But I don't necessarily think that translates to enormous, continuous mainstream success. I don't think that people were as interested after their first encounter and interaction with the band. I would say that it has been a healthy process for us to go big, experience that and also to experience what it's like to not be in the mainstream limelight as much. During that period, we developed our relationship with our fans, playing live in arenas and with our fan club on the internet. We've developed new methods of getting the music out to people.

You're known for making each show as unique as possible. For instance, you often design special posters for the shows. How many different posters do you think the band has created over the years?

Stone – I think we've done close to a thousand different posters, but not all of them have been for shows. We've been doing individual artwork for our t-shirts and shows for so long now that we've got a collection of images that is just amazing.

That's pretty cool. It's been a focus of ours for a long time, and continues to be. I think it's been one of the most interesting and cool things we've done. When you look back on it, it's like "Thank God that we kept all these designs." People have really embraced the artwork, and we're proud to have worked with so many talented artists, who have helped us discover new visual expressions for Pearl Jam. It's a very strong part of the band that I'm really proud of, and it brings a special energy, coming mainly from Jeff and Ed, who have been involved every step of the way.

In the past, you had incredible success and released a albums at very short intervals. Do you see that as your most productive and creative period in the band's history?

Stone – I think we released a bunch of albums because we didn't know what to do with ourselves. We were all restless youth and wanted to keep working. It never felt like we were doing more than we could handle. Now we probably do less than what we could handle. I think the tempo is a bit slower. Now we release an album every two or three years instead of once every 18 months. I think that we have the potential to be a band that people will look back on and say that our albums are still evolving, which shows that we're still in touch with the things we had going when we were young. The key to it all is our love of punk and folk, and how those things keep coming back again and again. Punk gives us the freedom to be childish, noisy and not as self-conscious – and then folk, which represents simplicity and poetry. It's been there for ages, people gathering around the campfire in the village. Those two things are the lifeblood of the band.

Ten – again

How do you feel about your greatest commercial success, Ten?

Stone – I have a hard time listening to it. It's not a record that I'd put on, if you know what I mean. We made that album right when we met Eddie. We had known him for three months or something like that. It was right out of the gate and a collision of styles. We tried our best to keep it all together and make it work given the circumstances. We didn't have time to dwell on the various styles and I think you can hear that. There are elements of classic rock and elements of what was going on in Seattle at that time. It lacks some perspective. But it's great to play the songs live and relive them, so to speak, but I don't really have a strong sense of what that album means to a lot of people. But I'm in the band, so I can't really judge it. What do you think?

I've always liked the album, but I think that Vs., Vitalogy *and* No Code *have more power and cohesion.*

The calm before the storm. Pearl Jam on stage.
Photo: © Danny Clinch/Universal Music Group.

Stone – Yeah, that's how I feel too.

[I have to interject here that since this interview, I've rediscovered *Ten* and in many ways I've really started appreciating it on a new level. A song like *Release* is one of the strongest, most vital and sincere expressions I can think of. I hold two quotes dear as expressions of my approach to life. One is from my Norwegian grandmother, who lived to the age of 103 and fiercely maintained her strength and dignity to the end: "I'll never give in" – and the other comes from Eddie when he sings: "I'll ride the wave where it takes me."]

Brendan recently remixed Ten. *What do think about the result?*

Stone – I was skeptical about what we'd get out of it and what it could add to things. But I'm really satisfied with the results. Maybe it also gave Brendan a chance to get to know us better as a band, because he wasn't originally a part of that album. It was interesting to hear the music from the original recordings and once again after Brendan had worked on the tracks. There's so much more direct output, so much more structure in the bass. He brought out a clarity and a tension in the tracks, as opposed to what we originally brought out when we mixed the album with Tim Palmer. The remixes were cool and definitely made an impression on people. We got a ton of positive feedback. It was an exciting journey, and I don't regret releasing it back then, but I feel like the sound and power of the band is much stronger in the new mix.

There are plenty of amazing songs on Ten, *but the record tended to be overproduced, with massive reverb on the guitars from start to finish. On the remixed version, the sound seems much more clear, powerful and direct.*

Stone – Good to hear. The album was remixed, not just remastered. That means Brendan went into every track and deleted all the effects. He worked with the bare original tracks and set new levels and so on. I would guess that he worked on the album for a couple of weeks. It was Brendan all alone. If we had been there looking over his shoulder, we would have never finished! [laughing] Brendan knows what he wants to hear, and barely needs any input.

Festivals
After Roskilde 2000, you said that you would never play festivals again. What led to you change that stance?

Stone – Well, I think that the nature of our security and our oversight, in terms of how much cooperation goes into a concert, engaging with the venue, engaging with the local security, engaging with an actual blueprint of the barricades. Really it comes down to oversight, and since Roskilde we haven't played any shows where we didn't feel that we were in complete control of communications and the layout of the venue. So basically, if we're involved in a festival or in a large-scale show, we're top-down. We want to make sure that all the exit avenues and all the barricades can withstand whatever they need to do, that the push from behind will always be met with multiple barricades. We do whatever we can to make that situation safe, although it can never completely be safe – that's impossible. But we have decided that we can play for a lot of people and that it can be OK. It was a big decision for the band, and it took us a long time to get there.

You mentioned U2 as a band that's never aimed small. Their stadium concerts are choreographed and planned in detail. But I guess the fact that you constantly change songs makes it impossible to have a classic, large-scale stadium production?

Stone – The best decision we ever made was choosing against a huge stage production. We tour with about five to seven semis carrying equipment, whereas artists like The Rolling Stones, U2 and Britney Spears probably tour with 60 to 70 semis. All of those built-in things take up a huge amount of space and cost a fortune. So in that sense, we have a huge degree of freedom. The best thing is when people come to our concerts and start off by thinking, "It will probably be boring to watch small guys far away on stage and nothing else." But the second the music starts playing and people sing along, they think, "I don't care about all the window dressing." We've started using some screens when we play, showing people close-ups and so on, and it's worked fine. But basically, we're very pleased with the way the concerts are performed and the response we get. And people appreciate the fact that we always change the songs in the set – it's the audience that convinced us to do it! You can make everything sound amazing when it's all kept in an electronic beat, with sampled background vocals and keyboard pieces. But there's also a charm in not having all those things. Like with us – we run around, miss notes and backing vocals, but at least we try. I think there's something fun about that.

Videos – and the lack thereof

After Ten, *you stopped giving interviews for a few years and you've been very selective about making videos through the years.*

Stone – We made one for *The Fixer*, which Cameron Crowe directed. But the thing is, nobody watches videos the same way now. We've made a few for each record, but people don't care. In the past we said, "We don't make videos," and now that we've started doing it again, people don't care. It's like it's too late now.

So when the Jeremy *video was plastered all over MTV, it got to be too much for you?*

Stone – There was a point where Ed realized that his life was changed forever because of a decision he had made six months earlier. It was a really hard time for him. "I've made this decision, but what has happened to me? I'm being watched around the clock, people are parking outside of my house all the time, I have to hire security guards, and wherever I go people ask me for something." It was really hard for him to navigate through it all, and because it was hard for him, it was hard for all of us. We were all trying on our own to figure out how to deal with all the situations around us at the time. Figuring out what to expect, and so on. It wasn't a particularly fun time.

Were you all in agreement about stopping with the videos and interviews at the time?

Stone – No, it wasn't like that. We expected that something would happen, but it was Eddie in the hot seat. We had our issues, but we weren't feeling it the same way he was. It was easy for us to have a different opinion. Of course, we also went through major changes, but if we thought that we were going through just as much as Ed, then we were fooling ourselves. It was – and is – different for him. He has an artistic ability to communicate with an audience that none of the rest of us have. It's just a matter of being honest and acknowledging that. We aren't just five guys on the same exact level. In some ways it's like that, for example in terms of our business decisions and how we treat each other. But in terms of sitting with an acoustic guitar in front of 50,000 people, he can do something that none of the rest of us can. It's a different experience.

Mutual love

What aspect of Pearl Jam are you the proudest of?

Stone – Probably that we're still a band, that we still like each other and care for one another, while we've witnessed the breakup of one band after the next. The foundation of our band is that we like each other. We're not always together when we're not on tour, but we're always in each other's thoughts. It's really amazing that we've been able to stick together for so long and that it's still strong. I think there's a tendency as artists to want to throw everything overboard when things get rough. When the vision doesn't take shape exactly as you had envisioned. But that's something you learn. When you work in a group, you have to find compromises. You don't get your way all the time, and that's OK. That's not to say that you shouldn't trust your instincts and your art. It's also about being open to the input of others and generally managing a balance of trusting your own ideas while remaining open to what others may have to contribute and what you can achieve together.

Looking back on it all, is there any one experience you would say was the best?

Stone – That's a tough one. We played four nights in a row at Spectrum Arena in Philadelphia in October 2009 – the last events held there before it was demolished.

We played virtually all of our songs. That brought everything together for me. I mean, who wants to hear your obscure B-sides? But people just went wild. The response was so immense, and we had so much fun trying to remember the songs we had practically forgotten. That was really cool. But I don't want to live in the past – I want to make new albums, and I think we still have the potential to keep slugging away and staying vibrant, getting better and more interesting. So I look forward to what the future holds.

Philanthropists and carbon conscious

You've chosen to lend your voice to environmental causes.

Stone – I think there are a lot of prominent people out there who feel like they have no other choice than to get involved. They feel like they have to do something. It's one thing that nations can try to agree on, treaties at the government level, but there are individual multi-billionaires who could really make a difference by having a vision about how new technology, clean energy and sustainability can make a difference. I think the best thing happening for us now is that there are people out there doing work that we don't know about yet, but which will turn out to be game-changing. We have to hope that governments will stimulate that development and help by providing resources and facilities to people who want to invest in those types of things at the national and international levels. A lot of companies out there are looking at their carbon footprint and thinking about ways to reduce their emissions. This can lead to radical changes that could sweep across the globe at lightning speed. I think that governments, legislation and regulations are one side of the equation, and I think that entrepreneurship is the other. A lot of people out there know that it's coming, and that the future is in integrated technologies that don't throw off our planet's environmental balance. We live in nature, we want the planet to function for the well-being of all, and if we want to continue to enjoy luxuries such as eating salmon, building houses and everything else we want to create and do, then we have to do these things in a better way.

Do you think it's been an important factor in your overall togetherness as a band that the big picture is about more than just music, such as the many benefit concerts you've organized and played since Pearl Jam's inception?

Stone – I think everyone in the band has felt like getting involved in various philanthropic activities, and an important part of that is not just raising money, but actively participating. If you look back on all the organizations we've been involved in and how much money we've donated as a band and as individuals, I'd say we've done a pretty good job. And it has done nothing but benefit us, this opportunity to express generosity and openheartedness and make a positive impact on people's lives. It has created a ton of goodwill, it's optimistic and reaffirming – these are things that make a difference. It's a position that we are blessed and fortunate to find ourselves in. We have so much to be thankful for, and when we give back in this way, we perform better. It's a good thing, and we can still give more. We're a middle-aged band, and as we get older we may find other avenues of philanthropy, so to speak. It's investing in causes, but not thinking about what's in it for us, other than seeing something succeed, seeing something do well and to see people's positive reactions.

Are there any causes that are especially important to the band and to you personally?

Stone – There are a few. Everyone in the band has their chosen causes, and when I look at the band's impact, I'm very focused on carbon emissions. I try to lead the way in showing companies that there are opportunities to recognize and minimize our carbon footprint. One thing is focusing on restoration of nature as a general strategy, which companies can voluntarily choose to support, and which would have an enormous long-term impact for the planet. In the past decade, we've been tracking our carbon footprint. We basically know what our fuel consumption is on a tour and we try to make offsetting investments in environmental projects. We were recently involved in the restoration of "green belts" in the Seattle area. Working with organizations and public authorities, we're helping to plant a bunch of tress that will absorb the same about of carbon dioxide over the next 20 years that we emitted on a given tour. If companies did the same type of thing on a large scale in various contexts, I think it would make a positive change in the world. In the US, we're discussing a carbon tax. Some say that it would kill the economy, while others say that it will kill the environment if we don't. I don't see it so black and white. We don't have to wait for somebody to tell us what to do – we can take the lead. That's what I hope Pearl Jam can do, and I hope to be challenged when other bands and other companies do it better and differently than us.

Pearl Jam Twenty

You're playing two anniversary concerts in early September – what can we expect?

Stone – I'm not exactly sure, but Mudhoney, Queens of the Stone Age, The Strokes and Pearl Jam will be playing.

That's a killer lineup.

Stone – Yeah, it's gonna be fun. And we're also going to have special guests and collaborations, but I don't completely know who yet. A lot of it is still in Ed's head. It depends a lot on how he wants everything to go down. But we're really looking forward to playing with the other bands. Julian Casablancas is an amazing vocalist. He's just so strong, his tone, his rhythm and his lyrics are all really fascinating.

You originally released Queens of the Stone Age's debut album on your own label, Loosegroove, back in 1998, and Josh Homme has showered you with praise the couple of times I've interviewed him.

Stone – Yeah, I think they're a fantastic band. Josh virtually does it all. He demonstrates his strength and dedication in so many different ways, and he has very unique and artistic taste. His side project [Them Crooked Vultures] has Dave Grohl and John Paul Jones as its rhythm section, which just about says it all. He's a hero in my book. I still love the first record we released – it's so simple and direct, and has some of the best stuff they've done. And Josh is a consummate gentleman – I've really enjoyed working with him. We don't see each other all that often, but when we do, we're always really happy to see each other. He's the type who's always on the go, in action. He's a very interesting and charismatic guy, and I love the fact that he's earned so much success.

QOTSA just toured with their debut album – did you see them play?

Stone – No, they didn't come to Seattle on that tour, but I heard that it was killer at SXSW.

Coffee table

A lot of writers have harbored ambitions of writing a Pearl Jam book over the years, but Stone previously said that the band isn't interested in anybody writing their biography, nor in releasing an official autobiography. But that stance appears to have shifted in connection with the band's twentieth anniversary and the release of an official book on Pearl Jam.

Stone – Well, I wouldn't really call it a biography, but more of a coffee table book. It basically contains a bunch of previously unreleased photos and a lot of information, primarily in chronological order, with quotes from the band alongside all the photos. I just saw a pre-print of the book, and it looks great. None of us were saying, "We just *have* to put out a book," but the opportunity came up in connection with the documentary, where we could put together some of our so-called historical materials into book form, and we decided to go for it.

From 1,000 to 2 hours
What kind of movie are we talking about?

Stone – Well, I'd say that it's funnier than I expected. I enjoyed seeing it, even though it's a bit strange to watch a film about yourself. But if you're interested in a band that has done quite a few things, then it's probably worth seeing. It has something for our fans, but I think it also offers something for people who don't like the band. One thing for certain is that Cameron is an amazing storyteller, he's an amazing artist, and the project would have never happened if not for his drive and vision. He had around 1,000 hours of raw footage, which he has whittled down to less than two hours. He has collected tons of old footage. We probably did about 20 to 30 interviews for VH1 through the years, where they usually used about 30 seconds out of an hour-long interview. Then you've got a bunch of material from channels like MTV and a ton of private recordings, following us in the tour bus, at concerts, etc. Hundreds and hundreds of hours of film. And he has also conducted a few interviews himself. There's a wide range of material and it's all told in an entertaining way. Cameron loves music and he tells stories from the heart. He has this warmth and sensitivity. We're honored that he wanted to work with us, and the result is the product of his efforts. I don't want to talk too much about the content, but I hope people will see the film – I think they'll like it.

Determination, stubbornness and loyalty

Unlike so many of the other big rock bands that broke up, Pearl Jam is now celebrating 20 years and still going strong. What do you think has been the key to your survival as a band?

Stone – I think there's a certain artistic stubbornness at play. We refuse to give up. We joined forces and tried to figure it out as we went along. We were determined and stubborn and loyal to each other, and those are underappreciated values in rock sometimes. You find yourself in all these storms – there were a million times where conflicts could have altered the band's course, and there were a million conflicts that did alter the band's course, but each time we decided to make a new record and continue. But besides that, it's the fans that have helped us through the times when we might not have been as connected to one another and the process. We would play a concert and see 15 to 20 thousand people so extremely into the band, which made it impossible to deny the past, and made it impossible to stop. So we found a very unique setup, in my opinion. Jeff and I started the band, and then Eddie brought in his artistic powers, taking us to places we never could have dreamt of. It was this completely new wild card. I'm not sure, but I think that the stubbornness, determination and loyalty were just stronger than the conflicts.

Differences and similarities

Apart from a couple of changes behind the drums, where Matt Cameron has been since 1998, the band has remained intact since its inception more than 20 years ago. What makes your creative bond so strong and enables it to keep developing?

Stone – I'd say that everyone in the band still loves the variation between styles. We still love heavy music, we play up-tempo and down-tempo numbers and a lot of ballads. The way I see it, we range from simple folk to pure noise. It's exciting to grow with the music and see and feel which songs become important to the band

and to audiences. There's always an element of surprise, even to this day, in terms of understanding who we are and what we're capable of. We've been around for a long time – people have an idea of who we are, but I still think that we have the potential to prove that we're more than that, or different than what people may expect. Everyone in the band still has a drive or a need to discover new things. It's a really good thing for the band, and I think that we've succeeded in many respects because we've embraced these challenges. It hasn't always brought us more success, but the journey as a whole has been an enriching and learning experience – it has given us space to evolve. I think we'll keep playing older songs, and I'm optimistic and hope that people will continue to enjoy them – but I'm also curious about what we can do in terms of new things that may define a new era for the band. I hope it's possible and I know that everyone in the band has a belief that it is.

The crew, the family and the future

You've worked with a relatively unchanged crew for 15 years. What has that stability meant for the overall atmosphere and working process?

Stone – Well, there's a guy like George Webb, who's Jeff Ament's best bass tech, and Ed's man when he tours solo. Jeff and I started working with him in Mother Love Bone, back in 1987, which was the same time we started working with our manager, Kelly Curtis. In addition to that, there are a lot of people who have been with us for 15 to 20 years, like our monitor tech, Karrie Keyes, who we met on the first tour with Red Hot Chili Peppers, and Dave Rad, who we've known for years. There's an incredible comfort in having a big group of people that we know really well and have worked with for so long. It means that we can be ourselves, and feel like a big family when we're on the road. We understand each other's humor and can work out any problems that arise. The history of rock is full of crew members getting fired all the time, but sometimes it's better to keep the people that you're thinking about firing on board. If you fire somebody, you may have just solved one problem but created two new problems. The dynamics between band and crew are incredibly important. If you've got the crew and they're all-in and they're feeling it, then it's ten times easier for us to achieve our goal, which is getting to a place where the music just happens.

In the future, do you see yourself bouncing back and forth between Pearl Jam activities and personal projects?

Stone – Yeah, I think that will be the situation for a while. We all like getting away from the band for stretches of time. When we go on a world tour, we're on the road for three months, unlike Metallica, who go on tour for two years. We're very focused in terms of the work we put into Pearl Jam. We all like playing music with

You don't stick together for more than 25 years if you don't enjoy each other's company. Pearl Jam, laid back, 2013. Photo: © Danny Clinch/Universal Music Group.

a bunch of different people. Ed's ukulele record was a big success, and I think that inspired him to think, "I can do Pearl Jam, but I can also make these other records that are nothing like Pearl Jam." I'm pretty sure that he's psyched about that. I also think it says something about him that he released his first solo album after eight or nine Pearl Jam albums, while a lot of the biggest vocalists are much quicker to think, "I might as well just do it on my own." I'm really thankful to him for his strong belief in the band. I know that he truly loves our tight-knit family.

If you were 20 years younger and Pearl Jam was just getting started, how well do you think you'd fare?

Stone – I have absolutely no idea. Everything is changing so quickly. You can go from obscurity to a huge success on YouTube overnight. On the other hand, I also think that you can go from being a huge star to obscurity just as quickly. I don't know the answer to that question. I think we started at very unique point in terms of the music industry. It was just before computers and the internet took over. I'm certain that we had a level of visibility that would be difficult for a band to achieve today. But the most important thing is that it has kept going, that people tend to go back to the music, and they still like what they're hearing – but it's been a long time since we were huge in the media. We still get coverage, but we're a middle class band – we really are – in terms of how many albums and concert tickets we sell. We're in the middle class. We're not the biggest, that's for sure. But generally speaking, I have no idea what would happen if we were younger and wanted to get started today. I doubt that we would have done it differently.

A lasting bond. Eddie Vedder & Stone Gossard. Forum, Copenhagen 2012. Photo: Susan Nielsen.

Eddie Vedder and members of the Polish fan group "Touring Poles." Forum, Copenhagen. July 10, 2012. Photo: Karen Loria.

Chapter 13

2012: BERLIN. COPENHAGEN.

I've just found out that Pearl Jam is coming to Europe next summer on a tour slated
to wrap up with a show in Copenhagen in July – the perfect news to bring some
warmth on a cold winter's day. I've established something of a tradition in the
past few years of visiting family in Norway with one to three of my kids – Tobias,
Celine and Lulu – and then taking Lulu on a short vacation to a European metropolis
of her choice. And by no small coincidence, these trips frequently coincide with
Pearl Jam concerts. Such was the case in 2012, with concerts in Berlin on July 4
and in Copenhagen on July 10, and we repeated the feat in 2014.

BERLIN
After a few e-mails back and forth with Stone, we agree to meet in Berlin. He's
looking forward to seeing Lulu again – it seems she made a lasting impression on
previous encounters. So the plan is to start with the concert, and then coffee the
day after. Lulu and I arrive in Berlin a few days ahead of the big show to enjoy life
in what might just be Europe's most intriguing – and certainly most paradoxical –
city.

I have so many memories rooted in this city through the years. There was an
insane school trip in 10th grade in 1980, romping through the city on both sides
– and practically on top of – the Berlin Wall. Tons of concerts and extended stays
with Sharing Patrol in the dying days of the Cold War from '85 to '89 are also

among the experiences I'll never forget. At the height of the city's squatter and anarcho-punk movement, we played a slew of concerts, including one show with a very young My Bloody Valentine. And everywhere in the midst of all this inspiring, decadent, extreme and potentially dangerous madness was the wall, symbol of separation, the great divide. Every day we rode on the subway under East Berlin, passing the empty stations like deserted ghost towns. On these stays in frenetic Berlin, I felt like a trapped zoo animal, driven by an urge to go crazy – which is exactly what we did. When we finally had a more relaxed day and visited our booker's parents a bit outside the city, it turned out that their small backyard had a natural boundary in the form of a wall – yes, that wall. It was inescapable.

I had so many amazing experiences in the Berlin of that era. It was the ultimate shining example of the bipolar world order, an order that virtually everyone believed would remain unchanged in our lifetimes – that is, if the world managed to outlive us.

As part of the school curriculum for virtually every Dane in my generation, we were shown the iconic German film *Wir kinder von Bahnhof Zoo*, known in English as *Christiane F.*, based on the true story of the young drug addict Christiane F. It's a frightening tale of what drugs can lead to, but at the same time it's strangely alluring and almost romantic. To this day, I would have a hard time coming up with a movie where music plays such a central role in tying together an artist, city and culture – in other words, David Bowie's concert and soundtrack to the film, and particularly the way that his *Heroes* album became a musical trademark of Berlin and a historical snapshot of a disillusioned youth culture from the Cold War on the brink of collapse.

Arriving in Berlin always triggers a special state of mind for me, and I have a tradition of buying a sausage and bun at the airport right after landing, just to get into the right German mood.

Since Astoria in London in 2006, my close friend Signe Glahn has moved to Berlin, where she works for the renowned artist Olafur Eliason on his sustainable solar energy project *Little Sun*. She also now has two children with her partner, Peter Busk, who is beginning to enjoy great acclaim in the international art world. It's blistering hot in Berlin, but it's great to see Signe with her kids for the first time, and she's going to join Lulu and me for the concert at the O2 World Berlin arena.

The venue is the epitome of my favorite setting for seeing Pearl Jam live: 18,000–20,000 people in a tightly-packed sports arena with good lighting and sound. We're standing to the side of the stage and the sound is superb, with a song like *Jeremy* hitting the bull's-eye. The crowd sings along at full blast, the venue's acoustics remain impeccable, the intensity continues to rise, and it all culminates with the expected 13 ai-ai-ai-ai-ai-ai-ai-ai-ai-ai-ai-ai-ai's. I later find a recording of the song on YouTube, filmed from just about where we were standing, where you see the back of a young girl who is totally into it, and the comments below filled with things like "who is that girl?", "I wanna marry her" and so on. She clearly embodies the joy and power of the music, whoever she is. The audience is 100% into it, the sound is on point, and I feel completely calm and warm inside as the final introspective tones of *Indifference* ebb out.

As he said he would, Stone has returned home to the hotel after the show. We hang out for a while and run into Mike, who introduces me to his wife: "This is Henrik – the author." That's not exactly how I typically present myself, but it comes as a surprise and an honor.

The rear exit

We head for home to get some sleep. The next day Lulu and I set off for the Hotel Ritz and our appointment with Stone. Lulu can't help but laugh at the extreme luxury of the hotel, juxtaposed with Stone's super summery attire and pronounced lack of formality. Stone suggests off the cuff that we take the rear exit, as a number of fans have already gathered outside the hotel. Lulu laughs as if we have suddenly found ourselves in a scene from an old Beatles clip. We haven't, but everything certainly seems to be buzzing with the fact that Pearl Jam is in town.

As we stroll through Berlin's city park, Tiergarten, and a group of five guys comes walking towards us – all of them wearing Pearl Jam T-shirts. Stone is in the middle of telling us a story and doesn't notice a thing, nor do the guys passing us by, so I just keep it to myself with a subtle and silent smile. After a good walk, we stop at a cafe on this dazzling sunny day. It's nice to have a laid back visit with Stone, free of pressure of any kind – two or three good hours with plenty of time to talk at length, and the time flies, given that we now know each other so well. We talk about Birgitta and her family, Stone asks a lot of questions about how it's going with me and my family, and tells me that he's also gone through some major changes.

Although they still share a closeness, and bond through their daughter Vivian, Stone and Liz are now divorced. Uncannily, he now has another Viv in his life, in the form of his new girlfriend. The two would later marry, and are still husband and wife today. Stone and I are only three years separated by age, but in terms of settling down and having kids, the gap is considerably wider. Whereas I practically can't remember what it was like to not be a father, and say to Stone that I think I'm done as far as having kids goes, he feels quite the opposite. Things are going well with "big" Viv and they're working on a new addition to the family. Stone and Viv go on to hit the jackpot twice within a short span of time. When I meet with the proud father of three daughters in Buenos Aires a few years later, he breaks out the family photos, but also mentions that he's also done making babies.

Returning back to Berlin in 2012: We order coffee and cake. A short time later, a man cautiously approaches Stone and says discretely, "Excuse me, are you who I think you are?" And, of course, he is. It turns out that the man and his friend have travelled from Israel to see Pearl Jam's two concerts in Berlin. He gets a selfie with Stone.

Stone invites us to see that night's concert, the second and last in Berlin on this tour. There's probably nothing we rather would, but the plane tickets are booked and we have other obligations in Denmark. Unfortunately, it's simply impossible. So it's a good thing that we'll be seeing each other again just five days later at the concert in Copenhagen. We stroll back towards the Ritz, and now a much larger crowd has assembled in front of the hotel, including one guy with the band's name tattooed on his arm. We say goodbye to Stone, who slips almost unnoticed through the hotel's rear entrance. But, as I said, "almost." Somebody yells, "It's Stone!" and a flock of 15–20 people run after him – but Stone has already made it through the entrance, and I actually don't think he even registers the commotion. Or he just intuitively knows when it's time to vanish into thin air.

COPENHAGEN

Our rendezvous in Copenhagen comes four days later. A sunny summer Thursday. It's a good day – a very good day. All told, I've probably managed to invite around 100 people to Pearl Jam concerts around the world thanks to Stone, and on this day I have a bigger group of guests than usual – many of whom are especially near and dear. All of my children are coming, Tobias's girlfriend Liv, my childhood friend Emma, Jonathan from Sharing Patrol, Kasper and his girlfriend Cecilie, and 19-year-old rock guitarist Mikkel, who was also at the Copenhagen show five years earlier. We start off at a local Thai restaurant before heading over to Forum and the bustling crowd outside the arena. This particular concert isn't one of the most memorable in my book, musically speaking – the sound lives up to the venue's terrible reputation, despite the fact that it has actually improved in recent years. But people definitely seem to be satisfied nonetheless. Pearl Jam reaps nothing but positive reviews from Danish concert critics and most of the people I talk to are totally jazzed. But of course, they don't have the show from Berlin just days ago to compare it with. As Stone puts it when we talk about it a few years later: "Oh yeah, that was completely different."

Rumbling bass or not, it's amazing on a very personal level to see how all of my guests thankfully lap in the band's attention and generosity. Celine falls ill and has to go home ahead of schedule, and Tobias, who is rarely star-struck, leaves with his girlfriend right after the concert because they both have to get up early for work the next morning. All of which means that I have three unused backstage passes for three of my *Gaffa* colleagues, all of whom are hardcore fans.

The first person we run into after the concert is Stone, who walks right up to me and asks, "Is your son here?" I tell him that he isn't, because he has to get some sleep before work tomorrow. Stone follows up with, "OK, well do you guys want some champagne?" as he fetches an open bottle and paper cups.

It's an offer that Lars, Michael and Morten from *Gaffa* can't refuse. We're talking about big-time fans here. I don't talk all that much with Stone, but focus more on making sure that everyone's having a good time. I can see that Mike McCready is in a festive mood. He starts chatting with Mikkel about Gilmour and Pink Floyd, and after a while I see Mikkel jokingly pointing at McCready's forehead and declaring "I'll battle you!" Mike is a man who would never back down from a challenge, but as far as I know, the time and place of said battle has yet to be determined. On the whole, I can tell that people are really happy and everything is good.

Edved

Out of the corner of my eye, I see Eddie in the distance, walking around the large backstage area. It's actually very rare to see him in an "open" area. I don't want to cramp him – or, actually, I want to, but it's just not very cool to chase down a man who's been chased non-stop for two decades. But my friend Kasper quietly implores me, "Come on! Go over and say hi."

I waltz calmly in Ed's direction, thinking "He probably won't recognize me." But when he turns around, he throws his arms wide open and loudly yells, "Henrik!" and then it's big hugs. We quickly start talking, jumping from one topic to the next, and spending a little extra time when the conversation comes to our respective daughters. I ask if he'd like to say hi to Lulu. And he definitely would, so I wave her over to us. Lulu walks over with a big smile on her face. The others backstage catch a whiff of what's going on, and soon the whole gang is standing there with us. Before long, Eddie says: "Ok, I've got five minutes, just tell me what you wanna do." The five minutes stretch out to ten, fifteen or maybe more – I don't remember exactly.

I stay off to the side, observing. The conversation bounces from topic to topic as Lars and his friends collect autographs and pose for an array of photos with Eddie, Stone and Mike. Mikkel takes a different approach. "Do you wanna take a picture together?" asks Eddie, to which Mikkel answers, "No, but I'd like to shake your hand." Mikkel takes Eddie at his word: "*Take my hand, not my picture*" from *Corduroy*. It's probably the Pearl Jam song above them all in terms of Eddie raging against the workings of the music industry and the alienating abyss that comes from aggressive and manic fan hysteria, all of which is so far removed from what he and Pearl Jam want to communicate.

It's a reply that appears to catch the lead singer's fancy – they fall into conversation, in any case. First Eddie gives a thumbs up to Mikkel's The Strokes T-shirt, to which Mikkel responds by bringing up the version of Marvin Gaye's *Mercy, Mercy Me* that Eddie, Josh Homme and The Strokes recorded to benefit the victims of Hurricane Katrina. Eddie then says that he had actually spent most of the day on the telephone with Josh, who is Mikkel's biggest hero.

As I later say to Mikkel: "It's the first time I've ever heard somebody say no thanks to Eddie Vedder." And maybe that's precisely why, in recognition of Mikkel's consideration of Eddie's position as eternally hunted by fans, that he earns the front man's appreciation and a personal story. "I could see that he was tired and wanted to give him a break," says Mikkel when we later talk about that night. The more you need, the less you get.

By chance, I discover some years later that my photographer friend – Mikkel's dad Morten – never even heard the story, because Mikkel never mentioned it. I've always admired the power in the understated approach this family seems to master.

After the concert, we go our separate ways. I bike home, satisfied and with a distinct feeling of peace. Stone gave me the opportunity to give tickets to a lot of people, all of whom were delighted with the gift and had an unforgettable evening. It's not only the less you need – but also the more you give – the more you get.

I've gone through some really tough years, with work-related stress evolving into depression, I got divorced, and for an extended period I was only capable of working part-time. Ultimately, I threw the towel in the ring – the best decision of my life – and took a deep look inside myself, with the help of many good people in my life (you know who you are). And I can't thank Birgitta enough for her long-lasting, stable and constructive support.

But for quite a while now, up to the point of this concert, I've generally been feeling pretty good, and only lacked the finishing touches of stability. This evening proves to be a true turning point. The inner peace I feel is different and much more clear than previously; it's just something I can sense. It's a little bit like when I was struck by Eddie and Pearl Jam in Barcelona in 1996. A gut feeling, a certainty. That feeling proved true back then, and the same can be said here. The going has only grown smoother ever since. And looking at my life, at this story, it seems only fitting that this monumental turning point came in connection with Pearl Jam and the hospitality and generosity shown to me by Stone Gossard though all the years.

Kasper and Cecilie are happy, Emma and Lulu took some nice pictures with Eddie and the other rock stars, Jonathan from Sharing Patrol, who was born and raised in Seattle, is there too, as are my colleagues from *Gaffa*. Lars Breum, a sales and distribution rep at *Gaffa* who's around 30 years old, had contacted me on many occasions in the past to talk about Pearl Jam and my relationship with them. He tells me that he was talking with his dad about the people he'd like to meet most, if he could choose from anybody. Coming in at third place was Barack Obama, number two was Nelson Mandela (still alive in 2012) and number one was Eddie Vedder. Lars thanks me profusely for giving him the opportunity to meet the two people he wanted to meet more than anybody else in the world, Eddie and Stone (causing some doubt about where that leaves Obama and Mandela). After the backstage gathering draws to a close, he exits Forum through the back door, passing the crowd of waiting fans and watching as they cheer and shout to

Lulu Høi Tuxen and Eddie Vedder. Forum, Copenhagen. June 10, 2012. Photo: Susan Nielsen.

"I'll battle you." Guitarists Mikkel Sylvester Larsen and Mike McCready. Forum, Copenhagen. June 10, 2012. Photo: Henrik Tuxen

the band members as they board the tour bus. Arriving at his car, he can't help but shed a tear.

At an industry party about a year later, I talk to Lars's girlfriend Lise (now his wife and mother to the couple's son, little Eddie!). It should be said that Lise is by no means a die-hard Pearl Jam fan, but she tells me that she was unexpectedly blown away and had the concert experience of her life recently in Amsterdam, where she and Lars saw Eddie Vedder solo. As we're talking about Lars, she looks at me with her big, beautiful brown eyes and says: "You'll never fathom how much what you did meant to Lars."

Mike McCready and Lulu Høi Tuxen. Forum, Copenhagen. June 10, 2012. Photo: Henrik Tuxen.

Chapter 14

2013: BRAD IN BERLIN. RELEASE IN LONDON.

Pearl Jam has pulled the plug for a time, as the band members primarily focus on other projects. Stone is recording and touring with his side project, Brad, which has existed almost as long as Pearl Jam. Around the time it came out, I listened to the album *Interior* quite a bit, but I've never seen the band live. So now, in the middle of dark and cold Danish February, I join forces with my tennis partner and good buddy Kasper, and we head for Berlin to meet up with Stone and see Brad in concert.

We make it to Berlin and find the venue, which has a capacity of around 300. The tour bus is parked outside the building, and it appears that Stone is taking a nap on board. As we're taking a look around the venue, we suddenly find ourselves in a loud argument, bordering on fisticuffs, with a short man with an extremely long red beard. He works for Ten Club, touring frequently with Pearl Jam, and right now he's Brad's tour manager plus an occasional musician in the band. He doesn't know us, and he wants to dictate our every move. We're not having it – not even a little bit. I know and understand that Pearl Jam's crew sometimes has to be fierce when staving off desperate fans trying to get close to the band, and I've witnessed it first-hand plenty of times, but at this particular moment, that's not really the thing at the top of my mind. Kasper and I sometimes have a quick temper (as some certainly know from the tennis court), and this time around our collective battle gene is activated. The tension eventually subsides to less combative levels, and shortly after we find Stone. Then we go for a bite at a small Asian restaurant, enjoying Stone's company, a beer and a meal.

BRAD

Kasper and I are staying with some of his friends who live in a collective in Berlin's Moabit neighborhood. They're nice people who Kasper ran into one night about a year earlier in Copenhagen, when they all had more than a few beers in their systems in Copenhagen. They didn't have a place to stay for the night, so Kasper lent them his apartment – and so now we're welcome in Berlin. We pull some strings with our insider connections and expand the guest list to include our host Erik and a number of the collective's other residents. Stone is really looking forward to playing.

It lives up to expectations and is a great concert. I've become so accustomed to seeing Stone in the role of the rhythm guitarist who holds everything together, with Mike as the classic guitar hero with flashy solos and rock star attitude. But in Brad, Stone has a freer role and plays full throttle. If you're among those who think that he can't steal the show as a lead guitarist, you should probably check out Brad the next time they come to town.

After the concert, we all meet in a cozy backstage room. There's time to talk, and I tell Stone that it was great to see him play so many different guitar roles, including his numerous leads. Drummer Regan Hagan is also with us backstage. He's goes all the way back in Seattle, formerly of the band Malfunkshun, and now on the Pearl Jam and Ten Club crew. Then the guy with the long red beard arrives. Stone introduces Mike and says with a smile: "I can understand that you've already met each other." We smile, shake hands with Mike and laugh heartily. It's all good. I understand and respect that Mike is taking care of the musicians – that's his job.

Stone is revved up, and after an hour or two we decide to go out for a genuine Berlin sausage – at 2 a.m. on a Monday morning in February. I'm not sure it gets any more miserable than that. But we're completely unfazed. Stone forgot his wallet, so for once I have the opportunity to treat him to beer and a sausage. It doesn't exactly cost a fortune – 5 dollars or thereabouts.

We're pretty much the only people in all of Berlin who are still awake. Before parting ways with Stone, Erik has an idea: We should take a picture in a coin-operated passport photo booth. Stone laughs a bit at the thought, but Erik insists, so that's what ends up happening. Like a bunch of teenage boys on spring break, we squeeze our four heads together at three in morning and capture the moment in black and white for time immemorial. Four pictures, one for each of us. That photo, equal parts amusing and absurd, spent a long time in my wallet.

RELEASE

After many years as a print journalist, I've diversified a bit, adding live interviews in front of audiences, talks and other activities to my repertoire. The flagship for this new focus is Gaffa Library Session, a series of events where I'm typically joined by a prominent Danish musician on stage, in front of somewhere around 300 people. The sessions are half interview, half music. There's also a variety of events I organize on my own and random unsolicited requests from various channels, giving me plenty of opportunities to share my personal experiences and explain why Pearl Jam holds a special place in my heart.

In 2013, I'm asked to give four talks at libraries about AC/DC – even though I had no idea I was an expert – as part of a collaboration between the Danish Broadcasting Corporation's P6 Beat radio station, the libraries and *Gaffa*. It turns out to be a total blast. After that, I hold similar events at libraries where I talk about Pearl Jam, and P6 Beat invites me into the studio for a six-hour live broadcast called "P6 Beat Loves Pearl Jam." Although the broadcast is right on the heels of *Lightning Bolt*, which came out on October 11, 2013, I happen to be rather obsessed with *Release* at the time.

Shortly before my first talk on Pearl Jam, I'm in London to interview the young crooner Sam Smith before he hit the big time, and while there I run into a Norwegian girl by chance in the Underground. We talk a bit and then go for a coffee. She tells me that she's just about the world's biggest Springsteen fan, having just returned to London from a Bruce convention, not to mention her strategically located tattoos relating to "His Bruceness" on large swaths of her bodily canvas (she works in marketing in the finance sector, so visible tattoos are a no-go). And when she asks if there's any music of special importance to me, I tell her about my relationship with the quintet from Seattle.

We part ways, and before heading for the airport I have time for a random movie at the cinema on Leicester Square. The next film starting is *Out of the Furnace* with Christian Bale playing the lead. As I take my seat in the theater, the bleak cinematography unfolds on top of *Release*. And then, as the credits roll on this heavy and excellent movie, we get *Release* again, this time from start to finish. It's the last song on the band's debut, *Ten*, and the first number Pearl Jam played live under the name Mookie Blaylock at The Off Ramp on October 22, 1990 in Seattle. Once again, I find there's always an unturned stone just waiting to be discovered in the Pearl Jam catalog. That afternoon, for the very first time – and an eternity after my maiden encounter with the band – I realize the unbelievable intensity of Eddie's autobiographical lyrics to the father he never knew: "*Release meeeeeeee.*" I go on to listen to *Release* daily for about the next two months, and start each of the library talks on Pearl Jam by showing the official trailer for *Out of the Furnace*.

The "P6 Beat Loves Pearl Jam" broadcast is a marathon of sublimity. I'm in the studio with host Anders Bøtter (a legend in the world of Danish heavy metal) and producer Christian Lundov. I get a piping fresh interview with Stone about *Lighting Bolt* in the can, and compile a bunch of other past material to pepper throughout the six-hour program.

We talk, analyze and laugh for six hours on end – and listeners call in and share good stories on the air. One of the callers is Henrik the driver from the band's first European tour in 1992 (the one where Susan sat in the passenger's seat). That tour took place at the exact time that *Ten* was going supernova in the States, without the band completely realizing what was going on. Their transatlantic correspondence was mostly by fax and the European tour was playing small venues like Copenhagen's Pumpehuset, whose capacity is 650. The driver also says that Mike had to be chaperoned at all times when he wasn't on the bus or at a venue, because he had absolutely no sense of direction. Henrik also spent a lot of time with Eddie Vedder at coin-op laundromats. The only clothes Ed had with him were two pairs of shorts and three T-shirts – and they needed to be washed along the way. While the band toured Europe with the status of your run-of-the-mill punk band, reports started trickling in from the US: *Ten* has now sold 500,000 copies. Now it has rounded a million, etc. Depending on the source you check, *Ten* has now sold around 18 million copies. It's pretty wild to hear the driver's story about being on the road with the band right as they were becoming superstars on another continent, and hardly even knew it – or, at the very least, hardly comprehended it.

Chapter 15

2013: NO SLEEP TILL BROOKLYN.

... She Got Pearl Jammed

"We also need your social security number, so we can send you a little payment for your participation," says the producer from P6 Beat, as we're wrapping up the six-hour show.

"Oh," I say, "I thought I was just doing it for fun."

The little payment turns out to be 5,000 kroner (about 750 dollars). Combined with the fact that I can get Universal to pitch in and can easily sell an article for publication, I decide to go to New York to see two Pearl Jam concerts at the newly-built Barclays Center in Brooklyn. It's always been a dream of mine to see the band in New York and in South America. And perhaps also some day in Seattle.

Sarah from the PJ office writes shortly before my departure from Copenhagen to let me know that I have a +1 on the guest list for both concerts. My ex-girlfriend Signe, who accompanied me to London about four years earlier, is on the verge of spontaneously joining me on a moment's notice, but she can't get the time off from work, so she ends up staying in Copenhagen. I end up taking the trip alone, but it's not long before I'm in good company.

Before taking my seat on the plane to New York, I fall into conversation with an enthusiastic Norwegian man (Kjetil Kristoffersen), who tells me that he's just bought an apartment in Frederiksberg (a small city nestled in central Copenhagen), and that his 6'5" 16 year old son (Jullan Kristoffersen) plays soccer for

FC Copenhagen and is going to be the new Andreas Cornelius (FC Copenhagen's brightest offensive star at the time). Kjetil also tells me that he's a successful Norwegian publisher.

We talk briefly about the book industry, and I mention that I've written a book about Pearl Jam. The publisher turns very serious and virtually on the spot he offers to release the book in Norway, asking almost as an afterthought if I thought that Norwegian Pearl Jam fans would buy it.

"Well, I would," comes a voice from off to our left, where a smiling Norwegian couple has sat down next to me.

It turns out that Asbjørn and Kamilla are die-hard fans on their way to the US to see the band five times while their daughters, ages 5 and 8, stay with their aunt in the Norwegian town of Sarpsborg. It's far from the first time that the friendly Norwegians are on the road to see their favorite band: Chicago for PJ20 in 2011, lots of trips around Europe, and a few more. They're well-aware of my book already, and ask if I know anything about a six-hour Danish radio program about Pearl Jam that was broadcast four days earlier.

Well actually, yes, I do. Maybe it was "destiny and meant to be," as Kamilla says the next day when we meet at Times Square. It seems that Pearl Jam fanatics pop up out of the blue and into my life all over the place. I don't know if the same is true of other bands' fans, but I know that when it comes to Pearl Jam there's a special dedication and loyalty. From Sarpsborg to New York. Or, for that matter, from Valencia to Maui. That's just the way it is.

When Pearl Jam is playing, people show up – and a lot of them go to every show on the tour. Nomadic fans, like a modern-day version of the Grateful Dead's legendary "Deadheads," as Stone once put it.

A fire in Ed

Back in the '60s, Eddie Vedder's biggest musical idols, The Who, sang the hymn of youthful angst *Young Man's Blues*, and the notorious line "Hope I die before I get old" from the song *My Generation.* Rock has long been synonymous with youth, but Keith Richards has now rounded 70 and the genre has proven capable of expressing the full gamut of ages, and not just "Teenage Riot" (to quote Pearl Jam's close friends in Sonic Youth).

Pearl Jam was absolutely representative of angry young men as they emerged in the early 90s, but in my view – and that of many critics, bloggers and everyday fans – Pearl Jam shows its growth, musically and personally, with *Lightning Bolt.* The album is not made for and by teenagers, although many of them also listen along; it's a mature rock album that remains passionate, fiery and intense in a different way than when *Ten* and Nirvana's *Nevermind* set the agenda in the early '90s.

Eddie Vedder still means what he says, and he's not all fuzzy and cuddly. The vitriol towards his stepfather (a man who has taken his lumps through the years, the moral of that story being that you better treat your kids right or hope that they don't become rock stars) is bitingly aggressive on *My Father's Son*. But the album ends on an almost spiritually euphoric note with the beautiful *Future Days*.

Stone is also highly pleased with the results when I talk to him one week before the show in New York:

Stone – I don't know what it is about Eddie. I think he just keeps getting better and better at expressing himself. Getting stronger in his lyrics and the rhythm of his vocals. *My Father's Son* is currently my favorite on the album. I love the intensity of his vocals and the way he's able to put his thoughts and feelings into words that ignite the listener's mind. There's still a fire in Ed, and he continues to burn.

+1?

Having arrived in New York, I find my hotel, get some sleep and relax to the max. When I wake up I think, "What was that again? Oh yeah, +1 tonight – but who is that +1 going to be?" Well, at the time being, nobody, here on a different continent. But who knows, maybe I know somebody who wants to join me here in New York. Facebook.

The replies come fast and furious. Everything from friends that are probably in New York, a son's friend, a distant colleague, and then, a suggestion from a close friend: Marianne Søndergaard, formerly of Sony Music and featured in three parts of this book already (Maui, Roskilde 2000 and Vote For Change 2004), writes that her little sister is in town and would absolutely love to see Pearl Jam. Marianne also says that I know her sister from a past trip to New York, but I know for a fact that I wasn't on that trip. But it sounds like a nice and easy solution, so that's that.

A very short time later, Marie and I agree to meet at Union Square in 90 minutes. And so it was.

I'm absolutely certain that I've met Marie before, just not in New York, and five minutes later it's like I've known her for years. A wonderful New York trip with excellent company. Truly the beginning of a beautiful friendship.

But at first it looks like I might have gotten a bit ahead of myself. When we arrive at the venue, we're sent from one window to the next as only they can do in the US. *Wrong line, wrong entrance, another list, you wanna call Seattle?* It just keeps on and on until at last, so close to the start of the concert that I know it will be almost impossible to get in, a messenger arrives with two tickets in an envelope with more than ten names crossed off – but not mine. We get in, great seats, fantastic concert.

Marie is blown away and ecstatic. I see an array of familiar faces dotting the crowd, including Asbjørn and Kamilla. I've arranged with Stone to touch base with him after the concert. But to no avail. We try to find the backstage entrance and try calling Stone and Sarah. There's no answer, and we practically get lost in the enormous building.

We eventually find our way out and take a seat at an outdoor cocktail bar in the neighborhood. While on our second beer, a text message from Stone ticks in on my phone: "Hey, was looking for you. Where are you? Love you!"

Jeff Ament

So that was a good way to start a trip to New York. I sleep like a log that night and the next afternoon I meet up with Marie in a part of Williamsburg that is grotesquely trendy. Everybody seems like actors on their own personal film set. But it's also nice to see that part of New York.

Later on, we're in a different area of Brooklyn with one of Marie's friends, who has a definitively posh pad. Two stories with a huge rooftop terrace and an unimpeded view of downtown Manhattan. Wow. Why do my friends live in shacks and tents? Anyway, back to the music.

The second day with Pearl Jam in New York. Now we're armed with personalized, laminated All Access passes hanging around our necks, which makes it infinitely easier to go anywhere we want in the arena. Before the concert, we wander around and come across a little backstage cafe, where we run into the always peppy, jolly and talkative Jeff Ament. I can't remember ever encountering him in a different mood.

Through the years, Jeff, his brother and Ed have produced the majority of the band's massive collection of artwork. Jeff tells me that we can expect about seven songs from last night's show and about 20 new songs (the band actually ended up playing an additional seven new songs). I know that this is by no means out of the ordinary, but as something of a "Pearl Jam rookie," Marie is amazed.

We talk a bit about Seattle, common friends, artwork. I show Jeff a picture on my phone of a 20-foot-tall painting of the *Lightning Bolt* cover on the wall of a building in Williamsburg, which he had no idea about, and we talk about the fact that *Lightning Bolt* went to #1 on iTunes in about 50 countries in the same week:

Jeff – It's funny. Neil [Young] once said to us, "First you have your hardcore fans, then they're gone for a while to have kids and so on. But if you hang on, their children will grow up and then they'll come back with their kids."

Later that evening, Stone also had a few words to say about Neil Young (*Lighting Bolt* is dedicated to Neil Young):

Stone – I just took a close look at the album artwork for the first time, and I hadn't noticed that dedication to Neil. But I support it 100%. I'd put it this way: If we had to choose a musical mentor for our band, it would be him. Even though two years may pass without us seeing him, we think about him in everything we do. He was a pioneer and exhibited the variation and stubborn individualism that we've tried to emulate. Not thinking about things too much, but just loving each other in the process. I'm all for that dedication.

Soundtrack for life

It's showtime for the second night in a row. This concert is light years above and beyond Copenhagen one year earlier. It's a show I wish every human on Planet Earth had the opportunity to experience.

As I'm standing and screaming at the top of my lungs with new milestones, spiritual hymns, old classics and non-stop rock'n'roll, I think about the overall audience experience. A soundtrack for life, rivers of emotional words that have embedded themselves in the souls of millions. Anger, disgust, hate, out-of-body catharsis from another world, and that voice. But first and foremost love, and plenty of it.

I've been regularly attending concerts since 1976, and this is my 17th Pearl Jam concert – and it's the absolute best concert I've ever seen. The sound of *Whipping* is pure whiplash. A 13-minute version of *Better Man* unites everyone in the building. The spiritual elements are like mass hymns. The punk is acidic and biting, the ballads make a beeline for my tear ducts, and the audience sings along to much more than just the biggest hits.

During this three-hour tour de force, which seems constantly on the verge of peaking, I reflect on the incredible richness of experiences I've had with this band since I saw them in Barcelona in 1996, drank wine and shook hands with Eddie Vedder for the first time. I drift back in my thoughts to relive the five minutes I managed to hear of the chaotic concert at Roskilde Festival in 1992, the night that Nirvana played afterwards and Denmark sensationally won the European Championships in soccer. I relive Roskilde Festival 2000, the visits to the friends and families of the victims with Stone, concerts around the world – everything. And all these years later, standing here with a sweet, smart and charming woman who popped up out of the blue, I think: "This is my life. Thank you."

I'm a guitarist

After the concert, it's crowded backstage as a mixed bag of people are mingling around. There's the towering Dennis Rodman with all his piercings, who at the time is in the media spotlight because of his "friendship" with the North Korean dictator, Kim Jong-un. Stone shows up, happy and relaxed, and says the concert was "pretty good."

"Pretty good?! What are you talking about? Did we just witness the same event?!"

We spend a moment catching up and expressing our joy to see each other, but some boisterous New Yorker in a baseball cap is trying to crash our conversation and get Stone's attention. I step in front of the guy demonstratively, offer him my hand and say: "Hi, I'm a tennis player."

He answers with a coy smile: "Oh yeah, I'm a guitarist." He thinks that Marie is Stone's girlfriend, but when she shakes her head no, he says, "Oh, so you're just a person."

By the way, I knew without having to card him that his ID reads John Patrick McEnroe.

As always, it's Fort Knox around Eddie Vedder, who gave so much of himself over the past two nights that it would be fully justified if he never lifted a finger again for the rest of his life. But he's not the only one carrying the load, as illustrated by one of his many comments to the audience during the show:

Eddie – We started off as a five-man band, then we became six [Boom Gaspar], and today we were a 17,500-man band, where all of you did the heavy lifting.

Take my hand – and my picture

Ed previously gave me his cell phone number and e-mail address, and I've been ritually photographed by the man, but nonetheless he can be extremely difficult to get in touch with. He's always being hunted down, so the crew is highly protective of him, especially when the band is on tour, and night after night he puts so much into his performances. And, of course, there's also the fact that New York is an absolute zoo.

At the furthest back of the backstage rooms, Eddie is hanging out and talking with a group of friends, his wife Jill McCormick, and their daughter Olivia. I stay at a distance, but suddenly he sees me and immediately comes over smiling, with an ebullient "Hey, my friend! So good to see you!" and gives me a big bear hug. Then he enthusiastically tells Marie, "We all love him," and also briefly expresses his love and appreciation for the contact with the Roskilde families.

Ed suggests that we take a picture together, and when I take out my phone, he sees the screensaver picture of my son, to which he says, "He's so handsome. Just like his father, no surprise," which although flattering, is obviously a lie (the part about me, that is). Then he smiles big and squeezes me tight around the shoulder. Tour manager Smitty takes the picture and then rushes to show us the door – friendly but there's no room for discussion. It's short and sweet, but unequivocally heartwarming. Can't find a better man.

The crowd backstage has thinned considerably by this time – Rodman and McEnroe are nowhere to be seen – which simply means plenty of time to relax with Stone. Suddenly, it's just the three of us left in the room. Stone shows us photos of his six-week-old baby and tells us that Pearl Jam will likely tour Europe again in June 2014.

Everything good comes to an end, and so too with this wonderful dose of Pearl Jam in the city that never sleeps. I give Stone some Danish vinyl and CDs, including Wave Of Stone (now Electric Elephants) and Baby In Vain, which he inspects closely. Then we run through the state of the world before he jumps in a car with tinted windows and is whooshed off to his hotel.

I've also got to find my bunk bed. I know that I have three hours to sleep

*Jeff Ament, Henrik Tuxen, Marie Hansen.
Brooklyn. October 19, 2013.
Photo: Private collection.*

*"A guitarist" and "Just a person,"
aka John McEnroe & Marie Hansen. Brooklyn.
October 19, 2013. Photo: Henrik Tuxen.*

before my flight to Pearl Jam's hometown. I'm going to spend five fantastic days in Seattle with Johnny and Lene. Pearl Jam continues on its US tour in connection with their latest album, about which Stone had the following to say:

Stone – I think we all feel that *Lighting Bolt* sounds more like "us" than anything we've done in a while. With age, it feels like we've gotten better at arranging songs, keeping it simple, and Brendan has helped us improve the clarity of the instrumentation, which gives Ed more room to express himself. There are things that are as extreme and intense as when we were 20 years old, but we also have this wisdom and broader perspective on life that you get with age, which enables us to have sentimental reflections on life and channel them into a kind of happiness. And when you bring those two poles together through a number of songs, the extreme and the beautiful, it feels like us, right where we want to be. I think we've found our own form of classic rock, which is definitely inspired by the epic artistry of Springsteen and the beauty of Simon & Garfunkel, combined with the power of Motörhead and punk. We combine all this input into a collective whole. You can do infinite things in a three- to four-minute song. The creative process in the band is constantly evolving and changing. That's what happens when you have five composers and an amazing front man, who really understands how to express himself verbally and continuously explore new perspectives in his lyrics.

Chapter 16

2014: EUROPE.

Stone's tip in New York proved to be true. Pearl Jam comes to Europe in 2014, and I set my personal tour record: 5 concerts out of 11. Seeing the band so many times in such a short time is an amazing experience, and at times like being on tour myself.

My trip starts in Amsterdam with two sold-out shows in the newly-built Ziggo Dome, whose capacity is around 18,000. Through the years, I've often worked with International Feature Agency, which was founded by my close friend Peter. He had often said that I was welcome to stay for free at his family's Airbnb apartment in central Amsterdam if I happened to be passing through Europe's capital for mind-expanding substances. And, as luck would have it, the apartment is available for my stay.

My brother Fredrik joins me in Amsterdam. Our everyday lives are worlds apart – he's an engineer and successful businessman, while I've devoted my heart to the financially meager, yet entertaining life of a rock'n'roll journalist. Despite our occupational differences, we generally agree when it comes to sports and music, and Pearl Jam is no exception. Although a huge fan of metal and hard rock in particular, Fredrik has been to surprisingly few concerts, and none of them featured Pearl Jam.

Amidst a summer heat wave in Copenhagen, we board separate planes to

Amsterdam, then meet up in city center before venturing out to the arena. The concert is a blast, and Ziggo Dome is an absolute gem of a venue. A ways into the concert, I'm about to go out for a new round of refreshments, but my brother stops me and says that he'll do it instead. Shortly after, rare but familiar tones fill the arena: *Light Years*. More than any other Pearl Jam song, it's the one that reminds me the most of everything that's happened through the years – and I get to hear it because my brother offered to go get the beer.

Thinking back on it later that night, I realize that of course they played it here in Amsterdam, Diane's home city. It's a song that has become synonymous with loss for so many people around the world, and was originally dedicated to Diane from Sony Music, who went to great lengths for the band in the Netherlands, and who died at the young age of 33.

AMSTERDAM, NETHERLANDS-SPAIN

The arena is incredible, the sound sublime, out seats are primo and we're singing along all the way. So too is everyone else in the crowd. Lots of humorous touches from the stage. *Animal* has a special meaning that day, with the line "*1, 2, 3, 4, 5 against 1.*" The day before the concert, the Netherlands national soccer team crushed the reigning world champions, Spain, 5-1 at the World Cup in Brazil. The victory was also celebrated on stage. After the concert, we dally down to the backstage area. No band members in sight, but a bunch of cool Americans, good wine and drinks. No complaints whatsoever.

We enjoy Amsterdam the next day, including a visit to the Van Gogh Museum with my brother and a sweet nurse from Dublin. To his great dismay, Fredrik has to return to Copenhagen before that night's show, so my Dutch host Peter accompanies me instead. He knows the route to Ziggo Dome, which is located close to the stadium where the professional soccer team Ajax Amsterdam plays its home matches. The band equals the intensity and excellence of the previous day's concert, though (unsurprisingly) with tons of different songs and only two repeats out of the first 17 – yet another testament to the constant variation of their setlists. Although a seasoned concertgoer, it's Peter's first time seeing Pearl Jam live. He gives an enthusiastic thumbs up to the band's performance and to Amsterdam for having such an excellent venue for the show.

This time around, we run into more familiar faces backstage after the concert. Mike rolls in with his eight-month-old son Henry in a stroller. I'm convinced that Mike named his son after me, but Mike assures me that the moniker comes from his grandfather. And when I ask if Henry can play *Eruption* lying on his back, Mike tells me of course he can. After all, any true McCready should be able to pull off Eddie Van Halen by the ripe old age of eight months.

Stone has his own private room, where a small yet festive gathering congregates for the next couple of hours. Stone tells his friend Steve, who's there with his family from Seattle, that he and I go way back, 18 years, and have been through thick and thin. Stone's arithmetic is on point, even though our encounter in 1996 was relatively short and I mostly spoke with Ed that time around. We talk about the concerts in Spain with Fastbacks. I add that my daughter was 14 days old at that time, and that I probably shouldn't have been there. "No, you probably shouldn't have," says Stone with a smile. But, of course, I was, and it's now part of my story – and Lulu's, for that matter. During my visit to Seattle about six months earlier, while visiting the pop culture museum EMP, I saw a T-shirt with Pearl Jam and Fastbacks that was dated "Paris, November 7, 1996" – the same day that Lulu was born in Copenhagen. Stone asks if I heard *Light Years* the day before, and he says that he was thinking of me as they played it. I tell him that I did in fact hear it, thanks to my brother.

Eddie pops into the room, but I don't notice because I'm sitting with my back to the door. I had caught a glimpse of him earlier, but he leaves the room before we manage to greet each other. Then, Mike and Jeff drop by and we all hang out for a while. Despite their appreciation for baseball, the NFL and all the traditional American spectator sports, Pearl Jam has really gotten into soccer and they're following the World Cup closely.

One week later, they'll be playing a sold out show at San Siro in Milan (the home field of Italy's professional soccer teams Inter and Milan), and Stone tells me that they're in dialog with the event organizer about showing Italy's World Cup match on the stadium's big screen before the concert. I don't know if those plans ever came to fruition, but I do know that things didn't go so well for the Italians at the World Cup that year. We take some pictures, everyone talks with everyone, and Stone and I know that we'll be seeing each other again soon in Berlin or Stockholm. My friend the nurse grabs me by the arm, looks me in the eyes and says emphatically, "You and Stone are *really* good friends."

BERLIN

I return to Copenhagen for about a week before I'm on the go once more. The first stop on this leg is Paris, where I'm going to interview Lenny Kravitz, who is renowned for being nice but extremely taciturn. I know this because I tried getting him to open up once before in New York, eliciting an equally lackadaisical response from both him and his dog. So I'm looking forward to a new chance to interview him in Paris. He turns out to have a lot more to say this time, without ever coming close to what could be deemed decidedly talkative. I tell him that I'm going to see Pearl Jam after our interview, and he expresses his great admiration for the band. He's seen them live recently and thinks they're at the top of their game. When I later talk with a Spanish fan and colleague who interviewed Lenny after me, she's genuinely shocked by how reserved Lenny is. "That's what I was trying to tell you," I say to her.

There's a bomb threat at Charles de Gaulle Airport, and the bomb squad has to come out and detonate a fake bomb, or something of that nature. Despite the commotion, I make it to my flight and land in Berlin, where I meet up with Kasper, who took the train from Copenhagen. He's with a couple of Swedish hippies that are on their way to a cult electronic music festival, but forgot their tickets back home in rural Sweden. We make our way to the same collective that we crashed at while in town to see Brad, and we get some sleep. The next day, June 26, is a fantastically sunny day. Sweetening the cocktail is Germany vs. the US in the World Cup, and Pearl Jam at Wuhlheide.

During the day, the half-mile path through the forest to Wuhlheide is lined with stands and big screen televisions. I can't get through to Stone by phone, and I'm not sure if I'm on the list +1 or +2. Nonetheless, we agree that Erik from the collective should join us on the way to the show, at the very least. We'll take our chances. He's able to celebrate the German victory over the US in soccer but, unfortunately, the envelope with my name on it only contains two tickets. Erik doesn't take it too hard, and heads back for Berlin.

Kasper and I pass through the entrance. The envelope with the tickets says that we're welcome in the backstage area, where things will be happening both before and after the concert. Not much of note is taking place backstage before the concert, but we run into Susan and Martin – a duo with whom I've seen my share of Pearl Jam concerts. We walk around together in the blazing sunshine, recognizing a few faces from the crew here and there, but it's by no means an organized pre-event gathering.

Suddenly I see Eddie in a barracks from a distance. He appears stressed. As he passes us by, he says something along the lines of "Sorry, I'm not doing too well right now. There are some problems, see you later my friend." Once past us, he yells "Fuck!" (among other niceties) and signals clearly that something is way off. We talk a bit with the tour manager Smitty and agree that it would be best if we made our way back out to the concert area. There's not really any reason to stay backstage right now.

A little greeting

The concert, on the other hand, has more than plenty to offer. We join up with Kamilla, Asbjørn and a group of their friends, where we enjoy the concert and the perfect surroundings. A meditative *Pendulum* opens the show in the blazing sun, and the opening set rolls on towards a roaring conclusion with *Rearviewmirror* as dark clouds take over the skies. Highlights of the encore include the insanely dynamic interplay between Mike and Boom on *Crazy Mary*, and *Comatose*, where they completely botch the intro and have to start over. We're two hours and nine minutes into the concert. I'm standing next to my soulmate, Kasper Schulz, surrounded by Norwegians who've downed more than their share of beer along the way.

Eddie's voice sounds out in the darkness: "We have a friend called Henrik here tonight, I just wanna say hi to him... and Susan, we didn't get to see you, but (...) Just friends from the old days, and we've been through a lot – and we're still going through it."

Some of the Norwegians turn around and yell, "Is that you?!" Others haven't heard a thing.

"Well, yeah, I guess so." I'm experiencing an utter sense of peacefulness that I just let linger. It's more than I can fathom. (YouTube: Pearl Jam LIVE @ Berlin 26.06.2014 (HD)).

The concert ends in encores packed with classics and a full-on rocking jam, surrounded by pitch darkness apart from the stage lights. As the final notes of *Yellow Ledbetter* disappear into the Berlin night, we head for the backstage area.

Stone and most of the others have already taken off, but Jeff is there and he's in great spirits. We get into a talk about Led Zeppelin and I suggest that Eddie could be a stand-in for Robert Plant, but Jeff shoots that idea down: "Ed's more of a The Who than a Zeppelin guy."

Unlike Ed, Jeff is a hardcore Zeppelin fan. He tells me that he was talking with a concert promoter back in 2007, who told him that he didn't have to rush to London, because Led Zeppelin was planning a 30-show world tour. But they only end up playing one show – *Celebration Day* in London in 2007. Only about 18,000 tickets were available to the more than 20 million people trying to buy them.

A couple of months before this show at Wuhlheide, Jimmy Page told me during an interview that all the others (apart from Robert Plant) thought they were going to play more than one concert. "We put a lot of time into practicing," as he said. I thought he meant that they expected to play four or five concerts, not 30. I found myself hating Robert Plant just a little bit that evening – couldn't he have done it for Jimmy's sake? After all, it was his life's work. Jeff also mentions that the balance of power between the two has shifted. In the past, Page called the shots, but now it's Plant.

Jeff also mentions the tumult in the crowd that night, and that every time Eddie said "Take three steps back, please everybody," there were a few people who demonstratively took one step forward. I didn't think all that much about it during the concert, but when I later watch the full show on YouTube, I realize the great responsibility that always rests on the band's shoulders. There appears to have been quite a commotion during the concert on several occasions, and I can't imagine the burden that must be felt by the band – and Ed in particular – and the worst case scenarios in their mind's eye as they try to keep the energy high, give 18,000 people a great concert for nearly three hours, and enjoy themselves along the way. In the midst of my euphoria over discovering this excellent video of the concert, which calls forth a river of great memories, I feel sorry for the band. Just think about having to fear for everyone's safety and the behavior of the crowd when you've been through what they've been through

Jeff also finds it funny that I work for a magazine called *Gaffa*. One of the names originally in contention against Pearl Jam was Gaffa, Pearl Gaffer or something like that, he says. On a more serious note, we talk about the Roskilde accident. Jeff tells me that he had seriously considered returning to the 2001 edition of Roskilde Festival as an anonymous guest to revisit the location and process the experience in his own way. But something came up, or he changed his mind – the idea never materialized in any case. I tell him that he should really feel free to let me know if he would like to revisit the festival or contact the people touched by the accident in any way. He thanks me for the offer, and we've later discussed this a bit via e-mail. But it hasn't come any further than that as of yet.

We take a few selfies, talk about sports and music, and then we realize that we're in the middle of a dark forest in the former East Germany, in a city where the public transportation workers are currently on strike, and we have absolutely no idea how we're going to get home. "You guys wanna ride along with me?" asks Jeff. "We'll just have to sit on each other's laps a little bit."

Speaking of transportation, that's why Eddie was so pissed before the concert. The driver had taken the wrong route, so Eddie arrived at Wuhlheide 90 minutes later than planned. That's less than optimal when you have to write a setlist and make sure everything's ready to go. But he managed to get everything worked out, and it was a concert to remember.

We all get into the black car with tinted windows. Kasper is loving it and thinks that Jeff Ament has got to be the world's coolest guy. Susan and Martin are with us, as is one of Jeff's basketball buddies through more than 20 years – a nice guy who doesn't seem particularly interested in music.

"Isn't Ed a pretty good basketball player?" I ask. "I don't think you could really say that," says Jeff, as his friend smiles coyly, but he adds that Vedder is a good baseball player and a fierce competitor no matter the game. Jeff talks sports, sports, sports – which combined with music and women makes up the world's three best topics – and he also reveals a few secrets. After a rough spill on his skateboard, Jeff had broken a bone in his hand or finger right before a tour or concert. He didn't dare tell the others about the injury out of fear that band would call everything off – instead, he faked it on stage as best he could.

It's about one or two in the morning by this point. We make it to Hotel Ritz at Potsdamer Platz, the same place that Lulu and I met with Stone two years earlier. We thank Jeff for the lift and exchange hugs, then we drop into a bar for a short bit before finding a taxi home to our collective crash pad. Kasper has to get back to Copenhagen for his girlfriend's birthday, so he manages about an hour of sleep on a chair, while I crash and sleep for a good long while.

When I wake up later that afternoon with a bit of a headache, I slowly run through the events of the previous evening. I check my e-mail, and there are messages from Jeff, Birgitta and Stone. Jeff sent the festive group picture taken after the concert, and Stone wrote an e-mail three hours before the concert asking "Are you ok for tix?" If the mobile network hadn't been so overloaded by the thousands of people flocking to the concert, Erik might have also got in to see Pearl Jam. In Birgitta's message, she writes, "Stone says you got a greeting from the stage last night."

Wuhlheide, of all places! I didn't jump up and down yelling when I heard those words. I felt at peace within, and then I was in doubt: "Maybe Ed knows another Henrik?" But when I read Birgitta's message, I know it really happened. I was kind of like, "OK, I humbly thank you and hereby cease 18 years of stalking. Mission accomplished." But in another way, it's so completely different, heartwrenching, heartwarming and more all-encompassing than I ever could have imagined 18 years earlier when I met Eddie for the first time and was nearly obsessed with becoming his friend. At that point, such an outcome was probably about as realistic as a newsboy from Mumbai who dreams of becoming a regular guest at the Obama family's Thanksgiving dinner.

STOCKHOLM

After another half-day in summery Berlin, I take the trip out to Schönefeld Airport and meet up with most of the Norwegian crew from the day before, plus a horde of other PJ fans. We're all headed to see Pearl Jam in Stockholm, Sweden.

Veronica picks me up at the airport in Stockholm. She's taken the trip from Norway and is visiting her close Chilean friends, Pepe and Mary, who also fled from the Pinochet regime. They're musicians by night and researchers in the pharmaceutical industry by day – a fascinating and sympathetic couple with four daughters. All the travel and shenanigans have taken a toll on my body that I can certainly feel, but it's hard to turn down their hospitable company. It turns out that they don't live in Stockholm proper, but in the suburb of Södertälje, about 15 miles outside of the city.

As we enjoy Chilean wine, Pepe and Mary inquire with great interest into all of my endeavors. I quickly discover that the couple is very politically active, and despite the fall of the dictatorship, they still do not view Chile as a well-functioning democracy today. They explain with great conviction how large international (often American) companies actually control Chile and large parts of Latin America. They tell of extensive and well-documented water contamination that has been proven to cause cancer, particularly in children and the elderly. On one hand, it's frightening and depressing, and on the other it's fascinating to get this kind of knowledge from people with such political and scientific expertise, and who have paid the great price of having to flee their home country because of their strong beliefs.

I crash on the sofa and get a ride into the city center the following day. Veronica accompanies me, and the first thing we do is meet up with Birgitta and Ebbe, who

Jeff, Martin, Susan, Kasper, Henrik. Wuhlheide. June 26, 2014. Photo (selfie): Jeff Ament.

are staying at one of the city's good hotels. They're with a number of young Italian friends, all of whom have a relation to Pearl Jam and the accident. The Gustafssons have already visited at length with Stone and Eddie, and they're both looking forward to the concert. But they're also a little nervous. There's a bit of a problem with an extra ticket that she doesn't like asking Stone for, and Pearl Jam has invited 15 of Carl-Johan's old friends to the concert, who will also be backstage after the show. Nonetheless, their joy outweighs their nervousness, and it's always wonderful to see the Gustafsson family – and it's also great to meet the friendly Italians for the first time, after hearing so many good things about them.

As always, Eddie shows Birgitta his love. He meets her at the hotel and takes a long stroll with his arm around her shoulder. It's clear that they share a deep mutual respect and warmth.

Chile-Brazil

It's a big day for my Chilean friends – and not only because Pearl Jam is in town. It's the day of the World Cup quarterfinals, where the underdog Chileans – who have exceeded all expectations to this point – will be playing the World Cup hosts, Brazil. Veronica tells me that the atmosphere in Santiago is ecstatic. When Chile plays a game of this magnitude, all public transport halts to a standstill – not a single bus driver could dream of driving during the match. Passion!

Here in Stockholm, Pearl Jam will be playing that evening at the gigantic, but much maligned Friends Arena, which is notorious for its terrible acoustics. Two years earlier, the band's concert at Globen garnered rave reviews, but many people are afraid of what tonight's concert in the "echo chamber" is going to sound like. But around 25,000 tickets have been sold, and most of the incoming crowd doesn't seem to be all that concerned.

Veronica and I go to the stadium well in advance, thinking that they might have a big screen showing the soccer match. At the guest check-in, I meet Susan, who has an extra ticket because Martin or a friend of hers cancelled at the last minute. Our stickers are labelled SG, while hers are labelled EV – Eddie's guest. Unfortunately, Pepe's daughters are unable to join us, so we walk around asking if anybody wants a free ticket. Many people smile in disbelief and say no thanks. Everyone has a ticket, so this one remains unused in our pocket.

There's no big screen at the venue, but a nearby hotel is showing the match. Our tickets say both pre- and after-party, but not much was happening before the concert in Amsterdam or Berlin, so I'm not counting on this being the case in Sweden either. And we both really want to see this soccer game. We can manage both the game and the concert, as long as it doesn't go into extended time and a shootout. Which, of course, it does. The game is unbelievably exciting, with Chile managing 1-1 against Big Brother, but we can't miss the concert.

We find our Italian and Swedish friends, including Carl-Johan's friends, and we see a by all means strong concert, but without the same electric atmosphere as in both Berlin and Amsterdam. The Swedes aren't quite as energetic, and the gigantic hall feels cavernous and alienating. But the setlist is incredible, and almost mirrors what it would include if I could write one for the band myself. There are a lot of emotional moments during the concert. Eddie mentions the Gustafssons and the accident, and he dedicates *Daughter* to young Judith – Sandra and Johan's daughter, and Ebbe and Birgitta's granddaughter. (YouTube: Pearl Jam Daughter --- Stockholm 28.06.2014). At the time, Judith is eight months old and backstage with her mother during the concert.

As he does virtually every time he takes a stage, Eddie shows many sides of himself: from the emotion and empathy relating to the accident, to the punk-rock abandon, and an extended humorous séance where he autographs the shoe of a woman in the audience and then uses it as a wine glass on stage (YouTube: Pearl Jam's Eddie Vedder drinks Wine from a Shoe / Stockholm).

Strong emotions

Veronica and I belt out the songs along with Eddie throughout the show, while checking updates from the shootout on our cell phones. Chile scores, Brazil misses – yeah! But then the opposite happens, and at last it's goodbye Chile and Brazil moves on to the semifinals (where they would suffer a historic and cruching defeat to Germany). Despite her strong patriotism, Veronica takes it all in stride and is delighted to be seeing Pearl Jam live again.

After the concert, we all gather backstage, where we are welcomed with great warmth. We're with all of Carl-Johan's friends in a room with plenty of food and beverages. I know a couple of people from Carl-Johan's circle. I have a good chat with his friend Richard about his band, Danmarck (named in tribute to Carl-Johan's death at Roskilde) and I greet many of his other friends and their accompanying partners.

Stone, Mike and Matt drop by to say hi, and spend a long time talking with everyone. A few years back in South America, Veronica had her picture taken with Mike, but otherwise she doesn't really know the band members. I introduce her formally to the Pearl Jam guitarists, and they're all on the same wavelength in no time. Veronica is one big smile, looking as if she couldn't possibly be any happier.

I talk with a lot of the crew members, who I know pretty well by this time, including one of the long-time security staffers, Sonny, who asks with interest about the book project and much more. I'm sort of halfway inside, halfway outside the room, and after some time I see Eddie walking towards me, waving to Susan and me as if to signal "follow me." I smile to Eddie, walk over to him and ask him if he was trying to give me a heart attack with that dedication from the stage in Berlin two days ago. He laughs. We pass by Jeff, who's relaxing after the concert, and I say, "Thanks for the ride yesterday!" "Anytime, man!"

Rock stars and relatives

I'm with Susan and Eddie – the ideal place on Planet Earth after an ecstatic concert. All the elements for a party are present, and the abundant amount of alcohol in my system is calling for more. But the band is on tour – at work – so the backstage area needs to be chill. There's a concert in Oslo the very next day.

Pelle Almqvist and another member of the The Hives, Stone, Mike, Ebbe, Birgitta, Sandra, Johan, little Judith and a dark-haired woman are in what must be Eddie's room. Birgitta introduces me to the dark-haired woman: "Meet Marie Spokes." Marie is the mother of Roskilde accident victim Anthony Hurley of Australia. So, obviously, it's a moment that calls for respect and attention, and letting the wine wait. Birgitta tells Marie about the book, and I add that a major reason for writing and publishing the book is to honor the victims, with whom many readers will be able to identify. Marie Spokes holds my hand firmly, looks me deep in the eyes, and I can see that tears are beginning to well up. Although more than half of the people in the room are closely related to the victims (and nearly all the rest are rock stars), the mood in the room is by no means somber. It's a room full of love, attention and respect. Yet it's still something of a balancing act, as all the people present in that room have very strong emotions relating to this particular evening.

I leave Friends Arena together with Veronica. My fourth Pearl Jam concert in 12 days is over. Outside, it's absolutely pouring rain. But who cares about that when you have a personal driver named Pepe, who drives us to the door in Södertälje. He's even so kind as to give a woman we've met backstage a lift so that she doesn't have to swim home.

The next day, I think that I probably had a few too many beers. The numerous photos taken that night certainly indicate a festive atmosphere. I find a picture of me, Birgitta and Stone, where I put my baseball cap backwards on Stone's head right before the photo is snapped, eliciting a look of surprise. There's a good joker picture of Mike, and one of Birgitta smiling wide with her arms around the two guitarists, one on each side. Eddie's also feeling playful and has clearly lifted Susan's spirits, which couldn't come at a better time, as she's been going through a rough patch. Good times, good company, and as usual, we also manage to catch up on how it's going with all the kids.

I have lunch that afternoon with Ebbe and Birgitta, who have been through a few very moving days. Eddie in particular reached out to Birgitta, almost always wrapping his arm around her shoulder. Birgitta shows me a bunch of photos, including one where Eddie is holding little Judith and inspecting her affectionately, both in them photographed in profile: a heartwarming picture. It has been wonderful for the Gustafssons to spend time with Carl-Johan's friends, but of course it's also hard. His friends are now in their mid-30s, they've graduated from college and they have jobs, wives and children. Where would their son be today if things had gone differently?

After our lunch, I take the bus to the airport and write a message to Stone expressing my respect for the crew's work, and that's when I get an almost immediate response that has become something of a framework for this whole story: "In general it's always good to try to be low key back stage so I appreciate your thoughts about Smitty and Pete. They are just making sure Ed doesn't get swamped by people cause he wants to visit with everyone but this isn't always possible. I think in general, with us, the more you 'need' the less you get. If that makes any sense. All right enough of that talk and more Rocking in Free World. Love to you big fella."

It's then that I realize, much more than ever before, just how much pressure is on Eddie, and how incredibly important he is to so many people. For the same reason, there are unwritten rules that you have to sense and accept for the sake of everyone's well-being backstage, and to ensure that everything runs according to plan.

A moment of weightlessness

At the airport, security takes the Chilean wine that Pepe gave me, of course. I hadn't thought about the fluids ban, and they offer me the golden opportunity to check it in at eight times the retail price of the wine. After clearing security,

Veronica, Stone, Henrik. Stockholm, Sweden. June 28, 2014. Photo: Susan Nielsen.

The drunk and the straight arrow. Henrik Tuxen & Eddie Vedder. Stockholm, Sweden. June 28, 2014. Polaroid photo: Mike McCready.

The guitarists with their "favorite lady" in the middle. Mike McCready, Birgitta Gustafsson, Stone Gossard. Stockholm, Sweden. June 28, 2014. Photo: Susan Nielsen.

*Cutting loose. Susan Nielsen, Eddie Vedder, Henrik Tuxen. Stockholm, Sweden. June 28, 2014.
Photo: Mike McCready.*

I find a random place to sit. I ask the Danish women sitting next to me something about the setup of the airport's departures hall. It turns out that they were also in Stockholm for the concert. "Your voice sounds a lot like the guy who talks in 'P6 Beat Loves Pearl Jam.' I've heard that podcast a bunch of times," says one of them. I then reveal the obvious explanation behind the similarity, but I can't speak of the podcast itself, which I haven't ever heard.

I later meet the two – Sisse and Natascha – at that year's Roskilde Festival, and six months later Sisse shows up at a Gaffa Library Session, where I'm speaking with the popular Danish singer-songwriter Tina Dickow. Later on, I pull some strings to get a couple of tickets to one of Tina's concerts for Sisse and her mother, and get an e-mail from Sisse telling me that she owes me a beer, which we should drink with Natascha. We've already washed one down, and there'll be more to come. Another good friendship via Pearl Jam. It happens all the time.

And now I'm airborne once again, headed for Copenhagen. For the first time since the flight to Paris to interview Lenny Kravitz, I have some time and space to reflect over everything that's happened – everything I've experienced and everything that has been said. Four concerts in a relatively few days. It has all happened so fast. I'm sitting with the old-fashioned Polaroid picture that Mike took of Eddie and me the day before – Eddie standing straight with a ballcap, and me with a drunken smile and a draft beer in my hand. I feel the warmth and a deep-rooted sense of gratitude. And I shed a tear or two.

Back home, but not much time for relaxing. I'm behind schedule on a two-page article and a cover story that's due the next day, and I haven't started on either. Meanwhile, Roskilde Festival 2014 begins three days later and I've promised to write a review of The Rolling Stones, who are playing on the festival's opening day. But all of that will have to wait until tomorrow. I plop down on the couch, happy but thoroughly beat. I think about Pearl Jam and how the band is feeling right about now. Shit, man. I realize that they're about to take the stage in Oslo. A fun life, but a damn hard one too. My fumes are running on fumes.

LONDON

After Roskilde Festival, it's time for me and Lulu to embark on our more or less mandatory big city summer vacation. She wants to see Pearl Jam – no two ways about it – and she's chosen the tour's final show at Milton Keynes Stadium. I've heard about the venue for years, but have never experienced it first-hand. I know it's a big place. Jeff told me two weeks ago in Berlin that they had sold 38,000 tickets, and on the day of show I'd guess that the crowd was about 50,000, but it's hard to say exactly.

Lulu and I are accompanied by a couple of friends: the man behind the camera, Morten, and his guitar-playing son Mikkel, both of whom have already appeared in this story at the two Pearl Jam concerts at Forum in Copenhagen. And

Marie is in London to visit a friend, check up on a guy and see Neil Young at Hyde Park the following day.

Given that it's such a big and popular venue for London concerts, I assume that public transport will run relatively smoothly for the 50,000 or so of us that need to get there and home again. Unfortunately, that's far from the case. Very far. Well, it did go OK getting out to the venue, even though it's a bit further away than expected. Much like Wuhlheide, there's a bit of a walk through some green areas before reaching the stadium. We end up sitting on the train next to a super hyped fan from Israel, but we don't mention the fact that we know the band. We find our tickets. Food and merchandise stands abound, and entering the stadium itself is something of a shock. There's not a chair or physical seat in site, but just a huge green amphitheater with the slopes formed by nature itself. It's gigantic and stunning.

The personal favorites, Black Rebel Motorcycle Club, open the show, and Pearl Jam ends up playing for more than three hours. Sublime. Yet another perfect rock'n'roll summer's night in the otherwise climatically unreliable Northern and Western Europe. It's the last concert on the tour, and Pearl Jam gives it their all. I'm rocking out with Mikkel and focusing intensely on the timing of *Go*, yelling "tunnel vision" in Mikkel's ear right when Eddie hits the unconventional beat. Morten captures the moment on film.

Stone already mentioned in an e-mail that he was flying directly to Seattle

"Tunnel Vision." Mikkel Sylvester Larsen & Henrik Tuxen. Milton Keynes, London. July 11, 2014. Photo: Morten Larsen.

after the show, so there's no real reason to go backstage – and with our public transport odyssey to get here fresh in our memories, we decide that it's probably best to try to get back to London as quickly as possible. Easier said than done. Thousands of people everywhere, every trains in sight appears to have been cancelled, and far too few taxis that all cost a bazillion anyway. It's all getting pretty dire and irritating, but at last we team up with some other Danes to get out of Dodge. We finally find an unlicensed taxi and pile into the ice cold and way-too-small car. Behind the wheel is a driver whose knowledge of London's streets is less than adequate.

It takes damn near forever, and all the while we try to talk ourselves warm. It turns out that I've previously corresponded with one of our new Danish friends in the car, and he previously met Stone in Seattle via my contact. It's just one of the many inquiries that have dumped into my inbox along the way. Another was from a woman who wrote and asked me to ask Stone if he would propose to her boyfriend at Wuhlheide.

Frozen to the bone and more or less drained of funds by the exorbitant taxi fare, we make it back to the big city. Everyone hobbles back to their respective abodes, which for Lulu and I means our hotel. We sleep like rocks and wake up with an e-mail in our inbox from Stone: "Thanks for everything." He's already landed at Sea-Tac Airport, back home in the Pacific Northwest.

Chapter 17

2015: DÉJÀ-VU. SCANDINAVIA.

Déjà-vu. That's the subject line of the e-mail I send to Stone in March 2015, about 11 years after I met him and Liz at Hotel Skt. Petri in Copenhagen. Lovely Liz has moved on to another phase of her life today, but it feels like Stone is right alongside me on this day in 2015, as I endeavor on a solo trip nearly identical to the one I took with Liz and Stone back in 2003 – a trip that will forever remain firmly etched in my memory.

I'm now very close with many of the people that I was only just getting to know back then. But this time we're going to talk while the recorder is turned on, and do a proper interview. No Skype or e-mail. Face to face, and on their home turf. There's a hint of symbolic ritual to driving this route that we took so many years earlier, heading for experiences that had such a lasting impact on me and many others.

The topic at hand is rather obvious: What now, after all these years? Where are you now, how are you doing, how did the accident change your lives, can you talk about the loss, etc. The recorder is running and there's no script or specific agenda.

In midst of an otherwise busy period work-wise, I find myself this late Wednesday evening in a gray Renault Megane rental car, with a tightly-packed schedule for the coming days. My first stop is a visit to the Gustafsson family in Tranås, Sweden, then it's on to the Bondebjers in Falkenberg, Sweden. After that, I'll be taking the ferry from Varberg, Sweden to Grenå, Denmark and stay the night at my friend René's pad in Aarhus, followed by a meeting with Leo's old friends Tore, Jakob and Martin the next day. Then I'll return to Copenhagen in the evening and meet with Michael Berlin the next day for coffee and conversation.

And then there were all those who declined my invitation. "No hard feelings" is the general response, but they've had enough. Finn Tonnesen is friendly but also very clear and concise: "No thanks, no more." Their son Alex would also prefer not to rip open the sores once more, and the same goes for Jakob Folke Svensson's mother, who appeared in the Danish Broadcasting Corporation's documentary, *24 Hours We'll Never Forget.* "It was more than enough to participate in that TV program," she tells me, adding that she doesn't want to comment publicly on the matter anymore.

I don't contact the Thuresson family – it doesn't seem appropriate, since I've never met them by this point.

The process is a bit different with Lennart's mother and sister, Sharon and Denise. I have a number of short but good chats with Sharon, who after some consideration declines to be interviewed. Despite the defeat in court, the never-healing wounds and other hardships, she remains strong and collected, expressing a joy to be alive. In the aftermath of the accident, she divorced Lennart's stepfather. She now works as an in-home caregiver and spends a lot of time with her children. Sharon says that she has learned from the loss, expresses her appreciation for my efforts and suggests that I try to contact Benita again.

I get a hold of Benita by telephone and have a very pleasant 45-minute talk that ranges from Jehovah's Witnesses to her asking if I want to tag along to a Tori Amos concert. Like most of the family, she has maintained her bond with Jehovah's Witnesses: "I'm one of those irritating people who come knocking on your door," she says, followed by a hearty laugh. Hers is the uplifting story of a happy woman, husband and three children, long sailboat vacations and good jobs, and she exudes the same sympathetic and thoughtful calm I first encountered ten years earlier. She doesn't downplay the family's past problems, but she says that things have improved for nearly all of its members.

Yet not all of Benita's experiences in the aftermath of her brother's death have been positive. For example, there's the ongoing press coverage and general attention directed towards her and the family. The icing on the cake came in the form of a TV program a few years back, when she suddenly saw a private photo of her little brother filling the television screen – a photo that nobody in her family had granted permission to use. But, fortunately, she makes a point of thanking me for my work; in my contact with both her and her mother Sharon, Benita has felt understood and properly represented. Nonetheless, she has no desire to run through everything again in an interview. And so, her response ends up being the same as that of her mother: "Thanks for asking, but no thanks."

It's also important to note here that Benita in addition tells me that she doesn't have anything against my conveying the general essence of what we discussed in this telephone conversation, and Sharon has also expressed a similar sentiment.

We round off our chat, wish each other all the best in the future, and I promise to drop her a line if I'm planning on seeing Tori Amos live that summer. She also asks me to pass on her greetings to Stone and Pearl Jam, and says that nobody in her family blames them for anything that happened.

First stop: Lunch with the Gustafssons in Tranås

The trip from Copenhagen to Tranås is further than one might think, given that Copenhagen is just across the water from Sweden. My plan is to depart from Copenhagen at 5:00 a.m., but despite my good intentions, the departure time ends up being closer to 6:30 a.m. It's good that my rental car has plenty of oomph under the hood. As I plow north through the Swedish countryside's green forests, with local radio stations on full blast, all the memories play out in my mind's eye.

I stop at the designated gas station and await my chaperone for the last few, potentially confusing miles. While there, my trip down memory lane is temporarily interrupted by a phone call from my *Gaffa* editor, who asks if I want to interview Blur (one of my other all-time favorites) in London a few days later, which of course I do. In the midst of talking about Damon Albarn & Co., I see a face that always brings a smile to my lips: "Hi Birgitta!"

I follow Birgitta's car along the last couple of miles to Regnvädersgatan. Entering this now familiar home feels like visiting family, and it's always filled with the enticing aromas of Birgitta's culinary feats. I greet Ebbe, who is calm and grounded as usual. I always feel warmly welcomed here.

This visit might be a bit unnecessary, I think. I've spoken with both of them, especially Birgitta, at length on countless occasions, and met with them – both with and without Stone and Pearl Jam – at least ten times. They've become "Henrik's Swedish family" as my mother puts it. But conducting an actual interview that aims to summarize, reflect and put things in perspective on the record turns out to be something different altogether.

I don't have to look long in the kitchen to find a connection with Pearl Jam. The elegant designer candleholders were a gift from Stone to Birgitta on the occasion of her 60th birthday the previous week. Hanging on the fridge are wonderful photos of the band members with the Gustafssons: the whole family with the entire band when the Gustafssons were guests of honor in Paris, Stone and Liz from our first meeting back in 2003, and a classic close-up capturing the strong presence of Eddie Vedder as he holds up their eight-month-old granddaughter, Judith. If you didn't know any better, it could just as well have been a heartwarming father-daughter portrait, and it reflects a bond that's just about as tight-knit as they come.

Birgitta – Our relationship got a lot stronger after Paris in 2007, where Eddie dedicated the entire concert to us. The contact and our relationship has grown much deeper. At first I was really nervous, but I feel none of that today. I FaceTime'ed with Stone yesterday. He talked about the kids and we talked about the fact that you were coming up for a visit – regular everyday things you talk about with family and close friends. But I know that he's busy – that's the way it is, but we probably touch base about once every two weeks. We really appreciate our contact with the others too, but of course it's particularly special with Stone. I always send birthday and Christmas greetings to all of them – and they always reply. It was funny – the last time they played in Stockholm, I told everyone in the band: "If any of you want a Christmas greeting, then you'll have to give me your e-mail addresses." Sandra said, "No mom, you can't do that!" But I got them all, and we all laughed a lot.

There's a steady stream of smiles, but it's all rooted in a very serious foundation. Birgitta and Ebbe try to focus on expressing what they've gained, since the loss is so obvious and ever-present.

Birgitta – It's a completely different life now. Stone and the others are in my thoughts every single day. It's wonderful that we've had the opportunity to spend so much time with them backstage, where the atmosphere is always so good. We don't have quite as much contact with Jeff and Matt, but they're all incredibly warm people. Mike is really funny and always makes me laugh. And to think that the loss of Carl-Johan has given us these warm and wonderful friendships, and so many incredible and amazing experiences. Others in the same situation have only experienced loss, without gaining anything. This contact is a source of positive energy for us. Eddie gives the warmest, most heartfelt hugs, just like Carl-Johan used to. Sometimes I feel extremely privileged.

Ebbe – One of the things that has shaped my perspective is their focus on doing something for the less fortunate in society. There's all the money they donate, but also the way they draw attention to issues that affect the lives of disadvantaged people. I think that's huge – as is the close relationship they have with their fans, and how much they do to make sure that their fans enjoy themselves.

Birgitta – We also talk about the fact that it never ends. I discussed that with Stone when we were talking about your visit. But the positive far outweighs the negative. The relationship has delivered such incredible consolation. And when you first came here in 2003, I was the one who asked Stone if I could have his e-mail address, which he gladly gave me. I've written and spoken with Stone during tough times, and the accident also affected him deeply. I think that we help each other. It's heavy, but I'm not overcome with grief. Life does go on, and our love for our granddaughter Judith is indescribable. It almost hurts when I hug her, because I love her so much. I took her for a walk in her baby carriage, and a woman came up to me and gave me a hug and said, "You deserve this, Birgitta."

Through the years, the family has had a slew of memorable experiences with the band, such as the time that Stone invited the family to Venice about five years earlier in connection with a Pearl Jam concert.

Birgitta – We were there for five days but didn't go to the concert, which was at a festival – we just couldn't, and they understood. We had a wonderful luxury vacation, and several of the band members also had their families with them. It was so enjoyable. I remember saying, "Even the toilet paper is fragranced," to which Mike answered: "Well, I don't usually smell my toilet paper." I thought I was going to die – first from embarrassment and then from laughing so hard! "That's so Mike," Stone said. [Birgitta laughs] The two of them spend so much time together, even when they're not recording and touring.

Just as my circle of friends relating to Pearl Jam continues to grow, Birgitta and Ebbe have gained some new and significantly younger friends, many of whom are from Italy.

Birgitta – Mateo is a jolly fisherman who lives in Terni, Italy. Sometimes he's actually in Tranås, because there are good fishing conditions here. Mateo has arranged fishing trips for Italians in Sweden. He talked a lot with people in Tranås, and it turns out that his wife is a huge Pearl Jam fan and has written a book about the band, mostly for herself. I got a call from his Swedish contact, who said that Mateo's wife would really appreciate if she could contact me. At first I was a bit reserved about it, but it turns out to be an extremely good contact. I'm naturally very cautious if anybody asks about my relationship with the band, and Stone also says that I should be careful and not let others pressure me. But they've always been so incredibly nice, and there have never been any problems. I also managed to get them backstage tickets in Stockholm. When we visited them in Terni last summer, they said that they had been thinking about the fact that we lost Carl-Johan and that he would have been then same age as them today, and they suggested that we could be a part of their lives as much as we wanted. Age isn't a barrier for them. We were all there last summer in Stockholm, including you Henrik, and it was a fantastic experience for them. And we're also in close contact with another Italian man, Danielle. He was injured at a festival where Pearl Jam was scheduled to play. A storm with heavy winds came in and blew over a stack of speakers on one side of the stage, which fell and hit him. He was badly injured and ended up having to be hospitalized – in fact, he still limps on one of his legs to this day. It was before Pearl Jam's concert, so they didn't have anything to do with it, but Nicole visited him on behalf of the band anyway. Stone wrote an e-mail to me, saying that they had contacted him. Danielle is also in his mid-30s and later wrote a long e-mail to me, telling me about his life. We've Skype'd a few times and have met up at concerts – he's always funny and ends his e-mails with special twist. Those Italians always make me laugh. Mateo is a former stand-up comedian, and practically every time he opens his mouth, something funny comes out. It's so liberating to just be able to laugh so thoroughly.

One thing that struck me the first time I met Ebbe and Birgitta is how instrumental their Christian faith has been in their grieving process. And their faith remains intact.

Birgitta – It's our foundation and will never disappear.

Ebbe – But it has probably changed some in recent years. There are Christians who say that if you believe in God, then everything will take care of itself. But that's not necessarily the case. The accident has changed our lives and our faith. The essence remains the same, but it's also different in a way.

Birgitta – All of the Italians we speak with are believers, but the way they practice their faith isn't necessarily the same as mine. It's an individual thing. In 2014 we met Marie Spokes. We didn't know that she was the mother of the Australian victim of the accident, Anthony Hurley. A Swedish woman came up to me and told me that her son had stood with Marie's son during the Roskilde concert. In 2012, we met the sister and brother-in-law of the young man from the Netherlands who died, and now we were standing there with Marie. It brings out the strong emotions, and we stood and cried together.

Ebbe – Marie was staying in Stockholm for a couple of days, and we invited her to our home in Tranås. She was a little hesitant, but her friend convinced her to come and visit us. She came here by train and spent the night. It was truly fantastic.

Birgitta – She's dealing with a lot. Her husband left her about six months before Anthony died. But she's also staying active. For example, she worked for a time as a teacher in New York, and she visited Eddie at his home and he has had a lot of contact with that family. She also hosted the entire band at her home when Pearl Jam played in Melbourne. I see a lot of myself in her situation. We've been in contact with many family members of the Roskilde victims. At first we were with the Swedish families a lot – that's what we needed at the time, but those meetings have kind of stopped. Gert Thuresson said he felt that he needed to stop the tradition of meeting up twice a year, where we took turns as the hosts. There were no hard feelings, but it was mostly necessary in the initial years after the accident.

Before I turn off the recorder, Birgitta ends with the words that also serve as the opening of this book.

Birgitta – I would like to say something about safety to all those who might read or hear about this book. Think about safety, think about each other, take care of each other, and get out of trouble in time. Help others when you can. I would like to say that to everyone. We don't want something like this to ever happen to anyone. You don't want to rob anyone of their enthusiasm, but be careful. I would very much like you to write that. That's from a mother who lost her son.

Second stop: Falkenberg, with Ann-Charlotte and Sven-Anders Bondebjer

Having a clear reminder of what all of this is about fresh in my mind, I continue on to Falkenberg, located about 60 miles south of Gothenburg on Sweden's west coast.

Hopelessly behind schedule and with a sense of direction that wasn't helped a bit by my degree in geography, I once again push the envelope and take my chances as far as the speed limit goes. We haven't set a specific time to meet, so when I start getting close to my destination, I try to call the Bondebjers several times, but only get their voicemail. I'm getting close to giving up.

I call Birgitta, who provides driving directions by telephone, and suddenly there's telephone contact with the Bondebjers. I find the house, which is larger than I had remembered. It's good to see the Bondebjers again.

The fine weather from earlier that day has now turned into heavy rain, wind and darkness – not exactly barbecue weather. Coffee, cheese and crackers are served in the kitchen. It's the same place and the same room where Stone, Liz and I sat in 2003, virtually paralyzed by the family's overwhelming grief that permeated the room. Rarely have I met people so deeply affected, and although they maintain that nothing will ever be the same, their faces reveal smiles from time to time in a different way now.

The two other sons are doing well, and the family now has three dearly beloved grandchildren. Unfortunately, I'm running short on time, as the ferry only departs once daily. We don't manage to talk all that much on this late afternoon, but we do reestablish our contact in a very nice way, which later leads to us meeting twice that summer for meetings that are unifying and emotional on a completely different level. But the following is a small excerpt from what we manage to talk about on this short visit, where we saw each other for the first time in many years.

Ann-Charlotte – It became a different life. Henrik is irreplaceable, he's always missing. But we have to keep on, after all.

Henrik's mother measures her words. Grief still weighs heavily on the couple, but life has also gone on for the Bondebjer family, with many new relationships and a different circle of friends materializing after their son's death. As when I visited the farm in Falkenberg more than a decade ago, the family is actively involved in an association for those who have lost children.

Ann-Charlotte – They're people we can communicate with, and it helps to talk with them.

Sven-Anders – Everyone is there on the same terms. Whether you're a business

259

executive or an unemployed factory worker, the pain and the emotion is the same.

Ann-Charlotte – We've been very active in the association, attending a lot of meetings, participating on the board of directors and things like that. But it's often a long drive to the meetings, and we're starting to get old.

The fellowship they discovered in the association has meant a lot to the couple. They've also gained a new perspective on their deceased son's rock'n'roll heroes from Seattle, thanks in part to their having met with Stone Gossard again after our original meeting.

Sven-Anders – We were in Copenhagen a couple of years ago and met with Stone at a hotel. It was a very nice meeting. He invited us to come to the concert in Stockholm, but it's not really our cup of tea. We said that we might come to Seattle one day, which he was really happy to hear, but it's a long journey.

Ann-Charlotte also maintains a degree of wit and humor, and doesn't hold back from getting a few digs in on the Pearl Jam guitarist and her son Lars, who joined them in Copenhagen.

Ann-Charlotte – And all these people lined up and looked at Stone, even though he's so short and thin! We were in Copenhagen just by chance with our son Lars. He's a "modern dad," so he didn't mind leaving his kids at home to take a trip with us for the weekend.

I pass on a greeting from Stone and ask about the couple's other social relations. As they said back in 2003, a lot of old friends fell by the wayside after Henrik's death. All in all, the Bondebjers say that the accident had life-changing consequences, and also brought about a lot of soul-searching.

Ann-Charlotte – We've reacted and responded in our way. But you get more critical with age. It's become more serious, deeper. You change – it's not something we've chosen, but it's the way it has happened.

Sven-Anders – Some of those we thought were our best friends may not have been such good friends after all. But others have come into our lives and the grandchildren talk a lot about Uncle Henrik. Lars talks about him a lot and they see photos of him and visit his grave when they're here.

The atmosphere is distinctly positive, and although their words are tinged with pain, Ann-Charlotte laughs quite a bit when the conversation turns to modern fathers, and she asks me if I genuinely like Pearl Jam's music. She admits that she can hear something of value in a song like *Love Boat Captain*.

Sven-Anders is a sixth-generation pig farmer, but there won't be a seventh generation. "You can't force people into a profession," as he says. The two other sons have had success in their careers, but Henrik's little brother Johan was deeply affected by the accident. He did well in school, but had difficulty dealing with the grief over his brother's tragic death and his mother's serious illness. His parents tell me that he suddenly felt all alone in his grief, and he often says that you can't change what has already happened.

Before this visit, the last time I saw the Bondebjers was in Denmark's Eastern High Court, where Tyge Trier was representing the couple. That case lasted several years and was finally closed on February 2, 2010. Roskilde Festival was not ruled to have been legally liable for the accident. Regardless of how one looks at the course of events, it can only be seen as a loss for the parents represented by Tyge Trier, and for the Tonnesen family in their lawsuit against the festival. Although the process was a prolonged and disappointing experience, the Bondebjers maintain a great respect for lawyer Tyge Trier.

Sven-Anders – He was the one who convinced us. We had a lot of doubts in the beginning. But Tyge believed in the case. The ruling was a stinging defeat for us. The management of Roskilde Festival could have at least apologized. Their lives go on as before. Our lives are changed forever. As our son Lars says, "We've aged by at least 10 years because of all this."

We don't go any further into the subject – there's no reason to dig deeper into these emotional wounds. And there's another topic that's more important to the family to talk about right now. Since our last meeting, they've seen the festival grounds with their own eyes. Their boys gave them a weekend stay at Dragsholm Castle, located near the town of Roskilde, as a 70th birthday present. And since they were in the vicinity, they decided to visit the grounds where the festival is held each summer, despite the deep sorrow such a visit might trigger.

Ann-Charlotte – We had been previously contacted by a film production team who wanted to bring us to Roskilde to see the area, but nothing ever came of it. But when we stayed at Dragsholm Castle, we gathered up our courage and did it. We met a woman who was walking her dog in the area. She led us to the place, and we were all very moved by the experience. It was incredibly touching. It's hard to express in words.

After seeing the site of the accident in person, including the nine birch trees and the memorial stone in the middle, an idea had grown on the Bondebjers to engrave the names of the deceased in the memorial stone. Sven-Anders even suggests that they would gladly pay to have it done. We agree that I will discuss the suggestion with the festival's staff.

Time is running out, and I have a ferry to catch. We shake hands as I leave, and Ann-Charlotte says, "Take care," giving me a hug and caressing my cheek. It's a heartwarming moment. And it's a really good thing that I came for this visit. Once again. In our short time together, I see that despite the devastating loss that dramatically changed their lives, the Bondebjers also show signs of joy when talking about their grandchildren and other things. We also briefly discuss the fact that they will be appearing in Tor Kolding's (at the time) forthcoming documentary about the accident.

I had heard about Tor and the film project here and there, but had never met him, and I wasn't quite sure what the project was all about. But our paths would soon cross, just a few short months later.

We've got to get a move on. Sven-Anders may be a laid-back senior citizen, but any true Swede knows how to put the pedal to the metal when needed. Meanwhile, the weather has gone from bad to worse – the rain is pissing down and it's pitch dark outside. I follow Mr. Bondebjer's car for a while, and I know that I'll be completely lost if he escapes from my sight. I just barely make it. A short time later, as I'm sitting onboard in the restaurant and the ferry is departing from the dock, I get a text message from Ann-Charlotte, who writes that Stone and I will always be connected with the memory of their son Henrik. She thanks me for my visit and concludes with the words: "Death is cold and inevitable."

Third stop: Leo's friends in Aarhus

Completely exhausted from all these experiences and impressions, I arrive 4½ hours later on the east coast of Denmark's Jutland peninsula, then drive through the rainy night to Denmark's second largest city, Aarhus. It's an area I know well, as it's home to the headquarters of my primary employer through the past 20 years, *Gaffa*. I almost always stay with my good friend and colleague René when I'm in town. It's great to be there, and soon I'm laid back with my feet up on the table. But since I've basically done nothing but race around behind the wheel of a car all day, I decide to go out for a quick beer before bedtime.

Although it's not my home town, I run into a bunch of people I know at the neighborhood bar. I get to talking with a colleague from the music industry, who asks about my trip and floats a couple of sharp but undocumented theories about shady ties between the public authorities and Roskilde Festival back in the day. He believes that an investigation would be in order, and that the true story hasn't been told. I tell him that it's not my errand, but also that I don't intend to treat the festival with kid gloves – instead, I'm writing down my thoughts, what I see and hear, and quoting central figures who want to speak on the record. He's far from the first person I've had this kind of conversation with, and it comes as yet another example of how strong emotions remain tied to the accident and its aftermath. It has left deep scars and shaken countless people, not just those in the music scene. I return to René's pad and, after an overwhelming day, I sleep soundly before my meeting the next day with Tore, Martin and Jacob.

I meet the trio at Tore's home in Aarhus, where there's plenty of cigarettes, coffee and conversation over the next couple of hours. At first, all three of them recount their experiences around the time of the accident, which occurred nearly 15 years ago at the time of this interview. They speak calmly and thoughtfully, without a hint of hesitation. But it's clear that it was a life-altering event in the lives of all three men. Youth comes with a sense of immortality, and they were no exception to the rule. On the night of June 30, 2000, that sense of immortality came to a sudden end.

Jacob – Our innocence evaporated in the blink of an eye, and right in the heart of our most cherished haven. We were a bunch of unemployed fuck-heads who drank too much, and Roskilde was the place where we could come once a year and act however the hell we wanted. Nobody was going to come and stop us, we didn't have to explain ourselves, and to think that it was right there that it happened.

Leo's spirit and nature has been covered earlier in this book, but new details are added to the story during this interview, and I sense the immense influence that he had on his friends. Neither Tore, Jacob nor Martin had known Lennart "Leo" Nielsen for a particularly long time, but nonetheless he had a similar impact on them all. Leo was a wild and strong character who always went his own way. He was naughty as a junkyard dog, bright as a button, the kind of person who always led the charge, a wild child and a good friend. But you could also risk getting clocked if you were acting like an idiot around him. Although Leo had his demons, he was full of life, wild abandon and energy. And he was a huge Pearl Jam fan. He was insanely drunk that evening and absolutely euphoric to be seeing his favorite band.

Martin recounts how they were initially informed that their friend wasn't among the dead, only then to get a description that indicated the opposite might be the case – and which turned out to be true. The others add details about Leo's personality and relationships in their circle of friends as a whole.

Tore – Leo had experienced more things than most of us, and had been through more things, like distancing himself from his family's involvement in Jehovah's Witnesses. That time represented an important development in our lives, and Leo played a big role.

Martin – We had no idea that we were going to have to bury a close friend. It wasn't like a grandmother or an old relative. We were a bunch of people who hung out together all the time. We lived in a collective in Aarhus, where we laughed and cried, talked about death, joked about the darkest shit and all processed what happened in our own ways and figured out what it meant to us personally. It was a really intense period that we all shared and went through.

Jacob – Leo started going out with Astrid, who was my girlfriend's friend, and we lived together for a period of time. The accident had a huge fucking impact on my life for many years after the fact. I visited his grave a ton over the next three or four years, every time I needed to reflect on something, meditate or process something.

Tore – Reality came crashing in. It was a wake-up call. It had a huge impact on me and so many others.

Martin – I usually visit his grave in the spring, and we've put a photo of him there with some of the lyrics from *Immortality*.

Jacob – When I think about the first meeting with Stone, where we all played that song together, I still get so moved and feel such a deep gratitude. Stone said that he only had two hours, but he ended up staying there for five. I was so relieved that it ended up being so fantastic, him taking the time to come and visit our trashy little apartment in Copenhagen.

Martin – That was when it first began to get easier. And it was good, because I had also been really annoyed with them. I thought they could have sent flowers to the funeral.

Tore – It hit me really hard. It took like four or five years before it started to fade on the horizon, but it still pops up in us, and we always think about it when we're at Roskilde Festival.

Jacob – It did something to our circle of friends, it brought us all closer. None of us were really heading anywhere in our lives, as far as careers and those things go. I ended up on the front page of the paper, crying my eyes out – that was a pretty strange experience. The accident and the pain have definitely shaped my decisions later in life, but we were also in the midst of developing and maturing, where a lot of factors come into play – and this was one of the big ones.

I stick around for a long time, chatting with the friendly guys, and our conversation flows in many directions: Pearl Jam, choices in life, where the various people in their circle of friends are today, Roskilde Festival and the way it has changed over the past 15 years. Everyone expresses appreciation of the festival's focus on safety, but Jacob also feels that it has diminished some of the festival spirit that he loved so much.

Jacob – Roskilde is overly cautious now because of what happened, and I have a problem with that. Security and safety have become the mantra, as it has in society as a whole, where much of the punk, anarchy and hippie spirit has disappeared. It might have happened anyway, but the accident has definitely accelerated the process.

Leaving Tore's apartment, I think that the conversation didn't necessarily reveal too many new perspectives, but it did reinforce the sense of how much the accident has shaped the lives of these three men and many of their friends. The end of youthful innocence and the start of a new phase in life. They not only lost a friend, but also their haven, Roskilde Festival, as their collective culture and gathering place was turned on its head.

Fourth stop: Michael Berlin in Copenhagen

When Pearl Jam played in Copenhagen in 2002, I tried to get a hold of Michael Berlin, but to my dismay, I couldn't find him on Facebook or through any other channels. I was extremely disappointed at the time, because I've always found Michael's story particularly moving. The unfathomable and macabre experience of being saved by two people who would both soon lose their lives. The potential mental anguish of such a fate could weigh heavily on Michael's shoulders.

Drawing on the help of journalist Janus Køster from the Danish Broadcasting Corporation (DR), I finally locate him. Janus contacts me in connection with his research and editing of an episode of DR's series, *24 Hours We'll Never Forget*, about June 30, 2000. In his program, Janus chooses to focus on the stories of two of the victims: Lennart "Leo" Nielsen and Jakob Folke Svensson. Those who primarily talk about Jakob are Jakob's mother and his friend, Michael Berlin. Janus gives me both of their telephone numbers, and Michael is up for an interview. We agree to meet after my trip to Sweden.

Michael immediately comes across as incredibly nice and considerate. Not only can I ask him about anything, but he's also brought along a small cardboard box with newspaper clippings, photos and other things relating to the accident. And what I think will be a conversation to mainly summarize all that has happened, it actually opens up a brand new chapter of the story. You never know what you'll find when you turn over a stone.

Michael – Jakob and I were inseparable. We had played soccer together, rode scooters, chased girls, we were wild and definitely on a slippery slope. Even though we went hand-in-hand everywhere, Jakob was the leader. I followed him through thick and thin no matter what. I was really slim and he outweighed me by 50 pounds. If he had continued drinking like he did, which all indications were that he would, I definitely would have followed the same path. That's also why I became a plumber. Jakob got an apprenticeship as a plumber, so I did too. It was hard those first years afterwards, being all alone like that. Jakob's home was always open – that's where we could go and do whatever we wanted. We also visited his house quite often after the accident. We were all together there on New Year's Eve 2000, which felt very natural and healing. We were there the next year too, but that felt a bit stranger to me. So much time had passed, and we were in different places in our lives.

Michael dramatically changed his life in the wake of the accident.

Michael – I've now made some completely different choices in my life. The last picture I have in my mind of Jakob is him with a big smile. He was feeling wonderful, he loved the music and was so psyched to be at the very front of the crowd, and to help me, his close friend, crowd-surf all the way to the stage. Based on what I later learned, I think that the accident and his death happened right afterwards, so I think it came by surprise and suddenly. But the fact that I survived because Jakob and that German guy helped me has given me a feeling of guilt and a feeling that since I survived, I have an obligation to live my life for two people. At the very least, I have to take care of my own life, change my direction and not waste it on meaninglessness. As far as processing what happened, I've decided to be open and expressive. I've always talked about how it changed me. But in relation to all that with the lawsuit and the legal stuff, I've checked out. It was an accident. I don't need somebody to be judged as responsible. A thousand factors were at play.

There's a long way from a life of heavy drinking and drugs to completing multiple Ironman competitions, but nonetheless that's the turn Michael's life has taken.

Michael – Whereas we used to smoke a lot of weed and pound beers and fix PVC piping at work, I almost completely abstain from those things. I now work in an office, and in my free time I'm a running coach. The coaching work is mainly about getting people to believe that they can absolutely complete various races, even though they've never run before, just by changing their daily routine and lifestyle – and, of course, a little training. It's because I don't come from a particularly sporty background myself, and I chose to turn things around the year after the accident. I use my own personal example as an inspiration for others. I've trained and participated in triathlons intensively for many years now, which requires long-term, systematic training – and I've completed a number of Ironman races. So you could say that the accident ended up charting the direction of my life. I've learned how fragile it is, how suddenly it all can come to an end, but also how valuable it is, and I intend to use my life to the best of my abilities. What happened will always be a part of me. But I'm happy about where I am today, and I appreciate my life.

And I appreciate Michael Berlin. The ultimate tragedy proved to be a game changer for him. He found his independence and destination, and today he is a peaceful, well-balanced man with an impressive drive. As we part ways, we agree to stay in touch and add each other on Facebook.

I go home and start leafing through the newspaper articles that Michael lent me. There's a lot of familiar material, with many variations of things I've already read or recognize. But an article headlined "The Witnesses," published on April 1, 2001 – nine months after the tragedy – comes as a complete surprise.

Chapter 18

2015: DÉJÀ-VU. ORANGE STAGE.

The article headlined "The Witnesses" contains the detailed eye-witness account of two sisters who were standing in the front row at the Orange Stage from 5:30 p.m. to 11:24 p.m. – to the right of the stage as seen from the audience (Stone's side), the presumed epicenter of the accident. They both escaped miraculously, but the older sister Lea still has recurring nightmares 15 years later.

The sisters' experienced extensive safety failures during the course of that fateful evening, with security guards repeatedly failing to act, react, and take action in time, despite clear indications early on that something was very, very wrong. It comes as disturbing reading to me, and I wonder how I haven't come across these accounts before.

The following may be difficult reading for people who lost somebody close to them that night, so they might want to consider skipping this section of the book.

The article is written by Kåre Quist, a seasoned journalist and news anchor for the Danish Broadcasting Corporation known for his integrity and clout. When I later get a hold of Kåre by telephone, he grants me permission to reproduce the article in its entirety, telling me that the story also continues to rummage in his mind.

I quickly locate Jane Jaqué, who would very much like to meet with me and talk. She confirms that the contents of the article are correct. Jane is a fan, and the article presents an extremely precise timeline of events. What follows here are excerpts from the article, as verified by both Kåre Quist and Jane Jaqué.

Pearl Jam, shortly after the start of the concert, rocking out and unsuspecting of the impending tragedy. Jane, who is in the middle of the tightly-packed and tumultuous crowd, realizes just a few minutes later that a tragedy is unfolding and her life is in danger. Henrik is standing off to the side, behind Mike. Roskilde Festival. June 30, 2000. Photo: Jane Jaqué.

Pearl Jam, Roskilde Festival 2000

About ten minutes before Pearl Jam takes the stage.

Jane – I notice that something is pressing up against my ankles. I think it's a backpack, and complain to my big sister that somebody was stupid enough to bring a backpack with them to the concert.

Pearl Jam takes that stage and opens with *Corduroy*.

10:40 p.m.: Pearl Jam is playing its second song, *Breakerfall*.

Lea – I tell Jane that I'm annoyed by somebody who keeps kicking me in the ankles.

10:43 p.m.: Pearl Jam's third song, *Hail Hail*.

Jane – The "backpack" moves closer to me. Suddenly, I realize that it's not a backpack, but a lifeless body lying up against my left leg. I can feel the body heat. I yell to a guard standing less than a yard from me that there's a person in the crowd behind me who's not moving, and that we have to get him up. The guard says that he doesn't have time to deal with it.

Lea – I hear Jane yell to the guard standing right in front of her, and I hear him reject her pleas because he doesn't have time. I'm worried that people are going to panic if they hear Jane say that a lifeless body is lying on the ground.

10:44 p.m.: *Hail Hail* (continued)

Lea – I realize that a lifeless person is also lying behind me – and that he must have been lying there for five to ten minutes. What I had thought were intentional "kicks" was actually the shoe of a "buried" concertgoer. I realize that when the "kicks" suddenly move closer. I can feel that the shoe is turned the wrong way – that the person wearing the shoe is lying face down. A prolonged chill runs through me. I tell a guard, who listens to me, but he shrugs his shoulders and stretches out his arms to the side to show me that he can't do anything about it. I can't understand that nobody else seems to have registered that the two people fell down.

Pearl Jam plays their fourth song, *Animal*.

Lea – Another guard comes by, and I tell him that two lifeless bodies are lying underneath me and my sister, and that he has to do something so that we can lift them up. He actually tries to look down behind Jane and me, but he can't see anything because people are standing so close to each other. So he gives up and walks away.

Pearl Jam plays their fifth song, *Given To Fly*.

Jane – My sister and I have started to panic. We're constantly trying to get the guards to do something, but they're either ignoring us or they don't believe us. One guard directly accused me of lying. He says: "You're just looking for an easy way out," as if I just want some help over the barricades because I don't want to see the rest of the concert. The pressure from behind is extreme, and I realize that it's only a matter of time before I can no longer remain standing upright. My legs are completely fixated against the lifeless body under me.

10:53–11:00 p.m.: Pearl Jam plays their sixth and seventh songs, *Even Flow* and *MFC*.

Lea – The guards have clearly begun avoiding us. But as two guards are reaching out to catch a crowd surfer I grab a hold of them. One of them bends over so that she can hear what I say. When I tell her that two people are on the ground underneath the crowd, she yells "oh no!" and seems very troubled by the situation. I think that they're going to do something, but they don't come back.

11:02 p.m.: Pearl Jam plays their eighth song, *Habit.*

Lea – Seven people fall about three yards to my left. I see it out of the corner of my eye. When I turn around to see exactly what is happening, another group of people falls, a total of 13 to 17 people. It's obvious that they're desperate and can't get back up. They're on their knees and throwing their hands in the air for help. For a short moment, a "hole" opens up in the crowd. People desperately try to avoid stepping on those underneath them. I get a hold of a guard to tell him what's happening, but he hardly looks at me. His arrogant and condescending attitude shocks me. After a minute, people are pressed together on top of those who fell, who are now buried under the crowd. I start yelling, "People have fallen and can't get up! You have to do something!" while pointing to the place where people are buried.

Pearl Jam plays their ninth song, *Better Man.*

Lea – While I'm standing and yelling, I try to come up with something to yell that will capture the guards' interest. My desperate yell finally causes two guards to come over to me. They look down in the tangle of desperate people who have fallen. The guards freeze and are obviously in shock. Then they leave again. I notice as a person next to Jane comes to, after having been passed out for most of the concert. Since the guards won't help me, I start yelling to people that they have to step back, even though it's completely impossible at that point. People seem to have heard me, because I hear someone answer, "We can't!" And other people start yelling "Step back!"

11:07–11:10 Pearl Jam finishes *Better Man* and starts playing *Light Years.*

Lea – I grab the guards' arms and clothes to force them to listen. I keep shouting again and again: "You have to do something. People are dying behind me. We're going to die." By this time, the guards are clearly at a loss. Many of them say, "We can't do anything!", putting their hands on their heads or spreading out their arms in helplessness. I remember thinking: "I'm not going to survive this."

11:15 p.m.: Pearl Jam finishes *Light Years* and starts on their eleventh song, *Insignificance.*

Lea – I get a hold of a guard with a headset. That guard later turns out to be the person who saved Jane's and my life. At this point, because of the immense pressure of everybody pushing, Jane is almost horizontal, and can't see much of what is happening. The guard bends over towards me and removes his headset from his left ear so that he can hear me. I yell: "Look behind me! We're dying, people are dead! You have to do something!" He looks straight into the crowd and goes completely stiff. He goes over to another guard near the middle of the stage and then returns to where I'm standing, going back and forth a number of times. That gives me the strength to resist falling down under the crowd. I start yelling in both Danish and English "Stop the music!"

Daughter is the last song of the concert, but Jane and Lea aren't quoted in the article about what happened during this song.

11:24 p.m.: The music stops, and a few minutes later Jane is lifted over the barricades with the help of Lea, who was lifted over right before her.

A female doctor affiliated with the festival's medical staff calls 911 and it later becomes clear that the accident took the lives of nine people. Eight of those who died were standing in the same area as Jane and Lea. The victims were suffocated by the pressure of people on top of their chests.

Jane and Lea in 2015

I meet with Jane at a café in Copenhagen in early summer 2015. She tells me there was a lot of pressure after the article was published, including many strange journalists who came knocking at her door. But she withdrew from the public sphere because she had already said everything, as collected in this one article, and it hurts to talk about it. Apart from the article, she appeared in an interview on the television news and one other news program.

Jane had been a Pearl Jam fan since the early '90s, but by 2000 she no longer follows them as closely, even though, in her own words, she would sometimes "caress my favorite album, *Vitalogy*." Lea is more into pop music. The sisters agree to accompany each other to the other's preferred concert in the summer of 2000: Michael Jackson and Pearl Jam.

Due to the bad weather, the sisters don't arrive at Roskilde Festival until the day of Pearl Jam's concert. They decide to try to get as close as possible to the Orange Stage, and end up front row, right in front of Stone, who Jane says didn't appear to see any of what was happening. They've arrived far ahead of time, seeing concerts by Ziggy Marley and Kent before Pearl Jam takes the stage. Leading up to the Pearl Jam concert, the crowd grows quickly and Lea starts to get a little nervous. As early as the Kent concert, Jane feels something under her feet that she thinks is a backpack. I ask again about that, and she says that she's certain. As I later write to Stone: It appears to be incorrect that nine people died during Pearl Jam's concert – at least one person was likely dead before the concert started.

Jane – The crowd was already packed for Kent's concert, so leading up to Pearl Jam, the pressure of people pushing against each other got really intense. I've been in a situation like that before, but usually the pressure will let up occasionally.

But during Pearl Jam it was constant, people were being pushed from all sides. I've never been through something like that before. My body was twisted sideways by the end, and I was almost levitating above the ground, thinking, "It's only a matter of time." Luckily, there was a post I could hold on to while my legs were pressed against a guy who was lying lifeless against the barricade.

The police report

Jane – I was interviewed by the Roskilde Police on the Sunday after the concert, and later by the National Police. But there's nothing new to add to what's already in the article. Kåre Quist also asked at the time, "Why doesn't anybody know all of this? Why isn't it clearly stated in the police report, if you've been interviewed and told them everything?" Everything in the article is verbatim. When I got home, I wrote everything down everything I said to the guards – 20 guards in all. We talked to every single guard, that's for sure. I said every word. I wrote everything we had seen and sent it to Ten Club, but I never heard back from them. I don't know if they read it.

Jane (cont.) – When I saw the police report, I couldn't see anything that we told them in it. I simply couldn't understand it. We could recall everything in detail and we already had. I've always wondered about what happened. In the first articles that were published, I couldn't recognize the course of events as they were reported – it didn't seem honest. Accusations were being hurled through the air, including against the band, and I really didn't like it. And what they wrote in the police report was very limited. "Why didn't you write all the details in the report?" I remember asking. "We'll get back to you," was their answer, but they didn't. I just think the truth should get out. I think a lot of people really need that.

Jane (cont.) – Personally, I was a little reluctant, because it had been such a horrifying experience. The feeling of powerlessness that grew as we saw the guards come and look at us, and then leave again. I've never felt so powerless in all my life.

The sisters survived, and Jane remembers it as follows:

Jane – We were lifted over the barricades right when Eddie said, "Take three steps back" for the second time. That's when a little bit of space opened up and a guard pulled me over. When I got on the other side, I could see that Eddie was in shock. I was standing between him and Mike, but it's all hard to remember, it was so unreal.

Responsibility

Do we have an innate responsibility as humans? Could one of the guards have stopped the concert earlier, even though they were further down in the chain of command? It's a question that Jane has often asked herself.

Jane – I've thought about it a lot. We had spent a long time earlier that afternoon talking with many of the guards who disappeared. After all, we had been standing there for more than five hours by that time. They were looking forward to the concert, and they also thought it was a big day. Maybe that's why I felt extra let down. We had stood there chatting with them earlier. I worked as a Champions League guard at soccer matches in the 90s, both at Denmark's national stadium Parken, and at Brøndby Stadium, and I've always been really focused on the fact that you're responsible for other people when you're in that situation. There was something wrong with the chain of command. I've never been contacted by any of the guards or anyone from the festival. Over the years, I've hoped that one of the guards would speak up, because I know that there were some people who didn't do what they could have done. We got in contact with of every one of them, and they responded in different ways. They simply had no idea what to do, and they ended up turning their backs on us.

The psychological aftermath
The accident has remained in the sisters' minds and has strongly impacted their lives.

Jane – It's been hard to live with that powerlessness afterwards. I was in crisis counseling right afterwards, but I was in shock. I didn't have an emotional reaction until four or five days later. I've chosen to talk about it and have worked through my trauma, in part by going to Pearl Jam concerts and standing on Stone's side of the stage. My sister has taken the opposite approach, but she also saw much more than me during the concert, since I was sandwiched sideways. Ever since, she has avoided tightly packed crowds and still has recurring nightmares about that evening – she has a hard time sleeping at night and doesn't like it when I travel, because it makes her so nervous. She says: "I was at Roskilde, so I don't know if you'll be coming home again." I think that I've recovered from it pretty well, but it took me 15 years. My clothes were totally ripped to shreds and the underwire in my bra had cut through my skin. I thought I was going to die, but the thing that kept me up was that if I did, and my sister survived, then I knew she would feel guilty. And my sister also carries a burden of guilt for those who did die. We both agree that we did what we could. I've gotten over it more, while she still carries more of the pain with her. And if we feel that way, I think there must be a lot of other people who have similar feelings. I once thought, "This is going to change me forever." And it has. Some people repress the trauma, don't dare to deal with it, while others may not realize the gravity of the events they witnessed.

The head of safety – Roskilde Festival
I didn't originally get an interview with Roskilde Festival, but Henrik Bondo Nielsen, head of safety for Roskilde 2000, would now like to participate in an interview. One

of the factors in his decision is the positive experience he had with film director Tor Nygård Kolding's documentary about the accident, *Nine Rocks*.

Bondo started as a volunteer at the festival in 1980, joined the festival organizing committee in 1986 and later the festival's management. He became a full-time festival employee in 1998, and was the head of safety for the music stages in 2000. Ever since, Bondo has been heavily involved in safety issues, both inside the Roskilde Festival organization and through outside activities. He explains that although the festivals compete to book the acts, they work together when it comes to safety. This includes two annual seminars and a number of festival networks relating to safety. For instance, if a concert promoter such as Live Nation in England develops a documentation system for dealing with extreme weather conditions, they share it with Roskilde Festival, and vice versa. The point of these efforts is clear to Bondo.

Bondo – We all have chosen our own way of processing what happened, and ever since, safety has been the primary focus of my life and work.

In the period after the accident, the press talks with virtually everyone who thinks they have some form of expertise relating to the accident. One of Pearl Jam's and the festival's oft-quoted critics is Paul Wertheimer from Crowd Management Strategies, who says that the band has encouraged tumult through the years, that the festival's safety precautions were lacking, and that both parties could be sued for the accident. Wertheimer is a figure who Bondo doesn't care much for.

Bondo – Paul Wertheimer makes his living by criticizing, so that he can be brought in as a consultant. He's completely unprofessional and his views are unfounded, but some organizations hire him as a specialist. On the other hand, there are some very good researchers who have spent a long time studying safety, such as Morten Thanning Vendelø from Copenhagen Business School, who specializes in Crowd Safety Management. He has interviewed many of our staff, and he even worked as a festival guard here for four or five years.

How did the festival organization assess your safety precautions for the festival in 2000?

Bondo – Our view – and the view of many of our colleagues – was that our way of designing a festival was very advanced. We had wave breakers to eliminate the pressure from those in the back of the crowd, whereas many of our colleagues just used ordinary arches. Our view was that we had a good and safe system. That's why we were really unsure about what to do afterwards. It was later said that if it can happen at Roskilde Festival, then it can happen anywhere.

What was your experience in connection with the accident?

Bondo – I was at the Ballroom Stage, so I didn't get to the Orange Stage until most everything had already happened. We had an emergency response team that could be activated in the event of a crisis situation. The team includes representatives from the festival management, the police and the fire department, and at one point also included a representative of the hospital sector.

What exactly did you do in that situation?

Bondo – We took action in response to the disaster. But the unusual thing was that as soon as we had the emergency response team assembled, it was already over. There was no longer any danger, unlike if there had been a fire, for instance. So the work was mostly about establishing an overview. The situation was so extreme that we didn't really have a detailed plan in place for responding to it. Another very important thing was notifying the public of whether the festival was going to continue. There are a number of other things – the police cordoning off the scene of the accident, confidentiality issues, not releasing the names of the victims, etc. There are some very specific procedures that you have to follow.

How has that event impacted the festival's self-image and direction going forward?

Bondo – In 2001, we were overly cautious, which is understandable enough. Since then, we've tried to find a balance, where the crowd has the freedom to cut loose and be spontaneous, but in a safe environment. Crowd surfing was previously the norm, but afterwards it was banned in most of Europe. Not because it's dangerous in and of itself, but because it prevents guards and safety staff from seeing what's going on and ensuring that people in the crowd are OK. But there are challenges. A lot of people crowd-surf today [2015], and the average concertgoer in the front rows was only five or six years old when the accident happened, so it's not in their consciousness. "That was in the old days. They were idiots. Today we're immortal." That's the typical youthful reasoning. It was totally different in 2001 and 2002 – everybody was completely tuned in to safety. We were practically drowning people with water, we had guards everywhere, and we can see in aerial photos that the pit was half-empty. But there's an interplay based on traditions. We have to keep up with our audience. Take "Wall of death," for example, where people run into each other – it isn't dangerous by itself, but it is if the other people in the audience don't know what it's all about.

The Roskilde spirit

Was the Roskilde spirit in danger of disappearing after the accident, and what about your own work and personal grieving process?

Bondo – We were very concerned that many people in our organization would give up after the accident. But on the contrary, a team spirit arose. "We can't leave off on that note." So we rediscovered our enthusiasm and drive. I also think that the experience we've been through gives us a certain strength. The inscription on the memorial stone says it all: "How fragile we are."

How do you see yourself in the Roskilde Festival organization going forward?

Bondo – I think that I have a lot left to achieve in safety, so I think it makes sense to stay here and do what I can. I still love being a part of making Roskilde Festival happen. My motivation has been that if something can be done, I want to contribute to the best of my ability.

Kåre Quist's article from 2001 raises some serious questions about the chain of command during the accident, as guards didn't react to pleas from the crowd. What went wrong?

Bondo – That's also what the police report points to: there was a lack of clarity and uncertainty about who was authorized to stop the concert. And that's also a balancing act. Historically speaking, if you look at stopping concerts featuring the most popular bands, people sometimes go berserk, which can be even more dangerous. Morten Vendelø interviewed many of the guards and found that there was great uncertainty. Now it is clear: there is one designated person who makes that decision. There's a security manager with the ultimate responsibility, and this person has a number of supervisors at strategic locations, and the ability to see everything in detail with remote-controlled security cameras. There are also supervisors at the entrance to the barrier system. If rank and file staff see a problem, they go directly to their supervisor. Another challenge is that it's hard to get experience with a situation similar to Roskilde Festival. It's not like in soccer, where you have 40 matches each season. So we also work closely with the artists. For instance, Lars Ulrich said something to the audience in 2003, in close collaboration with Metallica's tour manager and our stage manager. For the same reason, we have chosen a more formal and informative MC role than somebody who comes out to entertain and rile up the crowd. But on the day of the accident, things actually moved very quickly once the accident was recognized. The problem was that the recognition phase took too long. At the time, you could only see what was happening from the stage. Now we have many more options in terms of technology, cameras, the location of observers, etc.

There was a widespread view that Leif Skov was "the strong man." Was there a high level of control at the time, making people reluctant to take the initiative and go against his wishes, and which could have had an adverse impact on the course of events? After all, he left his life's work the following year.

Bondo – I'm not able to say anything insightful about that. I don't think that Leif as a person had scared anybody from making a decision, but I think that we weren't clear enough in our preparations and our communication at the time. I think the fact that Leif chose to stop in 2002 is closely related to the accident, but I don't think that any of the problems were a result of overly centralized power in the organization. In my view, all of the attention on Leif as the head of the festival was a very simplified portrayal by the media. When I look at the choices and decisions that were actually made, Leif played a big role, but he certainly wasn't all alone in the process. Henrik Rasmussen was also in the management back then, just like today, and all three us – Leif, Henrik and myself – can be really annoying and focused on every last detail, which can probably be said of many managers. But I've always seen Roskilde Festival's strength as a product of its being a collective effort.

The trial

Those who sued ended up losing, and many have been left with a feeling of loss, emptiness and powerlessness. How do you feel about that?

Bondo – That's the thing I find the most regretful – the fact that everybody was so far from being on the same page when they tried to talk with each other. At the time, it was compared to a lawsuit involving SAS and a plane crash in Milan. There's no doubt that, as the event organizer, we were responsible for safety and we still are to this day. Whether it was our full responsibility and our fault that people died that day, that was what people wanted us to say. I think there's a difference.

Did you visit any of the families after the accident?

Bondo – I drove with Leif in the car to visit the Bondebjers, among others, but we decided that he should go into the house alone.

The Bondebjers thought that he came across as very cold, whereas the Gustafssons had a much more positive impression of Leif.

Bondo – I would put it this way: I believe that the lawsuit Tyge Trier was pursuing was extremely unfortunate. I think it would have been better for all those involved if we had tried to figure it out together. You rarely achieve anything positive with a lawsuit, especially in a case like this one. What kind of settlement do you want to achieve? In my view, they sought to achieve something through the court system that would have been more attainable through a dialog. For example, we have close contact with the family from the Netherlands and they come here every year. We don't think that they should be made into some kind of special institution with a lot of attention, but we're extremely glad that they keep coming back to the festival.

In terms of the lawsuit, was there a fear of establishing a precedent regarding liability, and was it fear shared by other event organizers, soccer clubs, etc.?

Bondo – I don't know, but when a lawsuit is filed, the positions typically become more distant and rigid than reconciled. In the period after the festival, we tried to do what we could. I met with the Tonnesen family and showed them where their son died, and I also experienced a genuine desire on the part of Leif to do everything we could, which of course was mostly of a financial nature. We couldn't undo the accident. But much of what people remember has to do with conflicts. And I don't know how I would react if it were me in that situation. I have four kids around that age, so I have a pretty good understanding of why it broke people's hearts. At first there was one family, the Tonnesens, that wanted a lawsuit, and then Tyge Trier got involved and took on the case, probably without getting paid. But I don't want to comment further on that matter. But another thing I'd like to say is that there weren't any guidelines for an organization like ours to obtain a permit to hold a festival. In the permit conditions, it said that there had to be an "adequate number of guards," which was very imprecise. The requirements and specifications are now much more precise. Back then, the requirements varied greatly according to which police district had jurisdiction. Today there are standardized nationwide rules, including the rules on safety plans.

There were also critical voices that accused the festival management, the city and the police of being much too intertwined at the time. They claimed that because the festival is so important for the city's businesses, reputation and economy, the authorities were less critical. For example, Jane Jaqué found that her and her sister's very precise criticism was toned down in the police report.

Bondo – It's not true that you could just get away with anything because you were good friends, or that the festival and police shared ceremonial bottles of schnapps after the end of a festival. Instead, I would say that the norm in Denmark for documentation and regulation by the authorities was at the level that it was back then. The police in Roskilde are very experienced, so it's only natural that the police, event organizer and authorities have close cooperation, which can lead to a relaxed tone. That's how it was then, and that's how it is now. I'm going to Norway soon and giving a talk together with a policeman who also works in the field of safety. I firmly believe that this cooperation and common understanding improves safety at the festival, and not the opposite.

Have you, as the festival management, and we, as the audience and general public who experienced the accident, learned anything that we can pass on? For instance, to audiences and event organizers in South America, where similar major accidents have occurred?

Bondo – It's always difficult to transfer culture. But the accident has created a culture at the European level, both formally and informally, in terms of behavior in crowds, where taking care of each other is more explicitly discussed than before. And the fact that we as festivals have an ongoing cooperation regarding safety issues keeps us updated on the latest developments and enables us to predict and better prevent potential disasters.

Morten Thanning Vendelø

The storyline of this book is intentionally not one of investigative, in-depth journalism, but more a description of all the incredible events, connections and human stories I've encountered along my way – driven by equal parts coincidence and general curiosity, where the common thread for nearly all those appearing on these pages is a special affinity for the quintet from Seattle.

Nonetheless, I feel the need to seek out Morten Thanning Vendelø from Copenhagen Business School. I don't know any of the guards, and Jane Jaqué's fully verified narrative makes the guards seem somewhat cynical in my eyes. The story could use a more nuanced picture – something that gives the guards a voice, which Morten can help to provide.

I find him quickly, as his office is less than a half mile from my steady part-time job. The first thing he does when we meet is he takes my book in Danish about Pearl Jam from his bookshelf, and tells me that he's studied it carefully. Morten is an organizational theorist specializing in disaster management and crowd safety management, and for obvious academic reasons, he's spent a lot of time studying and trying to understand the accident at Roskilde Festival 2000, in collaboration with Associate Professor Claus Rerup from the University of Western Ontario in Canada.

He's spoken with numerous sources involved in or with the festival, including interviews with many of the guards, and he later worked a number of times as a guard at the Orange Stage to experience first-hand what it feels like when (as he puts it) "50,000 people are roaring in your face."

The researchers sought to examine questions such as: Why did it go so wrong? When did the guards realize that something was wrong? And why did it take so long before the music was stopped? Determining who was at fault was not among the issues they examined.

What have you previously found, Morten, about why the guards didn't stop the concert much earlier? At least some of them knew that the situation was extremely serious.

Morten – There were a lot of elements at play. First off, it's important to understand that there was absolutely no precedent for an accident of this nature. The festival had never before stopped a concert. The few times a concert was stopped ahead of time at Roskilde Festival, it was the artists themselves who stopped it. When we later asked about the "worst case scenario" that guards had imagined, they've said things like "a smaller person getting stuck who they couldn't help out," "a stage diver coming over the front barricade without them managing to catch him or her" – things of that nature. Nobody had imagined anything like what happened, and for the same reason they had no experience in dealing with that kind of disaster. Then there's the fact that the festival rightly thought of itself as a leader in terms of safety. Other festivals had inquired for years about Roskilde's latest safety initiatives and measures. However, there's no doubt that there was uncertainty about who was actually authorized to stop a concert. It is also a fact that the stage manager – a key person in the organization at Orange Stage – was talking on his cell phone with his girlfriend in France during the concert, but it's hard to say whether that had any influence on what happened. And it's important to understand that there were three layers in the safety organization. There was the front barricade arch, with about 40 guards – more came over from the side as it was happening – but there was only one supervisor who had radio contact with three guards on the stage. They had a different overview, and the contact between them and the supervisor of the front barricade arch covers things like whether holes are forming in the crowd, etc. Behind the stage was the production office, which could listen in on the radio communication, but it was unclear whether it was the production office, the stage manager, the guards on the stage or somebody else who was authorized to stop the concert.

But Jane's story makes it clear that some of the guards knew that things were very serious a long time before the music stopped.

Morten – Some of them knew that it was terribly serious, and others didn't. For one thing, the guards' experience varied greatly, and they were trained to have tunnel vision – which means that each guard was responsible for keeping a close eye on what was happening within a two- to three-yard-wide corridor of the crowd. As you can hear in the P3 radio documentary that tried to run through the course of events, there's a huge difference between what people who were standing very close to each other saw and experienced. And at the time, we're also talking about a history of about ten years of many wild concerts, which was part of grunge culture – it was an atmosphere that they were used to handling. Typical things they would say after a Sepultura concert or the like were along lines of, "Wow! Things were really wild tonight, but we did it." And the view for many of them that night was extremely poor because of the many crowd surfers, which made it really hard to see what was going on underneath, further back and to the sides. In the past, they had a lot of experience with audience members helping each other up when somebody fell. And in terms of guards, you also have to remember that the focus in the past was on the artists. Johnny Winter stopped a concert at Roskilde Festival in 1984 when somebody in the audience threw a bottle at him. That same evening, Lou Reed announced that he refused to play the next day unless a high fence was placed in front of the stage. They put up the fence, and Lou Reed played. You see, the focus was on the artist. The most recent example at the time, which many of the guards still remembered vividly, had been four years earlier, when the Sex Pistols stopped after 20 minutes and the crowd starting throwing all sorts of objects at the guards at the front barricades. They learned then that it can be rather dangerous to stop a concert. People often don't understand, and they get furious. As glass bottles continued to fly through the air, the guards were told, "Run away as fast as you can. Take cover!" And a lot of the same guards had been there for that concert. If all hell breaks loose, it's just a matter of getting away and finding somewhere safe. But back to the question. There are perhaps four guards who saw and understood that it was extremely serious around *Better Man*, which is when the major part of the accident occurs. It's estimated that a hole measuring about 3 x 4 yards formed for a short time about two to three yards in front of the front barricades [Morten Vendelø has maps and graphs where all of this is detailed]. This was caused in part by "trains," where one person pushes through people and others follow behind with their hands on each other's shoulders, so they push forward in a collective group. At the same time, a lot of people are crowd surfing, and suddenly there are no hands to hold them up, and nobody can manage to pick them up before an enormous pushing force comes in from all sides, and suddenly it's not two, but three or four people on top of each other, and that's when it goes terribly awry. But it's one thing to see it happen, and another thing altogether to get the concert with the evening's headliner stopped. Pearl Jam's tour manager, Roskilde's stage manager and the head of the production office collectively decide to stop the concert. Nobody from the festival management was present during the concert.

How have the guards generally reacted to the accident?

Morten – I've spoken with a lot of them, and some are very outgoing and talk about their experiences, emotions and thoughts, while others keep it bottled up, and others didn't work through the experience until years later. For all of the guards, it was a fateful and traumatic day in their lives. One of the safety supervisors didn't sleep for 36 hours afterwards, because he was trying to come up with a new safety system. He talked about how he became completely manic. Many people have stayed in the organization, and many are still guards at Roskilde Festival today. Others have left the festival forever. There was a joint meeting for all of the guards and staff involved that same night. A number of the guards said that they perceived the management's statement as a denial of responsibility. That made some of the guards feel like the burden of guilt was placed on their shoulders, which led many to cut ties with the festival and never return. Others have found it hard to represent the festival in the aftermath of the accident.

Chapter 19

2015: ROSKILDE FESTIVAL.

Not long after my deeply shocking conversation with Jane, I'm headed for Los Angeles on a journalist gig. First I'll be interviewing Muse, followed the day after by the rising Danish star, singer Lukas Graham – a guy I know pretty well by this time, and who is with his crew in LA to record the songs for their international debut. One year later, they would enjoy greater international success than any Danish band in history.

As on my previous visits to the States, I seize the opportunity to make a pit stop in Seattle, but this time around I only have a couple of days to do so. I write to both Stone and Jeff to hear if they're in town. It turns out that they're both in California – the place I just left. Stone and I could probably manage to wave to each other from the air above Seattle, since he's arriving at Sea-Tac around the same time that my plane is departing for Europe.

To top it all off, when I ask my host Johnny Sangster if anything of interest happened the day before I arrived, since it was Record Store Day, he tells me that Eddie Vedder played with The Sonics in downtown Seattle. "Timing is everything," as the lyric goes in *MFC* from *Yield* – and in this case, my timing couldn't have been worse. In principle, I could have made it to town in time to see Eddie and The Sonics.

Tor Nygård Kolding

I've been corresponding lately with Stone (and to a lesser extent Jeff) about my meeting with Jane and Henrik Bondo, interviews, this book and the coming launch of its Spanish translation in Chile, and about Stone and Pearl Jam's involvement in Tor's forthcoming documentary about the Roskilde accident. I also get a hold of Tor, who is well aware of my existence, and who says he considered contacting me on several occasions. Shortly after this initial contact, we arrange a rather unusual meeting, where we'll be interview each other. I've bring along my recorder and Tor brings a film crew with him to shoot our conversation. Tor's story is both special and frightening – and he has great empathy for the fact that the accident triggers many intense and difficult emotions for the many people whose lives it impacted.

In 2000, Tor is a 20-year-old Pearl Jam fan standing near the very front row when his idols from Seattle hit the stage on the last night of June. Unfortunately, he is standing in the exact location where a number of people would die a short time later. Tor quickly realizes the danger at hand, but like everyone else around him, he has zero control over the situation. When the crowd falls, Tor falls with them. He estimates that he had two or three people on top of him, and at least one person underneath him. How long it all lasted and what exactly happened remains unclear, but Tor believes that he lost consciousness two or three times and, paradoxically, experienced a sense of peace and calm, like a voice saying, "Just relax, lay down and sleep." And almost like the angel and devil battling on opposite shoulders in a cartoon, the angel implored him, "If you go to sleep now, you'll die!"

The angel watching over Tor Kolding that night comes out victorious. He struggles back to his feet and fights to breathe, breaking free from those laying on top of him and miraculously surviving the inferno of chaos, where the duration and sequence of events remains unclear to Tor to this day. Did it last 5, 10 or 30 minutes?

Although the angel won that initial struggle, enabling Tor to defy the odds and survive, the devil later plagues his conscience: He saved his life and escaped, but at what cost? What happened to the person lying underneath Tor, who unavoidably became Tor's physical springboard to escape from the tumult? No matter how illogical it may seem, this guilt gnaws at nearly all those involved in this accident and similar disasters. I've met so many of the people involved in the accident that I now recognize some archetypical patterns of reaction. Some people want to know everything, read every newspaper article, see every television program about it, talk with friends and family, and consult with psychologists and other therapists, while others choose to repress and forget the painful memories. Tor belongs to the latter category. Although relieved her son returned home alive from the festival, it becomes clear to Tor's mother that he is deeply changed. Tor is both wounded and hardened in the wake of the accident. His innocence, invincibility and youthful optimism are no longer.

Wake-up call

Tor doesn't return to Roskilde Festival for many years, and can react forcefully if somebody puts on a Pearl Jam album in his presence. He consciously and unconsciously distances himself from everything that happened on that tragic summer night. By nature, Tor is essentially a nice and amenable guy, so despite being hardened by merciless fate, life goes on and time heals all wounds and so forth – yet something remains unresolved. When an old friend, almost by chance, shows him some snapshots from Roskilde 2000, Tor sees a picture of himself after the accident where he's turning away from the camera, almost as if in shame. As if he has something to hide.

This experience comes as a kind of wake-up call. By this time, Tor has completed his studies in filmmaking and become a father for the first time. He realizes that there are still some things he needs to work through, not least for the sake of his young son. Tor spends the next five years working on the documentary *Nine Rocks*, a tribute to the nine victims. The film changes shape several times along the way, from an analytical overview to Tor's deeply personal account, where he shares his deepest emotions with a priest, his mother and others. Tor is the first person to conduct an interview with a representative of Roskilde Festival's management (Henrik Bondo) about the accident, and the documentary also presents an in-depth portrait of two of the families impacted by the accident – and their vastly different courses of action afterwards.

One of the families featured is the Dutch family, the Nouwens, who have attended the festival every year since the accident, celebrating and honoring the life of Frank, their deceased brother/cousin/son. As his sister Kathy puts it in *Nine Rocks*, "We think it's wonderful that we can come and pay homage to him here – the place we love, and which he loved most of all. It would be completely different if, for example, he had died in a traffic accident at some random intersection."

Tor and I quickly tune into the same wavelength, giving each other feedback on the other's work and process. Much like myself, Tor has received great assistance from Pearl Jam's management, and from Stone Gossard in particular. Without being privy to the exact details, Tor was granted permission to use Pearl Jam's music in the film, and Stone has been helpful with all the practical and legal aspects relating to a large-scale film production. Tor is disappointed, but also understanding of Stone's decision to not participate in an interview for the film. Instead, he offers to write a kind of introduction to *Nine Rocks*:

"June 30, 2000 is a date that I will never forget. What was meant to be a day of people coming together and celebrating their love of music, ended in the loss of nine lives with thousands more left deeply impacted by injury, grief and loss. Processing grief is a very individual thing. Tor Kolding's process included making this film about his experience in the months and years that followed. Tor conveyed to me in recent

correspondence that he hadn't spoken with one single guy or girl in the audience
that day that didn't feel some kind of guilt over what happened. I can relate. My
hope is that this film – and the journey he embarked on to create it – helps Tor and
others to process the horror of that day."

- Stone Gossard, Pearl Jam.

The Bondebjers and Jane

Tor and I talk at length about our common acquaintances, Sven-Anders and
Ann-Charlotte Bondebjer, and about my meeting with Jane, who was standing very
close to Bondebjer's son Henrik during the concert. After Jane shared with me
the details of her experiences in the front row that day, she reads through the first
edition of this book and can say without a doubt that she was standing nearby and
spoke with Henrik Bondebjer. I feel the need to pass on this information, writing to
the Bondebjers that I've met a woman who spoke with and met their son shortly
before the accident, and that she would like to contact the family if that is OK with
them. The family is clearly moved, and in her reply to me, Ann-Charlotte asks if
I think it would be a good idea for them to meet with Jane. I write that I have no
way of really knowing the answer to that, but that I found Jane to be a sympathetic
and honest person, although her story is not necessarily uplifting.

During this same period, Tor is in dialog with the Bondebjers, who are considering
an invitation to attend the premiere of *Nine Rocks* at Roskilde Festival on June 30,
2015 – the 15th anniversary of the accident and the last of the so-called "warm-up"
days before the official opening of the festival. (Roskilde Festival opens the campgrounds several days before it opens the festival grounds. People arrive early to
secure a good camping spot and to get a head start on the festivities during these
"warm-up" days.)

The Bondebjers decide to meet with Jane, and would prefer to do so face to
face in Copenhagen. I offer to host the meeting at my house, and on June 9, Jane,
Tor, Sven-Anders and Ann-Charlotte all meet in my dining room over a meal of
vegetarian lasagna. I'm rather nervous about hosting this meeting. How will the
Bondebjers react? Will it be too intense or cause a backlash, and what kind of
situation will that put Jane, Tor and me in? Deep down, however, I believe that it
will be a positive experience – and my gut feeling turns out to be correct.

We share a couple of heartfelt hours together, moving from the epicenter
of the tragedy to liberating laughter and telling stories from our lives. Near the
end of our meeting, Sven-Anders shares his fascination with Louis Armstrong,
and Ann-Charlotte, who previously teased Stone and me about our "youthful
rock'n'roll lifestyle," admits with a smile that Pearl Jam actually has a few pretty
good songs in their catalog. But of course, it's meeting with a predominantly
serious tone. It's clearly emotional for the Bondebjers to meet Jane, who respectfully
tells them how Henrik was initially so ecstatic to be near the very front row for

Pearl Jam at Roskilde Festival, only later breaking into panic as people futilely tried to help him, yelling "Help him over the fence, he's blind." Jane describes with conviction and honesty how Henrik seemed both lucky and happy until shortly before his death. Ann-Charlotte, Sven-Anders and Jane exchange long hugs, tears are shed all around the table, and Sven-Anders expresses how special it is for them to meet one of the last people to be with Henrik before his death. The Bondebjers have lost contact with Henrik's friend Anton, who accompanied him to Roskilde, and who has apparently also been plagued by guilt about the course of events.

The lawsuit and the forthcoming festival three weeks later are also discussed. Ann-Charlotte reads aloud from the letter she sent to the female attorney who represented the festival. The letter is written "woman to woman" and talks about how losing a son is a wound that can never be healed.

The attorney's response to Ann-Charlotte is no less personal and heartbreaking. Her deep personal respect as a mother and understanding of Ann-Charlotte's situation are incontrovertible, and the reply also acknowledges the cold and often brutal nature of the legal system when it comes to representing parties in dispute. It's beautiful, thought-provoking and thoroughly moving.

Nine Rocks is slated for screening at the festival three weeks later. I offer to help with all the practical details if the Bondebjers decide to attend, as I know that Tor will be very busy that day. When Sven-Anders and Ann-Charlotte are leaving later that evening, they say that they think they would like to attend the premiere, but that they need to go home and think things over and process their meeting with Jane, which has triggered a lot of strong emotions, both heartwarming and unpleasant.

Roskilde Festival, June 30, 2015

On June 27, the Bondebjers announce that they've decided to come to Denmark and Roskilde Festival. I coordinate the logistics with Tor and his dedicated press agent, Claus de la Porte (who has undergone seven surgeries due to larynx cancer and therefore speaks through a tracheal tube – a man with great will power and vitality). Bondo makes sure that a parking permit and tickets will be awaiting Sven-Anders, Ann-Charlotte, their two sons and cousin Frederik, who has been to the festival more than 20 times.

There's massive media interest in the event, which is much more prominent and explicit than five years earlier on the 10th anniversary. I publish a long interview with Tor in the Danish newspaper *BT* the day before the premiere. Numerous TV stations have broadcast clips from *Nine Rocks* in their news programs, including the interview with the Bondebjers in the film. These reports also mention that the family might be attending the premiere at the festival. The Danish Broadcasting Corporation (DR) is also very interested in interviewing the family. In cooperation with Claus, I ask the Bondebjers if they would like to participate in such an interview, and they say that they would.

Sven-Anders repeatedly expresses his surprise that there is such strong media interest in such an old case. But interest there is, and in the days before June 30, 2015, most Danes have probably learned through the media that this film about the tragedy will be premiering, and that family members of the victims will be present.

I also have a number of public engagements during the festival, but I've cleared my calendar for June 30 and will be meeting the Bondebjers at the festival's permanent offices about a half mile from the festival grounds. From there, we'll drive out to the festival together and meet up with Claus and Tor. This is also where the interview with DR will be taking place. In the days leading up to and during the festival, the surrounding area swarms with people and bumper-to-bumper traffic. Nonetheless, I manage to find Sven-Anders at the festival's offices relatively quickly.

Before meeting with the Bondebjers in Roskilde, I had been speculating as to their state of mind on the day of the premiere, but Sven-Anders seems to be composed and focused, asking about our route, parking, etc. There's not much small talk or dwelling on the gravity of the situation from Sven-Anders. I get into the tightly-packed car to give them instructions to the festival grounds, and to confirm that Claus, Tor and the DR News team will be awaiting them and assist with anything they need.

The family appears to be less emotionally burdened by the situation than I had expected – but that would come to change. On a purely practical and logistical level, navigating the festival can be demanding, but we glide rather smoothly through the process of presenting various permits and finding a parking space right behind the media's backstage area next to the Orange Stage.

I've already spotted Tor, Claus and the entire TV crew, who are headed towards us – and suddenly, the mood changes. Ann-Charlotte is suddenly deeply affected by the situation. Although I've spent much less time with them than with the Gustafssons, it still feels like we know each other well and share a mutual sympathy. As the slim 70-year-old Ann-Charlotte steps out of the car in the backstage area, she spontaneously hugs me tightly as she cries and trembles. While standing and holding her for a relatively long time, it almost feels like comforting one of my daughters when they were very young. Ann-Charlotte is understandably very emotional. I confer briefly with the family, and we agree that the TV interview will have to wait for the time being.

The TV crew waits respectfully, and the Bondebjers smile when they see Tor and Claus. Ann-Charlotte seems to be more collected now, and the first thing the family wants to see is the Memorial Grove. We walk a few hundred yards through the empty festival grounds, which are not yet open to the public, to the Memorial Grove, which is located to the right of the Orange Stage. The nine birch trees have now grown rather high, attesting to the many years that have passed since the unthinkable transpired. The mood is somber and calm. The family stands alone in front of the memorial stone and each of them lays a rose in front of the inscription "how fragile we are," followed by a silent moment of reflection. Tor and I stand close by, ready to provide assistance if needed, but also with respect for the family's need to have this moment for themselves.

The scene of the accident

Their eyes are red from crying, but the family members are composed. Ann-Charlotte asks me about the exact scene of the accident. I point to the area about 150 yards from where we're standing and ask if they would like to go it. They would. The TV crew remains respectfully in the background, but the family allows them to follow and film us. We take the at once short and very long walk with Tor and two cameramen, who are now filming close-ups of our faces. I've been a media professional for years and know "the game," but I wonder about how the parents must be feeling now, given that they live a completely different life, and have had almost only negative experiences with the press after the accident.

Tor guides us to the place where he and presumably also Henrik Bondebjer stood 15 years earlier to the day – and almost to the hour. The sun is shining and it's a wonderful warm summer's day, following what had been a terrible month weather-wise up to that point. Everything is peaceful and tranquil, so it seems almost surreally macabre when Tor, at the request of the Bondebjers, physically and verbally recounts and re-enacts what he remembers from the night of the accident: where he was standing to begin with, the place he moved to, where people fell and what happened then, and how he personally experienced the situation. All of this is filmed by the TV crew.

We take a deep breath and I think it's about time for the Bondebjer family to have a chance to relax a bit before the film's screening about two hours later. We walk with the family to the part of the festival grounds where there are already people, music, stands and events in the days leading up to the official opening. Ann-Charlotte looks around with a smile and says that people seem very calm, relaxed and happy. Her nephew Frederik shares many of his Roskilde Festival experiences. We cross the bridge to the Rising area, where the film will be shown; we find a stand with organic crepes and we all have a festival beer.

My impression is that Sven-Anders and Ann-Charlotte are feeling comfortable, which is the absolute most important thing. We visit *Gaffa*'s stand – the magazine that I've been a part of for ages, and the original publisher of my book about Pearl Jam and the accident in Danish. The managing director of *Gaffa*, Robert, who originally OK'd the book project, greets the family. We then seek a quieter refuge after a death metal band takes the stage. We're all enjoying ourselves, and I appreciate the opportunity to show the family what the festival is like. For many of us, Roskilde Festival has long been a haven and workplace – for the past 33 years in my case.

Nine Rocks

The time of the film screening approaches. Henrik Bondo comes by before the film starts and briefly greets the Bondebjers, politely asking whether everything was OK with the parking permits, access badges and so on – common courtesies in an all but common situation. The family that lost their son and a multi-year lawsuit against the festival, standing before the man with the ultimate responsibility for safety in the year 2000 and one of the festival's managers, both then and now. But it's far from impersonal, and it's an important meeting for all parties. Bondo is clearly attentive to reading the situation and sensing how much he should say to the family. He starts cautiously and it feels like the right approach.

A huge number of people have come for the screening. As a TV reporter later says during a newscast: "Never before have so many people sat down and been so quiet in the festival's 40-year history." Many people have recognized the family, who stick out somewhat compared to the rest of the crowd, and they're also familiar faces for those who have seen Danish television in recent days. One person comes up and asks if he can take a picture – a request that is denied – but otherwise the family stands undisturbed, holding one another throughout the 30-minute film. I try to stand discretely close to the family, ready to intervene if anything should happen, but I assume that the family would prefer to stand alone during the film, so I stay in the background.

Before the documentary begins, Henrik Bondo and Tor Kolding take the stage and both say a few words to the audience. Tor talks about his experiences and motivation for making the film, and Bondo reads Stone's statement as it is also projected on the large screen next to the stage. It's a beautiful séance, and the applause after the film is loud and prolonged. Tor comes down to us and is clearly relieved when he sees the family is doing well, all things considered. The next step for the family is an interview with DR News at the Memorial Grove. Henrik Bondo also comes over to us while we're chatting, and I ask him if he wants to join us on the walk over to the Memorial Grove. He would like to, if it's OK with the Bondebjers, which it is.

Bondo tells Ann-Charlotte that he has four children, all of whom are at the festival. We all talk with each other as we walk the approximate quarter mile from the Roskilde Rising stage to the Memorial Grove. It's a beautiful and peaceful summer's day at the festival. I talk quite a bit with Henrik Bondebjer's brother Lars and cousin Frederik during our walk.

The TV news crew interviews Sven-Anders and Ann-Charlotte, who make no bones about the fact that the accident has ruined their lives. The word "murder" is used, yet there's also a sense of underlying unity and peace, which the situation and the family's presence at the festival also reflect. Touchingly, Lars says to his mother that it's the first time he's ever seen the family talk to – and not about – Henrik.

The TV crew wraps up the interview, and Ann-Charlotte and Sven-Anders ask me to pass on their regards to Anna Rigas from DR News and tell her that it was the most positive meeting they've had with a journalist after the accident. Later during the festival, I get the chance to pass on that greeting, and Anna tells me that she was deeply moved by her meeting with the family. The situation is so special that it calls for a photo. To this point, it's the closest I've come to closure, resolution or reconciliation relating to the tragedy. We're at the Memorial Grove, the nine victims are present with us in the form of nine birch trees, it's the 15th anniversary of the accident, the victims' families are represented in the form of the Bondebjers, and Roskilde Festival's management in the form of the head of safety on the year of the accident and still a member of the management. Pearl Jam is symbolically present in the form of Stone's public statement, and the film director Tor, who very nearly lost his life, represents the audience and the survivors. And they're all standing there, arm in arm. The accident, the conflicts, the disputing parties, and the enormous pain that has filled the lives of so many people, including my own. This is a good moment.

A good moment. Lars Bondebjer, Henrik Bondo Nielsen, Ann-Charlotte Bondebjer, Gry, Sven-Anders Bondebjer, Tor Nygård Kolding, Fredrik Bondebjer. Memorial Grove, Roskilde Festival. June 30, 2015 Photo: Henrik Tuxen.

Chapter 20

2015: SANTIAGO.

During Roskilde, plans begin to materialize in connection with the South American launch of the Spanish translation of this book in its original form. I'm in ongoing conversations with Veronica in Norway/Chile, and with Trine Danklefsen, cultural attaché at the Danish Embassy in Chile. Our timing turns out to be incredibly fortunate. The official theme of this year's book fair in Santiago, which draws more than 250,000 visitors over three weeks, is Nordic/Scandinavian literature. The Danish Embassy has invited me to participate in the fair, as part of the fair's official program. In one fell swoop, I go from lowly music writer for a free magazine to an author on par with all the "real" Danish authors, including Pia Juul, Carsten Jensen and my personal favorites, Christian Jungersen and Sissel Jo-Gazan. Excellent company and an excellent event.

Mi nombre es Eddie Vedder

My luck only gets better when, a short time later, Pearl Jam announces a major South American tour that will open in Santiago, Chile on November 4 – smack in the middle of the book fair. I had a feeling that they might be headed in that direction when writing with Stone, but he's often the last one to know about these kinds of things, and the fact that Santiago is the opening concert is almost too good to be true. Veronica proclaims that the gods must be on our side, sending photos from Santiago's streets, which are plastered with PJ posters. She tells me that Pearl Jam is so popular in Chile that their music is used as the intro music for the TV news, it's played all the time on the radio, and it's often used in amateur and television contests. The latter not only turns out to be true, but soon leads to a special relation and even stronger ties with the wonderful Chileans.

Javier Diaz took second place in the national television competition "Mi Nombre Es," and first place in the regional finals. The essence of the show is that contestants must sing like their idols, while also mimicking their appearance, fashion style, attitude, etc. Every time Javier takes the stage, it's with the words, "Mi nombre es Eddie Vedder." And as a viewer, you really believe him. There's a stunning resemblance between Javier and Eddie – in a YouTube clip, Chris Cornell laughs that Eddie can now take a day off without anybody noticing. (YouTube: Chris Cornell Reacts to Eddie Vedder Lookalike // SiriusXM // Opie & Anthony)

Javier looks like Eddie from head to toe, but even more amazing is that his vocals are a dead ringer for Pearl Jam's lead man. The first clip I see is of him signing *Yellow Ledbetter* on the program – a clip that has been viewed more than 3 million times. Not bad for a cover version in an amateur competition.

Veronica knows the 33-year-old Javier, who by day is a veterinarian with his own clinic specializing in bulldogs. She says that she'll contact him to ask if he would be interested in participating in the book presentation at the fair. And as with any dramatic adventure, you have to go through a trials and tribulations before everything turns out happily in the end. At first, Javier can't get his band Piedra Negra to join him, so the presentation in the big hall is cancelled and moved out to a hallway. All of this is somewhat difficult to relate to, being almost 8,000 miles away in Copenhagen. But everything comes together in the end.

María Fransisca and Marie

My Chilean publisher, Curiche/Libros de Mentira, has hired a highly effective young lady named María Francisca Maldonado, who arranges interviews leading up to and during my trip. I've heard a lot of rumblings that these types of things in Chile are often subject to the whims of chaos and chance, but such worries quickly prove unfounded. I meet with talented and insightful journalists who fully live up to their reputation of being the country's leading music writers. The press coverage is overwhelming. When María Francisca later sends the press dossier on the book's coverage, there are TV reports, six radio interviews, and 29 pages of coverage from various websites and newspapers primarily based in Chile, but also outlets from Columbia and Argentina.

All dressed up and more or less ready to go, I meet up with my close friend Marie, from PJ New York '13, for coffee. Since New York, we've teamed up to develop ideas for various projects, exchanged e-mails and met up occasionally. She's been largely positive about my journey, reading and giving feedback on the first eight new chapters I've written since the first book, but she also works in an

"If I didn't know you, I'd think you were a little irritating." It's great criticism and I've tried to take it to heart in my re-writes. Marie also helped plan a strategy for conveying the book's message to the South American press in a way that the book and important figures will be remembered. But we've barely just sat down with our coffee when she asks: "Can I join you in South America for the whole trip? It's going to be an adventure, and I'd like to be a part of it. I'll pay my own way." And so it was.

From the very beginning, I've had great trust and interest in Marie's talents, ideas and ability to get things done. I know from our time in New York that she's an incarnate globetrotter who understands how to get by, no matter where she is, and that unlike myself, she's an ace at social media – a modern, funny, adventurous and effective woman, and I've never been blind to her feminine charm.

We agree to take the trip without "being married," and that we'll figure out the logistics along the way. Where there's a will, there's a way. The fact that we're suddenly two people about to take this journey, and that the other person is the highly effective Marie – who understands how to be friendly and accommodating while also cutting to the chase and getting things done – turbocharges the whole project. We plan a trip to Santiago from November 1 to November 18, with four days in Buenos Aires to catch Pearl Jam's concert there on November 7.

Time for reflection

In the midst of our euphoria, the book's impetus and many experiences behind it come to the fore. In other words: the reason for writing this book, what makes it important, its spirit, message, and so on. The story wasn't conceived as a book, and it was never the intention to "push" it to other regions, especially given its highly vulnerable content. The book is a labor of love, and it's essential to maintain and communicate that it was borne of this spirit. I also feel that it's essential to ensure that the two main figures in the narrative, Birgitta and Stone, approve of the content and angle before our take-off from Copenhagen.

"A main reason for putting out this book is to honor the nine young men who lost their lives on the tragic night. I wish that a new generation of fans can identify with these guys who were all just happy PJ fans thrilled to see a great show. Maybe their spirit can be a part of South American fans today – they were just like them/ you – filled with love for music, rock'n'roll, Pearl Jam. If the spirit of these fine young men can pass on to mental soul-mates on the other side of the world, and what they went through be a vital memory of the importance of always looking out for, and taking care of each other, the tragic loss of their lives, way before their time, would somehow seem less pointless."

I send these words to Stone and subsequently to Birgitta, who both respond with their support and high praise, giving me the peace of mind and the necessary backing to move forward with the project and convey what this story is about, in my view.

On all fronts, it's beginning to look like quite the trip. The only downside is that my daughter Lulu can't join us. She was 14 days old when I saw my first Pearl Jam concert in Barcelona, back in 1996. Lulu loves, understands, plays, sings and interprets the band, and she's seem them live and met them on many an occasion – and now Pearl Jam is playing on her 19th birthday, November 7 in Buenos Aires. That would have made a pretty OK present! But a tight school schedule and financial constraints make her participation a no-go. I bet another chance will come up in the future, though.

Prior to our departure, I exchange quite a few e-mails with Stone, who became a father for the third time in seven years in February 2015, and who takes pride in being an engaged father. Beyond the music, there's also his wide-ranging work relating to the band's social philanthropic commitment, which is always closely coordinated for each tour in cooperation with Pearl Jam's press manager, Nicole Vandenberg. In other words, Stone is a busy man. After Chile and Argentina, the tour will be going to Brazil, Columbia and Mexico for an additional five shows. I consider extending my trip to Brazil, but ultimately decide that that would be too expensive and chaotic.

Speaking of chaos

Time flies, as it usually does, and suddenly the calendar reads November 1. I pack my stuff, squeeze in one last table tennis battle with Kasper Schulz and, according to plan, I head for Marie's sister Marianne's place, who just happens to be taking the same plane as us from Copenhagen to Amsterdam. From there, we're connecting to Chile and Marianne to Kenya. On the way out the door, my telephone rings and a cheery voice asks me: "You do know that the flight is cancelled, right?" I wait a moment for the other shoe to drop and a "just joking," but no such relief arrives. Qué? Yep, sure enough – damn. Thick fog in Amsterdam and London has more or less brought all European air traffic to its knees.

To make a long and insane story short, two different flights are cancelled in Copenhagen, we arrive in Amsterdam five minutes after the plane for Santiago has departed, and we embark through a labyrinth of chaos, travelling back and forth between the airport and a hotel, five-hour long lines and never-ending changes to our itinerary. But there's not much to do, so we might as well relax and enjoy ourselves. María Francisca reschedules the interviews; I do one via Skype from Amsterdam and the others when I get to Santiago. Marie and I end up having a great time that evening in downtown Amsterdam at one of the city's oldest wooden buildings and pubs, In't Aepjen. I buy a beer and start chatting with a great bartender who spins tales from the 1600s. Back then, sailors docked in Amsterdam's harbor with exotic goods and monkeys from the East. The monkeys became a frequent component of barters, and were used as payment for accommodations at the building's hotel on the second floor. The only problem was that you were more or less certain to get lice and other goodies if you checked in. Therefore, the name of the place – "Are you sleeping with the ape?" – has become a Dutch saying for being broke, or at least for having lice and/or other tantalizing ailments.

After a 48-hour delay, it practically feels like a miracle when we're finally airborne. Sleeping like a log across the Atlantic, a one-hour layover in Buenos Aires, and then over the Andes to our final destination, Santiago de Chile. And everything starts great, right from the luggage conveyor belt. Marie's nice suitcase rolls out, and then the conveyor belt is bare. I'm left empty-handed, with only the backpack I brought with me as a carry-on. "Well," says an airport employee in Santiago, "your suitcase is in Paris. We've known that since yesterday." That's freaking great, or the exact opposite, what with not having contact lenses and other necessities. "Whatever," I conclude. The suitcase is supposed to arrive at our hotel within 24 hours.

At the arrivals hall, we're greeted by the smiles of Veronica and her *amor*, Sergio Dastres. The hotel room is nice, albeit rather small. We go out for Peruvian food and *pisco* sours in the fantastically beautiful city of Santiago. After visiting eight opticians and spending a small fortune, I get three sets of contact lenses that take my sight up to somewhere around 70% of what would be ideal. I also want to see, and not just hear, tonight's concert.

I know from experience that you have to get to a concert well in advance, since it can be hell to find the guest ticket window – and when you tell a venue's staff that you're on Pearl Jam's guest list, they think your full of shit *and* they have no idea where you would have to go if you weren't. So our party splits up. Veronica needs to stop by her home and change shoes, and Marie and I make our first acquaintance with Santiago's subway, together with Veronica's niece Sara, who is the photographer on our trip. She's a very colorful 27-year-old woman who poses artistically online in all sorts of different styles, including scantily clad, and who sometimes looks decidedly dangerous. It turns out that Sara is the sweetest, most charming woman, with a youthful spirit and a truly artistic soul. She designs and sews her own clothes, and looks like an original every day, while remaining calm and relaxed all the time. She's the type that you just can't help giving a big hug, again and again. That's how I feel when around her, anyway.

Estadio Nacional, Santiago, November 4, 2015

The time has come. The moment we've been waiting for. The area around the venue is dotted with stands and street sellers, and swarming with fans in an endless array of PJ T-shirts. One of the popular items being peddled is an Eddie Vedder mask, and suddenly five Edveds in a row are standing before us. As expected, it takes forever to find the guest list window, but we find it and our envelope has all nine tickets with stickers.

At the entrance there's a map of the stadium. On one side of the map it reads *Pacifico*, and on the other *Andes*. And the Andes mountains are clear on the horizon on this unusually warm spring evening. It's all a bit surreal for a Dane like me, who is used to November being about the darkest, rainiest and most miserable month imaginable. But here I am, walking around in shorts and a T-shirt under clear skies, together with 60,000 other hardcore fans.

The stadium is impressive. The Olympic rings on the front are apparently mostly there because the architect who designed the stadium took inspiration from the Olympic Stadium in Berlin. All of the Chilean national team's major soccer matches are played there. Soccer itself can be a violent sport, but on a much more chilling note, the stadium was used as a detention center under the Pinochet regime, during which time approximately 40,000 people were detained in the compound and an unknown number were tortured and killed on the premises. Pinochet's dark shadow hangs over the venue to this day.

I send Stone a text message right when we get the tickets. We then exchange a few text messages. He sends some info about catering during the concert and where we should stand, he hopes that everything is good, and says they have to leave right after the concert, but he hopes we manage to see each other in Argentina. The messages go back and forth, fast and furious. There are a few slightly strange questions, but he probably just didn't manage to read exactly what I wrote, since he's naturally very busy. It turns out that it was pure telepathy. Stone doesn't receive my text messages until they get to Argentina the following day. In fact, he's told that I didn't pick up the tickets, and he tells me in Argentina that he tried to call me ten minutes before the concert to check if something was wrong, or if we were stuck at the airport. He also gave my telephone number to their tour manager Smitty and put him on the case. Generally speaking, the telephone connections are rather shaky throughout our South American trip. There are Wi-Fi symbols here and there, but we never really know if there's an actual connection.

I doodled with a Duolingo program for a short time back home, but my Spanish doesn't extend very far beyond "*Dos cervezas, por favor.*" So explaining that we have to get to a backstage area before the concert and then to the area by the mixing booth is a pretty steep climb. But, as so often before, we succeed. We make it to a small area with beer, snacks and "Pearl Jam Wi-Fi," and everything is really cozy. Four spry Italians arrive and one of them says to me smiling: "Hey, you're that guy with the book. I've seen you on the internet." They're all friends of Eddie and spent the previous day with Mr. Vedder. That's pretty cool, but once again it causes Marie and I to steam about KLM and the 48-hour delay. I wonder what would have happened and who we would have had the chance to hang out with if we had been in Santiago on time?

Showtime

Five minutes before the scheduled show time, Pearl Jam's long-standing head of security, Pete Beattle, comes to pick us up. About six to eight of us are going to be escorted to the VIP area by the mixing booth. It's all pretty wild. I think we pass by Mike McCready, but I would have needed better contact lenses to be sure. We're led behind the stage and can see that the place is full of people everywhere. I'm at the front of the pack. We walk down a staircase right behind the stage, then continue to the area in front of the stage, where the hardcore fans have been waiting for hours. Some have even camped outside the stadium for as long as three days, we've been told. We continue along the stage and then turn left and walk about 50 yards along a six-foot-wide median through the center of the crowd, down to the sound tower. Our appearance from backstage signals to the crowd that the concert will be starting any minute now.

It's mind-blowing and a total rush, causing adrenaline to course through my veins. We should be completely tapped of all energy after the ordeal of the past three days, but instead we're primed and ready to go. And it's all about to begin. In the mixing area, we find Veronica, Sergio, Sara and staff from my Chilean publisher. Eddie's friends are there and, according to Veronica, all sorts of Chilean celebrities.

Marie films me, and asks me to guess the opening song of the concert. I start by saying *Pendulum, Release,* or *Corduroy*, but end up going with *Release*. The band takes the stage and people roar loudly enough to cause a rockslide in the nearby Andes. They start with *Pendulum*, followed by *Release*. A spiritual start. We're among the very few of the 60,000 spectators with room to dance around, and the large coolers are overflowing with wine, beer and whiskey. We sing and dance, drink, talk and shout. I manage to take some pictures, including of the many happy women from all over the world who are standing with me: Denmark, Norway, Chile, Argentina, Paraguay. I certainly can't complain.

During *Nothingman*, I entertain Marie with how deeply I've adopted the line "Some words when spoken... can't be taken back..." That line becomes forever changed as an arm bumps my beer bottle and propels the Corona right up into Marie's mouth, chipping off a piece of her front tooth. I feel terrible, but Marie smiles and we laugh at the paradoxical new meaning of the line: "Words when spoken – apart from the chip of tooth that disappeared – can't be taken back."

The first Spanish book

I have good eye contact with some cuties dancing who are singing along to every line, particularly a young, smiling woman with a classic European look and long, dark hair. We lock into something about each other; she sings to me and vice versa. I wander around a bit, greeting people, Eddie's Italian friends, who wave me over to stand with them, and then back to Veronica and the others. To my great surprise, the band plays *Light Years* at a relatively early point in the set, and I see that the

Eddies everywhere. Chilean fans. Estadio Nacional, Santiago. November 4, 2015. Photo: Marie Hansen.

dark-haired woman has tears running down her cheeks. In that moment, I think about the book. The Spanish edition. I haven't seen it yet, nor given it a thought. The whole process of getting to Santiago has been so hectic that I've had all kinds of other details on my mind.

Fortunately, Veronica has a copy of the book in her backpack. I walk straight over and give it to the woman, who later turns out to be my very good friend, companion and a bit of a guardian angel in Argentina. She's delighted and holds the book tightly for the remaining two hours of the concert.

Chicas locas. Leila Rausch, Laura "Pink", Veronica Bravo, Sara Vega Bravo. Estadio Nacional, Santiago. November 4, 2015. Photo: Henrik Tuxen.

It's a terrific concert and I'm feeling fantastic and totally relieved. We're here, taking in Pearl Jam live under warm and beautiful open skies, together with an incredible number of other people. After all the chaos we've been through in the past few days, it's almost too good to be true. And as with all Pearl Jam concerts, the band guides us through quiet and melancholy moments to full on singing and rocking with the rest of the stadium.

Leading the troops

One of the things that makes the biggest impression on me during the concert is the atmosphere around Pink Floyd's *Mother* and the subsequent version of *Imagine*. Darkness has fallen over Santiago, and when I look around, people have turned on their cell phones and are holding them high, while singing along to John Lennon's immortal lines, "I'll hope someday you'll join us / And the world will be as one." The second encore set nears its end with the hymns *Alive* and *Rockin' in the Free World*, and when Mike strums the opening chords to *Yellow Ledbetter*, I know it's the last song for tonight.

Stone wrote to me that the band is leaving after the concert, but I figure that it might be worth taking a look backstage after the show nonetheless. Maybe they'll have decided to wait an hour before leaving, or maybe some other fun stuff is going down. I seize this opportunity, thinking that if I look important and confident with my sticker, then I just might be able to go back the same way we came out to the VIP area. But I know that it's a matter of being quick and cool (earlier that evening, I was pulled down by a guard when I climbed up on a barrier between the crowd and the VIP area – nothing serious, but still). I give Veronica, Sara, Marie and the people from the publishing house the signal that now's our chance.

I lead the way, acting important, and to my surprise the guard opens the barrier. I continue to lead the way down the open walkway, directly towards the stage, as *Yellow Ledbetter* rings out into the inferno of noise from the band's most dedicated fans. Just as we near the stage, the whole band steps forward towards the audience, bowing arm-in-arm right in front of me as they are showered in applause. If only I had a ladder right there, I would have probably climbed up on stage and said hi. But waving to them would be like a drop in the ocean, and I have to keep moving so that we don't blow our cover. It's an amazing moment, just about ten hours after having set foot on the South American continent, in this jam-packed and storied stadium. By the time we get backstage, the band is gone with the wind. We have a quick beer and the day's festivities draw to a close. Arriving back at our hotel, Marie and I conk out instantaneously, completely and totally spent.

Our next morning, November 5, begins with a radio interview, followed by the presentation at the FILSA book fair. The first journalist, Alfredo Lewin of Radio Sonar and the program *Radiotransmisor*, turns out to know a lot more about Pearl

Jam than I had expected. He speaks excellent English, has seen the band live 17 times, and is especially fond of *Riot Act*, which reminds him a lot of New York in the days after 9/11, during which time he lived in Manhattan. The interview is live on the air, and his thoughtful questions are both personal and complex. I answer to the best of my abilities and within the limited time available. After this great experience, the radio station arranges a paid taxi to my next live interview with journalist Franciso Tapia of the program "Sordo como Tapia" on Radio Rock & Pop. There we meet up with Veronica and Sergio, and once again the interview goes really well. It's a big day at the radio station, and they have something else up their sleeve for their listeners: after my interview is over, they break the news to the people of Chile that The Rolling Stones will be playing at Estadio National in February. While at Radio Rock & Pop, we greet the head of the station, Pedro, and many others. It turns out that the relaxed, ball cap-wearing journalist is a bit of a celebrity in his own right, and is personal friends with Paul McCartney, whom he's guided around Santiago on multiple occasions.

Afterwards, we stop by the hotel to take care of a few practical errands. An hour later, there's an unannounced knock at the hotel room door, and in rolls my gigantic suitcase. I didn't see any point in travelling light, since it's one of the rare occasions where I've checked in luggage. I've got everything from suits, swimming trunks and indispensible comic books to sunscreen and a bunch of sketches for future projects. The day before we departed, I dropped by Marie's place and told her: "If you really want to work with me and know what I've got going on up in my dome, then here are a few examples." Those sketches include a long-read article on Lukas Graham that's mostly about me and my son, about 12,000 words on Jimmy Page written almost entirely in one go after returning home from interviewing him in London, and an inordinate number of handwritten diary pages from my rock'n'roll life in the Soviet Union in 1989, experiencing history in the making during the monumental weeks that culminated with the fall of the Berlin Wall. So if there are any readers out there feeling sorry for Marie right about now, I can only apologize and say I tried to warn her.

Feria Internationcal del Libro de Santiago (FILSA)

The weather is wonderful, so we decide to walk to FILSA – a trek with clear views of the snow-capped Andes all along the way. And here I am, walking around in shorts while those back in Denmark are freezing in the dark of winter – it feels fantastic. Marie and I suddenly realize that we have to pick up the pace, since I have a live radio interview in five minutes. We hurry and find Luis Hernández and Eduardo Fuentes from Radio ADN and just about die laughing in the process. The interview is in a temporary studio with glass walls, and since Eduardo is also the popular host of a children's television show, hordes of joyful and very loud uniformed schoolchildren have lined up around us to have a look. Some of them are also sporting Pearl Jam merchandise and they're extremely eager, to put it mildly. Veronica is our interpreter for the interview, which rolls on as the crowd of mostly young teenagers yell and scream on the other side of the glass. We take some photos along the way, including one of a smiling woman who comes into the studio with her arms raised high and gets Eduardo's autograph. To me, that photo symbolizes the pure zest for life, openness and love I experience everywhere in Chile and Argentina.

Afterwards, we have a bite to eat and take in a random book presentation – to an audience of four, which makes me a bit nervous: after seemingly endless wrangling in the planning, my book presentation landed in the big hall, Sala de las Artes, with a capacity of 600. I previously wrote to Trine Danklefsen of the Danish Embassy, "Better to fill a small room than hear the echo of a big and empty room, especially if Piedra Negra can't join me." On the way to the presentation, I come to terms with my worries, thinking: Well, whatever. I can't do anything to change it now, and Piedra Negra is here.

When I get to the hall, Piedra Negra is there practicing, and for the first time I meet Javier Diaz A (Eddie), Mauro Lobos Guede (Mike), Pablo Donoso (Stone), Gonzalo Espinosa (Jeff), Hillthsson Miranda (Matt) and Alejandro Calderón Espinosa (Boom). They greet me with great warmth and joy, and I like them all immediately.

The hall is super cool, with tons of chairs and a big stage decked out like a combination living room/concert stage. I had written with Javier in advance about possibly joining them on a song, but we never really hammered out anything concrete and I don't have a guitar with me. "Should we try *Immortality?*" asks Javier, who knows all of Eddie Vedder's often complicated lyrics by heart and with complete fluidity, even though he hardly speaks a word of English. "In E flat?" I ask. "Sí, sí," smiles Javier. We play it, and the only thing that needs adjusting is the solo – then it's ready to go. We go backstage and I greet our interpreter for the presentation. I also run into Henrik Friis from ROSA (The Danish Rock Council), who I've known for years. Next on stage after us is a presentation of Nordic music.

I tell Piedra Negra that I can also play on *Light Years*, if they think that's OK. Yeah, that sounds fine. But before we manage to run through it, somebody tells us that it's past 5 p.m. and that we have to go on stage right away. Things are moving really fast, with people rushing on and off the stage. On the way to the stage, I run into Jenny Rossander, aka Lydmor, who also gets a big hug. I just did a live interview with her back in Copenhagen three weeks earlier, and I'm going to be writing an article about her South American tour for the Danish newspaper *BT*. I manage to tell her that I'll see her afterwards before we take the stage. The rows of chairs are now full of people and people are standing up in the balcony –15 minutes later, every empty space in the room has been filled by a spectator.

The opening speaker is a representative from the publisher, followed by the respected Chilean music writer Fabio Salas Zuñiga. I later learn that he said a lot of nice things about me and the book, but I only pick up a little bit as he is speaking. I'm sitting next to Veronica on a sofa and a journalist asks me questions, with our conversation being interpreted both ways. It's a blast, but also a bummer that my Spanish is crap. Piedra Negra takes the stage for the last 18 minutes of our time slot, and they're a big hit. They start with *Love Boat Captain*, the song that more than any other is synonymous with the accident. The sound is good, people clap along, and Javier both looks and sounds like Eddie. I can now see first-hand that it's much more than just a YouTube gimmick. I return to the stage and we play *Immortality*. It's smiles everywhere, both on stage and in the crowd. I take the guitar off, but before the boys play their last number, Javier looks at me and asks, "Light Years?" Well, OK, why not? "Do you play it in D?" I ask. "Sí, sí," says Pablo, Piedra Negra's Stone. It's a total rush to play the song with these guys. When it's all over, we stand arm in arm as the crowd gives us a standing ovation. Pure joy.

Somebody says something in Spanish from the stage, and I actually manage to gather that they've said Henrik Tuxen will be signing books afterwards somewhere. I've spotted the two ladies from the concert the day before. I walk over to the woman with the long dark hair that I gave a copy of the book, and her friend with the pink scarf. We manage to briefly exchange something along the lines of "Hi and see you in a bit."

Veronica and I sit at a table in the hallway and sign books. To my utter surprise, we end up sitting there for more than two hours of signatures, hugs and selfies. The publisher later tells me that they sold more than 100 books at the presentation. I write lengthy dedications in the books, in an unsightly mix of Spanish and English. The most fantastic thing is their names, and especially the way they pronounce them. Besides all of the Chileans, there are people from Brazil, Argentina, Peru, Venezuela and even Palestine. It's one smiling face after the next, and a seemingly endless parade of beautiful Latinas. Perhaps I should consider emigrating. The two women from the concert have been standing off to the side and we've been making periodic eye contact, but suddenly they're gone. That's life, but then *whaddayaknow*, they show up again as the very last people at the table. They turn out to be Leila from Argentina and Pink, aka Laura, from Paraguay (her nickname comes from the fact that she owns the vegetarian restaurant Pink Cow in the Paraguayan capital of Asunción). There's no two ways about it: South Americans love Pearl Jam.

A Moment of Love

Everyone is delighted and the event is a success exceeding all expectations. Piedra Negra is still here, as is the majority of Veronica's family – nine sisters, her mother, a number of nieces and nephews – who invite us out to dinner. Veronica tells me

Chilean joy. FILSA book fair.
Santiago. November 5, 2015.
Photo: Henrik Tuxen.

FILSA book fair. Veronica & Henrik.
Santiago. November 5, 2015.
Photo: Private.

Two-hour book signing. FILSA. Veronica, Fe Ledesma and Henrik.
Santiago. November 5, 2015. Photo: Sara Vega Bravo.

Radio Rock & Pop. Santiago. November 5, 2015. Photo: Marie Hansen.

about six months later that it was the first time in 30 years that the family had gathered like that, due to past family disputes, but we hadn't seen any signs of tension whatsoever that evening. Piedra Negra joins us, as do Leila and Laura. We end up at a bar in town and take up most of the establishment. Piedra Negra, who are doctors, veterinarians, etc. by day, all express their great appreciation for being part of the event. On the contrary, I think: I'm the one who's thankful that they were there. Thoroughly likeable people. Our entire party ends up in the smoking section, breaking into song and playing guitar. I land next to María Francisca and a man who says to me, "Hi, my name is Luis. I'm your publisher." He turns out to be a great guy and he says he already has plans for an extra launch while I'm in Chile. Everybody mingles, talking and laughing all the while. Javier's girlfriend Aracelli and her friend Carmensita generously pour strong beer into my glass, and after 1½ hours I realize that we're sitting outside in a kind of covered courtyard. I had no idea until that point. I thought we were sitting inside. But then again, I'm probably not entirely sober right about now.

It's an honor for Javier to make sure that we make it home, and it's definitely high time that I call it a night. After a magic ride with about twice as many passengers as the car has seats and seat belts for, we head for the hotel, zooming over some bumps along the way that leave my rear end vibrating for the next few days. Piedra Negra is playing the following night at House of Rock & Blues, and they'd like to have me join them on stage for a few numbers. It's a highly emotional moment for all those involved, and I promise to pass on the story of this "moment of love" to Stone when I hopefully cross paths with him again in Argentina. To me, Piedra Negra and their friends are a living testament to how deeply Pearl Jam inspires people, enriching and strengthening their lives, and how the band brings people together across the globe – and to how great it is to be in South America.

The school class

At 9 a.m. sharp, we're picked up by a caravan from the Ministry of Culture and the Chilean library sector. They're all women and all at least a head shorter than me. They're all very sweet and friendly. I hug and cheek kiss with a number of people – in Chile, it's just one cheek kiss and only with the opposite sex, which Marie and I both get a lot of laughs out of, since we keep making mistakes with our air kisses. In Argentina, they also cheek kiss the same way with people of the same sex. One of the about ten cheek kisses this morning in front of the hotel is with a woman who then gets into a chauffeured car. I'm told that she is Chile's Minister of Culture.

We get into a tightly packed car and drive about an hour to the scenic but also economically disadvantaged area, Huechuraba. I'm sitting next to Laura from the Ministry of Culture, who speaks with great vitality about the Ministry of Culture's project to promote reading among school children in areas where having a book without having it stolen is almost unimaginable. These kids read the books in

The class in Huechuraba that read Tras la huella de Pearl Jam as part of their studies. Santiago. November 6, 2015. Photo: Marie Hansen.

school and then, as an added reward, get to meet the author for a conversation about the book. Today is the first time they'll be meeting a foreign author.

We arrive at the school during recess. The kids are playing in the blazing sun – volleyball, hopscotch and tag. At the library, we are greeted warmly by the head librarian and her staff. It's a beautiful and large library. They tell me that libraries in these parts are rarely this big, testifying to great efforts being made at the school. Everyone seems very enthusiastic and deeply devoted to their work. That also goes for the school class gathered at the library this morning.

I would guess that the students are around 14 years old, and after a long round of handshakes we all sit down. Veronica is our interpreter, and the class of about 20 students listens and asks questions. All of the uniformed school-children sit still with a copy of the book in their hands the whole time. It's a surreal experience. They're not usually so quiet, I'm told. I answer questions for about an hour. Along the way, I have the opportunity to reflect in depth on the wide-ranging questions on topics including life as an author and journalist, the joy of writing, believing in yourself, pursuing your dreams, dealing with grief, music, and why I don't like Nirvana more than Pearl Jam. Our spirits are high as we touch on many humorous and serious subjects. When it's all said and done, I have a really good feeling about the event. Afterwards, as I'm signing books, some of the women come up and ask if I'll also draw a heart in their books. Then, every student, without exception, returns their books to the library before going to their next class; otherwise, they would be stolen.

Piedra Negra, FILSA book fair. Alejandro (Boom), Mauro (Mike), Hillthsson (Matt), Henrik (wannabe), Javier (Eddie), Gonzalo (Jeff), Pablo (Stone). Santiago. November 5, 2015.
Photo: Sara Vega Bravo.

Piedra Negra, FILSA book fair. Henrik Tuxen & Javier Diaz. Santiago. November 5, 2015.
Photo: Sara Vega Bravo.

Sprechen Sie Deutsch?

The next stop is for lunch with the Danish ambassador, Jesper Fersløv Andersen, at a fine outdoor restaurant with the Danish authors Pia Juul, Thomas Boberg and Niels Frank, as well as Marie. The ambassador turns out to be totally chill and down to earth. We talk a lot about Chile and I learn that the country is both the wealthiest in Latin America and the country with the greatest gap between rich and poor, that the country has very low taxes despite a number of "socialist" governments since Pinochet, and that the country's enormous copper production has remained extremely lucrative and nearly unaffected by the financial crisis. The ambassador is extremely pleased with the book fair and says that it might just be the biggest cultural initiative ever for Scandinavian art in Latin America, and that the interest in my book has been particularly great. Every time they've had a like for one of the others, there were five for *Tras la huella de Pearl Jam*. This is heartwarming and great news, but I also know that it was blind luck that the book fair is at the exact time that Pearl Jam's concert is on everyone's lips.

We spend a couple of highly entertaining hours together in non-stop conversation. The three authors, who have released a collective anthology in Chile, are in a hoopla. They know each other well and keep intentionally – but also jokingly – provoking each other. Having served as chairman of the Danish Author's Association for six years, Niels Frank proclaims that the Danish language should be promptly abolished and that we'll all end up speaking German regardless. From there, the debate escalates. In the midst of their battle, I invite them to Piedra Negra's concert that night at House of Rock & Blues.

We're never going back home

Back at the hotel, there's a short window for crashing, but not for long. One of our new English-speaking Chilean friends, Fernando Belocchio, comes by and picks us up at the hotel. He's Piedra Negra's manager and a marketing professional who has been involved with various activities relating to Lollapalooza. He knows a bunch of rock stars, including Dave Grohl, he loves Pearl Jam and he seems to have a fondness for Marie. We drive to the venue, where the plan is that I'll practice a bit with the band before that night's concert. But only one band member has arrived, so Fernando invites us to barbecue at his home.

We have a great time, but things are definitely going at a very leisurely pace, and I eventually note that it's past midnight. We have plenty of time, Fernando reassures me as he flips steaks. Eons later, we finally leave for the venue. Zero time for practice and Piedra Negra is seven songs into their first set when we get there. I walk up to the stage and Javier says, "We're playing *Immortality* after the next song. Are you in?" I am. I play guitar with them on that song and the next, *Light Years*. During the break, the band asks if I also want to play bass. I say, "Yeah, that'd be great, if it can be on the first song!" We have to get up early the next

Playing Go on stage with Piedra Negra. House of Rock & Blues, Santiago. November 7, 2015.
Photo: Alejandro Andrés Calderón Espinosa.

morning to catch a flight to Buenos Aires, and we haven't exactly squeezed in much sleep so far in Chile. It's a total riot, with familiar faces speckled throughout the crowd, and many others who know me, but who I can't quite place. Happy people, beautiful people. The authors Thomas Boberg and Niels Frank are also there, as is Daniel Donoso from the Danish Embassy.

I join the second set and we start off with *Rearviewmirror*. I kind of forget that the bass drives the tempo, but it goes surprisingly well. By this time, it has long been November 7 in Denmark and thereby Lulu's birthday. Javier congratulates her in Spanish from the stage and we play *Go*, which has the coolest groove. People are generally way into it, both up on and down in front of the stage. Even though it's seriously time for us to be going, we keep getting delayed. Marie is having a great time and not exactly pining to leave, and I allow myself to get distracted, among others by an effervescent Brazilian, Gabriella.

Once again, we end up setting our alarm clock to ring in ten minutes.

Chapter 21

2015: BUENOS AIRES.

The past few days have been extremely eventful, overwhelming and emotional.
I've experienced interest in my life and story to an extent I'm not used to – or
had even imagined possible on the other side of the globe. But it's not something
that I've fully comprehended or had time to reflect on. My schedule has simply
been too jam-packed for that sort of thing. But as I sit in the plane from Santiago
to Buenos Aires, it all washes over me, much like one year earlier while in the
air over Sweden and Denmark on the day after Pearl Jam's concert in Stockholm.
There's no pressing business, nothing I have to get done, so I just hang here in
the air, looking down on the Andes, flying over the Argentinean plains and then
landing in the Argentinean capital city. There's plenty of vacant space in the plane.
Marie is sitting on the other side of the aisle, Veronica and sitting and dozing in
her own row, I have a row to myself, and Sara the photographer is fully captivated
by the scenery. It's just the second time in her life that she has flown. The skies
are clear, enabling Sara's camera to capture the spectacular landscape on film. I
smile to Sara, thinking about how we're so different in that way; I can't even count
how many times I've flown. Different worlds, yet it makes perfect sense that we're
together on this journey. I take my first real look at the Spanish version of my book.
I don't know Spanish, but can still figure out a little bit, since I'm obviously pretty
familiar with the content. I work my way through the epilogue, which I hardly
remember, and am moved by some of the passages, thinking: "Maybe it's actually a
pretty OK book." A good feeling.

A moment

A peacefulness sets in, and suddenly I find myself in a transformed state of mind, as if I've jumped two years in time in a split second. A blend of deep gratitude, joy, trusting and selfless love, devoid of demons, aggressions and inferiority complexes, as if they had been sucked out through the aircraft's jet motors. I see pictures in my mind's eye of Eddie Vedder, Stone, my children, scenes from Chile, an old girlfriend flashes by, and another woman is suddenly and vibrantly present in my consciousness. Tears roll down my cheeks. I know that this is just a glimpse, but it comes from within. Love is not bound or dependent on a woman, my son, Stone or any one person. It lives within me, comes from within and is a latent resource that I may one day be able to manifest on a different plane. A feeling, a state of mind that is inextricably linked to Pearl Jam and the way my life has taken shape and evolved as a direct result of everything I've experienced, all the people I've met and welcomed into my life, and all the places around the world I've visited because of this band and their music. I find Marie to share the moment with her. She's sleeping.

Several weeks after returning home, I check the photos on my cell phone. It turns out that I took ten photos looking out the window during the flight, which I had completely forgotten. The first four and the last five are completely clear, without a glare or anything else. In the fifth, there are large and very visible lines on the outside of the window. Where did those come from, and why in just the one photo and none of the others. I have no idea.

Buenos Aires

The drive from the airport to downtown Buenos Aires is stunning: a magnificent, colorful and impressive city, exuding both historic grandeur and visible poverty, and deeply intriguing in the blazing sunshine. I check my messages and texts with Stone – the ones that he didn't see until they got to Argentina – two minds on the same wavelength. Pretty wild telepathy there. I think again about the fact that it's Lulu's 19th birthday and that we're going Pearl Jam in Buenos Aires tonight. Or rather: we're going to see the concert in La Plata, the beach town that everyone in the capital city flocks to for sea and sand, situated about 50 miles from downtown. If not for the original 48-hour delay, we probably would've managed to plan things differently. But now we're headed into central Buenos Aires, where we've booked a hotel with fine cockroaches on the floor and where our doorknob later falls off. But it has two rooms and enough space for the four of us, so it's all good. Yet again, we don't exactly have time to spare, so it doesn't help things much when our ancient (and microscopic) gated elevator gets stuck between the 20th and 21st floors. We're dangling with nothing but a empty cavern below – nothing to stop a free-falling elevator. We're stuffed in this box. A local tries to kick the door open. It's over 100 degrees in here.

Arriving at our room, I get an e-mail from Stone who apologizes for the communication chaos and invites me and my friends to dinner after the concert (as I read it). Marie asks if I'm sure that Stone doesn't actually mean the day after the concert. But I don't want to disturb him more than absolutely necessary, and I've also clearly understood that they're continuing on to Brazil the following day.

Mr. Cab driver

But first we have get to that concert, which means the never-ending and familiar search for guest tickets and finding the VIP lounge. I manage to get a hold of Lulu via Skype and wish her a happy birthday from Buenos Aires, together with Veronica, who has always adored Lulu – and my other two kids, for that matter. As our (lack of) luck would have it, it's also the day of the annual gay parade in Buenos Aires (my tenant in Copenhagen just happens to be here), which in no way makes it easier to get out of town and head for La Plata.

We find a taxi driver who embodies the old adage, "Where there's a will, there's a way." No median or shoulder is too narrow and no degree of slaloming our way through traffic is too extreme. Road markings, traffic signs and other trivialities are of no concern. He has no problem pushing this car, which can't be geared to go more than 50 miles per hour, up to 80, driving with one hand and talking on his cell phone with the other. He's phenomenal, ice cold, brilliant. We survive, but to borrow a line from Dylan: "Don't even ask me how." The road to La Plata – the only one – is completely packed, but we miraculously make our way out there. I'm sitting in the back seat with Sara and Veronica, while Marie is sitting silently in the front seat. I assume it's because she's paralyzed by fear, but later discover that she was sleeping without a care in the world. As Stone later says about Marie: "She knows how to let go." Police and soldiers are driving around on motorcycles, mostly with two people per bike and armed with machine guns. At one point, one of the motorcycles drives up alongside of us as they yell, scream and wave their arms at our taxi driver, who hardly pays them any notice. "It's incredible that they're only now coming after him. He has been driving like a maniac the whole way," comments Veronica.

But it's not always a bad thing to travel by jalopy – after all, we make it there, or almost. The last mile or so will be on foot. Enticing yet dilapidated street kitchens with vendors peddling Argentine beef and canned beer make the trek pure pleasure. We arrive at the last minute, but for once we manage to find our tickets pretty fast. However, finding the VIP area after that proves completely impossible. We're on an seemingly endless wild goose chase. I joke with Marie that Stone should experience what this is all like – that he should be spend a day wearing a Henrik Tuxen (aka who-the-fuck-are-you) mask and try asking for directions to Pearl Jam's backstage area in a country where he doesn't speak the language. Stone can see the humor in this idea when we present it to him the following day, but he doesn't seem particularly interested in giving it a try.

The hammer

After dealing with one know-nothing security guard after the next, we give up on finding the VIP area. We're in a big, covered soccer stadium. There aren't as many people as in Santiago, but it's not exactly empty either. I later learn that the concert is sold out, so there must be some rules about the venue's maximum capacity. As in Chile, we have access to the area around the mixing booth – and who are the first people we run into, but Leila and Laura from Santiago. I've written a little with Leila about possibly helping with tickets, but it turns out that they've done perfectly fine on their own. This is the moment I've been looking forward to more than any other, and then the unavoidable happens. After six completely insane days in the fast lane covering thousands of miles, crises by the bushel, ample alcohol and sparse sleep, I suddenly grow tired. As in, shit-I-can't-stand-on-my-own-two-feet tired. I can also see that Leila and Laura's energy level is way lower than in Santiago, but it turns out to be a fantastic concert nonetheless.

The sound is impeccable. You can hear the bass incredibly clearly, which is often a problem at large stadium concerts, including some of those featuring Pearl Jam. Since I'm mellower than usual, I'm more relaxed and listen much more to the lyrics than normally. The concert evolves into a particularly spiritual one for me. In Santiago, I was on a mental trip around the world, one moment in Hawaii, the next in New York, then Berlin, so many concerts, so many impressions, the countless songs, various countries, all blended together in a wonderful cocktail of body and mind as Eddie and the boys opened the floodgates. In Argentina, my focus is more on the words, the moods, the sounds. The concert is not the out-of-body sing-along experience that I might have expected, but rather an intensely spiritual and extremely intimate performance. People are jumping, yelling and singing along – not necessarily in unison, as Stone says with a smile afterwards – but more for prolonged sequences than constantly throughout the concert. I seize an opportunity to lie down on a flight case for seven or eight songs as I come to terms with my fatigue. I alternate between standing with the others and on my own. Eddie, who's wearing a blue helmet, is really on top his game and walks all the way down the median (with Pete on his heels) to the area around the mixing booth where we're standing.

Ni una menos

When talking with Gabriella in Santiago, she tells me her greatest wish is that Eddie will address the extreme environmental problem of plastic waste on the Brazilian beaches. He later does just that, making big headlines in Brazil and elsewhere in Latin America. In Argentina and especially later Columbia, Eddie addresses another major problem faced in Latin America and throughout the world: violence against women.

As the second encore set begins, the big screen is filled with the image of a banner bearing the words "Ni una menos," eliciting huge applause from the crowd. These words translate to "Not one more" and refer to an Argentinean movement to raise awareness of the many women murdered by men, most of whom are current or former lovers. Eddie speaks on stage for a few minutes about a cool girl, about ten years old, wearing a Ramones T-shirt. He saw her on his way in, and thought that she must be about the same age as his daughter. Eddie and the band follow up with the modern feminist classic, *Better Man*, and then the old Motown classic, *Leaving Here*, which warns the men who don't treat women right and with respect that the women are getting fed up and will be leaving town soon.

It's really impactful to witness such a tangible expression of social commitment in front of a huge crowd that knows exactly what it's all about and may have experienced violence in their own lives. The moment is only heightened by the fact that I, as the only male, am in the company of five wonderful women with passports from as many countries: Marie from Denmark, Veronica, who is a Norwegian citizen, Leila from Argentina, Sara from Chile and Laura from Paraguay.

Two very different concert experiences for me: Santiago, in an absolutely fantastic setting, barely having left the airport – and Argentina, a more spiritual inner journey. Leila and Laura think the concert in Santiago was more high energy, while Veronica thinks the concert in Buenos Aires was light years better than three days earlier in Chile. Afterwards, there was quite a bit of criticism in the press and social media because they didn't play *Jeremy*, which is apparently the band's biggest hit in South America.

Time to die

And there was the whole dinner plan thing. I just saw and briefly greeted tour manager Smitty, but he's at work so it's nothing more than a quick "hello." Otherwise, I haven't seen any familiar PJ faces. We almost get lost again, but eventually find the backstage area, where I see Sara from Pearl Jam management, whom I have met many times before. She's nice and helpful, telling me that she sent me a lot of messages earlier that day about tickets and the VIP room with food and beverages – messages that reach my phone the following day. But she's pretty sure that the band has already left in the bus, and that they'll be travelling tomorrow. I try to call Stone, but there's no connection to anybody or anything.

Leila and Laura were tagging along, but they've said goodbye and left a short time earlier. The birds have flown the coop and, at the time, I'm certain that I'm not going to manage to meet up with Stone or any of the others this time around in South America. The busses for the crowd have also departed, there's not a taxi in sight, and everything is totally fucked. It's late at night, we're 50 miles from our hotel, and on the way down a street we're stopped by a uniformed policeman who says that it's far too dangerous to walk that way. Suddenly, everything I've heard all my life about how violent, criminal and dangerous it is to be in South America is materializing before me. But just when things seem to be at their most grim, a guardian angel arrives. From amongst the 40 to 50 thousand people at the concert who have now dispersed, Leila shows up again.

Amazingly, she's spotted us from a distance and can see that we're in a bind. As usual, Marie keeps a cool head as I'm freaking out and about to jump into the sea right then and there. Leila makes a bunch of calls – to her father, her friends, anybody she can think of. They're all gone, but she finds out that there is still a bus to a central station, which we manage to catch. From there, among endless lines, we find a taxi driver, or at least a driver, as taxi might be overstating things. Under the hood there's a big piece of cardboard to keep the engine from overheating, the hatchback pops open while we're driving, the police we drive past are basically indifferent, and the wheels are about to fall off. There's still heavy traffic and everyone except for me falls asleep. From the backseat, I can see that the driver's eyes have been reduced by heavy eyelids to two narrow slits. He's practically snoring. Unbelievably, we make it back to the hotel alive, and his parting words are these: "If you don't read in the newspaper tomorrow that a taxi driver died because he fell asleep on the highway, then I made it home alive." But we never did check the papers the next day.

Flowers by day, gourmet food by night

It's four in the morning and I'm finally in my bed. Hurray! And we have Wi-Fi. There's a message from Stone. As Marie suspected, he meant dinner tomorrow and not tonight, as I had understood it. We have a deal to meet up tomorrow. Apparently, he's not travelling to Brazil right away after all. Suddenly, everything falls into place once again, right when it seemed most hopeless.

It's wonderful to walk around Buenos Aires in the daytime, where movie-like settings are seemingly around every corner. Old American cars, murals, tango dancers, beautiful young women, busy businesspeople, picturesque old men with canes, children with balloons and strange hair, soccer hero posters, Evita Perón. Life in Argentina remains colorful, despite the country being more or less bankrupt since 2001.

We meet with Jenny aka Lydmor and her friend and cinematographer, Christina Amundsen, in the district of San Telmo. I interview Jenny for the Danish newspaper *BT*, Sara takes photos and life is good. Stone asks us to find a restaurant. Through a Mexican chef she knows, Marie finds a place; Leila, who will also be joining us, helps with all the practical details and gives the restaurant her stamp of approval. I had initially written with Stone about meeting and dining at his hotel, but for one thing the hotel is besieged by fans, and for the other, I definitely can't live up to the dress code in my shorts and sneakers. And all of my other clothes are in Chile.

We find the restaurant, Floreria Atlantico, which is a florist's by day and a super cool restaurant by night. We're running a bit late (Sara and Veronica are immune to being hurried). By chance, we meet the stewardesses who served us on the trip from Amsterdam to Santiago and the day before on our flight from Chile to Buenos Aires. They're dining at the same restaurant. Marie had told them about the book fair and Pearl Jam on the plane, which apparently sparked their interest. The first thing they ask about is whether we've seen and met the band while in town. At that very moment, I see Stone, wearing a backpack, step into the florist's/restaurant with Leila. Fortunately, she got there well ahead of time and met him on the street when the driver dropped him off.

It's wonderful to finally see him. We spend about three really good hours in each other's company, with some serious conversation and mostly lots of laughs. Veronica is dead tired, but it's a big moment for her to meet with Stone again – and Marie and Stone immediately tune into a common wavelength. He's so laid back and easy to be with, and as always he both praises and teases me all along the way. He has a gift for me: a huge bottle of wine. I introduce and present everyone to the best of my ability and it feels really good. He asks about the book launch and I tell him that I get the impression that people have really embraced its story and spirit. Veronica and the others say that I've received a star's welcome, and Stone comments with a smile, "Well, it's about time." He's just generally really positive about the situation, the book, the story. I say that it's been absolutely fantastic, but a bit strange when people react to me too positively, which can make me a bit uneasy. "Yeah, I know that feeling," says Stone. "That's how I feel sometimes." Two of a kind. Stone and I, in the same boat, like celebrities that practically have to flee from the masses. But let me put it this way: I can go to the supermarket without being mobbed by screaming teenagers. I can't help but laugh at the situation. But it's funny to hear Stone express those things, talk about those sides of himself and how he has tackled life as a rock star for a quarter of a century.

Although I'm tired, it appears that I haven't completely run dry when it comes to one-liners and biting commentary. Stone whispers to Marie, asking if she's ever able to get me to shut up. She nods in coy agreement. They've figured me out.

I tell Stone about Javier and Piedra Negra and tell him about the "moment of love" we shared in front of the hotel on our last night in Santiago. Stone wants to hear some sound bites and he just about dies laughing when he hears how much Javier sounds like Eddie. "Does he look like him too?" Stone asks. We show him a picture and now Stone is completely cracking up, and then we show him the YouTube video with Chris Cornell. Stone is really amped up about the fact that I played with Piedra Negra. "Can you really play the bass line to *Go*?" "Yeah, it's not all that hard," I say. Then the story about the time Stone messed up when playing *Immortality* with Leo's friends back in 2003 comes up, which just adds to Stone's amusement. Stone exchanges e-mail addresses with Marie and, in addition to asking her for restaurant recommendations in Mexico, he insists that she send him video clips of me playing with Piedra Negra. He points to the guitarist Pablo and asks with a laugh: "Is that supposed to be me?" Yes, it is. Just a really great atmosphere, excellent food and wine. Stone has complete respect for Piedra Negra and similar endeavors. He himself played covers back in the day, and we both agree that there are many ways of playing music. The most important thing is to do it and to have it as a companion in life. We don't all have to be Pearl Jam.

Stone leafs through the book and asks if it has also been published in English. We tell him that we're working on the case. Veronica asks him to sign her copy of the book, which he gladly does. Then I ask Stone if we should sign each other's books, or if that would be too weird. "No, of course we should!" he says. I can't imagine what to write, but I come up with something and get my book back from Stone, who spent a few minutes loudly enjoying the photo of me on the inside flap of the book's cover. He writes some wonderful words to me, with equal parts humor, respect and love. Wow, that's really heartwarming. I'll cherish that copy of the book, and in a way it's an indirect approval of the project as a whole, and that we can respectfully publish it anywhere and in any language.

We catch up on a bunch of things, I hear about his busy life as a father of three, he shows pictures of the kids and pictures of the entire family dressed up insanely for Halloween. We talk about the concerts and he's super glad that I thought Jeff played really strongly and came through clearly in Argentina. Stone says that he'll pass that on to Jeff and he knows that Jeff will appreciate it. Stone thinks that Jeff is the person in the band who has evolved the most musically over the past 20 years. He says that everyone in the band is doing well, shares a little bit about each of them, and I tell Stone that I greatly appreciate the things that Eddie has said to me and done for me. He doesn't have more hours in his day than any of us other mortals, but he puts them to use in a way that impacts the lives of others. I'm deeply grateful. Then it's time for group pictures and goodbyes – Stone must be moving on. Brazil is calling, and we need to go home and get some sleep.

I collapse back at the hotel, get sick and end up vomiting for the next day and a half. Veronica thinks that I went out drinking. It wasn't that evening's delicious food – none of the others have any kind of problems, so it might have been the street vendor in La Plata. But it's also symptomatic. The last thing missing to make the whole trip meaningful was to meet with people from the band – at least (and especially) Stone. We succeeded in spite of all the trials and tribulations. And afterwards – immediately afterwards – my body says stop, no more.

When I get back on my feet, I wander around with Marie, discovering the craziest places, streets, and shops, buying enough party hats to fill half a semi truck. There we are, two pale Danes in Palermo, Buenos Aires with our hats, Captain Kidd, exchanging currency on the black market in a Jewish fabric shop and attending a Lydmor concert with the other Scandinavian artists in the area. It's cool to see the South Americans react so positively to the Danish and Swedish artists, and that Laura and Leila are with us the whole evening. I actually have to return to Santiago with Marie the next morning, but because of illness I've missed out on all my sightseeing in Buenos Aires. So when Laura offers to be my guide the following day, I seize the opportunity and postpone my return to Chile by 24 hours.

Laura's Buenos Aires

As with nearly everyone I meet, Laura has a unique and special history with Pearl Jam. Ten years earlier at a PJ concert, the then 22-year-old woman from Paraguay with Argentinean roots met the great love of her life. Their relationship eventually ended, but the warm feelings and her friendship with the man San Figs remains intact. In many ways Laura has incorporated the band's words and music into many aspects of her life, emotions and decisions. She owns and operates a vegetarian restaurant in Paraguay and has eight employees. Laura later writes to me to jubilantly share the news that she's catered for the ultimate meat-hater,

Ni Una Menos. Front/back: Laura (Paraguay), Marie (Denmark), Leila (Argentina), Veronica (Norway), Sara (Chile). Estadio Unico De La Plata, Buenos Aires. November 7, 2015. Photo: Henrik Tuxen.

The trio. Henrik, Veronica, Stone. Restaurant Floreria Atlantico, Buenos Aires. November 8, 2015. Photo: Sara Vega Bravo.

Morrissey. And she's also an aspiring writer.

After a long, good day in the company of Laura in this fascinating South American metropolis, we meet up with hardworking Leila at a bar around 7 p.m. I think both of the women have been so helpful and such good company that they should have a gift. And what would be more fitting than the giant bottle of wine from Stone Gossard? After all, I wouldn't have anything but trouble trying to take it with me to Chile. They're ecstatic with the wine, and considering the original giver, it symbolizes our contact and connection. But they insist that if they are going to accept the gift, then we need to drink it together.

We walk through Palermo, which I instinctively fall in love with, and into Laura's ex-boyfriend San's vegetarian pizzeria. We sit outside in the balmy summer night as lazy hounds lounge about, amongst palm trees, fantastic vegetarian food and excellent company. It's just the kind of place I could settle down and write a couple of encyclopedias. San is a humorist and gentleman of the finest caliber. He also samples the wine, sending his thoughts to the band and love to Laura. We share stories and warm feelings. In just a short time, I've gotten to know both women really well, and they tell me things that open my mind and heart in new ways. It's a perfect way to say goodbye to Argentina.

It don't seem fair

I jump into a taxi and suddenly realize that I'm going to have to hurry to get there on time. I exchange a couple of bear hugs with the slender ladies and we hash out a hopeful plan to see each other on upcoming Pearl Jam US tour, which Stone confirmed two days earlier, saying "it just hasn't been announced yet." The announcement comes 2½ months later.

After a whole day of sightseeing with Laura, I'm pretty familiar with her relationship with Pearl Jam, but about six or seven weeks later, when I'm writing about the trip, I send an e-mail to Leila to make sure that I'm not exaggerating her relationship with the song *Light Years*. She previously said that if she had to pick just one song from the catalog, it would be *Smile*, so maybe it wasn't a tear that I saw on our first encounter. Maybe it was just a mosquito, a stray drop of beer or something of the like. But the reply I receive shows that my original intuition was correct, and it's yet another example of the emotional and potentially telepathic powers of music. And for many of us, the connection to Pearl Jam and everything they express and transcend is quite exceptional in this respect. Leila received the first copy of the Spanish book I had in my hands, three seconds into *Light Years*, at a point when we hadn't exchanged a single word and neither of us had any idea of who the other was. Here is Leila's reply about the significance of *Light Years*:

"My story about Light Years *is about my mother. She died in a car accident on February 15, 2009. We were extremely close and she was the one who held the family together. Shortly afterwards, my grandmother also died – I think it was from the grief. These emotions can't be explained, but I've had my ups and downs. 'Ups' when I feel that they're both with me and helping me, and 'downs' when I miss her presence, our conversations, everything we shared. So when I heard* Light Years *for the first time, I felt a special connection with the lines 'Every inch between us becomes light years now' and 'But now you're gone,... I haven't figured out why...' and especially 'It don't seem fair...' It seems like neither Eddie, myself, nor anybody will ever get over the losses we've suffered."*

Wow, my jaw dropped there for a moment, and the song now and forever has yet another dimension for me. I write to Leila that I'm deeply moved and almost shocked by the power of our first intuitive contact, and she replies that she gets chills thinking about the same. Music brings people, emotions and fates together.

Chapter 22

2015: BATACLAN. PARIS. HOW FRAGILE WE ARE.

Back in Santiago, the first thing on the program is a party at Veronica's apartment, which she kindly lent to me during my stay in Chile. There's a World Cup qualifier match between Chile and Columbia on TV, broadcast from the same stadium where we saw Pearl Jam play one week earlier. Almost all the members of Piedra Negra are there, together with some of their friends and our friend Fernando, who's in an exuberant mood. Aracelli and Carmensita are all smiles, and the latter tells me that her father lives on the eighth floor of this building, so if I ever need help with anything during my stay... Just another expression of the whole-hearted friendliness and hospitality that Marie and I encountered in South America.

When Arturo Vidal of the Chilean national team, which recently won *Copa de America* (an accomplishment they repeated the following year, leaving Messi and Argentina in tears), scores a goal to make it 1-0 in the dying seconds of the first half, the entire room – and Santiago as a collective whole – breaks into the most unbelievable jubilation. Columbia later equalizes for a final score of 1-1, which curbs the overall enthusiasm a little bit, but not the strong contact between all of us at the gathering. Although it's only the sympathetic, long-haired keyboardist Alejandro, our Santiago guide Fernando and one of their friends who speak relatively good English, the connection is strong. Javier and the others transcend the language barrier and clearly express how much our friendship means to them.

Stone has promised to put Javier on the guest list +1 for the concert in Mexico City, as the bulldog expert will be in town at the same time for a veterinarian conference. Pablo holds me tightly, looks me in the eyes and asks if he can take a photo of Stone's dedication to me in my book. Of course he can, but I ask him not to post it on Facebook or the like, and he confirms that of course he wouldn't do that. They express that I've become a kind of link to their biggest idols, both on a musical and human level. That's cool, but the best thing is that we're really becoming close personal friends.

Gourmet food

I enjoy my final, somewhat more relaxed days in mildly chaotic Santiago, spending most of the time with Marie before our flight home. We've had long discussions on world history, gender politics and much more, deciding in the process to form a duo for all activities relating to the Pearl Jam book going forward. But we also have other ideas and projects in the works for the future. Marie learns that there are no women's bathrooms at Santiago's strip clubs, we join Daniel Donoso Rasmussen from the Danish Embassy on a trip to the picturesque regional capital city of Valparaiso, and Marie invites me to dinner at one of South America's most esteemed restaurants, Boragó, where the service, food, stories and presentations are woven together in perfect harmony.

We wrap-up and say our goodbyes to our good friends and contacts, Veronica is glad, and we have a very promising meeting with the publisher Luis Cruz from Librosdementira, who is very satisfied with the process so far and promises at least one more release in April 2016 in Argentina. Luis is also working to ensure the wide scale release of the second book and/or a compiled version in South America in 2016.

Josh Homme

The only thorn in our predominantly rosy course of events comes from back home in Europe. On November 13, breaking news comes crashing in: Terrorists have killed around 140 people in Paris, two-thirds of whom are at the concert venue Bataclan during a concert by Eagles of Death Metal. In the midst of our euphoria about the power of music here in South America, a crushing blow comes from a Europe where many of the established structures of society seem to be eroding. Europe – and the Western world as a whole – is under pressures and experiencing a transformation that I hadn't imagined possible. And now a classic rock club has been attacked in the middle of a show by a festive, one-of-a-kind American band, where most of the concertgoers were around their mid-20s.

Eagles of Death Metal and Pearl Jam have more than their share of similarities and connections. One of the band's founders (who wasn't with them in Paris), Josh Homme, is amongst Pearl Jam's closest friends. Stone released the first Queens of the Stone Age album on his own label, and when they later became epic rock stars, Stone transferred all of the rights to his friend Josh Homme at no charge. As the towering, tattooed redhead said to me during a 2005 interview in Los Angeles, "That was the nicest unselfish thing anyone has ever done for me. And if anybody, anywhere, ever says something bad about him, I'll kill 'em." During the same interview, Josh flashed the legendary "Peace, love, death metal" hand sign featured on the Eagles of Death Metal debut album which had just come out at the time. The official celebration of PJ20 in 2011 is with The Strokes and Queens of The Stone Age as support, and at Lollapalloza in South America in 2013, Eddie and Josh make guest appearances with each other's bands (PJ and QOTSA) on stage.

One month after the massacre, I conduct one of my best interviews ever with Josh in Berlin, in connection with QOTSA's brilliant album *Like Clockwork*. Josh leaves no doubts about his amazing talent, charisma, wild abandon and heart, while also making it crystal clear that his relationship with Pearl Jam remains strong, lively and intense.

Roskilde 2000 vs. Bataclan 2015

On November 17, we depart from Santiago after two unbelievable weeks, heading for Charles de Gaulle Airport in Paris – the last city in the world that I want to visit right now. But we're just connecting in the airport, so everything's fine. Marie and I synchronously watch the 1983 movie *Ghandi* on the way home, bringing a fitting end to our trip with a glass of wine and a cinematic milestone paying tribute to one of the great humanists of our times.

The following week, I'm invited to appear on the leading nationwide morning television show "Good Morning Denmark" and comment on the links between what Pearl Jam experienced at Roskilde in 2000, and how the tragedy will forever haunt Eagles of Death Metal after what must be the worst Friday the 13th in history.

The friendly and popular host of the morning show, Morten Reesen, is highly engaged throughout our discussion – on an unrelated side note, he recently had a nostalgic rediscovery of *Ten*, so Pearl Jam is very present in his mind. We cover a surprising range of perspectives in the eight-minute conversation, during which a clip of Pearl Jam playing *Better Man* at Madison Square Garden on May 21, 2010 is shown (YouTube: Pearl Jam – Better Man (Madison Square Garden – New York, NY)), as are private photos of me standing arm in arm with Birgitta and Stone as we all laugh heartily. But I haven't come to the studio for knee-slapping laughs. Nonetheless, it feels good to share a few words about the extremely close ties between Pearl Jam and the many friends and relatives of the victims, particularly those between Stone and Birgitta, who are now like family.

Back to the matter at hand. I've attended Roskilde Festival 34 times and stood on stage with The Sharing Patrol in 1986 as a 22-year-old, playing in front of

10–15,000 people at what was basically one of our first concerts ever. A landmark experience of my youth. Roskilde Festival is coded into my DNA. To me, the accident at Roskilde 2000 initially felt like the death of a lifestyle, a youth culture and a rite of passage. Roskilde Festival and festival culture in general has had, and continues to have, a colossal influence on Scandinavian youth of all ages, shaping their culture, self-understanding and identity. The same can be said of festival culture in many countries and regions around the world. It's a way of being – on both an individual and collective level. My son Tobias expressed this poignantly a few weeks after RF 2016: "When I took the bus home from Roskilde this year, I suddenly realized how little people talk to each other in public and how reserved we are – the exact opposite of at Roskilde festival – how little we interact and open ourselves up to each other." A clear indication from a 28-year-old that the spirit of Roskilde is alive and well. It's where people let go and live. We need a space like this – and not just here in the cold northerly expanse of Scandinavia.

Is this form of gathering under serious threat? And is the attack on Bataclan a far more extreme attempt to destroy a music culture, a haven and a lifestyle? And what about the two bands? Are they forever changed? Pearl Jam is still, and will forever be changed. But what about Eagles of Death Metal? Will they ever escape the shadow of the Islamic State and Paris, and how strong is the bond between these two bands now? Can they help and relate to each other, and what happens to people – in this case, the bands – who are key focal points in connection with deeply tragic and fatal events?

Passing the baton

Although I unconsciously have many of the answers in my mind, it's completely different when you're asked directly and have to give a relatively brief and precise answer for a broad audience that doesn't necessarily have a deep and personal relationship with rock music. As Pearl Jam themselves stated briefly but unequivocally in Cameron Crowe's documentary, there will always be a before and an after when it comes to Roskilde 2000. It's an event that has forever changed Jeff, Mike, Eddie, Stone, Matt and the close circle around the band. For many, especially in Scandinavia, it's a ghost that will forever be associated with the band's name.

But the years go by, and for many people the accident is now a distant memory. As Veronica originally said about her motivation for releasing the first book in South America: "Everyone knows Pearl Jam, but nobody knows about Roskilde 2000." It's an exaggeration to make a point, but the point makes sense. With all respect, Eagles of Death Metal is a band without the same global history and impact. The very different political nature the Bataclan tragedy makes it an emblem of a world in deep geographical, economical, ideological and religious conflict. Eagles of Death Metal's name will forever be associated with this tragic event in a world of turmoil.

"Is it a good thing that the band is returning to Paris in record time and making a guest appearance with U2, and proclaiming that they'll play a new concert at Bataclan, as opposed to Pearl Jam, who never returned to Roskilde?" asks the host, Reesen. I answer: "The best I could say about that is that it's brave, fantastic, incredibly important, and a deeply symbolic act. Especially with U2, whose concerts in Paris in the days after the terrorist attack were cancelled, and who have has always been known for more than just their music, leading the way in philanthropic efforts. In a symbolic sense, Eagles of Death Metal are doing something similar to when U2 proclaimed prior to their version of *Helter Skelter* on the *Rattle and Hum* live album from 1987: 'This is a song Charles Manson stole from the Beatles. We're stealing it back.' Terrorists from the Islamic State briefly stole a music culture characterized by its openness and freedom. Now the Eagles are stealing back the spark and bringing rock music back to us again. Thank you."

It's impossible to compare Roskilde 2000 and the Bataclan in 2015. The latter claimed the lives of ten times as many people, and it was a brutal and politically symbolic attack. The Western allies' engagement and fatal lack of an exit strategy in the Iraq War have fanned the flames of conflict, but that in no way justifies barbaric fundamentalist violence using religious motives as an alibi. Terror and fear have become more tangible and present in the lives of Europeans than ever before in recent history. Having said that, Eagles are in a completely different position to take action and "steal back." Those guilty of the Bataclan attack have been identified, whereas the events at Roskilde were far more unclear, inexplicable and chaotic, leading Pearl Jam to say that they will never play at Roskilde Festival again. There will always be unresolved elements of this story.

And then there's the matter of guilt, no matter how fair or logical that may be. The conclusion, based on what I've experienced and described in this book, must be that the burden of guilt sticks with people far beyond that justified by basic logic. Should Tor Kolding feel guilty for saving his own life? Should Eddie Vedder feel guilty for not being able to see exactly what was happening in a crowd of 50,000 people from the stage, regardless of the blinding combination of spotlights and darkness? The same goes for the countless people who were present at Roskilde, the Bataclan and other mass events with tragic outcomes.

Perhaps this form of self-blame is similar to when children mistakenly blame themselves for their parents' divorce or women wrongly blame themselves for being raped. The nagging doubts. The subconscious workings of the human mind are mysterious. I've learned this firsthand from my experiences with the many people who have suffered after the accident at Roskilde 2000, including the irrational tendency to feel personally culpable. Those impacted never fully escape the demons of these experiences. "There is no closure," as Eddie Vedder said from the stage at the Forum in 2007.

That goes for the audiences, Eagles of Death Metal and Pearl Jam. But just as

Pearl Jam experienced the greatest tragedy of their lives, it has been followed by an insight and a love they had never imagined. I sense that the same is true of the musical jesters from Eagles of Death Metal. The historic and deeply emotional Vice interview (YouTube: Eagles of Death Metal Discuss Paris Terror Attacks), in which Josh Homme also participates, was followed by countless expressions of support and sympathy for the band (I'll refrain from commenting on Jesse Hughes's "pro guns" proclamations here).

Will they be able to live with their experiences and continue to grow as people? Will their musical presence alone be a symbol that life is stronger than death? Do the two bands have anything to do with each other, and does the tragedy at Bataclan have anything to do with this story at all? Yes, it actually does.

As Eddie expressed, the immediate personal support from Pete Townshend and Roger Daltrey after the Roskilde accident was key to Pearl Jam's ability to move on. The legends from The Who flew to Copenhagen to share their experiences after 11 people lost their lives during The Who's concert in Cincinnati in 1979. They're probably the only people who can fully comprehend Pearl Jam's state of mind in the hours and days after the accident. And, on top of all that, they're close friends with the band and Eddie Vedder's biggest idols. At Estadio Maracanã in Rio de Janeiro on November 22, Pearl Jam plays the EODM song *Want You So Hard*. And after having read Josh Homme's call to interpret and record *I Love You All the Time* – and to then donate the proceeds to the families of the Paris victims – Matt Cameron records a quick version in Mexico City on November 27. Both songs were released and promoted at PearlJam.com. And at the first concert after the attack in Paris, on November 14 in São Paulo, Eddie dedicates *Love Boat Captain* to the victims in Paris. On this evening, the song's original tribute to the Roskilde victims, "Lost 9 friends we'll never know,.. 2 years ago today," is changed to "Lost some of our friends we'll never know,.. oh again today." Just as The Who helped Pearl Jam steal back life, Pearl Jam is doing what they can to pass on the love baton to Eagles of Death Metal.

HOW FRAGILE WE ARE

After the TV appearance, just a few days after returning from South America, Morten Reesen's questions continue to simmer in my mind. I inevitably reflect on my life, Roskilde 2000 and more than two decades of walking in the footsteps of Pearl Jam, then occasionally side by side and once leading the way. In many ways, I'm the same happy-go-lucky rock'n'roller as the day I was star-struck and bowled over by my first meeting with Eddie Vedder in Barcelona in 1996, and in other ways my life and my personality are forever changed after the amazing journey I've taken, the extreme situations I've found myself in, and the people whose lives were shaken by tragedy that I've met and now followed closely for many years.

So much of all this is rooted in the band that I fell for more than 20 years ago, and who four years later found themselves at the center of a cruel tragedy that also became part of my life. A band whose songs and work are a voice giving symbolic meaning and providing hope and solace in a world in global conflict, as clearly manifested in the attack at the Bataclan about 16 years later – and now I'm the one asked to speak about these connections on national television.

The memories swirl furiously. Pearl Jam's power on stage, Eddie's presence and strength, Stone's humor, intelligence, vulnerability and groundedness. Birgitta's smiling, welcoming face, the Bondebjer family in the deepest sorrow, Matt Cameron's stone face backstage at Roskilde, lifeless bodies on the stage, beach party in Hawaii, Mike McCready's dazzling guitar skills and disarming humor, Jeff's vital and straightforward vigor, happy and cheering fans around the world, Eddie Vedder collapsing in tears on stage, the many times I've been plagued by doubt about whether my efforts were doing more harm than good. And what about myself? Things could have ended so differently. It was purely by chance that I was standing on stage and not in the front row of the crowd on the evening of June 30, 2000. Would the wounds and aftermath have been different if the festival had been called off immediately after the concert? I don't have the answers to these questions. But it's no secret that the closest thing I can think of in terms of closure – which by definition is impossible since the dead cannot be brought back to life – would be Pearl Jam once again standing on the Orange Stage at Roskilde Festival. It hasn't happened yet, but it's impossible to predict the future.

And what does all of this leave me with? First and foremost, a deep gratitude. The joy of having been able to take this journey, being able to play a part, being granted permission to tell my story as I've seen and experienced it. I think of everything I've learned and experienced, and how it has shaped and changed me. Joyous, optimistic people around the world, but also many who have suffered and continue to suffer. Of course, we're not all equals in this respect. As Stone said to me in 2001, reflecting on how the accident has impacted him and Pearl Jam: "The only thing I can think about is the families of the victims; how it has changed and impacted their lives. That's the only thing."

That is also my sentiment in the end. The families: the Bondebjers, Thuressons, Hurley/Spokes, Gustafssons, Svenssons, Nielsens, Tonnesens, Nouwens and Peschels. Their lives were changed forever on a summer evening in 2000. All those I have met have shown me the deepest trust. They have talked about their lives, their stories and their pain, as well as their hope and insight, and they have granted me permission to depict these things in my words. If this book can in any way help to relieve their pain just a little bit, and create new contacts and relationships, then these efforts will have been worth it. That's the most important thing.

Similar accidents and stories have unfolded both before and after, and will occur again in the future. Mass events can unite people in magical ways, be it soccer matches, demonstrations, parades or rock concerts. But history paints a clear picture: these gatherings are not always harmless. I think back to Birgitta's words that open this book: "We don't want something like this to ever happen to anyone. You don't want to rob anyone of their enthusiasm, but be careful. I would very much like you to write that. That's from a mother who lost her son."

Having said that, and this goes for public authorities, concert promoters, artists and audiences, I have personally felt the power of knowing and seeing my favorite band all around the globe over the past 20 years, and I know the enormous influence and importance they have for people worldwide – the power, insight, hope and commitment they represent and pass on. I've seen the global connections, joy and love that have followed in the wake of this journey, bringing together souls from cold Scandinavia to the north and Chile to the south. People who have enriched and touched the lives of myself and others, from fans around the world and the band itself, to the families and friends of the Roskilde victims. People who have shown me trust and love. But also people who, despite tragedy, have moved on, evolved through new friendships, relationships and a new understanding of others who live very different lives, from Christian Scandinavians and international rock stars to South American fans, heads of security, public authorities, attorneys, headbangers, teenagers, middle-aged and senior citizens.

We're all people, all with potential strength and power, but every person I've come across in this story has, at one time or another, expressed the wisdom of the words on the boulder at the Memorial Grove: "How fragile we are." Roskilde 2000 has become a symbol and everlasting reminder of this very fragility – but also a symbol of how we collectively uplift each other. The common link in this story is Pearl Jam – everything they express, give and represent. The words they sing and the music they play. Music is the healing power.

"How fragile we are." Memorial Grove, Roskilde Festival. Photo: Susan Nielsen.

Epilogue

Gudenåvej, Vanløse, Copenhagen, January 2, 2018

Since putting the final touches on this story, two years have passed and much has transpired in the meantime. The story is constantly evolving, but at some point you have to draw a line in the sand. Nonetheless, there have been a couple of events and some beautiful people out there that deserve a few words here at the closing bell.

In April and May 2016, I returned to Argentina and Chile in connection with the release of *Tras la huella de Pearl Jam* in Argentina. I spent nearly three weeks there this time around, with presentations at book fairs in Buenos Aires (Feria del Libro: Buenos Aires International Book Fair) and Puerto Montt, Chile. I also played live shows with the PJ cover bands Lost Dogs in Argentina and Piedra Negra in Chile, in addition to an all-night jam with Motherweiser in Buenos Aires in their practice room. It was mind-blowing to receive such a warm welcome the first time around, but coming back has only strengthened and deepened my friendships and relations with countless people. It's been an unbelievable, crazy, fun and absolutely wild ride. Chile and Argentina now feel like a second home, there's no doubt about it.

On this second trip, I meet Catalina, the 10-year-old girl Eddie talked about on stage during the concert in Argentina about six months earlier. She is accompanied by her parents to my presentation at the book fair in Buenos Aires. They give me two laminated posters with photos from the concert and we take pictures together.

Drawing by Catalina, entitled "Pearl Jam love". Buenos Aires. 2016.

Catalina and Henrik. Feria del Libro, Buenos Aries. April 26, 2016. Photo: Laly Garcia.

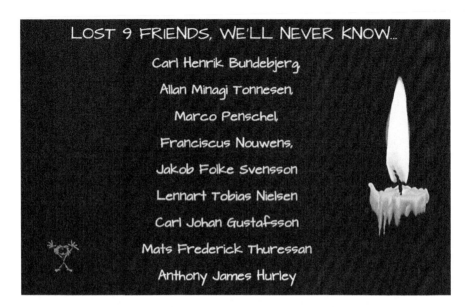

LOST 9 FRIENDS, WE'LL NEVER KNOW...

Carl Henrik Bundebjerg

Allan Minagi Tonnesen

Marco Penschel

Franciscus Nouwens,

Jakob Folke Svensson

Lennart Tobias Nielsen

Carl Johan Gustafsson

Mats Frederick Thuressan

Anthony James Hurley

Pearl Jam's Argentine fan club pays tribute on Facebook to the nine Roskilde victims on the 16th anniversary of the accident.

She's the most wonderful girl and has the nicest parents. Her mother later sends me a drawing by Catalina, entitled "Pearl Jam love," where Eddie, Anna Moon and I are named.

I've had reunions and encounters with many of the people portrayed in this book, and I've formed a bond with so many more who are not. My friendship with Piedra Negra and the circle around them is also much deeper now. Leila is once again on the spot in Buenos Aires, Indira, Dolores, Erica 'La Neno,' Gonzalo, Luis, Mariano, the table tennis club in Buenos Aires and many, many others: you know who you are, and I thank you all from the bottom of my heart. See you again soon.

I wrote to Stone while in Chile about how insane it was to be back in South America, and about all the love and enthusiasm I've been met with. I promptly received the following reply from Stone, who was on a tour of his own with Pearl Jam in the States: "Love love love Henrik, safe travels. Carolina today. Miss you. S." Pearl Jam is with me in spirit everywhere I go.

The thing that brings me the most joy when looking back on the overwhelming reception the book and I have received in South America is that so many people both reciprocate the love for Pearl Jam, and empathize with the loss and grief of the families. A touching example of this is when Pearl Jam Argentina posted a moving tribute to the nine victims on the 16th anniversary of the accident, June 30, 2016. Leo, Henrik, Carl-Johan and the six other victims shared the same enthusiasm for the band as fans in South America and around the world – and their spirit lives on through these fans. I can't even count how many people have come up to me and put their finger up to their eye, drawing a tear down their cheek. I can say – not only for myself, but also the families and Pearl Jam – that we are all very grateful for these expressions of compassion. Thank you.

In January 2017, I'm back in South America once more – this time at the Vino Del Mar book fair. It's yet another fantastic trip that could be a book in itself, but I'll spare you for now.

On October 30, 2016, this book was published in Danish, with a reception at the record and bookstore BEAT, located in the Copenhagen district of Vesterbro. At the reception, I play a handful of PJ songs with my daughter Lulu and Mikkel Sylvester. It's a beautiful day, and both the Bondebjers and Gustafssons make the trip from Sweden to be there. Thank you. Strong interest from the public and the media bring an array of moving moments. One of these comes when I join Michael Berlin (who miraculously survived the accident, unlike Jakob and Marco, who helped him out of the crowd) for an hour on the air at the studios of Radio 24-7, talking in-depth about the events before, during and after June 30, 2000. The entire first printing of the Danish edition is now sold out, and the second edition is available on Amazon.

From the very outset, the dream was to have an English translation of this book, but that's a prolonged and far from free process. In connection with other business, I was in contact with the chairman of the board for Roskilde Festival, Steen Jørgensen. Near the end of our conversation, I tell Steen about my and Marie's plans and ideas, to which he says, "You really ought to keep me up to date on that." To make a long story short, Roskilde Festival Charity Society has financed the entire cost of the English translation, without imposing any conditions or requirements whatsoever. I would like to pass on my deepest thanks to Steen, CEO Signe Lopdrup and Roskilde Festival, who have made the impossible possible. We also feel like we found the perfect man for the job, in the form of the Danish-speaking American expat, Michael Lee Burgess. In addition to his own long history with Pearl Jam, he has endeavored with great enthusiasm and dedication to brilliantly translate my Danish words into English. Greg Bennetts contributed his sharp eye and pen to the proofreading process.

In connection with Eddie Vedder concerts in Europe in the summer of 2017, and an invitation to the screening of the film *Let's Play Two* in London, I had ample opportunity to speak with central figures in Pearl Jam's management and crew over a couple of days – including a very warm and wet "Henrik, I love you!" hug from Eddie as he ran from the stage after his concert at Heartland Festival in Denmark on July 3, 2017 (my old "Pedal steel-friend," Maggie Björklund, Marie and I were standing on the side of the stage during the concert, alongside luminaries such as Michael Stipe, Cat Power, Glen Hansard and others). I also received an extremely warm welcome from Christian Fresno and manager Kelly Curtis in London two days later, as they enthusiastically leafed through the Danish version of this book. Kelly insisted that we immediately take a selfie and send it to Stone, who had no idea that I was in London. Stone quickly replied "Henrik!" and sent warm greetings from Seattle. We were subsequently in ongoing contact via e-mail with PJ Management, including Kelly, who wrote "Can't wait to read the English version," and Stone, who expressed his joy and appreciation that the book and story continue to touch people. It was fantastic to feel the continued support and backing from Pearl Jam and the people in their inner circle, and to be treated like a part of the family.

But a translation by itself is not enough. To realize our goal, including layout, PR and printing, we needed additional funds. On November 1, 2017, we launched a Kickstarter campaign to raise DKK 55,000. It was a 30-day campaign on an "All-or-nothing" basis. Without a single penny from secret donors arranged in advance, we reached our goal after just 13 days – not that this stopped many others from making additional contributions for the remainder of the campaign. A total of 250 supporters from around the world, countless shares, e-mails, messages, and supportive, uplifting comments from the global network have made all this possible in a way that Marie and I never imagined possible. Thank you to all of you – you know who you are – and an especially heartfelt thanks to Pernille Ravn and the rest of Pearl Jam Nordic, Simon Johansen and Dimitris PJ Kariotis.

And a warm thank you to my old friend Kristian Riis and NordicLA.

Thank you

Along the way, I've often wondered whether my efforts have done more harm than good for those whose lives were most affected by the Roskilde accident. Why bore into an open wound that will never heal regardless? But I've been propelled by the positive responses from those involved, and my experience that processing all of this through conversation, honesty and personal contact is helpful and makes a difference. If nothing else, this story illustrates that processing grief takes a unique and often unpredictable course for each individual person, and at very different speeds. At one point in this book, Stone Gossard notes that the accident is five years in the past, but that on the other hand it feels like it happened yesterday. Time does not heal all wounds, and some losses can never be replaced, instead becoming an integrated part of the people who suffer such loss.

In my work on this book, I've found that increased understanding and openness contribute to greater peace of mind and improved quality of life, while also giving rise to new thoughts, perceptions, friendships and relationships. Or, as Eddie Vedder puts it earlier in this book, when speaking on the process of going from deep and utter despair to a state of "suddenly realizing that the ashes of that which once had burned to the ground has blossomed into fertile soil. Unbelievable, life is unbelievable." I feel that this book is filled with incredible people, things and events, all of which are made possible through mutual help and support – not by standing alone. And with music as the common bond.

Originally, it was never in the cards that the meetings with the families would in any way be published or even made public, so I have found it absolutely essential to obtain approval of this project from the involved families and friends of the Roskilde victims. Fortunately, they have given their full support. Everyone has read and approved what they have been quoted as saying, and despite their enormous and heartbreaking loss, many have lent private photos for publication in this book. I give my utmost thanks and respect for these kind gestures. I would also like to humbly thank the families and friends of the victims with whom I have been in contact, and who have shown me the trust and granted me permission to tell their stories. Thanks to Birgitta and Ebbe Gustafsson, Sven-Anders, Ann-Charlotte, Lars and Johan Bondebjer, Eunice, Finn and Alex Tonnesen, Gert Thuresson, Jane and Lea Jaqué, Michael Berlin, Benita Rasmussen, Sharon Nielsen, Asbjørn Auring Grimm, Jacob Chapelle, Astrid Rørdam Ibsen and Tore Rask – and to the many others whose lives have been touched by the accident.

Special thanks to Stone Gossard for his admirable initiative, efforts and trust. Many thanks to Eddie Vedder and thanks to Liz Weber, Mike McCready, Jeff Ament, Kelly Curtis, Nicole Vandenberg, Virginia Piper, Sarah Seiler, Christian Fresco, the rest of Pearl Jam and their crew for their helpfulness, spirit and consistently nice treatment. Thank you for important help and assistance to Dorte Palle Jørgensen, and to Signe Glahn for thorough guidance and feedback on the first half of this book. And, of course, thanks to Marie Rose Siff Hansen, who in every way is a fully integrated part of *PEARL JAM The More You Need – The Less You Get*, and whose contributions have been essential to the book becoming what it is. And had it not been for Veronica Bravo's initiative, this book project would have become stranded in 2005.

And then there are all the parties, the music, the travels, fans, musicians, hangarounds, and rock'n'roll people of flesh and blood who have made my journey in Pearl Jam's tailwind an abundance of amazing experiences, with the South Americans in particular sweeping me off my feet. 20 years on the go – and the many people from near and far who have made it possible for this book to exist in English.

There are many people to thank, and also many to remember. I apologize if I've forgotten anybody. Thanks to Lulu Høi Tuxen, Celine Høi Haugelund, Tobias Tuxen, Anne Mette Degn-Petersen, Marie Dahl, Michael Valeur, Morten Larsen, Mats Johansson, Peter Ramsdal, Robert Borges and *Gaffa*. Veronica Bravo. Luis Cruz, Maria Francisca Maldonado Wilson, Fernando Bellocchio, Javier Diaz, all in Piedra Negra, Trine Danklefsen, Laura Vaca Pink, Leila Rausch, Gabriella Ullmann, Daniel Donoso Rasmussen, Jesper Fersløv Andersen, Leila Guerra, Sara Bravo, Veronica's family, Sergio, Aracelli Aguilar Alvarez, Cristian & Carmensita, House of Rock & Blues, FILSA, Anna Moon, Mia Ben-Ami, Kasper Schulz, Signe Dalsgaard Jacobsen, Lost Dogs, Motherweiser, Miguel Rojas, Elisa Katerina, Tor Nygård

Kolding, Claus de la Porte, Henrik Bondo Nielsen, Morten Thanning Vendelø, Tyge Trier, Kasper Schulz, Gonzalo Diaz, Mariano Mandrake Vespa, Karina Deschamps, Pearl Jam Chile Alive, Pearl Jam Argentina, Dolores Elortondo – Søren McGuire, Kurt Bloch and Fastbacks, Johnny Sangster, Jonathan Stibbard, Marianne Søndergaard, Susanne Heitmann, Lars Puggaard, Nicola Jackson, Emil Sprange, Thomas Helbig Larsen, BEAT, Hanne Lund Birkholm, Ted Shumaker, Simon Johansen, Steen Jørgensen, Roskilde Festival, Pearl Jam Nordic, Pernille Ravn, Linnea Nilsson, Cecilie Bolgen, Reeta Jalonen, Julia Nikiforova, Jimmy PJ Perú, Dimitris PJ Kariotis, Kristian Riis, Thim Steen Jensen, Michael Lee Burgess, Maria Elena Preciado and Greg Bennetts.

About the author

Henrik Tuxen (B. 1963)
Journalist, musician and ping pong player
Master's degree in Social Science from Roskilde University, 1995

Tuxen has worked as a journalist and editor since 1995 for an array of music magazines, daily newspapers and book publishers. From 1996 to 1997, Tuxen was a journalist at the music magazine *Wild*, and from 1998 to 2004 he was co-editor and journalist for the music magazine *Gaffa*. He has worked for the daily newspaper *BT* since 2014.

Tuxen now works as a freelance music and culture journalist, live interviewer, moderator, author, and librarian, in addition to having resumed his career as a musician.

Discography as a bassist and backing vocalist
Sharing Patrol 1984–1997
Dogfood 1995–1997
Chosen Few 1998–2001

Previous works
Kashmir: From Nirvana to Rocket Brothers, 2004 (in Danish)
In the footsteps of Pearl Jam – before and after Roskilde, 2005 (in Danish)
Gaffa's Cultural Canon, 2006 (in Danish)
And as contributor to various books.

About the translator

Michael is an expat originally from Denver who moved to Denmark in 1998 after finishing college. Once in Copenhagen, he began writing fiction and playing an active role in the emergence of a vibrant spoken word scene in the Danish capital around the turn of the millennium. After gaining a good grip on the intricacies of the local tongue, he shifted his focus to translating from Danish to English in 2006.

Ever since attending a small show on the advice of a friend on May 5, 1992 at the Glenn Miller Ballroom on the campus of CU Boulder, Michael has had a close affinity for Pearl Jam. He spent the rest of his junior year of high school wearing the long sleeve "rhino" t-shirt he bought at the concert, as PJ started getting more and more play on MTV and fewer and fewer classmates thought it was a shirt for fruit spread. He was also at the Roskilde Festival concert in 2000, which only adds to the gratitude he feels for being a part of bringing this book to a wider audience.

Printed by Amazon Italia Logistica S.r.l.
Torrazza Piemonte (TO), Italy

10818916R00203